I0594050

MACKENZIE CROSSING
Copyright © 2021 by Kaye Dobbie

2nd Edition
Published by Dobbie Enterprises

ebook 978-0-6489371-8-0
paperback 978-0-6489371-9-7

Cover Design and Interior Format

Mackenzie Crossing

KAYE DOBBIE

OTHER BOOKS BY KAYE DOBBIE

THE GLASS HOUSE
THE BOND
THE DARK DREAM
WHEN SHADOWS FALL
FOOTSTEPS IN AN EMPTY ROOM
WHISPERS FROM THE PAST
COLOURS OF GOLD
SWEET WATTLE CREEK
MACKENZIE CROSSING
WILLOW TREE BEND
THE ROAD TO IRONBARK

Also books previously written as Deborah
Miles
A PASSING FANCY
JEALOUS HEARTS
SWEET MARY ANNE

This book is dedicated to my daughter, Emma, who showed me Degraves Street and started me on Skye's journey.

CHAPTER 1

NEVILLE

Three pm, Friday 13 January 1939,
Mackenzie Crossing, Victoria, Australia

THE PITILESS FIRE had come roaring over the hill, while the wind that preceded it had been a hurricane of cinders and burning gum leaves. There was no point in the people from the Crossing staying to protect their homes, it was impossible to do anything but take shelter wherever they could find it.

Now, inside the tunnel of the old Union Jack mine, Neville pressed his face close to the muddy ground, where there was supposed to be more oxygen. With the hot air thick with smoke, it was hard to take a breath and he was choking.

In his head he could hear the fire bell still ringing its warning. There was no chance of winning the fight against the flames, and it would have been madness to try. In the circumstances, the mine had been the only option.

Funny, Neville thought, wiping the sweat from

his stinging eyes, how things turned out. Or ended, here in Mackenzie Crossing.

Earlier old Patrick had said he'd never seen a bushfire this bad and he'd lived through a couple. The tears had run silently down his grimy cheeks. They'd found him at the entrance to the tunnel, blinded, stumbling and calling for help. No one knew how many of the others were still alive. Some had gone into the millpond, he said, but he'd become lost in the smoke and confusion, and then the fire had cut him off.

Neville tried not to think, but the questions came anyway. Would he die here, today? Would these be his last moments?

He wished he'd spoken to Gertie before he'd left. Explained. She'd be eight now. Would she understand? His reason for walking away from her and her mother was complex. The Great War had played its part. He'd never been the same man since, no matter how far he'd gone or how hard he'd tried to outrun the horrors of the trenches. He knew they'd always catch up, eventually, and they always did, and today, well he could no longer run.

Beyond the entrance to the tunnel everything was black. He tugged the wet blankets over those around him, feeling the throb from his burns. No time to think of that. If they got out, then he could worry about how badly he'd been injured, but for now it was a matter of survival.

The woman lying on the ground beside him pressed closer and he could feel her hot skin and smell her singed hair. 'It's been nice knowing you, Pom,' she said, her voice a husky whisper. 'I wish …'

He put his arm around her and she didn't finish. She didn't need to, because Neville was wishing, too.

In Mackenzie Crossing he'd had a glimpse of a new beginning, a tantalising possibility of a fresh start. How ironic that, instead, he was going to die.

And how unreasonable, when he'd given the best of himself for his country, that he was going to end here, far away across the world.

But Neville Darling had long ago learned that life was never fair.

CHAPTER 2

SKYE

Thursday 5 June 1997,
Degraves Street, Melbourne

SKYE MADE HER way through the lanes. They were a bit like a maze. Old narrow buildings, once near to derelict, had become quirky eateries and bars, while small retail shops tempted her to browse inside.

The City of Melbourne was reclaiming this area, turning it into something modern and trendy, and at the same time drawing the people back into a part of the inner city that over the years had become seedy and somewhere to be avoided. Now, despite the chill of early winter in the air, groups and couples sat at the tables, chatting and laughing, reminding her of her student days which, she sometimes thought, were receding into the distance at an alarming rate.

Then again, she was a photographer from the firm of 'Fraser's Funky Fotos', and even at thirty-four years that meant she was allowed to dress like someone half her age in tight red jeans, red boots, a loose white sweater and a knee-length white woollen coat. Fraser encouraged his staff to be outrageous. This morning he'd been looking uber cool in a retro brown suede jacket, with his blond hair styled like a slightly rumpled Ralph Fiennes in *The English Patient*.

Skye paused, tucking back the curls of her own shoulder-length auburn hair. *Where was this place? Had she gone too far?* She glanced along the thoroughfare, checking the numerous business signs. She was in Degraves Street now, with more of the trendy restaurants and cafes, their outside tables sensibly set beneath festive canopies. Everyone knew Melbourne weather was not to be trusted.

And then there it was. Bookends.

It was where she was to meet Russell and she was running late. Someone had rung to change the date of their engagement photographs and there'd been the usual scramble to find an alternate time. When she'd finally finished pleasing everyone, the clock had already ticked past ten o'clock.

Skye stepped through the doorway and into a world of cosy tables, low lighting and books. Hundreds and hundreds of books, some in steel shelving or antique-looking cases, the rest in stacks on the floor. She could see old hardbacks as well as plenty of flashy, trashy paperbacks. Bookends was not somewhere Skye had visited before and from what she could see it was heaven for book lovers like Russell.

No one raised a hand towards her in greeting

and she was blinking in the dim lighting after being outside. As she edged along the row of tables, she saw him finally, and of course he was deep in a book.

Her eyes adjusted to the light and she realised he was losing his hair. She wouldn't normally notice, but at this angle it was obvious. She'd known Russell since she was at secondary school, when her family had moved from Northcote to Carlton. It was at a time when she'd needed a friend and he had been a good one, sticking by her when everyone else had given up on her. Afterwards, they'd kept in touch and although Russell had spent a few years in the north of the state, he'd recently transferred back to Melbourne.

'Russell.'

He looked up, grinned, and then got to his feet with some difficulty in the cramped space so he could give her a hug. He'd put on weight.

'You look great, as always. Just as well Julie isn't here. She goes green when she sees your clothes.'

'How is Julie?' Skye asked, as they sat down.

'She's good. Kids are fine. Enjoying being back in the Big Smoke. What about you?'

'I'm good. Working hard to keep Fraser living the life to which he's become accustomed.'

Russell smiled, though his eyes held a quizzical expression. 'You might as well have stayed married. Why don't you set up on your own?'

Skye shrugged as if she hadn't been thinking about it. 'One day I will. He's been good to me. After Mum died I needed to work and he was kind enough to offer. Anyway, weddings and christenings make the world go round.'

He paused. 'Sorry to hear about your mother.'

Skye looked away. It still hurt to know she'd never walk into her mother's house and see her sitting in her favourite chair with Milly the cat on her knee. 'It was a relief, really, when she passed away. And it was peaceful, after all the suffering.'

Her mother, Gertie, had been diagnosed with cancer only six months before she died. As her only living relative, Skye had borne the brunt of her care until she'd moved into the hospice, something she'd never regretted. Gertie wasn't old at sixty-six, and it all seemed so unfair, but her mother appeared to have few misgivings, unless it was the fact that she'd had no other children. Skye had come along when her parents were in their thirties and had just about given up. For a while now it had just been Gertie and Skye, and she'd believed they'd had no secrets, but shortly before she died Gertie had begun to talk about a man called Neville Darling.

'I wish I knew what happened to him,' she'd said one day, gazing at the view from her window, crisp white sheets tucked around her diminished form. 'After he left Glenelg, I mean. Where did he go?'

When Skye had asked her who she meant, her mother had stared at her with faded blue eyes—eyes that only a few months ago had been the same bright colour as Skye's—and said, 'My father, of course!'

'Your father? Do you mean Louis? Mum?'

But her eyes had closed and she was asleep again.

It had made no sense, but with Gertie in and out of consciousness, and often incoherent, it had been too late for Skye to solve the mystery of this man she had never heard of.

Afterwards, when Skye was looking through Gertie's bits and pieces, she'd made a discovery that had amazed and intrigued her. And this was the reason she was meeting Russell here today.

'So, Neville Darling, this mysterious grandfather of yours. What's that all about?'

'That's what I want to find out.'

Skye noticed Russell had already ordered himself a big mug of caffeine, and she thought he looked tired enough to need it. Russell Anatrelli was a detective constable who was currently working in the area of missing persons. Today was his day off.

'Sorry I was late,' she said belatedly. 'I got held up.'

'No worries,' was his laconic reply. 'You're paying for my coffee.'

Skye smiled and picked up the menu—a child's storybook with the inside transformed into a long list of beverages and snacks with literary names, such as a Samuel Johnson Sandwich with the Lot, or the Colleen McCullough Colosseum Feast. A waiter wandered down and she ordered an espresso.

'Neville Darling,' she began. 'From what I've been able to work out, he abandoned Mary, my grandmother, in nineteen thirty-five. When

Mum was five. Mary married again and I'd always thought Grandpa Louis was my biological grandfather, but when I was sorting through Mum's papers I came across her birth certificate and realised her actual father was a man named Neville Darling. He'd fought in the First World War and come back a real-life hero. He was born in Dorset, England, in eighteen ninety-four, and his father was a solicitor in a family firm that had been around for at least a hundred years. We're talking solid, respectable middle class. The sort of outfit you would've expected Neville to be a part of until he died.'

'Not head out to Australia and go bush?'

'Exactly. I also found Mary's marriage certificate to Louis, with the tantalising fact that her first husband, Neville, went missing in nineteen thirty-five—which is where I got the date—and was last heard of in Melbourne. And,' she leaned closer, her eyes lighting up, 'he was a photographer!'

'Just like you. Genetic, do you think?'

'Well, I have to think so. Mum had some of his stuff, too, and,' she shook her head, 'it's great. Really amazing. So I want to know more.'

'I can see that.'

'You said on the phone you'd found something?'

Russell gave her a conspiratorial smile as he patted the folder she now noticed on the table beside him. 'Your grandmother Mary *did* make inquiries about your grandfather. There's a file. I had to dig deep to find it. Not many of the historic missing-persons cases are given priority these days, but recently someone had been going through them. Trying to put the "Closed" stamp on a few of them, I suspect. That always looks good when it comes time for government funding.'

Skye sat up straighter. 'So there *is* a file on Neville Darling?' She could hardly believe it. When she'd first come up with the idea of trying to trace his whereabouts after he left Mary and Gertie, there had seemed little hope of finding even a grave to lay flowers on.

Through a variety of sources at the library she'd discovered Neville had sailed to Adelaide in the 1920s, and then she'd been given a copy of his war record from the British Archives. He'd been an officer, Captain Darling, and had won a commendation for bravery. He should have been set for life, but the war had messed with him. There were several notations by doctors as Neville spent time in and out of hospitals. The years went by but it was obvious he couldn't settle, and one day he had boarded a ship to South Australia.

By the time of his marriage to Mary he'd been running a small photography business in Glenelg. Once again, life should have been good. But then, in 1935, Neville took off again.

Russell interrupted her thoughts. 'I couldn't bring the original paperwork with me, but I made notes of the relevant bits. I gather that after Neville left your grandmother, she met someone else and was keen to remarry. For that she needed a divorce or some documentation to say she was a widow. Legally, if a spouse has not been seen or heard from for seven years then he or she can be declared dead. Mr Darling had been missing for over seven years when she made her request to Victoria Police, so it was academic really. She just needed to make a bit of an effort, and then the courts declared him dead and she got herself a new husband.'

Mary had remarried and moved on, and Neville was forgotten. Skye supposed she couldn't blame her grandmother and mother for putting the past behind them. Those times must have been confusing and deeply unhappy for them both—which was probably why they'd never spoken of them—and Grandpa Louis was a sweetheart. Like Skye a generation later, Gertie had been Mary's only child, and Grandpa Louis had treated her as his own, and as far as Skye knew, that was that.

Until now.

Had Neville Darling been a complete bastard as a husband and father? Skye just couldn't bring herself to believe it, no matter how naive this made her. Not when his photographs were so remarkable.

'So you're saying the police didn't find him?' Skye said now, unable to hide her disappointment.

'Not a trace.'

'But—'

'Hang on, let me finish.' Russell held up a hand to slow her down. 'There were notices placed in some of the major newspapers at the time. Asking for information. They had a few responses, but most of the sightings were so vague they could've been anyone, and I think that was the view they took. However, there was one that was never followed up. It arrived in nineteen fifty-seven, long after your grandmother remarried, so there was no reason to look into it, and they just filed it away. Here, take a look. I managed to get a photocopy when no one was looking.'

'Don't get yourself into trouble on my account.'

He winked. 'Why change a longstanding habit?'

It wasn't funny, not really, although she managed a laugh. There was a time when she *had* been trouble. Trouble with a capital T.

'Did you ever see them again? The Faradays?' Russell seemed to have read her mind.

'No.' She looked away and he backed off, just as she'd hoped he would. It wasn't something she talked about if she could help it.

The Faradays had been Skye's new next-door neighbours when her family moved from Adelaide to the Melbourne suburb of Northcote in 1978. Mrs Faraday was divorced and had two boys, twins. They weren't identical in looks or personality, but they had that strange twin closeness—finishing each other's sentences or knowing what the other was doing even when they were apart. Sixteen-year-old Dylan, the eldest by five minutes, was the ringleader, while the younger, Finn, thought his brother could do no wrong. And fifteen-year-old Skye ... sometimes even now she thought she'd been slightly in love with them both, but it was Finn who had held pride of place in her heart.

Afterwards, when it had all gone so horribly wrong, she'd moved to Carlton, started at a new school and met Russell and he'd been kind, a sort of big brother. He'd helped pick up the pieces and she would be forever grateful to him for that.

But that was all in the past, gone, although the memory was still there. A small dark spot. Which, most of the time, she was able to ignore.

She watched Russell pull a couple of sheets of paper from the folder. 'Here we are,' he said, pleased with himself, and handed them across the table. Eagerly she began to read.

Dear Mrs Darling,

I am writing not to distress you but because I recently heard the police were making inquiries about your husband, Neville. Do you still wish to find him? I have information that would be useful to you if you genuinely seek the truth. Write to me at the address below and I promise I will do my best to satisfy your curiosity.

Elysian, Victoria, Australia

'The signature at the bottom is a scrawl. As you can see, indecipherable. Maybe that was done on purpose. But the address is clear enough. And it makes sense.'

'Makes sense?' Skye was still frowning at the letter. She barely noticed the waiter put down her coffee.

'Elysian is up in the Victorian Alps. The High Country. It's isolated and remote and exactly the sort of place that your Neville Darling was likely to go to hide himself away. And maybe to take his photographs, do you think?'

Skye looked up, beaming. 'Yes.'

'Well, I'm glad to hear that,' and now it was his turn to smile at her, 'because this was attached to the letter.'

Skye had spent many hours poring over Neville's photographs. The formal portraits from his shop in Glenelg were interesting, especially as she herself was in the same trade, but they weren't the ones that fired her imagination. Neville had travelled all over South Australia taking his images. There were pictures of people in the arid inland, trying to subsist on drought-ridden blocks. And there were pictures of camps up on the Murray during the late 1920s, where men without work sat and looked at him through his camera lens without hope.

The photos were grim and gritty and very empathic.

Why her grandmother and then her mother had kept them she didn't know. Perhaps they just couldn't bear to throw them away? Like any great artist, he had a signature to his work. Nothing so simple as his name written across the bottom, although there was that, but an indefinable something that made any one of them instantly recognisable as 'a Neville Darling'. Recognisable to Skye at any rate.

Now, as she looked down at Russell's second photocopy, she felt her heart give an excited thump.

It was a sepia image of a girl—no, a woman—standing in front of a solid two-storey building with a crooked verandah. Smoke was drifting from a chimney against a setting of bush-covered mountains. The strange thing was that the woman was wearing trousers and boots teamed up with a man's shirt and loose jacket. If it wasn't for her dark hair, hanging in a long plait over her shoulder, Skye would not have realised she was a female. Then again, perhaps she would. The woman's face was ageless and very feminine. Delicate, with high cheekbones, and attractive, apart from the hard line of her mouth and the way her jaw was set. As if she was fully prepared to fight for what she wanted. Her eyes had a tilt to them, hinting at a mixed heritage, and she stared straight through the lens and into the future.

Skye was positive this was one of Neville Darling's. It just couldn't have been taken by anyone else.

Russell was watching her with amusement. 'Quite a character, yeah? Wouldn't want to tangle with her,' he added, although Skye suspected he probably would like to tangle with her, at some level.

'Who is she?' she asked. 'Where was this taken?'

'I don't know who she is. As to where it was taken, I'm sorry, but you're not going to like it.'

'What won't I like?' Skye asked with a hint of impatience. Russell always did have a flair for drama.

'Because it was taken at Mackenzie Crossing—written on the back was, *thirteenth of January nineteen thirty-nine, Mackenzie Crossing*.' He paused and then said, 'You haven't heard of it?'

'No, I haven't, but I'm sure you're going to tell

me.'

'Skye, if this was the last picture he took, and the date is correct, and he *was* in Mackenzie Crossing, then he must have been caught up in the Black Friday bushfires.'

That wasn't good. Though Skye had never experienced a bushfire, Victoria was the worst place in Australia when it came to them, and she'd seen them on the television news often enough. The Ash Wednesday fires in 1986 weren't all that long ago, and she still remembered the smell of smoke from her house in the inner city and the terrifying news reports.

Russell drew out a crumpled piece of paper from his pocket and held it up.

'Got this off the internet,' he said. 'Black Friday statistics. Seventy-one people died, around thirteen hundred homes and sixty-nine sawmills were burned, and three thousand seven hundred buildings were destroyed in total. Several towns were wiped from the face of the earth. Three-quarters of the state of Victoria was directly or indirectly affected by the disaster. They had a royal commissioner who said, and I quote, "… it appeared the whole state was alight on Friday thirteenth of January nineteen thirty-nine".'

'God, Russell.' Skye felt cold despite her coat. And yet when she wiped her palms on the thighs of her red jeans they were damp. 'So you think Neville was in that bushfire?'

'It would explain his disappearance. I've checked the list of dead and injured in that area and he isn't on it, but there could easily have been unidentified people there at the time who were killed. If he had no family to make a report immediately afterwards, then who would know?'

'And this place, Mackenzie Crossing. Was it one of the towns destroyed?'

'Completely. Some of them were rebuilt afterwards, while others were just gone.'

Gone, like Neville Darling.

Skye sighed and picked up her cup, but she didn't drink.

'I'm sorry I don't have better news. I'm sensing this is important to you?'

'Yes. Well, in a way. I was half hoping to persuade someone to put money into an exhibition I wanted to organise for Neville's photos. He seems to have flown under the radar and, well, I know he's my grandfather, but I think he deserves to be better known.'

That was the simple answer, although it was more complex than that. There was something about Neville's work that spoke to Skye in a way nothing else ever had. He seemed to have achieved what she had been trying to achieve ever since she was a teenager, when she had picked up her first camera. Neville didn't just take photographs of people, he opened them up, putting their hearts and souls on display.

Russell was wearing that irritating little smile again. As if he had a secret.

'What?' she demanded. 'Russell, come on. Tell me.'

'You haven't twigged,' he said with pretended disappointment. 'The photograph. The woman at

Mackenzie Crossing. If Neville Darling was dead then who developed it? Where did it come from? Who sent it to the police?'

'Oh. Then he could've survived! But wouldn't someone have heard? Wouldn't they know?'

'Depends how hard he wanted them not to know.'

Skye tucked a bright curl behind her ear while she thought about that. Neville Darling was turning out to be even more of an enigma than she'd imagined.

When Skye discovered photography—after she'd climbed out of the mess left by the Faraday brothers—she'd taken to it with a passion. She shot photos of urban scenes—grotty streets and hungry dogs, a bleak canvas that seemed to express the way she was feeling at the time. Neville might have taken professional portraits, but his real love was the photos he took outside the studio. The further away from civilisation the better he seemed to like it, which was surely a strange thing for an Englishman.

In some elemental way she connected with him.

Skye sipped her espresso. 'I'd really like to see this Mackenzie Crossing. I could drive—'

'Skye,' Russell interrupted, looking dubious. 'We're talking about one of the most isolated places in the state. Assuming your car made it that far without getting lost or bogged or falling down the side of a mountain. The roads are unsealed and they can be treacherous, not to mention the weather.'

'Russell, I'm not a complete city girl.'

He raised his eyebrow. 'What happened the only time we went cross-country skiing at Lake Mountain?'

'I fell over and sprained my ankle.' She sighed. 'Yeah, well, maybe I am.' She thought for a moment then brightened. 'Why can't you take me up there? I only need a few photos of the places Neville would have seen. Just to show a contrast between then and now, and give people some sort of idea of what he was up to.'

Russell sat, watching her, and she could almost see the wheels turning in his head. 'If you really want to do this … What will Fraser say?'

'I don't care what Fraser says. You just told me I need to get out from under Fraser's Cuban-style heel. Remember?'

'I did, didn't I?'

He drank the dregs of his coffee and set it down as if he'd made a decision. 'Here's the thing. Elysian is a few kilometres from where Mackenzie Crossing used to be. Remember the mysterious letter that came from Elysian?'

'Elysian? Doesn't that mean something to do with the afterlife?'

'Heaven, yes. Not exactly appropriate, I would've thought—unless they meant its altitude—but whoever gave it that name must have thought it was a pretty good place. The thing is, Elysian has a police station. Only one for miles and miles, so it covers a hell of an area. I don't know the officer in charge and I don't know if he can help you, but once you're up there, maybe you could follow up whoever sent the letter? In between snapping your camera.'

Skye tried to curb her excitement and failed; it was bubbling out of every pore. 'Russell, thank you, that sounds—'

'As long as you're not expecting to find anything,' he warned her. 'Don't get your hopes up. You don't even know if there's anyone still alive who remembers Black Friday.'

'I understand. I won't get my hopes up.' Only she was, she couldn't help it.

He nodded as if the matter was settled. He hesitated and then held up the book he'd been reading when she arrived. '*All Quiet on the Western Front*.'

'And your point is?'

'I'm not judging Neville. He ran off when he probably should've stayed. But the war destroyed lots of lives, and maybe you should look at it that way. Hero or not, the war destroyed Neville's life, too. It made him unfit for peacetime.'

Sudden tears stung Skye's eyes. Russell covered her hand and gave it a squeeze.

'I'll give you a ring in the morning. Transport,' he added, at her puzzled stare. 'Up to Elysian.'

'I don't know if I'm ready, Russell. I have to rearrange my schedule and—'

Again he stopped her with the upheld hand. 'Then you'd better get ready. This chance won't come around again.'

When he'd gone, Skye lingered. She stared down at the photocopy of the woman with long dark hair, thinking there was something intriguing about her face, not to mention her outfit. What was her background? Had she had a difficult life? Evidently she felt the need to dress like a man, but was it for protection or simple practicality? And yet there was her hair, proudly proclaiming her womanhood.

Neville Darling had been in Mackenzie Crossing on 13 January, Black Friday 1939, when much of the state of Victoria was alight. He'd looked through his lens and photographed this strange woman, and then … what? What had happened to him during that terrible, chaotic day?

Rightly or wrongly, Skye had formed an attachment to her vanished grandfather, and what had happened to him was something she very much wanted to know.

CHAPTER 3

NEVILLE

Saturday 7 January 1939,
Elysian, Victoria

SOMEONE HAD GOT hold of a Melbourne newspaper, the *Herald*, and it was causing a bit of disquiet in the Elysian Hotel. The journalist was reporting dire predictions for the days ahead, with northerly winds and tinder-dry bush. Some found this shocking, but others, the bushmen who had come into town for a drink, were more inclined to shrug their shoulders and down their beer.

It was hot enough for anything, Neville thought. He'd heard the temperature was over one hundred degrees Fahrenheit, and it felt like it. Or hotter. The thing was, with heat like this, you didn't get used to it. You just suffered through it.

There had been no proper rain for years now. Barely a drop of moisture was left in the state's dams, and Melbourne was currently on water restrictions. To make matters worse, this had been a particularly hot summer, and the heatwave that had started before Christmas seemed determined to carry on unrelenting into the new year.

There were already several fires burning around the state, and fire was not something to be taken lightly in the mountains. This was timber country, too, and the men and their families who worked in the mills or lived in the bush might be stoic and enduring, but the Bush Fire Brigades Association was close to broke. Neville had been told by a couple of the men employed by the Forestry Department that it was the government's lack of foresight, not to mention funding, that had left them so ill prepared.

It seemed strange to him that even with the *Herald*'s sombre headlines, most of the occupants of the bar were more interested in what Hitler was doing, or the civil war in Spain. Perhaps it was easier to think about faraway problems than to dwell on the situation facing them over the next few days.

As they said in the local vernacular, 'She'll be right, mate.'

Neville had become an observer of human nature. These days he preferred to keep a distance between himself and the world, and his Leica camera lens helped him to do that. He knew he was a very different man from the boy berated by his mother for being too lively. She'd barely recognised him when he came home from France. He'd hardly recognised himself. His camera had saved him, and now these mountains were proving to be a balm to his troubled soul.

Today the staff of the Elysian Hotel were run off their feet. The afternoon trade was escalating as the heat outside drove thirsty patrons inside. He was sitting at a long table, on the end, out of the way. He'd been in Elysian for a week now, and when he'd first arrived he'd thought it was rather isolated, but since then he'd heard of other places far more worthy of the name.

Like Mackenzie Crossing.

The boarding house where he was staying catered for Forestry workers, and the two who had told him about the troubles with the fire brigades had also been regaling him with tales of the Crossing in the old days. Evidently, a character called Big Jim Mackenzie had run it as if it was his own personal fiefdom. Things were very different now. According to them, Mackenzie Crossing, like many of the old settlements in the High Country, had become barely more than a ghost town. A survivor of a past that was fast disappearing and would not return.

It sounded exactly like the sort of place that Neville needed to photograph and document— make a record of the people who lived there, before they were gone.

A group of patrons at the bar were arguing among themselves, and as far as Neville could tell it was about a woman. One of them was keen on her, and his mates were warning him off, telling him she was nothing but trouble. They didn't appear to be getting through to him, hence the raised voices.

As often happened, Neville's own thoughts

turned to Mary and Gertie, his wife and daughter, away in Adelaide. Did they ever think of him? Or were they simply relieved that he had gone?

'Love is blind, isn't that what they say?'

The comment came from the chap sitting opposite him. The man was probably fifteen years Neville's senior, in his late fifties, with short-cut greying hair. His face was thin and bony, and there was an intent look in his grey eyes as he held out his hand to shake Neville's.

'Miller Brown,' he introduced himself.

Neville noticed that Brown had a cup of tea in front of him, just like Neville, and they exchanged a smile. Two teetotallers in a bar seemed reason enough to start a conversation.

'Do you live here or are you just passing through?' Brown asked, but there was still that sharpness about his expression that made Neville think the answer was important to him despite his casual tone.

'Passing through,' he said, and left it at that. 'What about you?'

Brown hesitated and then leaned closer, as if what he was about to say was in confidence. 'I *was* a Detective Inspector of Police,' he admitted, lowering his voice, although no one nearby was interested in them. 'Retired now. But I sometimes like to amuse myself by following up my old cases.'

This was a surprise, and Neville was suddenly much more involved in what Brown had to say. 'Though not officially?' he asked at the same time as he was considering what sort of photograph the man would make with his piercing, rather disconcerting gaze.

'No, not officially,' he admitted, with a frown, obviously not liking to be reminded of his current status. 'But if I came across something then I could make it official.'

'So you're in Elysian following up an old case?'

'I am,' Brown said. 'It's been lying around unsolved for nearly nine years.'

'Good heavens. Why have you decided to follow it up now?'

Brown stirred his tea. 'Some new information came to my attention and it seemed important. To *me*, anyway,' he added, and Neville knew then that this was a personal crusade for the man, perhaps made all the more attractive because it had been dismissed by his superiors. He looked the type to get a bee in his bonnet about that sort of thing.

Brown went on. 'I was the officer in charge of the case and at the time I had my suspicions. I'd like to prove them right. Murder isn't pretty, Mr Darling, not pretty at all. I don't have any sympathy for those who perpetrate it, even if they are of the so-called "gentler sex".'

Which explained his comment a moment ago, Neville supposed, shocked despite himself. 'So it was a woman who was involved in this crime? What will happen to her? If you find out you're right?'

Brown took out a handkerchief to blot the sweat from his face. It was hot in here, very hot, but Neville thought he did it to draw out the moment, increase the drama of it.

'Women don't hang very often, Mr Darling, but in this case I wouldn't be surprised. Not at all surprised. In fact, if it was up to me she certainly would.'

That was sobering. 'And you say she murdered someone?' he asked, and then wished he hadn't. Gossip like this left an unpleasant taste in the mouth and Brown's obvious enjoyment was making it worse.

The other man gave him a look over the rim of his teacup. 'She killed a man with a knife,' he said with a level of sangfroid that Neville couldn't help but admire.

The ex-Detective Inspector set down his cup and reached into his pocket, and took out a photograph. 'This was found among the murdered man's belongings. His wife didn't know who it was and neither did his friends.' Neville eyed it with interest, and wasn't averse to taking it when it was offered.

'Is this the woman you think killed him?' he asked unnecessarily.

'Yes. Do you know her? It was taken on the pier at St Kilda. Not a particularly good likeness, but it's all I have. I don't know her name, but my information is that she lives somewhere in these mountains, although no one I ask seems to recognise her, or if they do they don't want to tell me about it. Some sort of misguided loyalty, perhaps? I've given up trying to understand the ways of …'

His voice faded into the clamour and Neville

found his attention fixed on the face before him. Brown was right, it wasn't a particularly good photograph. The woman had half lifted a hand to brush a strand of hair out of her face. She was standing on the pier with the bay behind her, and the wind was blowing her skirt against her legs, moulding it to her slim body, and yet she was smiling. A half-smile, as if the situation amused her, and as if whoever was behind the camera was someone she was happy to be with. A secret smile just for him. Because it had to be a man, didn't it?

'What do you think?' Brown said.

Neville had forgotten he was there. Because the face before him was unforgettable for so many reasons that he could never explain them to Brown's satisfaction. The eyes with their slight slant, hinting at an exotic ancestry, the soft shape of her cheek that made his fingers itch to touch it, and the long dark hair. They were only a part of it. She was, he thought, young. Perhaps twenty, but she appeared younger. A girl in the first flush of womanhood, and although that sounded trite he thought it was probably true. And the man behind the camera? Was he her first lover?

'Who took this?' he asked, tapping the sepia photo.

'The gentleman she murdered, most likely.'

Neville looked down at her face again, noting how the curve of her mouth was shy and hopeful and all the things a girl of that age tended to be. He shook his head. 'She should be punished for that, of course, if she did it, but to be hanged …'

'You don't approve of hanging?' Brown spoke

sharply.

'I … I don't approve of murder by either side.'

'You weren't one of those conchies?' Brown leaned forward, seeming to quiver with outrage.

Neville felt himself go cold despite the heat. He understood the stance of the conscientious objectors, although he was never one himself. But there was something about the other man's self-righteousness that drew up those feelings of anger and pain from the well inside him. Memories of the war and the hospital, which despite being years in the past were things he still struggled with every day. He forced them back down into the murky depths, slammed shut the lid, and took a moment to regain himself.

'I did my bit,' he said, and reached for his cup, pleased to see his hand only had a slight tremor. There was a time when he'd been quite unable to drink any liquid without spilling it all over himself.

Miller Brown seemed to relax. 'Me, too.'

It was obvious the other man was getting ready to launch into his own wartime experiences, so Neville changed the subject without making it too obvious. They chatted for a while about the weather and the state of the government with the popular Joseph Lyons at the helm as prime minister.

The heat in the hotel was becoming so oppressive that Neville excused himself and went outside to light his cigarette. That was when he realised he still had the photograph in his hand. He considered whether he'd held on to it on purpose, because the woman—the girl—intrigued him.

He knew he should return it, and yet he found himself walking away, down the long sloping hill that led from the hotel and into the town proper. He told himself then that he'd taken the photograph because he wanted to save the girl, or at least delay Brown in finding her. It wasn't entirely true. The image was compelling and he wanted to keep it.

Neville thought he heard a shout behind him and he quickened his pace, until he had left the hotel far behind.

CHAPTER 4

SKYE

Saturday 7 June 1997

WITHIN TWO DAYS, Russell had arranged for her ride to Elysian, which had given Skye enough time to sort out her schedule. And Fraser.

Her ex-husband had appeared at the door of her Carlton terrace house on Friday night, after he'd promised to look after her cat. He didn't look happy. Skye had done her best to reschedule her appointments and, for any that couldn't be moved, she'd arranged for other staff members to take them on. So he really had no reason for complaint.

'What is this?' Fraser gave her his best mocking smile. 'An adventure? Are you going all *Alice in Wonderland* on me? Down the rabbit hole?'

Fraser knew Alice was one of Skye's favourite childhood books.

'Ha ha. Fraser, you know about my real grandfather. You know I want to find out what happened to him. This is my chance. Russell has teed up a lift with one of his colleagues going my way.'

He scowled, leaning against the doorjamb. Milly wrapped herself around his legs and his face softened. When her mother had died, Skye had taken on the cat, but Milly was closer to her ex-husband than she had ever been to Skye, and it was clear the love was reciprocated.

'I've bailed you out more than once,' Skye reminded him, adding another sweater to her bag and then jamming in her suede boots. She hesitated over a chic black dress with long sleeves and a lace insert below the knees. Would there be anywhere in Elysian to wear it? Still, better safe than sorry, she decided, and tucked it in.

Elysian had a hotel—she'd looked it up—and she was planning to ask her lift to drop her off there. When she'd rung them no one had answered so she'd left a message on their machine. She'd booked for a week with the possibility of longer, just in case. Who knew, she may never pass that way again.

'What about when you wanted to take Helen to Broome for a romantic holiday for two?' she jogged Fraser's memory.

He shuddered. 'You should've stopped me.'

Skye tried not to smile. 'I did try. She was never for you.'

'You were always more my type,' he said, bending to stroke Milly. 'Tell me, why did we get divorced?'

'Because you couldn't keep your hands off the customers, and they couldn't keep their hands off you.' At the time Skye had called him a deviant, but she'd long since realised the problem was he lacked the moral fibre to say no. Charming and gorgeous as Fraser was, women were drawn to him, and that wasn't his fault, as he so often had informed her. 'We're still friends though,' she told him, 'that's better than being married.'

He heaved a sigh. 'All right. Go off on your adventure. I can manage.'

'Thank you, Fraser.'

'Take care, Skye,' he added, as he scooped up Milly and turned to leave. 'That's wild country you're going to, and you're a woman who likes neatness and order. Don't get lost.'

She'd laughed, but his words had left her with a sense of unease.

Now it was late Friday night and Skye couldn't sleep, and finally she gave up just before midnight and logged on to the internet to search for Elysian and Mackenzie Crossing.

There wasn't anything on the latter, but the former seemed better known—if you could call a couple of terse pages on road closures and information on weather conditions from the local cop, Sergeant Galloway, a mark of recognition. There was also a forum run by a four-wheel-drive club with hair-raising descriptions of their adventures on the mountain tracks around the town, and a summertime panorama of the country beyond Elysian, with mountain tops receding into the distant hazy sky. One of them in particular, Mt Elysian, rose up a few kilometres north-west of the town.

Beautiful, yes, but also uncomfortable for a girl who preferred tower blocks and department stores. And yet, she told herself, surely being there would help her to understand what had drawn Neville to such isolation?

Or maybe she would just have to accept that, as photographers and people, they were poles apart.

The next morning Skye's ride—Detective Constable Chang—was supposed to have picked her up by eight, but instead she received a call to say that he had been delayed and couldn't get away until the afternoon. So she hung around the whole day, kicking her heels. Then when he did arrive he informed her that he was only driving her as far as a place called Lockington.

'Means I can go straight on to Cumberland,' Chan explained. 'Save myself a bit of time. Although Lockington is still *way* out of my way. Russell is a good friend of yours, is he?'

Which seemed to imply his arm had been twisted.

Detective Constable Chang was thickset, his dark hair cut very short, and he wasn't wearing a uniform. When he noticed her glance at his civilian jeans and jacket, he explained he was a plain-clothes detective with the Armed Offenders Squad.

'Apologies for the wait,' he added, not sounding sorry at all.

'I'm just grateful for the lift,' Skye replied, smiling to show how understanding she was. Now they were finally about to set off she just wanted to get in the car and go.

His four-wheel drive was parked out the front of her house, and when he slung her bag carelessly into the back she tried not to wince. Her Pentax digital camera was carefully packed, she reminded herself, and he couldn't hurt it. They both climbed in and as he manoeuvred his vehicle out of the narrow street and into the traffic, he explained the situation.

'You're lucky. There was a hold-up a week ago and one of the offenders was from Cumberland. I have to go and take some statements. The locals could do it, but my boss wants all the t's crossed and i's dotted for when we get to court. I'd drop you off there—it's more direct for me—only Sergeant Galloway can't get down to Cumberland tonight. He can meet us halfway, though, at Lockington. That's where he'll collect you.'

Sergeant Galloway, she knew from her internet search last night, was the police officer stationed at Elysian.

'I feel like a parcel delivery,' she said with a laugh, hoping he wouldn't just leave her on the side of the road. 'It's very kind of you to do this for me.'

He shrugged modestly, as if Russell hadn't been the persuader and this was all his idea. 'That's me. Mr Generosity. Not sure about Galloway. He has a bit of a reputation as a hard man.'

'Oh?'

'My advice? Don't let him intimidate you. He

has a difficult job to do and I reckon you need to be tough when you've got a thousand square kilometres of rugged country to watch over.'

Skye could understand that, but all the same she wasn't going to be intimidated by anyone. This was about her lost grandfather, a journey of discovery, and if Sergeant Galloway wasn't happy about her walking into his 'patch', then she'd be happy to stay out of his way. Then again she was going to need his help. She was a stranger here and she couldn't afford to put the sergeant's back up. It might require some careful juggling, and Skye knew from her work as a photographer that she was good with difficult customers.

Detective Chang—his name was Mark—chatted off and on as he weaved his way out of the city and along the busy highway, heading northeast. They soon left the suburbs behind, and Skye could see the hills getting closer. She wanted to ask him detailed questions about Mackenzie Crossing, but he didn't seem to know any more about it than her. She'd have to keep her curiosity for Sergeant Galloway and hope he wasn't as unapproachable as he sounded.

They made a stop for coffee in Warburton, a pretty little town on the Yarra River, and a gateway to the mountains. The sky had a cold look to it now, and Skye was glad to get back into the cabin and the heating. Despite her eagerness to reach her destination, and the caffeine, she began to nod off. Because she hadn't slept very well the night before, and the day so far had been an anxious and tense one, she was paying the price and now her eyes were closing.

When she woke it was to find the lowering sun playing peekaboo with the trees outside the windscreen. She stretched as much as she could in the cramped space. They were climbing through a set of switchbacks and hairpin bends on a road that was much narrower and less well travelled than previously.

'Too many late nights, huh?' her companion teased. He had the music on low—something with a bass beat—and was tapping his finger against the steering wheel. 'Another couple of hours and we should be at Lockington.' He pointed ahead and she could see snowy peaks against the darkening sky. 'This place has more National Parks than you can poke a stick at. Keep going and you'll hit the Snowy River.'

Skye nodded. The country was certainly grand. And wild. She could understand why it was called the Victorian Alps. While she'd been asleep the bush seemed to have gone from something away in the distance to being right there in her face. The trees weren't the sort of trees she was used to, either. These were tall mountain ash, their trunks straight, while their crowns of smoky-grey foliage loomed high above. Among the understorey were lush tree ferns of varying sizes, bracken and a variety of scrubby bushes. And it was also cooler, despite the heating.

Suddenly, she wished she'd left the chic black dress out of her suitcase and added another sweater.

The setting sun was stabbing at her eyes through

the windscreen, giving her the beginnings of a headache. Sleeping in the car hadn't helped, and she reached up to rub at the knots in her neck, when abruptly there was a break in the trees at her side. She found herself looking down into a valley and there at the bottom was a ribbon of water. Further over the land rose up steeply to a spur that had her tilting her head. And all around them the dense bush covered everything. It seemed unrelenting and rather disturbing to the city girl she now accepted she was.

How on earth could Neville have felt at home here? Perhaps he hadn't. Perhaps he'd died longing to get back to the safety and familiarity of Adelaide. Would she ever find out?

'Do many people live around here?' she ventured.

The further they went the less traffic they saw until it seemed to her they were the only ones left on the road.

'Not many,' Mark answered her easily. 'You know this is one of the most isolated areas of Victoria? Lockington is on a High Country plateau, so we'll keep climbing for a bit. I'm hoping the roads aren't as bad as Russell warned me.'

Skye hoped so, too.

'It must take a certain kind of person to live up here,' Mark went on, as if answering an unspoken question. 'Not sure how I'd cope. I like the city. Hustle and bustle suits me.'

'And Sergeant Galloway?'

'I reckon he'd *have* to like it.' He laughed. 'He's been stationed in Elysian for five years now.'

'Five *years*!'

He gave her a humourless grin.

Soon even the glow in the western sky was gone and clouds covered the stars and moon. Darkness seemed absolute, and the car headlights were barely able to penetrate the wall of night in front of them. Skye looked anxiously about her and wanted to ask Mark how much further, but she'd already asked him that question. She was starting to sound like a frightened child.

'It's this country,' he'd explained. 'Takes time to get anywhere.'

They seemed to have reached the plateau now. The roof of the world, or that was what it felt like. At least there was no more climbing or switchbacks, and they were driving on a level surface, but she couldn't see anything apart from the strip of bitumen in front of them, picked out by the glow of their headlights.

Skye was just beginning to wonder if she'd inadvertently strayed into one of those movies, where the woman steps through a hole in the space-time continuum, and is doomed to drive forever, when Mark slammed on the brakes.

'Bloody dog!'

Skye's heart jumped as she lurched forward. She clung to the dashboard, feeling the sharp tug of her seatbelt across her chest. In the headlights she could see the lean animal in the middle of the road.

It sat very still. Watching them.

It was a greyhound. But that only made the situation odder, because didn't greyhounds belong on race tracks and in kennels? They surely didn't reside out here in the empty darkness on top of the world.

Impatiently, Mark gave a blast on his horn. The dog took its time getting to its feet, and then turned and trotted leisurely off to the side and into the night. The detective shook his head and started to drive forward again, muttering, 'Now I know I've seen everything.'

Skye peered over her shoulder in the direction the greyhound had taken; it was too dark to see anything. Although … was that a cottage? Yes, and there was another. She realised that among the trees there were houses strung out along the road. Dark and silent and empty.

'Is this Lockington?' she asked, twisting in her seat, trying to see if there was anyone awake, anyone at all.

'Yep. I had a friend who stayed here once. He said there weren't any permanent residents anymore. Just holiday rentals. Hikers. People who like their own company.'

He sounded as if the breed was a complete mystery to him.

'Ah, here's your man.'

Up ahead a pair of glaring headlights was approaching. Skye squinted her eyes against them, watching as slowly the two vehicles drew closer to each other. She could recognise another four-wheel drive now, although this one was white with blue markings, and it had the word 'Police' printed across the bonnet.

Mark stopped a few metres away and left the

engine running.

She'd finally reached her destination, and all of a sudden Skye wasn't at all sure she wanted to get out into the unknown. Out of her comfort zone. As Fraser had said, she was a woman who liked neatness and order, and she had a strange feeling that what she was about to find in Elysian was going to test her.

'Ready?' Mark looked at her uncertainly. Perhaps it happened all the time, people coming up here and then chickening out and running off back to the city. Where it was safe.

Well, Skye told herself, she wasn't going to be one of them. 'Yes, I'm ready,' she said in her best confident-sounding voice.

Mark opened his door.

The air was cold and Skye could smell the astringent scent of eucalyptus, mixed with some recent rain. It was so lonely, and so eerie. She climbed out, and immediately shivered and folded her arms. Right now the hum of engines filled the silence, but when they were gone, Skye thought this place would be so quiet she could probably hear her heart beating and the blood rushing through her arteries and veins. She could probably hear her own mortality.

Mark had brought her bag from the back of the four-wheel drive and now he carried it past her, towards the other vehicle. Skye fell into step behind him. Sergeant Galloway still hadn't exited, although as they drew closer she could see his dark shape behind the windscreen.

'Sergeant Galloway?' Mark called out.

The door opened and light illuminated the cabin. Now Skye could see that Galloway was talking on the handset of his radio.

'I'll get back to you on it,' she thought she heard him say, and then he terminated the call. As he climbed out and walked towards them she noticed that unlike Mark Chang he wore a police uniform. Dark-blue trousers and a zip-up jacket with the Victoria Police insignia. He was also tall. Her overriding impression, before he stepped in front of the headlights and became a silhouette, was of dark hair and a frown.

And yet there was something else …

Something that made her feel disorientated.

'Here she is,' Mark had a cheery note in his voice. Skye supposed he was happy to offload her so that he could get back to his proper job. She wanted to turn and make a joke of it, except that something was holding her to the spot.

She couldn't seem to move.

The man in front of her hadn't moved either.

'Skye Stewart.' Remembering her manners even if he had none, she made an effort and took a step forward and held out her hand to him. 'Thank you for meeting me, Sergeant Galloway.'

His hand closed over hers in a hard, strong grip.

'Hello, Skye, it's been a long time,' said Finn Faraday, the boy she'd loved when she was fifteen years old.

CHAPTER 5

NEVILLE

Tuesday 10 January 1939,
Mackenzie Crossing

NEVILLE DARLING STOOD catching his breath at the top of the downward track to Mackenzie Crossing. Unfortunately, the dire warnings he'd read in Saturday's *Herald* had been fulfilled, and fire had overtaken several Victorian towns and bush settlements. All over the state warning bells had been ringing, and there were reports of houses and timber mills lost, and with them lives. By Monday the heat had waned slightly, although it was still uncomfortable. No one was quite sure what would happen next.

Sweat rolled down his back beneath his shirt and there was a drip from beneath the brim of his hat. As he reached up to wipe his arm across his forehead, he could taste the salt on his lips, and the smoke.

Tossing his swag into some shade, he carefully placed his scruffy leather camera case on top, before reaching into his trouser pocket for the makings of his cigarettes. Neville crouched down on his haunches, and began the unhurried process of rolling up the tobacco in the paper. Once it was done, he lit it, putting the spent match back into his pocket. One couldn't be too careful in this weather.

Back in Elysian they'd been waiting and watching. Would the fires stay away, or would they come roaring down upon the town? No one was leaving, not until they knew. Nonetheless the anxiety was palpable. Last night, as he'd camped on the lonely track, Neville had seen the flames in the distance, like evil red eyes, but they were still a long way away and he wasn't particularly worried.

Again he reached into his pocket, and this time took out the photograph of the girl standing on the pier with the salty wind tangling her dark hair. He'd left Elysian almost immediately after his conversation with Miller Brown. He wasn't sure why he hadn't wanted to run into the man again. Now, after a couple of nights alone in the bush, he decided he'd acted rashly in taking the photograph. Had the ex-Detective Inspector been telling him the truth, or was he just another of the odd characters one met in this isolated part of the country? Perhaps it had been a hoax and he'd been taken in by it. He felt slightly foolish, remembering how he had thought himself a hero, and that by taking the photo he was saving the girl.

It was a relief that Brown and his strange story

were now behind him, Neville thought, as he straightened. He tilted his head and looked up at the hazy, grey sky. Hardly any birds. Lately he'd seen a few fall, dead on the wing. It was the heat that did it. Not many wallabies about either, or anything else for that matter. It was very quiet and all creatures, whether they flew or hopped or crawled, were lying low.

Neville took off his hat and wiped his forehead again, glancing at his camera case. He was modestly pleased with the work he was doing. Lately he'd even been thinking about an exhibition of his photographs, although it seemed strange that something he'd begun as a way of helping himself get through the bad patches might now bring him a little bit of fame.

Would Mary hear about him, if he was famous? Would she and little Gertie seek him out? His thoughts started down their well-worn path.

Neville had never tried to explain what he had seen on the Western Front to his wife and his little girl. He didn't talk about it, not to anyone. Because when the men around him—friends and comrades—had died and he'd remained standing, something in him had broken.

Even when they'd called him a hero for the way he'd taken his men all the way across no-man's-land to the enemy trenches ... well, it had meant nothing. He'd known that after the sights he'd seen he could never be the same again. In his heart he'd known he was a dead man walking.

And then one day in 1926 he'd seen the new Leica 1 (Model A) in the window of a camera store in London, and on impulse he'd gone in. The salesman had been so enthusiastic—full of the possibilities of this new era of photography. Until now, he'd explained, cameras were large, unwieldy beasts, not for carrying about with you on a whim. With this little beauty it would be possible to go on holiday and bring your memories home with you in a tangible form. Reporters could carry it along with them and record important news events. Record history! Neville had listened and learned, and he'd been hooked.

He'd paid the sixteen pounds on the spot.

Photography became a distraction, a way of occupying his brain, of replacing with new images those awful pictures that seemed to churn up inside him, spewing out of the well, over and over again.

The camera became his closest companion.

His new hobby hadn't pleased his father, who had wanted Neville to knuckle down to workaday life. It was impossible, of course, although he'd tried, but being 'normal' put an unbearable strain on him. His mother had looked at him when she'd thought he wasn't watching, and he'd read the sadness in her face for the son she had lost. And then someone had said Australia was the place to go if you wanted to leave your past behind, and so he'd taken passage on a ship to Adelaide.

His family hadn't been able to disguise how relieved they were to see him go, and Adelaide was elegant and the climate very different from home, with its long, hot summer days. In a short time, he'd turned his distraction into a career and built himself a nice little business. That was how he'd met Mary.

She'd come to him to have her portrait done—it was to be a present for her parents—and he'd been smitten. She was young and innocent, and to his amazement she didn't seem to see anything wrong with him. When she gazed at him with her big brown eyes, she saw Neville Darling, English gentleman and war hero, not the dark, shattered character he knew lurked beneath his skin.

So he'd lain awake night after night, tossing and turning. Should he take a chance? Was this girl going to heal him? And he'd thought the answer was yes.

But he'd made the wrong decision. He'd been too ambitious too soon. Maybe the time would never be right for such a step. Once the marriage service was over, the old sense of claustrophobia came rushing back. That feeling of being hemmed in by some unnamed danger. And then the dreams. Over and over, every night, the trenches overflowing with blood and bodies.

Mary was afraid when he woke up sobbing and screaming. She hadn't married *this* man. She didn't know how to cope with him.

Neville had to face the truth then. His young wife was already starting to fear him, and soon his daughter would learn to fear him, too, or worse, hate him, and he knew he couldn't bear that.

He began to go off on his own, walking mostly, taking photographs of the land and its people. Especially the people. He told Mary he was planning to sell the images, but really it was to give her a break from his presence. He could see she was glad of it. She had her parents and Gertie, and her friends. Every time he came home from his little trips she seemed less enthusiastic to see him.

And then one day he didn't come home.

Neville caught trains and buses, and he walked, and eventually he ended up in the Victorian High Country. He did miss his family, terribly. Over time, though, being out here in the never-never, the isolation, the stillness of the bush and mountains, began to restore his battered soul. Not completely—he'd probably never be completely mended—and why should he, when so many were dead? But there was a sense of renewal that he'd never expected.

Neville finished his cigarette and put it out on the heel of his boot, then slipped the butt safely into his pocket. He picked up his swag and the leather case. Inside was his precious Leica 1 (Model A) camera. As the years had passed, cameras had changed. 'Improved', some said. The newer models didn't need an expert behind the lens. They could focus a shot for you, judge the distance accurately, and all you had to do was push the button.

Neville preferred his old Leica. Perhaps he'd become a purist, but he believed that some things were too important to be made easy. By now the camera he'd seen in the store window all those years ago had become almost an extension of himself.

He also usually preferred to develop his own

negatives, but that wasn't possible out here. Nowhere to set up a dark room, or store his equipment, and it wasn't a simple matter of taking the print from the negative by contact, not with 35-mm film. He'd need an enlarger. So he normally sent off the rolls of film to the laboratory in Melbourne—he had a fellow enthusiast there—and they would come back just as he wanted them.

It was the chap in the laboratory who had begun to talk about an exhibition, and how he had friends at the State Library who would be interested. Neville had smiled politely and said he'd think about it.

That was for the future, perhaps. Right now he was looking forward to Mackenzie Crossing, the place he'd been wanting to visit ever since he'd heard about it. Neville was hoping he might get some interesting photographs. He was always on the lookout for that special something. He wanted to know what it was that made these people able to withstand the loneliness and hardship of the country in which they lived. Lately he'd begun to believe the country itself had a lot to do with shaping that character. Toughness and resilience, certainly, but there was something more he was yet to fully understand. He saw it in their eyes when he looked through his viewfinder.

If only he could immortalise it on film.

And he had a feeling that here, he just might find what he was looking for.

The bush and ferns along the dirt track that led into the valley seemed to droop more with each passing moment. A lizard eyed him warily from beside a rock before scuttling further into the shadows. For a moment Neville questioned if he was doing the right thing. Maybe he should head back to Melbourne and wait out the summer?

He hesitated on the brink, as if some sixth sense was telling him to turn around. But Neville had survived one of the bloodiest wars in history, he was alive when he should by rights be dead, and he didn't feel the need to play it safe. So he started down the track, the dust puffing up under his boots as each step brought him closer to Mackenzie Crossing.

CHAPTER 6

SKYE

Saturday 7 June 1997

THERE HAD BEEN times, moments, when Skye had wondered if she would recognise Finn again. Maybe she had passed him on the street already without knowing it. Nineteen years was a long time and people changed. They'd been teenagers back then, and although she couldn't imagine not knowing him it was more rational to think he'd be a stranger to her now.

And yet there had been that moment when she saw him silhouetted against the headlights … that sense of time shifting. Of knowing.

There was nothing rational about that, or the way she was feeling right now.

'Finn? But … you're Sergeant *Galloway*.' She knew it sounded stupid, as if somehow he'd mistaken his own identity.

'My father's name's Galloway,' he explained gruffly. 'Legally I've always been Galloway.'

He let her hand go and she felt the tingle left

by his grip. Skye folded her arms, not knowing what to think or how to feel. Finn's dark eyes slid over her—she was wearing the same outfit she'd worn to meet Russell two days ago. Tight red jeans and matching boots, white sweater and the woollen white coat. He probably thought she was as out of place here in Lockington as a pair of high heels on a hiking holiday, and suddenly she wished she'd chosen something more practical.

As if that might have made a difference.

Finn's gaze finally shifted beyond her to Detective Chang, who was watching them with interest. 'You heading on to Cumberland now?'

'Yep. Don't want to be too late getting there, the locals are probably used to being in bed by sundown.' He said it with a laugh that wasn't quite derisive.

Finn didn't reply, though his disapproval was obvious.

Detective Chang cleared his throat and rubbed his hands together. 'Well, then.' He turned to Skye with a smile. 'Good luck. I hope you find your relative.'

Finn Galloway shot her a quick glance, as if he was speculating on which relative she was searching for. He didn't ask, he just reached for her bag and made his way to the back of his police vehicle.

Skye was glad he hadn't said any more. She wasn't sure she was up to having a conversation with him. She was starting to think she should be angry. Surely he had known who she was? He must have! There weren't that many Skye Stewarts around, and yet he hadn't warned her.

'Bye!' Detective Chang called, and she turned to see him lift a hand in farewell as he climbed back into his vehicle.

'Thank you,' she replied, lifting her own hand in response as her voice was swallowed up by the rev of the engine.

She stood a moment, watching his red taillights disappear into nothingness.

Here she was, all alone with Finn Faraday. Whatever he called himself now, he was still the person she hadn't seen since she was fifteen and who she'd thought, well, she'd *hoped* never to see again. That time had been such a mess of emotions and she didn't want to revisit it.

What the hell was she going to do?

'Skye? Are you getting in? The temperature must be just above freezing.'

Did she have a choice?

When she turned he was standing beside the open driver's door, and she had to wonder if he was really as calm as he looked. Maybe it didn't bother him at all, seeing her again. But she didn't think that was true. There was something about the set of his shoulders and his watchful eyes that made her certain that Finn, like her, was wishing himself anywhere except here.

Still, there was no help for it. She could hardly ask to be left behind, could she? Skye strode up to the vehicle, noting the mud splattering along the side and caking the tyre rims, and got in. So did he. Immediately she realised how big he was, much bigger than she'd remembered. He'd been a boy when she knew him before, she reminded herself, and now he was a grown man. It didn't help. She felt as if he was sucking all the air out of the space.

'Skye,' he said, something between a plea and an order, and waited for her to look at him. When she didn't he went on anyway. 'As far as I'm concerned the past is the past. We don't have to mention it. We can be strangers. If that's what you want.'

'Yes.' Skye nodded decisively. 'That's what I want.'

He lifted both of his hands off the wheel and held them up. 'Sorry.'

'You should've told me.'

Skye sensed him still watching her and it seemed safer not to look back.

'Who's missing?' he asked casually, changing the subject and buckling up his seatbelt. 'Chang said you had a missing relative.'

She was tempted to tell him that was none of his business, but of course it was. How could she do any of the things she'd planned to do without his help?

'My grandfather,' she answered reluctantly. 'He went missing a long time ago. In the thirties. At Mackenzie Crossing.'

Then Skye made the mistake of turning to face him and discovered he had fixed her with the full force of his attention. He'd always been able to do that, she remembered with a jolt. Pin her with his dark eyes and make her think she was the only one in the world that mattered. For a moment the memories of their last night together rose in a wave of emotion, threatening to swamp her, but she forced them back into the imaginary box in which she kept them.

And that was when she realised what she should have seen from the first, and if she'd been in her right mind she would have. He looked tired. Older, also, because he was nineteen years older. But it was more than that. The shadows under his eyes were grey and the lines on either side of his mouth were deep. He looked as if he had been up for days on end without rest.

Somehow seeing him like this made her feel less panicked.

'Why did you let me come?' she demanded.

He seemed to be working on an answer that wouldn't make the situation worse. Maybe being in the police force had taught him some negotiating skills, but then she remembered he'd always been measured in his conversation. As if he was holding back.

'What should I have done, Skye? I was given a message last night that a woman needed to be collected at Cumberland. I couldn't do that. We arranged for you to be dropped off here instead. Then I heard this afternoon that it was one of those scratch-my-back sort of favours, and the woman was Skye Stewart. You were on your way by then. It was too late.'

'You still should have said no.'

The cabin light had remained on, and her reflection stared back at her, wide-eyed and, if she was honest, a little crazy.

He gave a humourless laugh. 'Right. I thought we might be able to act like adults after all this time. Anyway, what does it matter? What happened, it was years ago. Forgotten.'

She was silent a moment longer but her anger was fading and the churning shock and emotion with it. She felt a bit sick. In essence he was right, it was years ago, and it didn't matter. Except obviously it did, to her.

But Finn didn't have to know that, and actually it was better if he didn't.

'All right,' she said, proud of her even tone.

'Good.' He sounded relieved.

'But only because I might need your help.'

He laughed again; there was humour in it this time. 'Fair enough. What happened to your grandfather?'

'His name was Neville Darling. I always thought my grandfather was Louis, but when Mum was dying she said some things and afterwards I found out Louis wasn't her biological father. Neville was.'

Talking seemed to be helping, so she went on, explaining about the missing person's file and the possibility Neville had come up here to take photographs.

He was a good listener, and a memory stirred and reminded her that he always had been. While she'd been talking, he'd turned the vehicle around, but they'd only travelled a few metres when he stopped again and she saw the greyhound. Once more it was in the middle of the road, ears pricked, staring at them. Before she could comment, or express her concern, Finn reached behind him and opened the back door. Immediately the dog came at a run and jumped inside, front paws going up onto Skye's seat. She ducked to avoid a pink tongue.

'Down. Sit.'

The dog did as it was told, arranging its slim grey body on a blanket. So it belonged to Finn. That made sense. He'd always had a dog—there'd been an old kelpie that used to follow him about when he came home from school.

They set off again, and about a mile further on they left the plateau and began to head down a gravel road—more like a track—that quickly became dirt. He drove very fast as they twisted and turned in the darkness. Well, he must have good night vision, Skye told herself optimistically. She had planned to ask questions about Mackenzie Crossing, but her previous need for conversation seemed to have dried up and now she stayed quiet.

A burst of static on the CB radio made her jump. Finn reached for the handset, eyes on the road, not slowing down even one bit.

'Yeah?'

'Finn?' A male voice. Young. 'Are you nearly back?'

'I have a passenger to drop off. I'll be there as soon as I can.' A pause. 'You okay, Taylor?'

Some throat clearing. 'Yep, thanks, see you soon.'

Finn hung up and glanced at Skye. 'Temporary staff,' he said, as if she needed an explanation. 'Alison, my usual operator, is down with the flu.'

A question popped into her head so she asked it. 'How many people do you have working for you?'

He considered it a moment before he answered, as if she'd set him a trap. They were both stepping around each other like cautious cats.

'Normally there's Alison and me and two constables. No constables at the moment, one's been seconded to an investigation outside the area, and the other position is still pending. The government likes to pretend it's going to cut our funding now and again, until the outcry forces the pollies to rethink.'

'It happens the world over.'

Finn nodded, giving her another glance. 'We're just about there,' he said.

'Mackenzie Crossing?'

His surprise was genuine. 'Mackenzie Crossing doesn't exist anymore. I'm based in Elysian. It's the biggest place for miles, which isn't saying much.'

'How big is it?'

'Population of a hundred, which includes the surrounding area, although that multiplies during holiday times. There are a few tiny settlements further out, but Elysian is the service centre. Next place of any size after us is Westcott. Even though we're part of Westcott Shire, most of the time we're on our own.'

It was surreal listening to him speak so confidently, and yet she shouldn't have been surprised. Finn had always been clever—the most grown up out of the three of them. Skye, Finn and Dylan, the three crusaders, trouble with a capital T.

She almost asked where Dylan was, but luckily before the words could form—and it would have been a huge mistake, she realised almost at once—she saw the lights.

They'd been travelling on dirt roads up till now, when abruptly the sound of the tyres changed as they hit bitumen, and there in front of them was a long sloping descent. To either side she could see buildings. Actual proper, inhabited buildings. She noticed a two-storey hotel on her left, while beyond it was a string of shops and there, at the bottom, was a modern-looking box building with an illuminated sign that said 'Police'.

Civilisation, Skye thought with relief.

Finn drove through the town without stopping.

'I booked at the hotel. I left a message.' Skye turned her head anxiously. The greyhound met her eyes and yawned.

'Sorry. Undergoing renovations. No running water or heating at the moment.'

'I don't mind. I can make do.' She sounded desperate.

He seemed almost amused. 'The owners are away.'

Reluctantly she turned to face the front again. 'Then where are we going?'

His hands tightened on the wheel and then he let out a breath. 'Look, I know this isn't ideal. I had to make a decision on the run. Alison was going to put you up, but now that she has the flu I can hardly drop you off at her door. So you'll have to stay at my place, just until she's better. Don't worry, you'll hardly see me,' he added quickly, sensing her rising consternation. 'I'm out most of the time. You'll have the place to yourself, Skye.'

'Your place?' she repeated. 'No, Finn, I … no.'

He turned off the main road and suddenly they were on another dirt track, back in the thick of the bush. Skye hung on, her incipient headache beating time with the bumpy road. Just as it reached the point of being too much and she thought she might scream, they pushed through into a cleared area, and there before her was the dark shape of a house with a verandah.

The greyhound whined and stood up, sleek body turning in circles. Finn's shoulders rose and fell, as if he was taking another deep breath and preparing himself for whatever she might have to say.

Skye had never been one to hold back.

When he turned to her she could barely see him in the darkness, just the shape of his face. 'I'm sorry,' he apologised yet again. 'I know this is the last thing you want, but there's really no alternative.'

He sounded sincere and it helped. Skye told herself she needed to be reasonable. Adult. And anyway what choice did she have? 'I suppose it's only a few days. Are you, um, with anyone? Is your wife …?'

'In Perth, last I heard.'

And he opened the door and got out.

She'd touched a raw spot, Skye thought wearily,

as she climbed out and followed. Maybe it was her turn to say sorry? By the time she'd reached the house he had the lights on. Now she could see that it was a classic Australian homestead, with a wooden verandah all the way around and a sloping roof. The greyhound loped along beside her as if it was showing her around.

The house felt warm. Inside the front door a central passageway was gleaming with cream paint and polished floorboards, but there didn't seem to be much in the way of furnishings or pictures on the walls. Finn was standing by a room further along, and Skye made her way towards him, glancing in the open doorways as she passed.

A sitting room with an open fireplace, and a bedroom with a pink bedspread on a cute iron-framed bed. Added to that were Little Pony curtains like Russell's daughter's bedroom, and Skye abruptly realised that Finn's wife had taken more than just herself off to Perth.

Strangely, seeing the little girl's room actually quietened some of Skye's doubts about being alone in the house with this man who had once been on the most intimate terms with her, and who she hardly knew now.

They were strangers and admitting it was a relief. She didn't have to try to be his friend, she didn't have to discuss what had happened, she could just be a polite visitor.

'This is it,' Finn said, his deep voice cool and equally civil.

The bedroom was sparse in comforts, but it had the bare essentials—a bed and a wardrobe and a mirror. There was also another fireplace with logs neatly stacked ready to light. She imagined it could get cold up here.

'You shouldn't need the fire in here tonight. I have a firebox in the kitchen and it's adequate most of the time.' That explained the warm house.

He'd put her bag beside the bed and was standing with his hands in his pockets, letting her take it all in. Skye went to the window—the curtains were still open—and looked outside. It was dark, though the verandah lights shone out far enough for her to see there was a grassed yard running down to a line of trees. For a moment she thought she could hear water running, as if there was a creek, but maybe it was her imagination. She was used to Melbourne, and the noise of traffic and people had become so familiar it no longer bothered her. She pondered whether the quiet would keep her awake.

'Okay?' he sounded impatient, as if she was wasting his time. She turned back and found him frowning again, his dark eyes watchful. The shadows under them were greyer and his features even more drawn. Not that she was looking much better. A glimpse in the mirror had been enough—white face and reddened eyes and her hair sticking up. She ran a hand over it now, pulling it back to her nape.

'Yes, fine, thank you. I'll stay out of your way. I know you're a busy man. A lot on your plate and so forth.'

He looked surprised. 'At the moment I do. Have a lot on my plate. There's an ongoing operation and I need to keep tabs on things.' He shrugged. 'In fact, I have to get back to the station now. But none of that should affect you. Tomorrow morning we'll work out some sort of plan for your stay.'

A plan sounded good, so she nodded.

'Right, well the bathroom is next door, and the kitchen is at the back. I've stocked up on what I thought you might need, but if there's anything else let me know.'

'Thank you. Again, I'll try not to get in your way.'

'No worries. Goodnight, Skye.'

He smiled. It softened his face and unexpectedly there was more of the boy in him than she'd thought. It threw her, and his next words unsettled her even more.

'Sorry to hear about your mother. She was a nice person.'

To her dismay tears stung her eyes. *No, no, no.* She bent down to fumble with the opening to her bag. 'Thanks, er, Finn.'

To her relief he turned and left, closing the door behind him.

Shortly afterwards she heard him talking on a telephone somewhere in the house, voice muted. Not long after that the police vehicle started up again, the engine fading as it headed once more down the rough track.

Finn was gone and Skye was alone, which seemed like a good thing right now.

Well, almost alone, she thought, as the dog whined at the door and she heard the scratch of its claws on the wooden panels. She opened it and the greyhound pattered in, heading hopefully over to the rug by the fireplace, where it lay down and curled into a neat ball.

'I don't even know your name,' she told the dog. The wiry tail thumped once and went still. It had a grey coat with one white paw, and there was a shiny silver androgynous collar around its throat. Although her knowledge of dog anatomy was sketchy at best, she thought it was a girl.

The house seemed deathly silent. Apart from the greyhound snoring everything was still. Skye went to the bathroom—utilitarian with a scattering of male toiletries but clean—and then on to the kitchen. There was food in the fridge, except she wasn't hungry enough to bother cooking a meal, so she made herself a mug of tea and found some biscuits in a tin. The kitchen looked as if it had been renovated, all shiny in silver and black. Perhaps Finn's wife had wanted the latest, or perhaps Finn had tried to hang on to her by offering enticements. Obviously it hadn't worked, not if she was in Perth, which was a very long way from Elysian.

Finn married? It seemed almost as unexpected as Finn being a policeman, and yet she shouldn't be surprised. They were strangers. Still, she knew curiosity would get the better of her at some point and she would probably ask him. Just not tonight.

She took a headache tablet, and carried her tea back to her room and unpacked. And then she had a shower and attempted to unwind her tense and tired muscles under the hot water. After that there seemed nothing else to do but go to bed.

The shock of seeing Finn again had pushed away her real purpose in being here, just for a time, but now Skye felt the growing thrum of excitement building inside her.

She was here, ready to follow in Neville's footsteps, and tomorrow she'd start on her quest. She might be a city girl, and the landscape in Elysian might be very different from what she was used to, but surely the people were similar. Someone must remember Neville, or have heard of him.

Tomorrow we'll make a plan, Finn had said. Despite her past and present colliding, and the complications that ensured, she found herself looking forward to it.

CHAPTER 7

DYLAN, FINN AND SKYE

December 1978,
Northcote, Melbourne

AS SKYE STEPPED off the school bus she was near to tears but holding them in, so that the other kids couldn't see she was upset. It seemed important to pretend she didn't care, even though she did. Since she'd moved from Adelaide she'd only made one genuine girlfriend, and now Susanne had dropped her. The cool kids were having a party down at the beach at Sorrento on the weekend, and she'd thrown aside her loyalty to Skye to cosy up to them for an invitation.

She'd even called Skye a Croweater—that ridic-ulous old insult against South Australians. Skye had always laughed when the other girls said it, putting on a brave face. It was harder to be tough when it was your supposed best friend who was leading the pack. Skye knew they'd put Susanne up to it, that she was only doing it so they'd ask her to the party, but it still hurt. And it hurt to know the Christmas holidays were stretching out before her and Susanne wouldn't be there to hang out with.

So she had spent the whole of lunchtime sitting on her own, pretending to read a crappy book and wishing her family had never left their house in the South Australian seaside suburb of Glenelg. Why had they, anyway? She wanted to despise them for it, although, reluctantly, she supposed her father had seen the possibility of a better job and more money, and her mother had said something about finding someone called Neville, whoever that was. When they'd noticed Skye listening they'd shut up.

It wasn't fair, it just wasn't.

Further along the street from the bus stop, Finn was sitting on a fence, waiting, his scruffy schoolbag at his feet. He was holding a McDonald's thickshake in one hand, and his school shirt was hanging out of his shorts—he did it on purpose, she knew, because he hated wearing the uniform. She didn't want to talk to him. She didn't want to talk to anyone. Without a word he got to his feet and fell into step with her.

Did he know about Susanne and Sorrento? She wasn't sure how she'd feel about that if he did. She didn't want to think he was sorry for her and that was the only reason he was hanging out with her.

'Got some tickets for the movies,' he said, turning the straw upside down before offering her the shake.

Skye eyed it suspiciously. 'You know they use

pig fat in those. That's what I heard.'

Finn frowned. 'Nah,' he said at last. 'No way.'

She grabbed the cup from him and took a sip. It was good. Vanilla, her favourite. Finn always chose vanilla.

'What movie is it?' she asked him, handing it back.

He put the straw in his mouth without turning it, then saw her notice, and looked away. '*Jaws 2*,' he said.

Skye thought about saying no. She didn't want to see sharks in bloody water, but then she thought that at least it would be something. Otherwise while the others were partying down on the beach, she'd be sitting at home with homework and telling her parents everything was all right when it wasn't.

She knew they loved her, and she loved them, but it was hard being an only child. They were always watching and worrying. It made her sneaky, it made her feel guilty. It made her into a person she didn't want to be.

Things were different for Finn. His mother, Melissa, didn't care what he and Dylan got up to, she was always busy with her own life. She thought they were old enough to look after themselves, and Dylan used his freedom to run wild; however, Skye knew for certain that despite his don't-care attitude, Finn always did his homework on time. There was something unusual about him, as if he was older than his sixteen years. Dylan was the crazy one, and he was the one all the girls wanted to be with. Despite his good looks, Finn was too serious for most of them.

Like now, meeting her at the bus stop and walking her home. As if she couldn't look after herself, as if she was still a little kid. Skye turned to tell him so, but the words stuck in her throat and she couldn't do it. Maybe because she was just as serious at heart, even when she was pretending otherwise. Like when Dylan dared her to do something stupid and she did it.

Finn hated that. Once, when she'd shoplifted because Dylan kept on at her to do it, Finn hadn't spoken to her for two days.

'Why?' he'd asked her, when she'd knocked on his door and his mother, a glass in her hand and none too steady on her feet, had let her in.

He was sitting on the bed, staring at the poster of The Angels on his wall. Doc was in full flight, jumping in the air, energy uncontainable. The poster was the only thing that was new in that room, with its patchy paintwork and cracked linoleum.

'Why? I don't know. Because it's exciting.'

He'd turned to look at her then and she'd avoided looking at him. Was he upset with her because she'd stolen something, or because she'd done what Dylan wanted her to? She wasn't sure and she didn't want to ask.

'Dylan isn't someone you can trust,' he'd said at last, and then she'd had her answer.

'What do you mean?' she'd demanded, suddenly angry on Dylan's behalf. 'Why would you say that about your brother?'

Finn had tightened his arms around his bent

knees and she could see that there was something burning a hole in his tongue that he wouldn't say. After a moment he sighed.

'Nothing,' he'd said. 'It's nothing. But don't do something just because Dylan tells you to. Okay?'

'Where is Dylan?' she asked him now, glancing sideways at him as they walked along the footpath. She was watching for that frown, Finn's trademark, and how it made his young face look old.

He sucked deep on the shake. 'Around.'

'Wasn't he at school with you?'

'He wagged.' Now the frown. 'Why?'

'Just wondering.'

Wagging was normal for Dylan. The truant officer had been around to his house on more than one occasion. Dylan always went to classes for a while after that, long enough to lull them into thinking he'd reformed. He was always walking a fine line.

'Will you come? To *Jaws 2*?' He sounded as if he couldn't care less whether she came or not, but it was an act. He did care and that's why, even though she'd rather see *Grease*, she wouldn't tell him that.

'I s'pose.'

He smiled at her and she smiled back. Finn seemed straightforward, but sometimes he was tricky, and she felt as if she had passed some test. Her mood lightened, and she decided the Christmas holidays were going to be okay after all.

Without warning Finn caught her hand in his and held it. His fingers were warm and sweaty—

the sun was blazing. The feel of his skin against hers gave her a jolt right down into the pit of her stomach, as if she was imagining him touching her all over and not just her hand. Some nights she lay awake thinking of him, dreaming of them together in a way that made her body ache and her heart pound. Skye and Finn. Even their names sounded right, together.

So she didn't pull away. She meshed her fingers with his and held on until they turned the corner to their street and only then, reluctantly, did she let him go because she was worried her mother might see.

CHAPTER 8

SKYE

Sunday 8 June 1997

SKYE HAD HEARD that people from the city didn't sleep well this far out in the sticks. Although it was true her Carlton terrace house was built just back from busy Lygon Street, she hadn't thought of it as particularly noisy. But now she learned the truth. She was simply accustomed to it. Because here she was in her bed in Elysian, tensing up, waiting—almost longing—for the sound of passing cars and trams, or the voices of late-night partygoers.

On the plus side, the bed was comfortable. As she lay there on her back, staring at the ceiling, thinking how quiet it was, she gradually became aware that it wasn't really quiet. There were little crackles and rustlings and squeaks; there were moans and whispers and shrieks. The possum that ran back and forth over the roof sounded as if it was wearing Blundstone boots.

The variety of noises was unnerving, but eventually she was so tired she fell asleep. She only woke once after that, when Finn returned. It must have been either very late or very early, and although she registered the sound of his vehicle and his steps in the house, she went back to sleep soon after. And stayed dead to the world until the morning light shone through the chink in the curtains and onto her face.

If she'd been a coward, she might have stayed there rather than face the day, but Skye was no coward. There were things she'd come here to do, and she meant to do them.

Anyway, Finn was moving around in the kitchen, and before long the tempting smell of bacon and eggs wafted into her bedroom.

The greyhound had left during the night, per-haps when Finn came home—she'd propped the door slightly ajar to accommodate it. Skye pulled on blue jeans and a cream-coloured Aran sweater she'd bought in Britain on her one and only backpacking holiday. It was old now but still a favourite, and more importantly it was warm. She ran a comb through her shoulder-length hair—the rich auburn colour went with her pale skin and blue eyes. A glance in the mirror showed she looked reasonably okay.

But the lines reminded her that she wasn't fif-teen anymore, that was for certain. She let herself ponder, just for a moment, whether Finn ever remembered those long-ago times with anything other than regret and disgust.

During the night she'd decided that if she was going to survive these next few days, living in his house, being in his company, then she couldn't allow herself to dwell on any of their shared past. Even the good bits. And to be totally honest with herself, there had been plenty of 'good bits', it was just that it was difficult to separate them from the rest.

Finn was in the kitchen, his back to her. He was wearing blue jeans and a checked long-sleeved shirt over a white tee-shirt, and he was busy with a frypan on the gas ring. The crackle and sizzle of eggs and bacon was plain to hear, and Skye's mouth watered. He'd set one end of the table—which was just the right size for the space—with cutlery and white plates, and there was toast and butter and a variety of condiments.

It seemed as if he'd gone all out. Fraser's idea of breakfast was a visit to a cafe, but if he had to stay in, then it was cereal eaten straight from the box. She didn't know what Finn used to eat for breakfast, that wasn't something she'd ever known. Probably he'd been lucky to get anything. In those days shopping for groceries hadn't been as high on his mother's list of priorities as getting drunk. Or stoned. Or both.

For a time the relationship between Skye and Finn had seemed so close, so intense, but might not that be because she was seeing it through the eyes of a teenage girl?

Damn it. And hadn't she just told herself she wasn't going to remember the past?

'Good morning,' she said in what she hoped was a polite voice. One distant acquaintance to another.

Finn's shoulders tensed, as if she'd surprised him, or maybe he'd forgotten she was there. And then he turned around and her face must have shown her shock.

He had a black eye, or it would be soon enough. Right now it was red and puffy with streaks of purple around the socket, and even his cheekbone had taken a battering, with a scabbed cut across it.

'It's not as bad as it looks,' he said with a grimace, and reached up to touch it.

'My God, what happened?'

'Illegal deer hunter. We've had a few lately. He took a swing at me. Usually I dodge in time, but I must be getting slow.'

'Are you all right?' She found herself wanting to reach out and touch him and clenched her hands into fists, realising how inappropriate that would be. He might take her concern for an advance, and that was definitely not a complication she needed.

'I'll live,' Finn said, shrugging it off as if it was nothing. Perhaps to him it was. Perhaps he got beaten up every Saturday night.

Skye hovered for a moment, unsure what to say or do, and then decided that if he wasn't bothered by it then neither was she. The electric jug was full and she switched it on to boil. 'Do you want a coffee? Tea?'

'Coffee, thanks. One sugar.'

She obliged as he finished cooking, and then followed him as he carried the pan to the table and divided up the contents onto two of the waiting plates. It was far more than Skye usually ate for breakfast, but she was starving and didn't argue. After setting down the mugs, they pulled up their chairs and tucked in.

For a while there was no need for conversation.

'Good,' she managed at last, with an awkward nod and a smile. She noticed he had a few scrapes on his knuckles, too, as if he'd punched the deer hunter back.

'Do you work on Sundays?' she asked, glancing at his eye.

'I work most days,' he said evenly.

Of course he did. He was under-staffed and had a very big area to police. He probably never had a day off. Was that why his wife had left him? Skye wondered, and then told herself to back off. She wasn't here to analyse Finn's personal problems.

'We were going to come up with a plan of attack.' He picked up his mug and took a sip.

She must have looked blank because he added, 'Mackenzie Crossing. Your missing grandfather.'

'Oh yes. Neville.' And then, as an afterthought, she added his surname, 'Darling.' He looked a bit startled. Realising how that must have sounded, Skye hurried awkwardly on. 'No, I mean that was his name. Neville *Darling*. I wasn't …'

Now his eyes had a gleam in them as if he was trying not to laugh. It was a lighter moment and it should have helped the discomfort between them, except it ended up making her feel ridiculous. Skye rearranged her cutlery.

Finn cleared his throat. 'So … when exactly in the nineteen thirties did he go missing? You didn't give me a date last night.'

'Thirteenth of January nineteen thirty-nine, I think.'

'Thirteenth of January nineteen thirty-nine,' he repeated softly and it was his turn to fiddle with his cutlery. He moved his knife a fraction of an inch to the left and then moved it back again. 'Look, Skye, I hate to be the bearer of bad news—'

'I know about the Black Friday bushfires. I'm not expecting happy news.'

'Okay,' he said. The way he said it seemed familiar and for a moment she had that strange sense of crossing time zones, as if the past and the present were trying to merge. But it must be her imagination—she told herself she couldn't possibly remember such a thing.

'So is he missing or is he deceased?' Finn's voice broke through her reverie.

'There's a chance he survived the fire. There was the photo in the file Russell found, the one I told you about last night, remember? Someone had to develop that. That's why I'm here. To find out.'

'Wasn't there a list of the victims at the time?'

'Yes, there was, but Neville's name isn't on it. Russell thinks it's possible no one knew he was in the area, that he might never have been identified.'

Finn scratched his chin. He'd shaved since last night, though with his dark hair he would probably be showing a five-o'clock shadow before lunchtime.

'That makes sense. If he was alone in the bush and got caught up in the fire …'

Skye's spirits dived before she forced herself to think positively. 'That's possible, of course it is, but I'm hoping someone will remember. Fifty-eight years isn't quite a lifetime. I can ask around town and … and I can go to Mackenzie Crossing and take photographs. That's one place we definitely know he was at.'

Finn scratched his chin again and eyed her doubtfully. 'Might be a bit tricky, Skye. Mackenzie Crossing was completely destroyed in the fires. Never rebuilt. I'm not sure what happened to all the people who survived. Some of them might have moved over here to Elysian. That's something I can find out for you. And there's Archie Manning. I'm sure—'

'Archie?'

'He runs the local museum. It's really just a couple of rooms at the front of his house, but it's amazing what he's been able to cram in there. He should definitely be on your plan of attack.'

'Okay.'

She could see his mind ticking over. He was staring across the room to the floor-to-ceiling windows. There should have been a view through the glass, only this morning the mist was lying eerily upon the ground, enclosing the house in a world of white. Out of the blue, like something from *The Hound of the Baskervilles*, the greyhound came bowling out of the fog and up onto the verandah. It stared through the glass at them, pink tongue lolling.

Finn got up to let his dog in.

The greyhound was wearing a warm dog coat in a tartan which Skye suspected was Galloway. It came pattering across to greet her.

'Lightning, leave her alone.'

'No, it's all right. I wondered what her name was.' Skye stroked the sleek grey head. 'Hello, Lightning. It suits you.'

Finn leaned back against the kitchen bench. There wasn't an ounce of fat on him, it was all lean muscle. His blue jeans hung low on his hips and his shirt had been washed so often that the red-and-blue check had faded to pastel. When he crossed his feet at the ankles she noticed he was wearing socks, thick black Explorer ones, without shoes.

'She was never a champion, but she ran in a few races. When these dogs are no longer any good for running most of them are euthanised. Or worse, taken out and shot. A friend of mine in Westcott who's a vet decided Lightning'd make a good pet and thought of me. I spend a lot of time on the road and it can get lonely. So me and Lightning keep each other company.'

'She's a lucky girl.'

He smiled. The smile changed him into a different, more approachable man. Skye felt herself relaxing a little bit more.

'You had that dog, the kelpie.'

'Old Dixie.' His eyes were warm as he remembered. 'She went with me everywhere. Darryl wanted to take her to the pound, afterwards, but I wouldn't let him. Came home with me and

I buried her a couple of years later under her favourite tree.'

Something stirred in Skye's heart, a feeling that had no business being there. Nostalgia, she realised. Her teenage years were full of angst and high passion, and they'd left their mark. Of course she'd feel emotional now that she was revisiting them, but that was all it was, a half-remembered scent of something long gone.

'You said Russell was helping you,' Finn went on after a moment. 'Who's Russell? Husband?'

'No. Just a friend I met at school, after I moved from Northcote Secondary. We've been close ever since.'

'Right.'

This time the silence was longer and more awkward. She might have explained about Fraser then, but decided against it. Her life was no concern of his, not anymore.

'So.' Skye forced a businesslike note into her voice. 'Will you be going into town this morning? Can I hitch a ride?'

'Of course.' His answer was equally professional. 'I'll be ready in about an hour.'

'Perfect.'

Just then his telephone rang. He looked over to where it was attached to the wall, and there was something about his expression that made Skye think this wasn't a call he was looking forward to. 'I have to take this,' he said.

Skye stood up. 'I'll get ready.'

'Sure.' By the time she'd reached the door Finn had picked up the handset and was listening, his shoulders rigid, his free hand clenched. She couldn't help but overhear his first words and his tone of voice. Harsh, painful and angry.

'What the hell do you think you're playing at, Laurie? You said she was coming to stay for the holidays. You promised.'

Skye returned to her room. She could easily work out what was going on. Finn's daughter had been coming to stay and her mother had changed her mind. But really, if he was as busy as he said he was, Skye could understand his wife's reluctance.

It wasn't her affair, she reminded herself as she gathered together her toiletries and headed for the bathroom. His life may have briefly intersected with hers many years ago, but it was done and gone. Over. It was well past the time to move on.

Yeah, sure, only she was having trouble obeying her own instructions.

Skye was ready before the hour was up. When she checked the kitchen Finn wasn't there. Then she saw him outside the window, Lightning at his feet on the closely mown grass. The fog had begun to lift and there was even a gleam of sunshine, although it was only a promise right now. Finn was in his uniform, staring towards the line of trees at the bottom of his garden, hands stuck in his pockets, standing perfectly still.

There was something about that stillness that warned her off. She was about to leave him to it, when suddenly he turned and came striding towards the house. He was so deep in his own thoughts, he didn't see her through the glass as he stepped up onto the verandah, and when he did he gave a start.

Maybe he'd forgotten she was there. Well, she told herself, that was a good thing surely? It meant she was as unimportant in his present-day life as he was in hers.

Skye stepped back as he pulled open the window, a mask settling once more over everything he might be feeling. The damage around his eye looked even more red and angry.

'Ready?' he asked her in a cool voice.

'Yes. But look, uh, you don't have to do this. Maybe I could get a taxi? I don't expect you to chauffeur me around.'

He couldn't quite hide his exasperation. 'No taxis here, Skye, and I wouldn't advise walking. They're forecasting wild weather later on today. When you're done at the museum, just head down to the station. Someone will be there.'

She nodded because he was waiting and he seemed to require a response. She was tempted to salute. Honestly.

He stopped her as she went to push past him, and she looked up in surprise.

'I know you think I'm being a pain. It's just easier for me to handle it. And I'm not expecting you to strike off on your own into the bush, but … we've had a few hikers go missing lately and it required a lot of time and manpower to find them. I can't really spare either right now.'

Well that shows me, Skye thought wryly. Aloud she said, 'I understand. I promise I won't wander off the path.'

'Not without me, anyway.'

For some reason that made her face feel warm, which was ridiculous. Thankfully he was already walking away. 'Let's go, then.'

Lightning seemed to think that meant her as well, and the dog took off after him, tail wagging furiously, while Skye brought up the rear.

CHAPTER 9

NEVILLE

Tuesday 10 January 1939,
Mackenzie Crossing

NEVILLE TOOK A moment to catch his breath, and to once again wipe the sweat from beneath his hat. His mouth was gritty and dry, and he reached for the bottle of ginger ale he'd carried from Elysian. Leaning against the post and rail fence behind him, he took a swig of the warm, overly sweet drink and grimaced, but at least it was wet.

Mackenzie Crossing was laid out before him and, although he could see that once it must have filled this valley, perhaps when the gold mine was operating in the late 1800s, now it had contracted. Seeing the half dozen or so ramshackle cottages and their falling-down sheds, one could call it a shantytown.

At least, one could, if it wasn't for the rather grand two-storey wooden building with a sign across the crooked verandah that stated emphatically, 'Mackenzie Crossing Inn and Hostelry'.

It looked so out of place that he couldn't help but stop and stare and speculate. For instance, how did it make enough money to stay open for business? And why hadn't it fallen into ruin like the rest of the place?

Neville remembered hearing there was timber-getting around here. Somewhere on the timbered slopes above him was a sawmill, as well as a camp for the men who worked it. Possibly it was they who kept the Mackenzie Crossing Inn and Hostelry going. He smiled, leaning against the fence and imagining the sort of photograph he would take. The building was so incongruous, as if it had been set down here by mistake when it should have been part of a much grander setting.

Something knocked against his shoulder.

Neville turned, surprised, and then he laughed. He hadn't noticed the white-and-tan horse in the paddock behind him, and now it had come up to see what he was doing. It tossed its head as if asking him what his business was here. It wasn't a big animal, although it had the look of a Clydesdale, with feathery feet.

A mixed-up breed, he thought, like most Australians. He didn't mean it in a derogatory way, and he'd never say it aloud, but he often thought that the intermarrying of immigrants had created a tougher race, a people who could handle life in this difficult land and climate, whereas their ancestors may have wilted and perished in the same conditions.

Survival of the fittest. An interesting study,

something he could observe from a distance, without getting too involved. Because Neville preferred to keep his distance from the humanity around him, to not allow himself to get personally entangled, and the camera lens was perfect for that.

The horse was still waiting, and he noticed there didn't appear to be much feed left on the ground. However, it was clear that someone was looking after the animal, and had filled the trough with water. Neville found an apple in his swag, shrivelled and dry, and tentatively he held it out. The horse removed it delicately with its lips, and then quickly crunched it up, before looking at him for more.

'Sorry, old chap,' Neville apologised. 'That's all I have.'

The horse tossed its head, before letting him stroke the soft nose and the white blaze on its forehead.

'No hard feelings, then,' he murmured with a smile.

Neville pitied the animal in this heat, but there was a large tree further down the paddock that gave some shade. He thought that was probably where it had been, before it spotted him.

'He'll take everything you've got and more.'

The tone was dry and the voice was close by his side. Neville turned, startled, wondering what it was about Mackenzie Crossing that allowed its inhabitants to creep up on him unnoticed.

The owner of the voice had bent down to open a bag of feed. Loose shirt and trousers fastened around the waist with a thick, tooled leather belt, and a broad-brimmed hat much like his own. A man, obviously, or a lad. The soft, husky voice had sounded like a lad, and yet … The figure straightened and Neville tried not to stare.

It was a woman.

If he hadn't known from her features then her hair, which hung in a long dark braid over one shoulder, would have given it away. He'd noted since he stepped off the boat from England that the glare of the sun, with its drying effects on the skin, tended to age people much faster than at home. But this woman's skin looked smooth and ageless.

And then she narrowed her hazel eyes at him in the shadow of her hat and he realised she had the high cheekbones of someone with Asian ancestry. His senses seemed to sharpen. Was it … could it be the girl in the photograph he'd taken from Miller Brown? Older, of course, and dressed so strangely, and yet there was *something* about her.

She'd noticed him gawping and raised her eyebrows. His certainty wavered as he stammered an apology—which she ignored. More cautiously, he continued to observe her as she reached over the fence, but the longer he looked the less certain he became that this was the same woman.

The horse took some oats from her hand, and when she smiled lines appeared about her eyes and mouth, giving her a maturity that made him think she was in her late twenties or early thirties. Yes, the age was more or less correct, and yet how many women of that age with dark hair were here in the mountains? No, he decided, him coming upon Brown's suspect was extremely unlikely, a coincidence far beyond the realms of possibility.

However, by now Neville's professional interest had been well and truly captured. Whoever this woman was she'd make a compelling subject. He found himself planning the photograph he would take of her, considering the angle, the background, the fall of the light on her face, and the way he'd pose her before he clicked the shutter.

'What's his name?' Neville asked, not so much because he wanted to know but because he wanted to hear her voice again.

'Aesop,' she said, and then, seeing his expression, her eyes danced. 'My father named him.'

She reached into the sack and found a piece of apple, more withered even than Neville's had been, and held it out on her flat palm. Aesop took it neatly and, as if he knew from experience that that was all he was getting, turned and trotted back to the shade of his tree.

The woman was staring after him, still smiling, and once more Neville was able to examine her surreptitiously. There was a scar on the side of her neck, not quite hidden by the collar of her shirt. A nasty one, by the look of it, as if someone … Once again she caught him looking and reached to draw up the concealing collar, and then bent down for the feed sack.

She had lifted the sack and was preparing to leave, and suddenly Neville didn't want her to. Another question would delay her.

'Aesop is a working horse, then, is he?'

'He used to be. After my father died he was sent up to the mill to haul timber. When he couldn't do that anymore, they were planning to send him to the slaughter house, so I said I'd have him back.' She turned away, adding over her shoulder, 'More fool me! He costs a small fortune.'

Neville couldn't stop himself. He strode after her, catching up and falling into step.

'I don't think you mean that,' he said. Quite clearly she had a fondness for Aesop that went beyond him earning his keep.

She glanced sideways at him, an amused expression on her face. 'What are you doing here in the Crossing? English, aren't you? A long way from home, I'd have said.'

He would have answered her. Not the truth, but some story or other to keep her interested, until he got up the courage to ask if she'd let him photograph her. He had a feeling she wouldn't be a pushover. In the end he didn't have to.

An unholy racket erupted, and out of nowhere a rooster came running around the side of the hostelry, and right behind it was a young boy in shorts and bare feet, his long dark hair flying.

The bird was flapping its wings as it ran, without gaining much height. The woman at Neville's side clicked her tongue in annoyance and hurried to block the bird's path, but it easily outmanoeuvred her. Neville stepped around her and reached out to grab it; he received a slice from a razor-sharp spur for his trouble.

Bird and boy ran off, leaving Neville staring

after them, holding his hand and dripping blood.

'Don't you know better than that?' the woman said, shaking her head at him. 'Come with me and I'll fix it up for you. Can't leave it,' she added. 'End up with lockjaw.' Her mouth tightened, as if the word had meaning for her, before she headed for the doorway into the grandest building in Mackenzie Crossing.

Neville slung his camera case over his shoulder, picked up his swag with his uninjured hand, and followed.

The room inside was not so splendid, being dingy and full of the aromas of smoke and beer. At least it had a floor, not just packed earth, something he'd seen in other establishments with names that weren't so grand. Whether it had a licence was another matter, and wasn't something he was about to ask; however, it was cooler in here than it was outside in the sullen heat of the day.

The woman had gone through a door at the back of the room, and now she came out with water in a bowl, and cloths, and a small bottle of something white, which—when she pulled out the cork—smelled pungent of a herb he couldn't name.

Neville sat down on a bench, as she directed, and placed his hand palm up before her. She examined it with a frown, her touch firm and brisk. Had she been a nurse in another life, per-haps? She took off her hat, and he marvelled at how he ever could have thought she was a boy. The shape of her head, the delicate curve of her cheek and ear, the dark arch of her brows and long lashes, made it obvious she was of the female sex.

He did still wonder about the scar on her neck, and about her past, but Neville was a private man and he understood the need for privacy in others. If she wanted him to know, then she would tell him, otherwise he would just have to speculate. He could make a guess, though. Someone had cut her. Perhaps even tried to kill her.

Unless she'd done it to herself.

He'd known a man who had done that once. During the war some of the soldiers shot themselves on purpose, usually in the foot or the hand, in the hope they could get out of the trenches and go to hospital, or maybe even that holiest of grails, home. But this fellow went further than that, and cut his own throat. It was early in the war, and he remembered thinking he would never do such a thing, that it smacked of cowardice and even a weakness of the mind. A couple of months down the track he knew exactly why the poor devil had done it.

The thought of this woman taking a razor in her small hands and laying the cold, sharp edge against her throat … Despite all he had seen on the Western Front, Neville found it unexpectedly shocking.

'Not too bad,' her husky voice interrupted his thoughts. She'd finished her inspection of his wound and now she nodded at the bottle. 'Tea tree. I use it for Aesop, but he won't mind.' Then she smeared some of the ointment onto the cut and proceeded to wrap it in a clean strip of cloth, tying it neatly so it wouldn't easily come off.

'Thank you,' he said and meant it.

She nodded again and almost smiled. Quickly and efficiently she cleared away the mess, and then went to the front door. Frowning, hands on hips, she looked out. 'Where is that boy? We were supposed to have that bird for our tea tonight. Nothing but trouble. The bird, I mean, not the boy. This morning he flew at Aesop and would've taken out an eye if I hadn't been there.'

'Is the boy your son?'

She turned back to him and for a moment her face was blank, and then she put on a smile as if he'd made a joke. 'What, Tiddler? No. He's a cousin. His parents are dead, so I look after him.'

She was lying, he knew it, but he told himself it didn't matter to him. He only wanted her permission to take a photograph and then he'd be gone. She was more than welcome to keep her secrets.

'Did you come by way of Elysian?' She continued to peer out of the door. 'What did they say about the fires?'

'They're burning to the north-west, in the Blue Range. I didn't see anyone from Elysian evacuating when I was there.'

'Well, you don't want to leave if you don't have to,' she murmured, more to herself than him.

'So do you think the fire will get this far?'

'Who knows? I doubt it. We've been lucky in the past. Anyway, it's all right at the moment. Maybe it'll rain.' She laughed, to show how unlikely she thought that. 'What's your name?'

'Neville Darling.' He got up and held out his uninjured hand, and she looked at it in amusement before giving it a quick shake. 'How do you do, Mrs …?' he asked with a questioning pause.

'Miss. Georgie Mackenzie. Short for Georgina. My father's little joke.'

'Joke?' It suited her, he thought. She fascinated him, even while he found her conversation bemusing. He felt himself being drawn in by her. Like a puzzle he had yet to put together satisfactorily.

'Well, it's hardly the name for a girl living out here, is it? I should've been something plain and simple, but no, he had to call me *Georgina*. After his mother, he said. A grand lady with a grand house. He thought I'd take after her, but as soon as I could talk I decided on Georgie.'

'And you said you were a Mackenzie? Does that mean you're related to the Mackenzies of Mackenzie Crossing? I've heard mention of Big Jim.'

Again, her hands went to her hips. 'I *am* the Mackenzie of Mackenzie Crossing. Big Jim was my father and he gave this place its name last century when he came through looking for gold. The Union Jack mine dates from then. You wouldn't believe what a bustling place it was in those days.' And she smiled that smile he was beginning to crave for his camera. 'When the gold began to dwindle, he started sawing down timber instead. I'm the last Mackenzie to live here, and when I'm gone I wouldn't be surprised if the whole town vanished in a puff of smoke.'

She was quite a character, Georgie Mackenzie. All the more reason to take her photograph so that she could be immortalised. Would that please her? Neville wondered. Or would she refuse his request outright?

He was just considering making his approach when there was a commotion outside, and the boy, Tiddler, arrived with the subdued rooster under his arm. He looked as if he'd had to fight and, judging by the scratch on his cheek, he hadn't won easily, but he was grinning from ear to ear.

Georgie laughed and clapped her hands. 'Good boy!' she said, reaching out to smooth back the lock of hair that had fallen into his eyes. It was obvious to Neville that she loved the boy whatever she called him.

'Come on, then,' she said bracingly, 'let's get the axe before he runs away again.'

Tiddler hurried out and Georgie followed, pausing briefly at the door. She was just a shadow against the light so he couldn't read her expression, only hear the husky sound of her voice.

'You might as well stay for tea. Plenty of room at the inn, as my father used to say.'

And then she was gone.

Neville hadn't planned to stay. He usually camped out and shifted for himself when he was on the track; however, the offer was too tempting to pass up. Staying would allow him to make friends. It would be more difficult for her to refuse him then, he told himself. And he wanted her photograph, more than he'd wanted anything for a long time.

CHAPTER 10

SKYE

Sunday 8 June 1997

ELYSIAN WAS BUSIER than Skye had been expecting. Perhaps this was the day when the more adventurous city travellers left their safe homes and came all the way out here for a Sunday drive? There seemed to be a lot of mud-splattered SUVs parked along the front.

The locals were about, too.

When Skye walked past the quaint timber-framed, combined cafe, post office and general store, she couldn't resist peeping inside. There were people chatting by the racks of vegetables and shelves of tinned food, or else reading the newspapers over their morning cuppa.

After Finn had dropped her off she had declined to come into the station with him. He was preoccupied and it just seemed better to set off on her own, and as he'd already pointed out the museum, it wasn't as if she could get lost.

Elysian consisted of the one main street, and

facing onto it were buildings with mostly timber frontages, although there were a few others further back, higher up the steep hills that ringed the town. Some of them looked quite precarious to Skye's eyes. The morning air was cold and damp, and while the fog was gradually lifting, she could still see it clinging to the hilltops, making the trees look ghostly. At lower altitudes, in places like Melbourne, the autumn weather was probably still lingering, but up here it definitely felt like winter had arrived.

Lucky she'd put on her white woollen coat and was wearing gloves, but now, with a shiver, she decided she might need to buy a hat and scarf. Surely there must be a suitable shop catering to the tourists somewhere around here?

The coffee in the cafe smelled good, but she didn't go in, eager to reach the museum. Finn had assured her it was open, and if it wasn't then she should simply ring the bell. Elysian didn't stand on ceremony.

There *was* a touristy-looking store that didn't open for another hour. She paused outside, peering through the glass at the knitted gear and souvenirs, before she told herself she'd have time to browse when she came back.

Skye headed further up the hill, towards the hotel, and on the way she passed a wooden building with 'Community Health Centre, open two days a week' written above the door. It was all locked up, so evidently Sunday wasn't one of the two days. By the time she reached the museum, she was puffing.

You're out of shape, she scolded herself. She worked hard at her job. In fact, and she wasn't sure whether this was a good thing or not, it was her whole life. The time she'd spent with her mother, before she died, had cut her off from her previous group of friends, and until Fraser had offered her the job she'd been adrift. Now, when she socialised, it was with the same people she worked with, and even socialising had become less important lately.

She was stale. She probably needed a change. The exhibition idea was one way of achieving that, but sometimes it was easier to talk about doing something than to actually *do* it. Skye admitted she harboured fears that it wouldn't work out, and she'd end up creeping back to Fraser, begging for her old job. Taking photographs for a living was very different from choosing photographs for an exhibition, and then inviting the world into your private space and laying yourself bare to whatever the critics might say. She wanted to do justice to Neville; she didn't want to fail.

Skye sighed. Maybe she needed to join a gym and make time for the treadmill in the evenings, instead of collapsing on the couch in front of the television with Milly and a glass of wine. Or she could find a hobby? The trouble was she didn't seem to have time for either, and it irritated her sometimes how Fraser managed to meet numerous women and break their hearts, when she couldn't find even one man who seemed worth the effort.

Her life was in a holding pattern until she decided on her next step. She told herself that coming up here to find Neville was going to help with that. Yes, there was definitely a sense of anticipation, of something about to happen.

Skye just hoped it was something good.

Elysian's museum was an ordinary house, but the front had been altered to include large glass windows. They were currently jam-packed with paraphernalia, including a tin wash tub and a mangle. There was a sign board hammered into the front lawn, and Skye walked in through the open gate to read it.

'Elysian was settled in the 1860s, when gold was discovered in the surrounding creeks and gullies. The town was badly damaged in the 1939 Black Friday bushfires, but a determined effort was made to rebuild. Elysian continues to thrive. Come in and see our past and our future.'

Skye smiled—that sounded friendly and welcoming—but when she tried the door, she found it locked. She hesitated. There was a bell attached to the wall—a proper bell with a metal clapper. Before she could ring it, a movement inside one of the windows caught her eye. An old man was staring out at her from behind the glass.

She had just begun to raise her hand when in a flash he'd gone. Skye was left standing and was wondering what to do next, when the door behind her was thrown wide open and a voice invited her to, 'Come in, come in!'

The elderly man was craggy-faced, with white hair and hazel eyes that shone with pleasure. He must have been at least seventy, and he wore trousers that were too big for him, as if he'd recently lost weight, and a green cardigan that could easily have been just as old as him.

'Thank you,' Skye said with a smile, stepping inside. This was exactly who she'd been hoping to find here in Elysian, someone who was enthusiastic about the past.

'I hope you have plenty of time because there's lots to see!' he assured her, and she could have sworn he was hopping from one foot to the other in his excitement.

The museum smelled musty. It was the sort of odour she always associated with the second-hand bookshops her mother had frequented, searching for a bargain and coming away with more stories than she'd ever have time to read.

There was a laminated sheet of cardboard to one side of the door and her attention was caught by the heading: 'Victims of Black Friday'. She paused, running her eye down the names and places—only those in the local vicinity, she noticed—until she came to Mackenzie Crossing. Here there were about half a dozen names, and of course Neville *wasn't* one of them.

'Come in, come in!'

A narrow walking path ran through the clutter, ending at a counter whose surface was a confusion of pamphlets, booklets and postcards. The elderly man raised a wooden barrier, slipped through, and took his place behind it.

'Right,' he said, picking up a metal tin that looked as if it had once held Arnott's biscuits.

'It's a dollar for entry.' He struggled with the lid. 'Bugger.'

'Do you need some help?'

'No, no, I can manage.' Just then the lid came free and coins burst out and rained down around him. As he scrambled for the escapees on the floor behind the counter, Skye's attention was caught by a large framed picture hanging on the wall behind him.

A painting perhaps? A landscape? But the cover glass reflected the electric light bulb dangling in front of it and she couldn't make it out. Just as Skye was about to ask the old man what it was, a door opened to her left and a woman hurried out.

She was young, barely in her twenties, and she looked anxious. Her anxiety only increased when she saw the elderly man struggling to gather up the scattered coins.

'Oh, Grandad! What are you doing? You're supposed to be resting.'

Archie—because Skye was pretty sure that's who this was—gave her a furtive look.

'Now, now, Saskia, I can't be resting. I need to sort through that trailer load we got the other day from Mr Rutherford's place. You never know what treasures I might find in there.'

'Junk, you mean,' Saskia retorted, but she sounded exasperated rather than angry. 'You paid far too much for that. Mum will be livid.'

'Your mother doesn't know everything, sweetheart.' The old man tapped his nose and winked at Skye. 'My daughter, Nancy, can be overly protective.'

'Enough of that. Come on.' Saskia helped him out from behind the counter. 'We'll both be in trouble if Mum finds out you're not following the doctor's orders.'

Archie heaved a sigh. 'My heart is perfectly fine,' he said.

Skye smiled at him. Saskia, on the other hand, wasn't impressed. 'Your heart isn't fine. No, Granddad, no more arguing.'

And she took his arm and steered him back to the doorway through which she'd entered. Archie went, dragging his feet like a recalcitrant child and muttering to himself. Just as his granddaughter moved to close the door on his retreating back, he turned around and gave Skye one of his 100-watt grins.

'Don't let her put you off, will you? There's lots to see.'

Saskia finally got the door closed. 'He's a terrible man,' she said, but it was spoken with such love and affection that Skye felt quite teary.

Saskia noticed and made a sympathetic noise. 'Oh, I'm sorry. Do you want to sit down?'

'No, oh no. I just ... my mother passed away not so long ago. The way you were arguing, well pretend-arguing, reminded me. That's all.'

'And your father?' Saskia gave her another sympathetic look.

'Died in a car crash about ten years ago. It was sudden, but ... my mother died of cancer and sometimes I wonder which was worse.'

'At least you got to say a proper goodbye,' Saskia

said knowledgeably. 'I'm training as a nurse,' she added, with an intent look from her green eyes. 'Are you an only child? I am. So was Mum. It's lonely sometimes.'

Saskia was a brunette, with her hair tied back in a ponytail, and she had an open, honest face. The sort of sweet, scrubbed-clean face you saw in commercials for wholesome foods. Her skirt was short and she'd teamed it up with black stockings and Doc Martens, and a sapphire-coloured sweater.

'Well the thing to do is to have lots of children of your own,' Skye recommended. 'That's what I planned to do, anyway, but … I never got around to it.'

Saskia blushed, as if she thought Skye expected her to go out and multiply immediately. 'Oh no,' she said, 'I'd need to finish my training before …'

Time to change the subject, thought Skye. 'Are you on holidays?'

'Yes, from uni. I'm staying here looking after Granddad. Mum usually looks after him, but she's been so busy at work. As I'm on a break I said I'd come and keep an eye on him for her.'

She seemed eager to share. Maybe she was missing her friends and feeling lonely with only one old man to talk to.

'That's very generous of you,' Skye offered. 'It can't be very exciting here in Elysian, uh, running the museum and looking after your grandfather.'

'Well,' she was obviously torn between loyalty to the town and telling the truth, 'there *are* compensations. Taylor is here.' And then she blushed again.

Skye turned away to hide her smile, pretending to examine a set of old glass bottles with stoppers, lined up on one of the shelves. Was Taylor the preferred father of the many children?

'Are *you* on holiday?' Saskia was sticking to her side. 'Granddad says there are always tourists around, no matter the weather. A few of the more challenging tracks will be closing once the snow comes, but that doesn't stop them.'

'No, I'm not a tourist. Actually I'm here to find *my* grandfather,' Skye said, taking the plunge. 'I was hoping that Archie might be able to help me. Your granddad *is* Archie, isn't he?'

'Archie Manning, yes.'

'So, has he lived here long?'

'I'm not sure *how* long, but a long time. He was from Sale, originally, in Gippsland. But he's very interested in the history of this area. The museum has been his passion.' She leaned closer, as if Archie could hear her through the wall, and for all Skye knew he could. 'Unfortunately, he contracted rheumatic fever as a child and it affected his heart. He's never been strong and now he's getting worse. Mum's had to ban him from the historical society meetings in Westcott. There's talk of a big new museum being built there, you see, and he thinks they'll steal his customers. He gets so upset at the meetings, she's worried he'll have a heart attack.'

'Oh, that's a shame.' Skye considered her next words carefully. '*My* grandfather was last seen in a place near here called Mackenzie Crossing. He came from England, originally, and he married my grandmother in Adelaide. My mother was born there. She never really knew her father. He left when she was little and he never came back. He was a photographer and I think he was up here with his camera.'

While Skye was explaining about Neville, she couldn't help noticing that Saskia's expression, at first politely interested, had begun to grow steadily more anxious. She smoothed her sleeves and shuffled her feet. Finally, the girl could no longer hold her gaze and turned away, pretending to straighten the pamphlets on the counter, but it was clear to Skye that something was very wrong.

'You know him, don't you?' She took a step closer. 'Neville Darling? You know him!'

Saskia shook her head, still refusing to meet Skye's eyes, yet she looked so worried and guilty. 'No. No, I don't. I'm sorry. Anyway you said he was staying at Mackenzie Crossing?' she went on, sounding a bit breathless. 'There's nothing there now. It was an awful thing and I wish …' Again she glanced at the door through which Archie had departed. 'I'm really sorry, but I can't help.'

It was so obvious that Saskia knew something. However, for some reason, probably because of her grandfather's weak heart, she wasn't prepared to share it.

Skye wasn't normally rude, at least she tried not to be, but it didn't seem fair to be on the verge of making a great discovery about her grandfather, only to be sent away again, empty-handed.

'I don't believe you,' she said desperately. 'Saskia,

tell me what you know.'

But Saskia wouldn't answer, straightening a stack of the same brochures over and over again.

Skye took a deep breath and let it out slowly. Releasing the negative, breathing in the positive. She needed to tone it down. 'Do you think your grandfather might be able to help if I came back later? After he's had his rest?' she suggested sweetly. 'Please?'

Tears filled Saskia's eyes as she shook her head. She was probably a nice girl who hated to disappoint people, and just for a moment Skye thought she'd won her around. But her next words, spoken in the firmest voice she'd heard Saskia use, brought her hopes crashing down. 'No, you can't. And he can't help. I'm sorry, you'd better leave now.'

Skye swallowed. Once again she felt close to tears. She thought about arguing, and she thought about begging, except it didn't seem fair to either of them. Saskia was only following orders— probably her mother's—and it would be wrong to browbeat her.

A flush had risen up the girl's neck and into her cheeks, and she doggedly continued with her reorganisation of the museum's advertising matter. 'I'm sorry,' she said with quiet finality, 'but we can't help.'

Skye told herself this wasn't the end of her search. It couldn't be. She'd come all this way and she wasn't giving up. She had a whole week here in Elysian, and she'd be back.

She'd reached the gate to the street when she

turned, and, as she expected, Saskia was there. The girl was watching her through the window, half hidden by the mangle, and darted back guiltily as soon as their eyes met.

Skye hesitated, wondering what would happen if she marched back up the path and pounded on the door. Archie would have a heart attack, that's what might happen. She couldn't risk it. Finding Neville Darling was important—a quest, she realised it had become—and then there was her hope, her *dream* of an exhibition. Neville's photographs getting the acknowledgement they deserved. Right now, though, if she was going to get anywhere at all, she needed to give Archie and Saskia some space.

After her encounter at the museum, Skye needed to shop and to drink caffeine, in that order. The knitwear in the tourist shop kept her busy for over an hour as she inspected the scarves and hats and sweaters, before choosing one of each for herself and an extra scarf as a thankyou for Russell, and a hat with a fake set of deer's antlers for Fraser. An apology present for going off at such short notice. He'd appreciate the sentiment and it would make him laugh—he might even wear it. She hesitated over something for Finn—he *was* putting her up—but the idea of her handing him a gift-wrapped scarf he didn't want and him stumbling over his thanks, and … Best not.

The woman who ran the business said she was from Warburton, not a local, and she only came up for the weekends when the tourists were about. Skye, who had been hoping to grill her about Neville, smiled and let it go.

Next, she lingered in the cafe, finding herself a nice seat at the window so she could watch the world go by. The street was almost empty of cars and people, the earlier crowd having long gone. She had it to herself as she ordered a sandwich and another good strong coffee.

For a long time Skye stared out at the gentle rain which had started to fall. The light had begun to fade, too, and now the streetscape resembled a sepia photograph—one of those old ones like Neville's—and meanwhile the questions went around and around in her head.

What did Saskia know about Neville? And what was the point of speculating when she couldn't get an answer? She sighed. Could Finn help? It was he who had put her onto the museum and Archie Manning. But then again did she want to ask him for any more help than he was willing to give? Things were awkward enough as it was, with the two of them tiptoeing around each other.

No, what she needed to do was go to Mackenzie Crossing. It might seem silly, but she had the feeling that if only she could just walk on the ground where her grandfather had walked, then the truth would reveal itself.

Skye sighed again as she picked up her cup and realised it was empty. One of the overhead lights went out. She looked up in surprise. Had the bulb blown out? That was when she finally noticed that the man behind the counter was eyeing her impatiently, and it must be obvious to anyone less caught up in their own thoughts that he wanted to close.

She got to her feet and went over to pay.

Outside the rain was heavier. Maybe she should get the waterproof jacket she'd seen in the tourist shop? By the time she'd trudged all the way back up the hill, she found it closed and dark inside, so she turned down again.

There was no choice but to return to the police station and face Finn. Until she'd formulated the thought, Skye hadn't realised just how apprehensive it made her. Was that why she'd been drinking coffee and dithering over scarves, because she was afraid of facing Finn? Was she such a coward?

She should be embracing the chance to clear away the cobwebs of her past. Next time they met she would come straight out and ask him about Dylan, and then they could have a full and frank discussion.

No, she wouldn't. The very thought of it made her squirmy inside. *Just leave it alone,* she told herself. *Don't lift the lid, keep it jammed firmly on. Don't let something out that you can't put back in again.*

Which meant, Skye supposed, that she *was* a coward. A coward with Finn and the past that they shared, and a coward in the future, content to stay in the same rut rather than take a risk and launch out into something new, in case it might fail.

By the time Skye had crossed the road, the rain was soaking through her coat and turning her hair into a dripping mess. She was clutching her purchases, none of which were waterproof, and when she reached the station she was shivering.

There were two cars parked in the designated spaces outside the building. One was an old Datsun with a poor paint job, and the other a dirty-looking white Toyota LandCruiser. So she was pretty sure that, unless the police vehicle was hidden around the back somewhere, Finn wasn't here.

Her sense of relief was quickly followed by irritation. Because no Finn meant waiting and Skye was very much used to arranging her life to her own convenience. Waiting meant time wasted and she told herself she couldn't afford to waste one single moment of her precious visit.

She considered walking back to the house, despite Finn's warnings, but the rain was getting heavier. And where was the sense in setting off into the elements, just to prove a point? Finn would be annoyed with her and she would have to apologise and … No, there was really nothing else she could do but grit her teeth and go inside and wait.

Skye pushed at the glass door, but it was one of those airtight ones and needed a good shove before it opened with a whoosh.

The interior looked modern and new. A faux wooden counter, with an area behind for filing cabinets and a bulletin board covered in helpful flyers on weather conditions and ways to prevent intrepid visitors from getting lost, as well as a wanted poster of someone who looked liable to terrify small children. A beige-coloured partition closed off her view into whatever was at the back—maybe Finn's office and an interview room. Were there cells, too? Perhaps whoever had given Finn his black eye was locked up in there awaiting transport to Melbourne?

A pity there was nobody to ask.

At least it was warmer in here. Her hair began to dry and curl, and she stopped shivering. She walked to the counter and rested her hands on it and waited, but nothing happened, so she went over to the door through the partition and listened. Silence. Should she peep inside, or call out? Was it against the law for her to leave the public area?

'This is ridiculous,' she muttered to herself, and was just about to open the door when there was a whoosh behind her as someone entered.

Relieved, she turned. She was hoping to see Finn with his black eye, which she quickly told herself was perfectly natural and meant nothing more than a ride back to the house.

But it wasn't Finn.

This was a thickset man in a leather jacket and bike helmet, which he was removing as he came towards her with big strides. Through the glass behind him she could see a macho-looking motorcycle, parked in front of the station.

Any thought she had of smiling died. He looked aggressive. His removal of the helmet disclosed brown hair sticking up and a mixture of dirt and rain on his face. There was a thin white scar running from the corner of his mouth to his ear, and another one cutting his eyebrow in half. A serious-looking tattoo peeped up at her from under his collar.

Skye backed away until she was pressed flat against the partition wall.

'I'm here and I wanna make a complaint,' he growled and thrust his face into hers. He smelled of sweat with an after tang of leather.

He thought she worked here. Worse, he thought she was police. 'I'm sorry, I'm not … that is, I don't work here, I'm …'

He wasn't listening.

'Police harassment, that's what it is!' He was jabbing his glove-covered finger at her and in a moment he'd actually make contact with her body. It occurred to her that the man responsible for Finn's black eye wasn't locked up after all. That maybe he was right here in front of her.

Skye braced herself. Normally she wasn't the screaming sort, but in these circumstances a scream seemed the best option.

Before she could open her mouth and let loose, he froze. The expression in his dark eyes changed from anger to amazement, and then to disbelief. He blinked.

'Skye?' he whispered. 'Jesus, Skye, is that you?'

CHAPTER 11

NEVILLE

Tuesday 10 January 1939,
Mackenzie Crossing

MACKENZIE CROSSING SEEMED to con-
sist of more ruins than liveable dwellings.
While he was waiting to join Georgie and Tiddler for their tea of the unfortunate bird, Neville
went for a walk along the creek. He could see
that Georgie was correct when she'd told him
that once upon a time there had been a lot of
people living here. Many of the mine shafts were
still visible, although some weren't, so he was
careful where he put his feet. There were also the
footings of buildings that had once been quite
substantial, and he stood and smoked and wondered who had lived in them and where they had
gone.

It was clear to him that the Mackenzie Crossing Inn and Hostelry wouldn't have looked so
incongruous in those boom years.

He got out his *Victorian Handbook*, a tattered

copy he'd carried with him since he'd purchased it in Melbourne. It had been printed in 1903 so it was well out of date, but it still offered some interesting insights into the towns he passed through on his travels. Neville turned the pages until he found Mackenzie Crossing.

'*Rugged country makes this a place not easily reached but it can be done, and well worthwhile once it is achieved. Mackenzie Crossing lies in a valley some ten miles from Elysian, with a good water supply from Silverfish Creek. Mining is what brought the population to this isolated spot in the early days, but apart from a few single-handed operations, the main gold mine—the Union Jack—is closed and the miners have all gone. During those halcyon days there were several hotels and a school, as well as the usual paraphernalia of stores and businesses. Supplies had to be carried in by horse, but now a train runs to Westcott and then a coach to Elysian, and horse or foot thereafter. The Mackenzie family, who established the town in 1878, remain, but the rest of the population is in decline. Big Jim Mackenzie still welcomes visitors with a chilled drink and stories of the old days, and when they leave it is with a sense of regret that times are changing so quickly.*'

'You stayin'?'

The man was wiry, his brown hair too long, his face unshaven, and his gaze held a hefty dose of suspicion. He had noticed Neville's book and his mouth quirked with what could have been derision. 'On holiday, then, are you, mate?'

When Neville had explained his reason for being here to the man's satisfaction, he introduced himself as Hector Kennedy, and said he lived at the Crossing with his wife, Marie. Hector fell into step beside him. He walked with a decided limp, but he glossed over the explanation—as if an accident in a timber mill years back, when he was eighteen, was something that could have happened to anyone. Neville enquired how he made a living, and Hector explained he picked up a bit of work here and there, and that he and Marie grew vegetables for those who wanted to buy them.

'Once you've lived in the mountains you don't want to be crowded in,' he said.

'The fires …' Neville glanced up at the sky, which in normal circumstances would have been streaked with evening colours, but right now was covered by a gloomy, smoky haze. 'Are the townsfolk going to evacuate?'

Hector snorted a laugh. 'Some have. Georgie says she'll look after us, though, and Marie believes her.'

Neville speculated on just how Georgie could do that if the fire came through, but perhaps he was naive. People in the mountains experienced bushfires every few years and they must be well able to take care of themselves.

'So you're staying?' he asked Hector, as they approached the hostelry.

Hector looked towards the surrounding hills and frowned. 'I'm not sure,' he admitted at last, 'depends on the wind and the weather, and Marie.' And with that, he turned and walked away.

Georgie's door was open. Neville knocked and hesitated, but there didn't seem to be anyone around to ask permission of, so he took a step inside, and then another. The smell of the meal cooking wafted towards him, and he followed, through a door at the back of the bar. A passageway, crammed with a table and a dresser and a whatnot, took him past some stairs, and Neville glanced upwards into the shadows at the paintings on the wall. They, and the elegant furnishings, seemed to confirm that Big Jim had had a taste for expensive trappings. And, once upon a time, the income to indulge it.

'Mr Darling?'

It was the boy, Tiddler, smiling shyly from the landing. A moment later Georgie herself appeared, looking flushed, and led him into the kitchen. Neville told himself he must be getting used to her odd attire because he hardly noticed it anymore.

It was stifling in here even though the fire was no longer going. Sweat ran down his back as he sat down at the large table beside Tiddler. He glanced at Georgie, her own face shiny from the heat, and wondered about her mother. Was she one of the Chinese miners who flooded into the goldfields in the early days, or at least a descendant of them? There was no doubting Georgie had an Asian ancestor somewhere in her tree.

Neville was so engrossed in his thoughts that he started guiltily when Georgie spoke to him. Her past was none of his business, he reminded himself, but it was becoming harder to listen to his own advice.

'I saw you with Hector out there.'

'Yes. I asked him if there were plans to evacuate to Elysian.'

She glanced at the boy, tucking into his meal, and shrugged. 'I'll probably wait it out. There're always fires up in the mountains. If you ran away every time there was a bit of smoke you'd never get anything done. Mostly they burn themselves out, or head the other way. There was a bad one back in twenty-six, but it missed the Crossing. Maybe my father is watching over us.'

Neville had heard something like this before, and he knew it came from familiarity with the summer fires, and possibly the 'she'll be right' attitude, which he found in equal measure frustrating and endearing. He reminded himself that Georgie Mackenzie must know the situation better than he did.

People here called him 'Pom', not without affection, but often with a derogatory note. He was different, a stranger, and that moniker underlined the fact that he did not fit in. He tried not to be offended, though there were times when he couldn't help but remember the respect shown to him by his father's employees and his mother's servants.

Not that he deserved any such respect then or now. What had he done to earn it? Fought in a war that killed most of his generation, failed to join his father's firm and instead wandered the country. He'd crossed the world and tried to make a new life for himself, and when that didn't work he'd run away from his wife and daughter. No, Neville thought, he certainly didn't deserve respect.

He realised he'd been lost in his thoughts and a silence had fallen. Neville glanced up, a little startled, as if he'd woken from sleep, and found Georgie and Tiddler watching him curiously.

Georgie smiled. 'Thought we'd lost you there for a moment,' she said in her low, husky voice.

'Sorry, I …' He shook his head, embarrassed to be caught ruminating. Sometimes the past was so strong it felt more real than the present. 'I was remembering,' he said at last, and took up the glass of water she'd placed in front of him.

'I understand,' she replied, sombre.

Neville met her eyes and felt a jolt. Because he saw that she really did understand. She smiled again before she turned away, and just for a moment it was as if they were in perfect accord. Shock gave way to confusion and puzzlement, and the same questions he'd been asking himself ever since he first met her by Aesop's paddock resurfaced.

Georgie was mopping at the gravy on Tiddler's chin, such a domestic and commonplace action, and Neville refused to believe this woman could be capable of murdering anybody.

'What did Hector say?' she asked.

It took him a moment to remember what their previous conversation had been about. 'I think he's more afraid of his wife than the fire.'

Georgie gave a carefree laugh and sat back in her chair. 'They've been at the Crossing forever. I'm glad they stayed. Peggy and her son, too. Peggy's father came to work for Big Jim in the

Union Jack mine, and never left. It does that, the Crossing. Gets its claws into your soul so that you find yourself missing it whenever you go away, and then you can't wait to get back.'

'Have you been away?' Neville asked her curiously.

'I have,' she said, 'and I came home.' She changed the subject before he could ask more.

The conversation meandered along, and Neville wanted to know how such an isolated place received its supplies and news of the outside world.

'Horse, usually. In the old days there were bullock drays. One memorable day a truck got through, driven by a couple of fellows out to prove something, but it never happened again. When there were more of us we used to keep the track in better condition. Big Jim would send out working parties every few months. Nowadays it doesn't seem worth it, and anyway we manage.'

They'd finished eating. Tiddler had disappeared out of the back door, which he'd left wide open, and now the air was stirring faintly.

'Do you have to open the bar?' Neville asked, watching her face in the flickering candlelight.

'Not tonight. Not officially anyway. Did you want a beer, Mr Darling?'

'I don't drink, and please, it's Neville.'

She gave him a curious look. 'Did you never drink?'

'Rarely. After I came back from the war I didn't like the way it made me feel. I needed all my wits about me, I'm afraid.'

'I don't understand. Why did you need all of your wits about you, Neville?'

He didn't want to talk about his time in hospital, his struggles with illness and shifting sanity, and all the dark places he'd been. And yet she'd shared a meal with him and he felt she deserved an answer, but apart from that he found he *wanted* to tell her. The acknowledgement surprised him. 'I was afraid I'd lose myself,' he admitted at last.

And now she'll ask me what I mean, he thought anxiously, but she didn't. Instead Georgie nodded, and that smile was back, teasing at the corners of her mouth.

'I know what you mean,' she said, and he could see that she did.

He must have stared too long, because Georgie cleared her throat and looked away, and then stood up to tidy the table. Neville's birth and training brought him to his feet, too, and Georgie laughed. 'You really are a proper gentleman, aren't you?' she declared, but it was kindly meant. 'Let's leave these. I want to show you my father.'

She meant one of the paintings, Neville realised, as she took up the candle and led the way to the staircase. She glanced over her shoulder, saying, 'He's up here,' and Neville found himself following her up the stairs and into the shadows.

They passed a couple of landscapes, too gloomy to make out properly, and then they reached the upper floor and he saw that a chair had been placed in a recess, as if for contemplation, and on the wall above was a modestly sized portrait. He'd been expecting something larger and more suitable for a man of Big Jim's status, and yet there was a real power to the painting.

Big Jim looked out at him with a clear gaze, his mouth set, his arms folded over his barrel chest. He had a neat beard and a full head of dark hair peppered with grey, and his sun- browned face was deeply lined. Georgie held up the flame and Neville decided that her father's expression wasn't exactly welcoming but nor was it stand-offish. It was no doubt his vivid imagination, yet Neville felt as if he was sizing him up, trying to decide whether or not he was good enough for his daughter.

'He used to host dinners here, in the old days.' Now Georgie had led him into a small panelled room with barely enough space for an oval table and some wooden chairs, carved and polished to a soft gleam. The window was framed by grace-fully draped curtains, tied back on either side. 'I don't remember them, but I've heard the stories. You can imagine how crowded it could get in this house, despite its size. People came from all around and sometimes they'd still be here the next day, and the one after.'

Neville tried to picture it. The laughter and music, as the people from the mountains made merry. A different world, a different time, and one he doubted would come again to Mackenzie Crossing.

Georgie had gone to open up the window sash and the smell of smoke drifted in. He could see outside to the tall gum tree, and the paddock where Aesop was a mere shadow. There was a lamp on a table nearby, its pedestal made of brass and its shade of yellow-coloured glass, and now she lit it, setting it directly in line with the open window at a safe distance from the curtains. Seeing his puzzled expression she explained.

'This lamp has always been lit in the evenings, ever since I can remember. It's to guide any travellers who might need a place for the night.'

Neville doubted there would be many travellers coming this way tonight or any other night, and perhaps his expression gave him away.

'You think it's ridiculous,' she said, hands on her hips. 'I don't care. It was something Big Jim believed was important.'

'Do you still follow your father's dictates, even now that he's dead?' Neville asked her, not meaning to sound dubious.

'Of course. It's the least I can do.'

An awkward silence fell. Neville thanked her for the food and said it was time he retired. 'I like to look up and see the stars,' he said, in case she thought he was suggesting she offer him a bed.

She didn't follow him downstairs. As he walked from the hostelry, he noticed that those still occupying their cottages had dragged their mattresses out onto the verandahs to sleep, it being too hot inside. Hector lifted a hand in a half-wave and Neville saw the glow of his cigarette.

No one missed much at the Crossing.

As Neville spread his blanket by the privacy of the fence, Aesop came trotting over to investigate him but plodded off when he realised there were no more apples. Neville used some of the water from the trough to wash his face and clean his teeth, and then he lay down on his back.

This was what he loved about his time alone out here in the wilderness. The sense of being at one with the country. He still had his dreams about the war, they never went away entirely, but he was able to better handle them. The peace and quiet around him were a solace to his heart and mind.

What a larger-than-life character Big Jim Mackenzie must have been, and perhaps it explained Georgie's wanting to keep his memory alive. And yet it was more than that. She seemed to have taken her father's place. Why? What was driving Georgie to step into her father's shoes so literally?

Neville was finding that his naturally reclusive habits were at war with his desperate need to uncover all of Georgie Mackenzie's secrets.

He began to wonder where Miller Brown was now, and then wished he hadn't. It would be too much to hope that the man would return to Melbourne empty-handed. He was like a fox on the scent of his prey, and he would never stop. And why, if he'd decided Georgie could not possibly be the woman Brown sought, did that make him so uneasy?

He turned his head and his gaze found the hostelry. No stars tonight. Everything was in darkness apart from the faint light from the upstairs window, the lit lamp meant to guide travellers to safety. The sight of it was oddly comforting and Neville closed his eyes with a smile.

CHAPTER 12

SKYE

Sunday 8 June 1997

'MR TENNYSON!' The spell was broken. Someone behind Skye was trying to open the door in the partition, and she slid to the side to let them through. The angry man in front of her stepped back, looking confused and shocked, and probably everything Skye herself was feeling.

'Mr Tennyson, *I* called you in. She doesn't even *work* here.'

Dylan Faraday stared at her. He used to have the same nose as Finn, but now she could see it had been broken and was mashed at the bridge. He was older, too, just like Finn, just like her. His hair was either going grey or he'd had blond streaks, and there were lines around his eyes and a deep crease between his brows, and the scars …

Now he'd backed away she could breathe again, but her head was still spinning. The owner of the voice moved to stand by her side and some part of her brain noted that he was young, with brown hair that was a bit long and a body that seemed all gangly arms and legs in a suit he'd almost outgrown.

Dylan had dragged his gaze away from Skye and turned his attention to the boy, who, as if he thought he might now be the one under threat, put up a hand. Skye noticed it wasn't quite steady.

'Sergeant Galloway *told* me to call you in. Sir.'

Dylan shot a sideways look at Skye. 'Sergeant Galloway, eh?' he muttered. 'You met him yet, lady? He's a smug bastard, that one.'

She probably blinked but otherwise she didn't move a muscle, although in contrast her brain was tumbling over and over like clothes in a spin dryer.

He doesn't want me to tell anyone who he is. He doesn't want anyone to know that he and Finn are brothers.

He widened his eyes at her in warning. Oh, God, was she staring? Skye glanced down, just as Dylan banged his bike helmet on the counter and made her jump.

'Get him,' he growled at the boy. 'Sergeant Galloway. I want a word with him.'

'He's out. I'm sorry. If you want to wait he shouldn't be more than an hour. I did tell your wife on the phone. Sir.'

His *wife*?

As Skye edged away she heard Dylan mutter something uncomplimentary about the woman. She moved further out into the waiting area and sat down, giving her shaky legs a rest. Dylan stood a moment, clenching and unclenching his fists—he was certainly putting on a masterful performance and she might have applauded if she hadn't been so shocked. And then she wondered if it was a performance, or if perhaps Dylan had turned into this testosterone-driven monster for real. He had always been crazy and it had been nineteen years.

'I'll be back later,' he said threateningly, leaning in close to the boy, and then he turned and marched out. As he passed Skye, his back to the room, he gave her a wink. The door whooshed shut behind him.

She stared after him and then, remembering herself, looked down at her hands.

What the hell was going on? First Finn and now Dylan. She was owed an explanation.

'Phew.' The word was heartfelt. The boy gave her a grin, fingering his hair out of his eyes. 'That was one angry man. I thought I was about to get a shiner like Finn's.' He was looking at her now with interest. 'Are you Ms Stewart? Finn said you might drop in while he was out. I'm Taylor Mac-Rae.'

Skye knew his voice. This was the temporary staff member who'd been on Finn's police radio yesterday evening, when they were driving down from Lockington.

'Please. Call me Skye. Finn said you were filling in for ... Alison, was it?'

'Yeah. I'm home at the moment, and Alison is off sick. He thought it would be good training for next year, if I do decide to join the police force.'

Considering the scene they'd just been a part of, Skye had to question whether he was being sarcastic, but he seemed sincere.

'If they'll have me,' he added a little anxiously, as if he was worried her silence meant she wasn't sure he was up to it.

'Well, you certainly dealt with Mr Tennyson,' she said approvingly and tried not to smile as he straightened up proudly.

'I did, didn't I?' he agreed, tugging his too-short cuffs down over his wrists. 'I don't think he would've clobbered me though. Finn says his bark is worse than his bite. Still, I wouldn't like to square up to him in a dark alley.'

Were there many dark alleys in Elysian? It was hard to imagine. A thought occurred to her. 'He wasn't the one who …?'

Taylor laughed. 'No, despite his carry-on he wouldn't dare touch Finn. No one in Elysian would. That was a deer hunter. He was making a nuisance of himself, didn't even have a licence, and another shooting party called for Finn, but when he went out there the man was drunk and took a swing at him. I think it was an accident that he connected—the bloke could hardly scratch himself.'

So it had been nothing to do with Dylan, Skye thought. Although that still didn't explain why Finn and his brother were pretending not to know each other. Suddenly Skye felt tired. She had enough on her plate right now without worrying about what the Faraday brothers were up to.

'You *did* say Finn would be about an hour, didn't you?'

'Well, that's what he told me. But you know him. If something else comes up he won't be able to say no.'

'So he's a workaholic,' she said.

Taylor looked genuinely shocked. 'Oh no. I didn't mean … Finn just likes to help out.'

Skye thought she preferred her explanation, then she could dismiss him. Thinking of Finn as a man who was admired by others wasn't helping her to relegate him to the past as she wanted.

'So, are you all right here?' Taylor was glancing at the door through the partition, as if he needed to get back.

'Is there anything I can do while I wait?' Skye gave him a hopeful smile. Anything rather than be left here on her own to wallow in her own thoughts. 'Filing? Man the desk? You look like you could do with some help.'

Taylor's gaze flickered to a pile of paperwork beside one of the cabinets that looked as if it was about to tip over and, like an avalanche, go rolling across the floor. He chewed his lip. 'Well, strictly speaking, you're not police personnel,' he said. 'Not that there's anything there that's top secret. Parking fines, mostly. And some paperwork on loss of demerit points for drink-driving. Finn likes to spend the occasional Friday night sitting outside the pub, making sure no one who drives home is too far over the limit.'

'Must make him popular.'

'And saves a few lives.' Taylor cleared his throat again and avoided her eyes, but by now it was clear to Skye that he had a bit of a hero-worship thing going on with his temporary boss.

'Look, if you want me to do some filing then just tell me. I don't mind and I promise not to look at any names—well, except to find out which letter of the alphabet to file them under.'

He hesitated a beat and then shrugged. 'Righ-tio. Go for it. I have to get on with some other stuff. As long as you don't mind being alone out here? Give me a shout if someone comes in.'

Skye got to work. Taylor hovered a moment, but when he saw she was reasonably competent, he left her to it. However, this time the adjoining door remained open. The phone rang a few times over the next hour and once Finn checked in on the CB radio, asking if she was there, and Taylor said she was. He dropped his voice, so she didn't know what else he said. After she'd finished her filing, she turned her attention to cleaning the small kitchen. Keeping busy seemed to help, and what was the point of dwelling on the past? Although she had more than enough to keep her brooding for days. Dylan and Finn, firstly, and secondly, what Saskia and Archie knew about her grandfather and wouldn't tell her.

Outside the rain had set in and every now and again there was a gust of wind that splattered hard droplets against the roof and windows of the sta-tion. Skye was glad she'd had more sense than to set off on foot. If she had … well, by now she'd have been shivering and soaking wet, and probably knee deep in mud, and then she'd have to front up to Finn, the saintly cop, and explain herself.

That thought made her smile.

Russell had left a text message on her mobile, wishing her luck and asking how she was getting on. She tried to ring him. And then she tried to ring Fraser, imagining him home alone with Milly. It would have been nice to hear their voices, but the signal dropped out before the calls could connect. She supposed poor reception must be a constant problem up here in the mountains. Just another reminder of how far out of familiar territory she was and how good it would be to get home to her terrace house and her job and her ordered, comfortable life.

Lonely life.

'Stop it,' she muttered, just as Finn finally walked in the door.

He looked damp, his hair flattened to his head, and he was wearing his habitual frown. Also he seemed to barely notice her, which was irritating when she'd been impatiently waiting, questions at the ready. But all he did was give her a nod as he took off his jacket, shook the water from it and hung it up, and then strode straight through to Taylor.

They had a muted conversation.

The door was still open and she noticed with interest that Taylor kept glancing at her, so she was pretty sure they were talking about her and 'Mr Tennyson'. Then Finn was looking at her, too, and when Taylor noticed her interest and glanced away, Finn kept his gaze fixed on hers.

For a moment she stared back at him, letting him know she *knew*, and then she turned away.

The kitchen wasn't finished. She'd lined up the freshly washed and dried coffee mugs to one side of the electric jug, in size order. She'd collected dirty ones from all over the station, and they'd been tucked into the strangest places. There had even been one in the filing cabinet out front, under N, which used up some thinking time before she decided it was probably a reference to the brand of coffee the station used.

Skye suspected that, with Alison away with the flu, things had slipped a little, standard-wise. She couldn't believe it was always this grotty—even the tea towel looked as if it had been used to wipe the floor. So she hunted in the drawers for another one, and was just arranging it neatly on the railing when he spoke right behind her.

'Taylor says there was an incident.'

She jumped. She turned so quickly she would have bumped into him if he hadn't reached out to steady her. He dropped his hand immediately, which was just as well, because she was on the verge of shaking it off. For a moment she was distracted by the sight of his eye, which had darkened to a plum colour over the intervening hours, with the swelling around the periphery rather than in the eye socket itself.

He probably had a headache.

I hope so.

Then the thought popped into her head that if it was Fraser who had the black eye, he would have been in bed demanding attention, not out on the road doing his job. And that made her angry with herself as well as him, because why was she measuring Fraser's worth as a man against Finn's?

'Skye?'

'"An incident"? Is that what you call it?' She lowered her voice, glancing at the door. She could see Taylor at the other end of the room, stapling together some pages. 'I think you need to tell me what's going on.'

'Yes, I suppose I do.' He also glanced towards Taylor.

'Finn, what *is* going on?'

'I'll tell you what I can. Later.'

'What you *can*? What does that mean?' And then she connected some dots. 'Oh, please don't tell me this is some undercover police operation?'

He was giving her that concentrated stare, and she really wanted to look away. The times they'd played that staring game, each of them trying to outlast the other, trying not to blink. He'd always won. Well, not this time.

And then she thought how childish she was being.

As if he'd had the same thought, a smile twitched at the corner of his mouth, and he looked down to check his watch.

'I can drop you off at home now, if you're finished.' He gave the rows of clean mugs a puzzled glance, as if he'd just noticed them. 'Did you get what you needed from Archie at the museum?'

Something in her expression must have warned

him that the visit hadn't been all she'd hoped for, because he tilted his head to see her better. He really was tall. And his eye did look sore. She clenched her fists, just in case her fingers disobeyed her and touched him. What was that all about? she thought impatiently. She was getting very tired of her lack of self-discipline.

'So … the museum?' he repeated with a lift of his eyebrows, and then winced when the injured eye hurt.

'I saw Saskia. Archie is ill, his heart, evidently, so she sent him back to bed. I explained about Neville. She said she couldn't help me. But Finn—'

'That's odd. Archie knows everything there is to know about this area. He—'

She put her hand on his arm to stop him, but something about that contact caused her to just as quickly remove it. 'I was going to say that I'm sure she did know something. It was … well, it was strange. Is Archie really that ill? She said he'd had rheumatic fever as a child. I wouldn't upset him, just ask him a couple of questions. You'd think I was planning to use electric-shock therapy on him, the way she got rid of me.'

Finn scratched his chin. 'He was away in hospital in Westcott last month. Although he's never been all that robust, I thought he was back to normal. Do you want to talk to them now?'

Skye considered how it would seem to Saskia if she arrived at the museum with a police escort, and shook her head. Better if she handled this herself, in her own way. 'Perhaps not right now.'

He shrugged. 'It's up to you. But Archie knows

me. I can be sensitive. We're not all into police brutality, especially when it comes to pensioners.'

She shot him a look and this time he gave her a proper smile.

A joke. Or … was he flirting? Oh, God, don't let him be flirting.

Her voice was cool. 'Okay, Finn, I admit it. I was thinking that arriving in your cop car would be a bit over the top. I'd prefer to try again myself before I call in the big guns.'

His smile was gone as if it had never been. 'Fine.' He moved towards the door. 'Tomorrow morning I can take you out to Mackenzie Crossing. Might have to be early.'

'Thank you. I can manage early. I'll bring my camera.'

This was a chance that may not come her way again, at least not for a long while.

Skye had followed him back into the public area. If he was going to explain about Dylan, then maybe she could cook dinner. She could cook and listen at the same time, and she told herself it would also assuage her discomfort for freeloading on the man.

'Finn …'

He was looking over her head, through the glass to the outside. And yes, he was frowning. A moment later the door whooshed open and a familiar voice growled.

'I want a word with you.'

Finn glanced a warning at Skye, before he stepped forward and held out his hand. 'Mr Tennyson, just the man I wanted to see. Please come through.'

Dylan shook his hand, but he was looking at Finn's black eye. He gave an evil grin. 'Suits you,' he said.

They had always looked quite different to each other and now time, and Dylan's broken nose, had changed them so that there was only a passing similarity between them.

As they went by Dylan kept his gaze to the front, but Finn paused briefly by Skye. 'I'll get Taylor to run you home,' he said.

Then the beige door closed behind them, leaving Skye on the outside.

A moment later Taylor appeared, pulling on a jacket, car keys in his hand. He handed Skye a separate key. 'Finn said this will get you into the house.'

The old Datsun parked at the front was Taylor's, and he shoved some food packets and other rubbish off the passenger seat, before he folded his gangly body inside the vehicle.

'Maybe I could hire a car while I'm here?' Skye suggested as he worked on getting the engine started. 'Then I wouldn't have to hang around waiting for Finn.'

'You'd have to go to Westcott to get one. Or Cumberland,' Taylor said, giving the car a satisfying rev. 'And you'd pay a premium for the damage these roads do to a shiny new duco.' A gust of wind and rain hit the windscreen, and he turned on his wipers. 'Anyway it probably isn't worth it,' he added, and rubbed off some of the inside condensation with his hand. 'Finn's out and about all day, so it's no bother to him if he's dropping you off and picking you up.'

Saint Finn. He'd probably relish the chance to do more good. Skye bit her lip and told herself not to be sarcastic, even if it did improve her mood.

As he backed out onto the one sealed road in Elysian, the weather eased up just for a moment, and Skye spotted a sapphire-blue sweater in front of the cafe. Saskia. Taylor saw her as well, because when the girl looked up, evidently recognising the car, he waved. She lifted her hand with a smile, and at the same time she saw Skye in the passenger seat. Even from this distance it was obvious her smile wavered and then, more to the point, she turned her back.

Taylor gave a curious sideways glance at Skye but didn't comment.

'Are you and Saskia friends?' she ventured as Taylor crunched the gears.

'I suppose. We used to go to the same school in Westcott. We still meet up when she's home from uni.'

Was there a flush in his cheeks, a studiedness to his voice? Skye remembered how Saskia had looked when she'd spoken of Taylor, and it seemed to her that the two of them were on the cusp of being more than good friends.

'I met Archie and Saskia today at the museum.'

He chuckled. 'I really don't know how he fits everything in. He brought home another trailer load the other day from Mr Rutherford's house. None of the family live here anymore and they're going to sell the place, although I reckon it needs some work first. I was thinking of putting in an offer.'

He slowed down, waiting patiently as a couple of pedestrians with backpacks and hiking boots crossed the road in front of him. Whereas drivers in the city would have gone crazy beeping their horns, Taylor seemed to accept this as simply part of life in Elysian.

'Putting in an offer? So you want to live here permanently?' Skye couldn't help being curious. 'I thought you said you were going to join the police force?'

'Well, I need somewhere to come home to now and again, and this is where I want to live, eventually.'

'Maybe when Finn retires you can take over from him.'

Taylor shook his head and said in a serious voice, 'No one could ever replace Finn Galloway.'

There was nothing Skye could say to that, and anyway just then he swung the car onto the rough track that led to Finn's house, and her teeth were rattling too much to talk. Thankfully, the torture was brief and a moment later they'd reached their destination. Taylor drew up with a scatter of stones.

'Thank you, Taylor.'

'No worries.'

She reached for the door handle and then paused. Taylor knew Saskia and her grandfather, and it seemed crazy to miss such an excellent opportunity.

'Saskia mentioned that Archie has been unwell. His heart. The thing is, I wanted to talk to him about Mackenzie Crossing. My grandfather was there before the Black Friday fire and I thought Archie might have heard of him. His name was Neville Darling.'

It meant nothing to Taylor. 'Did you ask Archie?' he said.

'I tried to, but Saskia didn't want me bothering him. I think I upset her. Do you know how sick he is?'

He scraped his thumb over some peeling plastic on his steering wheel. 'Nancy, Saskia's mum, has left her in charge while she's away for work. If anything happened to Archie she'd get into big trouble. Maybe that was why she was upset.'

'She did send him back to bed.'

Taylor chuckled. He was a nice boy. He just needed to grow into his body and he'd be a handsome man.

'Sounds about right. Look, it might be best to ask Nancy. She should be back by the end of next week.'

'I doubt if I'll still be here then.'

But Taylor had run out of suggestions. After he drove off, Skye hurried inside out of the weather. She stood a moment with her back to the door, listening. The house felt very desolate and she thought again of her own home in Carlton, empty and dark, waiting for her, everything in its place.

With nothing else to do, she went to her room and flopped down on the bed.

Outside the rain was falling heavier than ever and she could hear the wind moaning in the trees. The light was fading fast.

With a sigh, she got up again and went to take her camera out of the drawer. It was a Pentax K1000. She also had an older 35mm Kodak as a backup, but she was used to the new model now and, unlike some more senior photographers who were more set in their ways, she much preferred digital.

She checked the monitor. Her last shot had been of Milly in her kitchen at home. The way the light glowed through the cat's whiskers was clever, and she reminded herself to get the print from the memory card and have it enlarged for Fraser.

Her heartbeat quickened at the sound of the rain on the roof and the possibility that the conditions would be just as bad tomorrow. In the past she used to worry if the sun wasn't shining and the sky wasn't blue, but these days she looked upon the vagaries of the weather as a challenge.

She may never find out what happened to Neville, why he left Mary and Gertie, why he disappeared. Perhaps, as Russell had said, it was to do with the war and his experiences on the Western Front. Or perhaps it was just something in him, something that didn't allow him to buckle down to responsibility.

But she was a photographer and so was he, and it created a connection between them. Part of him was in her, a link of blood.

And just like that, she knew she had to do the

exhibition.

She'd been dillying and dallying, but in her heart of hearts she now accepted it was the only way forward. Even if it was a flop, she had to make the attempt, because if she didn't she would regret it all her life.

Skye wasn't entirely sure how she was going to get the backing—Fraser might offer, but maybe not. Maybe she could get an arts grant from the government or look for a sponsor with an interest in what she was doing. She'd have to work something out. The idea just seemed so *right*, which frightened her, because she was normally an organised, cautious person and one of the reasons she'd held back was because this had initially seemed like an insane leap into the unknown.

She hadn't always been afraid of risk. But after she'd met Finn and Dylan, after that had ended, her life had shut down. She hadn't wanted any more drama, and she'd obeyed her parents and gone down the conventional track. Apart from her photography, that was. Her choice of career had been the one and only thing she'd stood firm on, resisting when her parents were pushing for her to go into business studies.

Maybe it was time to release the tight restraints she had put upon herself.

Thunder rumbled overhead and Skye went to the window, watching the darkness roll in. Her terrace house seemed a long way away right now and she was in a place at once unfamiliar and unsettling, with a man she'd known when she was fifteen and had never really got over.

Was that an admission? And if it was, then what was she admitting? That he still meant something to her, and that there were unresolved issues between them?

Well of course there were. How could there not be? And before she left Elysian Skye knew she was going to have to sit down and have a long talk with Finn.

And then, finally, she was going to forget him.

CHAPTER 13

DYLAN, FINN AND SKYE

December 1978,
Northcote, Melbourne

'FINN! FINN, COME *on*!'
Dylan Faraday was laughing at his brother. It was just about dark, nearly ten o'clock day-light-saving time. He took a step, his legs not quite steady, and stumbled against the playground slide, clinging to the ladder to keep himself upright.

The bottle in his hand was doing its job.

Skye had taken a couple of mouthfuls of Southern Comfort and Coke, just enough to make her mellow, but she didn't really like it. Although she knew she should say no, the couple of times she'd tried, Dylan had made her feel like a silly little kid.

She glanced sideways at Finn. She wasn't sure how much he'd had. Unlike Dylan, however, he seemed in control.

It was the first day of the holidays. School was done for another year and for their various reasons they were all glad to see the back of it.

Throughout this last term they'd all had their ups and downs, mostly downs, and their small group had grown tighter.

Dylan staggered over to join them, dropping down on the picnic bench where they were sitting, pushing himself in between them, a bit like a toddler with his parents, so they had no choice but to make room. He grinned and slung his arms over their shoulders.

'Come on, Finn,' he said again, and shook the car keys in front of his brother's face. 'We can be back before Darryl clocks it's gone. You know Mum and him'll be out of it till morning.'

'And what if Darryl wakes up and sees his car's gone and calls the cops?'

'Nah, I saw him through the window. He's out of it, man, just like her. Anyway Darryl won't call the cops. They caught him with that stuff last month and he went to court and only just got off. He hates 'em.' He leaned in closer to whisper in Finn's ear, but Skye heard him. 'Let's teach him a lesson, hey? Show him he can't push us around.'

She could tell Finn was starting to waver. Dylan seemed to know just which buttons to push in order to wear down his brother's reserve.

At first Finn hadn't wanted to drive his mother's boyfriend's car down to the bottle shop, and then he'd resisted parking by the playground. Now he was refusing to go to the bay for a swim despite the sweltering summer heat.

Skye wondered sometimes what it was all about, this tug of war between them, but she didn't ask and they didn't say.

'You're no fun, Finn,' his brother said in disgust. 'Skye needs some fun.' He pulled a silly face at her and Skye giggled. Mostly it was nerves, though Dylan had the ability to make her smile at the most unlikely moments.

Like now.

'Aw, Finn, don't be a sook. Boo hoo!' Dylan pretended to sob on her shoulder.

Before Finn could do more than frown, his brother had grabbed Skye's hand, pulling her, shrieking, towards the car. The world was tilting. Either she'd drunk more than she'd realised or Dylan had added something else to the bottle before he had handed it to her—something Darryl had given him or he'd found in his mother's room.

She half fell in through the open door, onto the cracked vinyl of the back seat. 'Ow!'

Darryl's box of tools dug into her leg. He was supposed to be a handyman, but Finn said he spent more time dealing drugs than mending things.

Dylan leaned in beside her. 'Skye, aw, Skye, are you all right, Skye?' She felt his warm breath against the side of her face.

And of course she giggled again. She couldn't help it. Dylan grinned back at her, his eyes not as dark as Finn's, his hair a lighter brown.

Sometimes she believed that Dylan and Finn were engaged in some sort of tug of war and, in Dylan's mind anyway, she was the prize. Except she'd already chosen Finn as the winner.

She blinked. Dylan was still leaning in through the car door, watching her. He gave her a know-ing smile. *Crap.* She looked away, hoping he hadn't read in her eyes what she was thinking.

'Let's go to the beach,' he said quietly. Then, louder, 'Let's go skinny dipping!' He looked back at Finn over his shoulder as he said it.

Trying to make him jealous, Skye thought, and to her shame a hot bolt of pleasure shot through her. Was Finn jealous? She knew he liked her. He said he did, and the way he looked at her … But she'd heard from other girls that boys could pre-tend to like you and once they had what they wanted then they walked away. Worse, they told their friends about it.

Skye didn't think she could bear that. What she felt for Finn wasn't plain and simple friendship, although that was part of it. What she felt was more. It was *love*. The acknowledgement gave her that familiar achy sensation in the pit of her stomach, the awareness she had whenever she was with him, or thought about him, and she hugged the insight to herself. It had to remain a secret. She couldn't tell anyone she loved Finn. She was only fifteen and her parents disapproved of their next-door neighbours—she'd heard them talking in hushed tones about the house next door and the word 'disgrace' had been used. If they knew she was out here now instead of with her former best friend, Susanne, as she'd told them she was, then there'd be a whole load of trouble.

They mightn't let her see Finn ever again.

He'd kissed her tonight, when Dylan was in

the bottle shop. His lips on hers, his arms loose around her waist, her arms tight around his neck. She'd felt the excitement of it right down to her newly painted toenails. Not seeing him again, well, she may as well be dead.

'Finn!' Dylan roared, and made her jump. 'Come on, please, Finn. If you don't,' he gave her a sly look, 'I'll tell Skye what you told me.'

Finn was on his feet. 'Shut up, Dylan.' He reached the car and lost his balance, falling against it. He must be drunker than Skye had thought. That was worrying. Because if Dylan was crazy and Finn was drunk, then things could get quickly out of control.

Dylan gave his head an exaggerated shake. 'Your choice, brother.'

Finn glared down at him as if he hated him. Despite being the younger twin, he'd grown taller than Dylan over the last few months. The tension she sometimes felt simmering between them leaped to a new level.

'Finn,' Skye murmured, suddenly not liking this at all. Dylan tended to make situations go off in unexpected directions. Like this one, when a walk to the shops for ice cream had turned into a ride in their mother's boyfriend's car. Usually Finn could calm it down, he could control his brother's wild behaviour. Not tonight, it seemed.

Finn looked at her, reading her fear, and then back at his brother. 'If Skye says yes, then we'll go down to the bay. The cops will be at that concert at Waverley, looking for drunks. They won't be hanging around here.'

This wasn't what she'd wanted. She didn't want to be the one to make the choice, and she resented Finn putting her on the spot like this. Although the boys liked to tell her about the wild rides they'd had around the paddocks at their dad's farm, before they moved to live with their mother in the city, this wasn't the bush.

They were both watching her, waiting for her answer.

'I'll go to the bay,' she said at last, 'if Finn drives.'

'Then I'll drive,' Finn said, holding out his hand for the keys. 'Hand 'em over, brother.'

'Aw, Finn.' Dylan pulled a face, a parody of his brother's frown. 'Don't you trust me?'

He held up the keys and gave them a defiant rattle, and the challenge was back in his voice.

'If you want to drive then come and get them.'

CHAPTER 14

SKYE

Sunday 8 June 1997

THE KITCHEN WAS well stocked, but then Finn had said it was, and Skye knew that as a boy he'd always done things to the best of his ability. He obviously still did. That, at least, hadn't changed. If anything he was an over-achiever. Afraid of getting it wrong. She'd never thought about that in the past, but now she couldn't help deliberating on what had made him so serious at such a young age.

With a sigh she opened the fridge.

Well, he was still a meat eater, but he'd moved on from burgers and fries. There were two steaks in the freezer and she found a variety of vegetables, including potatoes and carrots and beans. Mushrooms, as well, which she'd use to make a sauce for the steak. There were also a couple of stubbies of beer, and a bottle of dry white wine, half full, in the door. She poured herself a glass of the wine to sip while the steak and vegies cooked.

She hoped Finn wouldn't mind her making free use of his home, but then she decided it was too bad if he did. She was here alone and she was hungry and so would he be, when he finally got back. At first she told herself she would demand answers. How dare he bring her into another dodgy situation involving his brother? But as the time ticked by, no matter how she tried to hang on to it, she found her anger receding. Perhaps she'd be generous and let him eat before he began explaining.

By seven-thirty it was quite dark and she lit the fire in the sitting room. There was a clock ticking on the mantelpiece. It looked old, like a family heirloom. Had it belonged to Finn's mother? She didn't think so—she would have sold it for drugs, or to bail Darryl or Dylan out of jail. Perhaps his father? Or maybe it was Finn's wife's treasure and she hadn't been able to fit it into her suitcase when she left for Perth.

Skye ate her steak and left his in the oven to keep it warm. She tried to picture what Finn's wife and daughter looked like, and almost immediately she spotted their photo on the table under the window.

It was one of those photographs you can have taken in a shopping mall. Smile and click. Finn looked younger, and less tired, and he was standing with his arm around a dark-haired woman in a low-cut blouse. She was holding a little girl of about two, in a frilly dress with sandals on her feet, and her toenails were painted the same pink as her mother's fingernails.

They looked happy, in a guarded sort of way. Even though they were smiling, there was something about the set of Finn's shoulders and the woman's mouth that spoke of unresolved tensions.

They'd probably just had an argument. Skye knew all about that. She and Fraser had argued in the most inconvenient places and at the worst possible times. She used to tell herself that that was what kept their relationship fresh, but in the end it had just been exhausting.

Was that how Finn had felt?

By nine she'd washed the dishes and got ready for bed. By ten she went into the kitchen and switched off the oven, and then the lights. On her way past the sitting room she looked in at the photograph of Finn and his absent family, and rethought her version of events.

They were on holiday away from Elysian and Finn was worrying about work. His wife was telling him if he went back then she wasn't going to stick around.

It was a picture of an ultimatum.

When next Skye opened her eyes, it was morning, and Lightning was sitting by her bed, staring back at her, unblinking.

Skye smiled.

The greyhound took that as an invitation to lick her face. Laughing, she reached out to capture the dog's head, struggling to hold it at bay.

'I don't need a bath, thank you very much!'

Then she caught sight of the clock on the bedside table. It was nearly ten.

'Oh crap,' she whispered, and leaped out of bed while Lightning jumped out of the way.

This was the day they were going to Mackenzie Crossing and she'd slept in. Finn had probably already given up on her and left for work.

Quickly Skye pulled on her underwear, blue jeans and a white long-sleeved shirt. Her toes were frozen and she paused long enough to drag on some pink socks, before she took off down to the kitchen, still carrying her shoes. She was moving so fast she skidded on the polished floor and it was only by grabbing at the doorjamb that she stopped herself from landing on her bottom.

Which would have been embarrassing, considering there were two other people in the kitchen besides Finn.

At the table, a brunette in a smart-looking skirt and jacket looked up in surprise—the flash of anger in her eyes came and went so quickly Skye wasn't even sure she'd seen it. The man adjacent to her was dressed in a suit that looked as if it had seen better days, and his iron-grey hair needed a cut. There was a nervous energy about him—she could see his knee jiggling—and his blue eyes held a glitter that made her think he was on a short fuse. She almost backed out of the room again. There were papers spread in front of them, and now the woman began to tidy them into a pile.

Finn was standing, leaning back on the kitchen

counter, a mug in his hand. He wasn't wearing his uniform, instead blue jeans and a pale-green button-up shirt, and his favourite black socks.

'Oh, I'm so sorry.' Skye tried to back-pedal, except Lightning was right behind her, and she stumbled again, nearly falling over the dog.

A strong hand closed over her arm, steadying her, and Finn gave her the benefit of his searching gaze. 'Okay?'

Before she could answer, the man pushed some of the papers away and growled impatiently, 'Can we get *on* with this?'

The woman shot him a look and then spoke politely. 'Are you all right?' Despite her good manners, there was an expression on her face that made Skye think she was as irritated at the interruption as her companion.

'Yes.' She glanced up at Finn. 'Sorry. I saw the time and I was worried I'd missed you. You said early.'

'I did, didn't I? These are two of my former colleagues from Melbourne. Detectives Lois Petersen and Gary Grey.' He'd released his hold on her and turned back to the others, who seemed to be watching their interaction with some interest. 'Skye is staying with me for a few days. Her reason for being in Elysian is … personal. Nothing to do with this situation.'

It was an odd thing to say. Lois Petersen looked down with a smile, as if something about his explanation amused her. 'We have no secrets from each other, surely, Finn?' she said in a voice that could only be described as coy.

Finn didn't reply, and the woman looked up at him. There was something cold about her smile now. What the hell was going on? Skye couldn't shake the impression of danger.

'I think we're finished here, aren't we?' Finn's voice was cool, too, and Skye saw the other two exchange a glance.

'We'll leave you to think about what we've discussed. You have my number. I really advise you to …' Gary Grey's voice trailed off and he flicked a look at Skye, obviously not trusting her with what must be privileged information. Instead, he leaned forward and the sense of menace grew. Had the man slept recently? In that regard he looked worse than Finn.

'You need to think hard, Finny-boy. Long and hard.'

His gaze swivelled around to Skye and he bared his teeth in a grin that wasn't at all nice.

Suddenly Skye didn't want to be in the room. 'I'll go and get ready,' she said and turned to leave.

Skye was halfway to her room when she heard Lois Petersen laugh. 'You always were a bit of a dark horse, Finn,' she said, and it didn't sound like a compliment. 'I never did believe that squeaky-clean image you like to project.'

Skye didn't like the insinuation or the way it unsettled her. Perhaps Finn was now a serial womaniser, although she couldn't imagine it, not the boy she had known, but then, she reminded herself, people changed. Quite a lot. She should just concentrate on finding Neville.

She was checking her camera again when she

heard a car drive away and shortly afterwards Finn knocked on her door. 'Skye?'

'Yep, I'm ready.'

She grabbed her camera bag, slinging it around her neck. The white coat hadn't dried out properly overnight, so she was wearing her one and only warm jacket—wool-lined blue-and-gold check—the one she usually took with her when she went out for jobs at chilly times of the year. Putting it on this morning had made her feel like a professional, less vulnerable, as if she was here on business.

Quickly, Skye glanced at herself in the mirror, tucking her auburn hair behind her ears with her gloved hands, and pulling on the blue knitted hat she'd bought in the shop yesterday.

She went to open the door.

Finn was standing right outside and his expression was severe.

'Look,' he said before she could ask what the matter was. 'This isn't important, and I don't want to go into detail, but I've been suspended.'

She certainly hadn't been expecting that and she didn't know what to say. He didn't give her a chance to answer.

'I can't go into the station and I have to stay put in the area. So today I'm all yours. I suppose that's one good thing.'

Skye shook her head, ignoring the 'all yours'. 'There are no good things, surely? Why … what …?'

What have you done? she'd been about to say, but thankfully hadn't blurted it out.

Finn was watching her. His injured eye was an array of colours this morning, sickly yellow among them.

'It's something that happened back when I was with the Drug Squad, years ago. I was cleared then and I'll be cleared now. Meanwhile, I have to go through this crap.' He took a deep breath and let it out, and slowly relaxed his clenched hands.

'But why are they reinvestigating you, Finn?'

'It's complicated,' he started, and then changed his mind and shook his head, turning away.

After a moment she followed him to the door. Lightning was there waiting, clearly intent on joining them on this adventure. Finn crouched down to pat her, and then rested his head against the dog's.

And just like that her heart ached for him.

He had been suspended from the job he loved and he was being investigated for God knew what. Maybe he was a brute who beat up his prisoners every night and ran a racket on the side. As quickly as she'd formed the thought she rejected it. She simply couldn't believe it.

'Weather hasn't improved,' he said to Lightning, but Skye assumed he was talking to her. 'Might even snow before the day is out.'

'You think?'

He looked up at her, probably trying to figure out whether or not she was serious, and then he smiled.

'Thanks for the steak.'

'Wasn't it dry and inedible by the time you got

home?' Skye heard the sharpness in her voice, and knew she was compensating for the way his smile affected her.

'I got home just after midnight, and it was delicious. It's been a long time since anyone cooked me a meal.'

'Oh.' What was she to make of that? Any pleasure she gained from his comment she quashed by remembering the photo of Finn and his family in the other room. 'I'm glad you enjoyed it,' she told him matter-of-factly.

He seemed to be considering his next words. 'We'll go to the Crossing this morning, no worries about that, but there's a side trip I have to take on the way. You can stay in the car if you like. In fact, I'd understand why you might prefer it.'

'You mean Dylan,' she said, her voice flat.

He nodded and straightened up, waiting for some response from her.

'Then I'll wait in the car.'

'I thought you wanted me to explain …?'

'I've changed my mind, Finn. I really don't want to know.' There was such a thing as self-preservation and she had a feeling that if she let this wave break over her head she would drown.

His mouth closed in a tight, straight line and he nodded his head. 'Right,' he said. 'We'll leave it at that.'

Finn was right. The weather was worse. Skye huddled into her jacket as they drove through

Elysian and out again. Though the lights in the museum were on, she couldn't see any faces through the windows.

The police four-wheel drive was evidently back at the station, and Finn was using his own vehicle, the dirty white Toyota LandCruiser she'd seen yesterday.

There had been an unbroken silence between them for about fifteen minutes and she was looking for some way to ease them through this awkwardness.

'Taylor said that Archie's daughter is keeping an eye on him,' she said. 'He has a weak heart.'

He nodded, staring ahead through the windscreen. 'I heard she wants him to leave Elysian. She has a job in Warburton so she has to travel. Makes it hard for everyone.'

'And Archie won't leave?'

'He's spent forty years of his life here and he wants to die here.'

That was sobering.

Skye looked around her at the cold cloudy sky and the sombre bush, still dripping from last night's storm, and wondered if she could spend her days in a place like this. Finn did. He'd obviously grown to love it. Perhaps it took a certain type of person to do that.

'How on earth did you become a cop, Finn?'

He gave her a humourless smile. 'When I landed back with Dad I was a bit of a mess. He'd never been much good at inspiring his sons— he was an old-fashioned man who just got on with it and expected us to do the same. I needed some plain speaking, but I wasn't going to get it from him. Anyway, I met up with some of my old crowd, decided I was bad through and through and might as well not fight it.

'Then one night I got pulled over on a lonely road by a young traffic cop. I was by myself and driving an unregistered vehicle without a licence, and at first I thought he was going to beat the crap out of me.'

It had begun to rain again and he put on the wipers, letting the pause lengthen.

'And?' Skye asked impatiently. 'Did he beat the crap out of you?'

'No, he didn't. It turned out that he knew about my circumstances so he decided to cut me some slack. He came around a few times after that, just to see how I was getting on, and I started to look forward to his visits. Despite the way my mates treated me because of it. A long time afterwards, he said he saw something in me that made him believe I was worth saving. He suggested I think about becoming a policeman. At first I wasn't so sure, but it seemed a better plan than doing nothing and getting into trouble. I've always been glad I listened to his advice.'

'You were never Dylan, Finn. You would never have ended up—'

'In jail?' He shook his head at her. 'I'm flattered you think that, but I'm not so sure myself, Skye.' He paused, slowing down. The rain had turned to sleet, and all the world was grey. 'What about you?' he asked. 'I used to wonder what happened to you.'

She shrugged because she wasn't going to tell him her life story. She was in enough trouble just being in the four-wheel drive with him, without letting him into her secrets.

'I got on with it.'

He nodded. 'Good for you,' he said, but he said it gently, as if he really was glad for her, and she had to turn away so he wouldn't see how that affected her.

Finn manoeuvred the car onto an unmade road he informed her was called Desperation Track, and the vehicle bumped and twisted its way along. Skye felt as if she was sailing on a rough sea, and clung to the door, hoping they'd hit clearer water soon. In the back Lightning whimpered.

A few more kilometres and there was a fallen tree on the side of the road. Finn eased around it and turned left onto a narrower track.

'Most of these tracks were put in for the timber industry,' he explained, glancing at her clenched white knuckles. 'A few of them are no longer in use, except by thrill seekers. In the summer we get a lot of call-outs from people who are lost.'

Eventually, they came to a stop in front of a fall of boulders, at what looked to Skye to be a dead end. The scrappy bush to the side was a screen, but behind it smoke wafted and Skye could just see the outline of a cottage behind a wire fence. Lightning growled, staring, and that was when Skye noticed the seriously savage-looking dog chained to the gate.

Finn sat with his hands on the wheel for a moment, as though gathering his thoughts, and then he turned his dark, serious eyes on her.

'It might help. To talk. Are you sure you won't come in and …?'

'Finn, it was a long time ago. I'd rather wait here.'

Really, she told herself, the last thing she wanted was to have a deep-and-meaningful conversation with Dylan. Yesterday she'd thought she wanted to know what he was doing here but today she'd changed her mind. It felt like she was getting dragged deeper and deeper into something that wasn't healthy for her. Skye remembered what it had been like all those years ago, and the consequences of that, and she had no desire for history to repeat itself.

'Okay, stay here. I won't be long.' He opened the door and freezing air gusted in before he closed it again. He'd left the motor running so that warmth continued to blow out from the vents around her.

She watched as he made his way towards the gate. The dog was pulling against the chain, snarling and showing its teeth. A glance behind her showed that Lightning was as appalled as she was by its bad behaviour. Above the noise of the engine, she heard Finn call out something, and the next moment the door in the sunken porch opened and Dylan stepped out.

He called the dog to heel. Finn opened the gate and went in and for a moment they stood together, talking, their heads bent towards each other in a manner that struck a chord.

What was Dylan up to now? Skye wanted to

know. He'd always had the ability to draw his brother into things that he'd be better left out of. And Finn had let it happen. It was as if he believed that by joining him in his crazy escapades he could save Dylan from himself. How long could he keep doing that? They were brothers, yes, and they were close—or they used to be—but how long could Finn keep stepping in to rescue Dylan from his own stupidity?

As she watched, Dylan led the way into the building and Finn followed. Just before he vanished inside, Finn paused and glanced back, and Skye sensed he was wanting her there. Maybe he thought she should make her peace with them both.

Well that wasn't going to happen.

'What do you think they're up to?' she murmured to Lightning.

The dog gave an anxious thump of its tail.

'Yeah, you're right. Better not to know.'

CHAPTER 15

NEVILLE

Wednesday 11 January 1939,
Mackenzie Crossing

AS THE SUN set in a strange and bloody smear of red, a group of men from the timber camp came trooping down the track to Georgie's hostelry. The beer was warm, nothing else it could be in this weather, but they drank it down without complaint.

They were a rough-looking lot to Neville's eyes, though surprisingly respectful to their hostess. Or maybe not so surprising, he thought, watching the way she treated them. More like a sister or a mother, she scolded them, teased them, and praised them when they'd done something she approved of. These weren't local men—some of them were far from their homes, while others may never have had a proper home.

And they all lapped it up.

Neville had spent the day at the Crossing, again wandering around, and had sat for a while with

Hector on his verandah. The heat was much the same as yesterday, and now and again the wind brought thickening smoke from the burning ranges to the north. Hector was still tossing up whether or not to leave.

'I'm not going,' Marie said in a voice that dared him to contradict her. Her reddish hair had been tied back from her face with a scarf, and her skin seemed to have been bleached of colour by the high temperatures. 'Georgie said she'd look after us and that's good enough for me.'

As if in agreement, the white-and-black goat they had tethered to the post let out a bleat.

'Georgie can't stand in front of the fire and send it back,' Hector retorted, but he had lowered his voice as he glanced towards the hostelry. 'We should be talking sense into her, love.'

'Peggy and Arnold are staying, too,' Marie said, as if that settled it.

'You know Peggy would do anything Georgie tells her, and as for her son … a shingle short, that boy.'

'Well if you believe she's wrong, *you* knock some sense into her,' Marie dared him. 'Go on.'

Hector shifted uneasily in his chair. He flicked a look at Neville and seemed to brighten. 'Perhaps you could talk to her? I reckon she'd listen to you, Neville.'

'I doubt it,' Neville said. 'Why should she listen to me, when I'm just a stranger from England?'

Hector didn't seem to know the answer to that, but Marie smiled to herself, making Neville wonder what she was thinking. They were still bickering when Neville left them. He found Georgie about to chop some wood for her kitchen fire. When he insisted on doing it for her, she laughed. 'You really are a gentleman, aren't you, Neville?' she teased, and there was something in her gaze that made him think she was flirting with him. It gave him a ridiculously warm sensation in his chest.

Last night as he lay under the stars, he'd decided he should show Georgie the photograph he'd taken from Miller Brown. It seemed the right thing to do, especially as he kept telling himself it wasn't her and had nothing to do with her. Then, in the light of day … Something stopped him, some niggling sense that if he did show her then he would break whatever spell had been cast over him. It was as if, whenever he was in her company, he felt lighter, less weighed down by his past, and that was something to cherish.

So instead he asked her the question that was on everybody's lips, 'Is the fire heading this way?' Sweat dripped off the end of his nose as he rested the axe head on the ground and leaned on the handle.

'Which one?' she asked him wryly. 'I've heard there are several.'

'So you're leaving?'

She sighed and put her hands on her hips. 'People keep asking me that and I keep saying the same thing. I'm not going anywhere. The Crossing is all I have and I plan to keep it, and the people in it, safe.'

It was on the tip of his tongue to ask her how

she meant to do that, but he could see she was ready to keep arguing with him. So he picked up his axe again and got back to work. When he was done he went to find her in the kitchen and she handed him a glass of water.

'Come over to the bar tonight,' she told him. 'The boys from the mill will be here. One of them has a birthday and they want to celebrate.'

'Thank you, I will.'

He was tempted to prolong the conversation, so that he could ask if she'd mind him taking her photograph, but she seemed busy. Tonight, he told himself. He'd ask her tonight.

Now here he was, seated in the corner with his camera in its case, while the mill workers sang 'Happy Birthday' with plenty of loud enthusiasm. He was itching to record some of these moments; he had yet to ask Georgie's permission and he didn't want to put her back up. He was aware that Georgie had secrets, he knew it instinctively because he was the same, and he knew that people with secrets didn't give their trust easily.

Tiddler had crept into the corner beside him. He was sleepy, his face freshly washed, and even his long hair had been given a good combing.

'How's it going, Tiddler?' a booming voice demanded.

The man who strode over to them had a cigarette dangling out of the corner of his mouth and a beer in his hand. He was eyeing Neville curiously even as he greeted the boy.

'Good,' Tiddler mumbled shyly.

'How's it going with your arithmetic? That

Georgie cracks the whip, doesn't she?' He chuckled at his own joke while the boy dutifully smiled. Abruptly, he stuck his hand out towards Neville. 'Phillip Appleby, mill foreman.'

Neville rose to his feet and took the proffered hand. He was taller than Phillip, but the other man was broader across the shoulders, and his arms were hard with muscle beneath the rolled-up sleeves of his shirt.

'Neville Darling,' he said, feeling the squeeze of Phillip's fingers.

A gleam came into Appleby's brown eyes. 'You're Pom!' he said and laughed out loud, turning to share the news with the others. 'Hey, it's Pom! You're famous, mate. Everybody knows about Pom Darling and his camera.'

Everyone? Neville looked over Appleby's head and encountered Georgie's amused stare. 'A photographer, hey, *Pom*?' she said with a knowing smile. So much for waiting for the right moment, he thought wryly, she was already on to him.

'What are you doing here in the Crossing?' Appleby demanded, sitting down at the table and plonking his glass clumsily onto the pitted surface. Some of the beer slipped over the side and pooled in a dip. Tiddler reached out a finger, encountered Neville's gaze and withdrew it.

'I thought it might be a good place to take some photographs,' Neville explained, and then thought how feeble he sounded.

Appleby didn't seem to mind. 'Nowhere like the Crossing,' he offered with pride. 'That right, Georgie?'

'Too right, Phil,' Georgie called back.

'Come on up to the camp before you set off again,' Appleby invited him, eager as a boy showing off his prize marbles. 'We wouldn't mind our portraits being taken, would we, boys?'

There was a rowdy consensus.

'What do you think of this heat, eh?' Appleby said, not waiting for an answer. 'Heard on the bush telegraph there was a fire over Toolangi way. Went through so fast they only just got out by the skin of their teeth. The machinery at the mill melted together.'

'How far away is Toolangi?' Neville asked.

Appleby eyed him with amusement. 'Afraid you'll get your camera singed, Pom? It's about ninety miles by road, and the road isn't too good. Whereabouts in the mountains have you been so far?'

Neville started to tell him but the other man interrupted every few words to say something of his own, and in the end it seemed better just to let him talk. Then Georgie announced the beer had nearly run out, and who knew when they'd be getting more in, and Appleby hurried over to the bar with the others for a last drink. Neville and Tiddler exchanged a mutual glance of relief. Neither of them, it seemed, was inclined to socialise.

'Are you good at arithmetic?' Neville asked the boy.

Tiddler nodded and smiled at him. He had a good smile, so broad it took over his whole face, and you could see he meant it. It wasn't just for show. Neville had seen children on his travels and some of them bore all the hallmarks of having miserable lives. You could always tell. Not Tiddler though. Whether or not Georgie was his mother, she treated him like a much-loved son.

'Hmm. What's twenty-six plus forty-seven?' Neville asked.

He didn't even hesitate. 'Seventy-three.'

Neville had just plucked the numbers out of the air and he had to search a moment for the answer. 'Right,' he said appreciatively.

The game went on for a while. Then Tiddler started testing Neville. It was late when the men began to leave, heading back up to their camp in the bush. Phil called out, reminding him about visiting the camp, and shortly afterwards the hostelry was empty. Georgie set about clearing up and Tiddler looked like he was half asleep in his corner.

Finally, Georgie came and rested her hand on the boy's head. 'Bedtime,' she said, and he didn't argue.

'Goodnight,' Neville called after him.

''Night.'

Neville stood up, stretching, and moved to the door, pausing just outside. It was still very hot, and the air was pungent with the smell of burning from the fires. Down here in the valley there wasn't even a puff of breeze.

Across in the paddock he could see Aesop silhouetted against the smoky sky and, above him on the skyline, that strange red glow from the ranges, where the numerous fires marked time. If this calmer weather kept up the fire brigades might be able to beat the fires back from the towns and smaller settlements that dotted this country. And if they could turn them away, then the flames could burn themselves out in the rugged places, where no one lived.

'So when were you going to ask me?' Georgie was standing behind him, one hand on her hip. 'I know you want my photograph. I can see a look in your eyes, like you're already working out how to get me to pose.'

For a moment he thought she was angry with him, and then he realised she was teasing. Maybe even flirting again. Uncertainly he shifted his stance. He'd resisted getting involved with women since he'd walked away from his wife and daughter. He knew his limitations and Mary had shown him he wasn't much good at relationships. It seemed wiser, and a lot less trouble, just to remain on his own. And yet with Georgie Mackenzie he felt different, as if he was on the threshold of something very unexpected. No, that wasn't quite right, Neville decided, it was exhilaration he was feeling. He was standing on a precipice, and the next step forward might send him soaring up into the air on an eagle's wings … or tumbling down into nothingness. And yet, imprudent as it might seem, he was still inclined to take that step.

'Sorry if you thought I was being dishonest,' he said, hearing his voice get stiffer and more proper, as it always did when he was nervous or hesitant. His public school education had given him the right accent—his father had wanted him to practise law, and eventually take over the family firm. When he came home from the war he'd tried, but it was soon evident he wasn't suited for that anymore. In truth, he wasn't much good for anything.

Neville cleared his throat and tried again. 'I was going to ask you, but then Appleby and his men came in, and … I didn't want to do it in front of them. I didn't want you to feel you were being pressured. I thought it could wait.'

She was looking at him, and with the lamplight at her back he could only see her silhouette. He couldn't read her expression, and he wanted to.

'It's been a long time since anyone asked me for my photograph,' she said softly, and there was a wistful note in her voice. 'Not for years.'

Not since one day on St Kilda pier with the wind blowing her hair? This was the opportunity he'd been waiting for, the perfect moment. All he had to do was reach into his pocket for Brown's photograph.

'Neville?'

She was close, her eyes on his. There wasn't much difference in their height and if he'd shifted forward, just a little, he could rest his lips on hers. The thought startled him and he would have stepped back, except she reached out to lightly grasp his arm.

'Will you have supper with me?'

'Supper?' he asked, bemused.

She looked away, as if the intensity between them disturbed her as much as it did him. 'In case the fire does come.'

Neville realised then that she wasn't as certain of the Crossing surviving as she pretended. Was it all an act, the way she dressed, the way she exuded confidence? And if it was, then he was flattered she trusted him enough to give him a glimpse of the real Georgie.

'We haven't had any supplies for weeks,' she was explaining, and then she smiled. 'I do have a tin of peaches and some milk from Marie's goat. Not necessarily to put together, but I'm game if you are.'

Neville smiled. 'Sounds like a feast, Georgina.'

'I like that,' she said in her husky voice. 'You calling me Georgina. No one has called me that for ever so long, Neville.'

'And I like you calling me Neville. It seems I'm Pom to most people.'

'It's meant as a term of affection. Pom, I mean. You know that, don't you?'

Georgie was closer, although he didn't remember moving towards her, and then his arms were around her, and he didn't remember that either. Her lips were soft and warm, and when he tightened his hold she made a little sound that made him think she liked this.

'Georgina,' he whispered, and rubbed his cheek against hers, glad he'd taken the time earlier to shave off his whiskers.

She turned her face again, her mouth searching for his, and he felt that tightening low in his belly, that physical need.

'Georgie ...' Tiddler's voice drifted down from his bedroom upstairs, rising to a crescendo.

'Georgie!'

She pulled away with obvious reluctance. 'Bad dreams,' she murmured and gave a tight smile, as if she was suddenly self-conscious or embarrassed.

At once Neville felt the doubts slithering out of his well, all of the memories and fears and disappointments, daring him to take this chance when he knew he must fail. He heard himself saying, his voice very formal, 'Then you must go to him, and I must go to my bed.'

Was that disappointment, swiftly hidden? 'Of course,' she said. 'Goodnight, Neville.'

'Goodnight.' She'd already gone by the time he got the word out, and he heard soft voices on the upper floor. A door closed.

He'd had his chance to soar, it seemed, and instead he'd fallen.

CHAPTER 16

SKYE

Monday 9 June 1997

SKYE REACHED INTO her pocket and took out the copy of Neville Darling's photograph of the woman with the long dark hair from Mackenzie Crossing. She wasn't sure why she'd brought it. For luck, maybe, or because of some wild hope that by holding it up she could locate the spot where Neville had stood and taken it. Maybe even the exact place and moment he went missing.

Which was plainly ridiculous.

A photocopy wasn't as good as an original— the details weren't as sharp—but she didn't need it to be precise to see that the building behind the woman was a one-off. The house was quite grand; however, the verandah roof was made of timber shingles, and it was sagging in the middle, perhaps hinting at happier days. Like a *Gone with the Wind*–type lady past her best—the house that was, not the woman.

The door to the house stood open behind the woman, but it was impossible to see inside. And did the house even belong to the woman or was she just passing by? It was a pity there wasn't more. Skye would have liked to see what was on either side of the building, whether there were more houses or a street, or other people. It seemed unlikely it was just sitting there alone, although she supposed anything was possible.

So what function did this house serve in an old mining town in decline? A hotel? An inn? A bawdy house? Or was it just somewhere the small population could gather and chat and share a glass of red?

As she examined the grainy image, Skye noticed there was something edging into the far right-hand perimeter of the shot. She hadn't noticed it before because the woman had taken all of her attention, but now that she was seeking answers about the location it was obvious.

She held the paper up to the light, frowning in concentration. Whatever it was seemed blurred, as if the click of the camera had caught it in motion. An ear, could it be an ear? And part of a mane and an eye … She smiled. It was a horse. Maybe it had moved into the frame the moment the photograph was taken. Maybe Neville had been concentrating on the woman, too, and, uncharacteristically, hadn't noticed.

She was so deep in her own thoughts that when the driver's-side door suddenly opened she jumped and let out a gasp.

Finn was back.

As he climbed in, she turned to look through the passenger-side window and saw Dylan standing at the gate. He had one hand resting on his dog's head and he was watching her, and as soon as he saw her looking he gave a mocking little wave.

She nodded. That was as far as she was prepared to acknowledge him. No smile; he didn't deserve one. Then Finn was easing them out of the tight space, turning around, and heading back onto the main track.

He was obviously preoccupied—maybe the talk with Dylan hadn't eased his mind. As if aware of her scrutiny, he gave her a glance, and then made an obvious attempt to shift his thoughts away from whatever was bothering him.

'Okay,' he said, 'that's done. I'm all yours.'

Skye cleared her throat. He'd never been all hers. She knew that now, although at the time she'd believed he was. Time and distance had shown her that it was Dylan who had pulled the strings, and if his brother said 'jump' then Finn asked how high.

Depressingly, it seemed nothing had changed.

'Is it far?' she asked. 'Mackenzie Crossing, I mean.'

'Twelve k's from here, but the going gets rougher further on, and the road gets worse, especially after rain. It could be tricky getting in.'

Although the sleet had stopped, the sky looked as if it was brooding and about to unload its angst upon them. Fabulous weather for some moody photos, Skye thought, her heart giving a skip of anticipation. Some people prayed for blue skies, but she preferred wild, and the wilder the weather the better she liked it.

The vehicle tipped to one side, tyres spinning. Finn expertly turned the wheel and righted it before she had a chance to be frightened. He must be used to driving in these conditions and on these roads, so at least that was something. He gave her a feeling of confidence, and that wasn't new either, only these days she was older and wiser, and she wasn't sure she could trust it.

The CB radio sent out a burst of static and Taylor's voice filled the cabin. 'Finn? You there?'

Reluctantly, Finn looked at his handset, but there was never any way he wasn't going to pick up. 'Yeah. What is it?'

Taylor seemed fired up, and, Skye suspected, less than cautious about what he was saying.

'It isn't true, is it? I can't believe it.'

In contrast Finn was carefully calm. 'The bit about me being suspended is true, Taylor. The rest is rubbish. But I have no choice but to go along with it. Alison said she'd be back today, and Doug is being released from secondment. You'll just have to do your best.'

'I know. It's just … This is so *wrong*, Finn. You don't deserve this. And for something that happened five years ago. Don't they realise—'

'Evidently not,' Finn said, cutting him off. 'It'll be fine, Taylor. You know what it's like in this job. There's red tape and there's dickheads, but it's still worth doing.'

'I suppose.'

'I know I can rely on you.'

Taylor mumbled something about a group of tourists at the desk wanting a map and a road-conditions report for Mt Elysian, and then he was gone.

'He's a good kid,' Finn said.

'He thinks a lot of you.'

'I've taken the time to listen to him, that's all. There are so many ways a boy can go wrong. Taylor's family are a bit dysfunctional. His mother walked out on him when he was about twelve, and then his father went off the rails. He brought up himself and his sisters, and I can identify with that. I remembered the help given to me when I needed it, so I've spent some time with him, keeping him on the straight and narrow.'

'Well it seems to have worked.'

Skye wondered what had happened to Finn and Dylan's mother. She knew after the accident they'd been removed from her custody, and Finn had told her he'd gone back to his father. Once Skye and her parents had moved houses, she'd never tried to find out about Melissa Faraday, although for a time there, whenever she'd seen a homeless woman on the street or someone on a tram obviously affected by drugs, she'd remembered her. Melissa, with her gaunt face and too-thin arms and legs, as she'd weaved her way unsteadily through life. And Darryl, the part-time handyman, always so angry. Skye hadn't seen him that often, but her memories of him were sharp and clear. He'd either been yelling and waving his arms, or else flaked out and dead to the world on whatever illegal substance he'd just acquired.

She considered asking Finn whether Melissa was still around. It seemed the right thing to do. To her relief, he changed the subject before she could fashion the question. Her relief changed to anxiety when she realised he'd decided to delve into *her* life.

'You haven't told me anything about yourself, apart from your friend Russell,' he said. 'You call yourself Ms Stewart. Is that because you're single or is it your professional name?'

'I'm divorced, but we still work together. Fraser's Funky Fotos. Don't suppose you've heard of it?'

He gave an apologetic shake of his head. No, Skye thought, of course he wouldn't have. Fraser's life and work were about as far from a man like Finn as it was possible to be.

'Well, I'm a photographer. I do christenings and weddings and everything in between. It's fun and I love it, but, well, I'd like to do more than take pictures of other people's happy moments. Lately I've been thinking that an exhibition of Neville's work would be nice.'

'Okay. What about you?'

She shook her head. 'How do you mean?'

'Well, you could turn it into a joint effort, your work and Neville's. A family reunion sort of thing. A journey of discovery.'

Skye took a moment to mull over the suggestion. 'You mean like, uh, Natalie Cole when she made that album with her father, Nat, despite him being dead?' She felt a spark of interest begin to flicker inside her, but it was too soon and she shied away from it. 'I don't know. Anyway, it's in the early stages,' she waved a hand to gloss over the detail, 'I have to work it out.'

'Sounds interesting,' he seemed to mean it. He gave her a curious glance. 'When did you decide on photography? You used to say you wanted to be a teacher.'

'Did I? God, I'd have been a dreadful teacher. Probably teach the kids all the wrong things. My classes would be chaotic.' She laughed.

He pulled a face, as if he didn't agree.

'No kids of my own,' she added, to save him asking. 'Fraser and I decided to hold off on a family. He was still growing up.' She smiled to show she didn't have any ill feelings towards her ex-husband.

'You make it all sound very mature.' He smiled back at her. 'When I saw you the other night up at Lockington I couldn't help noticing how fashionable you looked. Like one of the kids we used to pretend to despise at school, although we were probably just jealous that they were cooler than us.'

So he thought she was *cool*? Skye laughed softly.

'It's nice to get dressed up,' she explained, 'and Fraser likes us to be trendy. It's part of his signature for the business.'

He nodded, but she could see his thoughts were again elsewhere. Probably with Dylan, and his suspension from the job he loved.

'What about you?' she asked, telling herself she was trying to distract him, but the truth was she wanted to know his story. She was going to end up asking him at some stage so why not now?

He hesitated. 'Laurie, my wife, she wanted some space. That's what she told me when she left nearly two years ago. She needed space. So she went to Perth, and that's a whole lot of space. When she didn't come back I knew it was over. If it wasn't for my daughter, Ashley, I wouldn't be in contact with her now, but when you have a kid you have to make the effort.'

And Finn, Skye thought, would make the effort.

'It was Fraser who asked me for a divorce.'

He gave her one of his long looks. 'He asked *you*?' he repeated, as if he was finding it difficult to come to terms with that.

Which was flattering. No doubt about it, Finn was good for her ego.

'I know, hard to believe,' she agreed wryly. 'Honestly? We'd been over for a while, but you know how it is, you just travel along, stuck in the same old rut, because to make the change seems so tough. He'd been playing up. I knew he was like that when I married him, but … You don't realise how much it hurts. It must be in my nature to keep trying to fix a thing, no matter how badly it's broken, or maybe I'm just stubborn. But when Fraser told me he wanted a divorce, I was so relieved to know it was really over. Not that things have changed all that much. I'm still working for him and we still spend a part of nearly every day in each other's company. I think we get on better now than we ever did when we were husband and wife.'

She'd probably said more than she meant to—she just hoped she hadn't been gabbling—but she found him easy to talk to. Finn had always been a good listener.

'Sounds good. Great,' he upped it, with a glance at her.

The LandCruiser dropped into a culvert, and for a moment he concentrated on keeping them on an even keel, easing their way through some churned-up ground. They were getting higher, travelling along a mountain he'd said was Mt Elysian, and she didn't want to look over the side if she could help it. She needed distractions and his voice was a welcome one.

'Laurie hated it here. She'd always been a city girl and she didn't want to leave Melbourne. But I'd had enough of the Drug Squad. It wasn't what I'd had in mind when I joined up, and once the thrill had worn off I could pretty much see that. There were things going on and I didn't want to be a part of them.'

'Things?'

He looked at her, his face grave. 'You don't want to know the details, Skye. Let's just say I didn't want to join in and I knew I couldn't stop any of it, so I got out, and they were happy to help me on my way. There's only so much crap you can bathe in before it begins to affect your own life.'

'You mean corruption?' Skye shook her head. She didn't listen to much news, but she thought she would have remembered if there'd been talk of police corruption. 'Is that what this suspension is all about? Those two detectives this morning …?'

She was horrified and couldn't hide it. Whatever she thought of Finn, however many years had passed between them, she did not believe he was capable of doing anything criminal. Despite his mother and Darryl and what they'd got up to, it just wasn't in him. Which was strange, really. Considering how short their time together had been, she shouldn't have such a solid image of who and what he was.

He read the expression on her face and reassured her. 'Not me, I'm squeaky clean. That's the trouble.'

'Oh.'

There was an awkward moment, but he obviously wanted to move on, so Skye didn't ask any more questions, although by now her brain was reeling.

'Anyway, about Laurie. We'd only been here a couple of weeks when she went home to Melbourne for a visit. Over the next three years she spent more time there than here. She thought I'd get sick of Elysian and when I didn't she tried to get me to transfer back. Even though Ashley loved it, or I thought she did. So I said no. I wouldn't. I couldn't. I knew if I did then I'd probably end up … well, I would've taken leave and once you do that, if they think you can no longer hack it, or you're a bit of a liability, then they don't want you back. That's the cold, hard, uncomfortable truth.'

'But that's so unfair.'

He shrugged it off. 'Being up here away from

everything suits me. I feel more centred. And I'm probably a bit of a control freak, so I can run my little empire exactly as I want to.'

She thought about that. Did being in control include Dylan? She opened her mouth to ask him and then changed her mind. They'd moved on from that subject and she was quite happy not to revisit it.

'How old is your daughter?'

His answering smile told her he was a fond dad. 'She's seven. I worry ...' he hesitated and then took a breath. 'I worry she'll forget me. You know,' he turned to her, 'I don't usually talk about this stuff. You were always a bit of a witch, Skye.'

'I don't know about a witch,' she murmured, asking herself what he meant. 'I don't have second sight.'

'No. If you did ...' He shrugged.

And what did *that* mean? Skye sighed. Did he think if she'd known what Dylan was going to do that night nineteen years ago, she could have stopped it? Did he think they might have still been together?

It seemed a bit of a jump. They'd been kids, and who knew what turn their lives might have taken, even if they hadn't been broken apart? They could have naturally drifted away, and Skye's parents had worried about her friendship with Finn. Probably worried more about Dylan. At some point they would have stepped in and insisted she not see him. Or would that have had the opposite effect and made her want to see him all the more? The Romeo-and-Juliet effect was still very powerful when it came to the teenage view of the world.

She didn't have any photos of that time, but she tried to imagine the pair of them as they were then. Finn, tall, a bit gangly like Taylor, with his dark hair and serious eyes. He'd just started to shave, she remembered, and was self-conscious about it. She'd told him it was nice, rubbing her cheek gently against his. He'd said he loved her hair. The wild red locks made her look like a witch, he'd said …

Ah. That's what he'd meant just now. She'd forgotten. And fancy him remembering after all this time. But perhaps Finn had more time to think up here, alone in the wilderness. In his own little kingdom.

The conversation had fallen away, and apart from the windscreen wipers going like fury there was silence. It was sleeting again, and the combination of rain and ice struck the vehicle with relentless fury. Finn began to slow, although he wasn't going very fast anyway, and she knew they were close to their destination. The vehicle was heading downhill now, and when the wheels slipped, taking them closer than Skye would have liked to a line of trees, not to mention the clear air beyond, he stopped.

'I don't think we can get down the last bit,' Finn said. 'And even if we did, I may not be able to get us up again. We'll have to walk. The trail is a bit steep, but once we're down the weather should be better. More sheltered in the valley,' he explained, seeing her clueless expression.

'So this is …?' She was peering through the windscreen, trying to see beyond the weather.

'Yes, this is it. We're here. Mackenzie Crossing.'

There was no use in hoping the weather would clear. Although it had eased up slightly, the sleet turning back into rain, and then into drizzle, it wasn't going to stop. And according to Finn, if they waited, it could well get worse.

He'd reached over to the back seat and found a yellow plastic wet-weather coat, which he handed to Skye. It had 'Police' stamped on the back.

'Mine's waterproof,' he said, seeing her hesitation, 'but I don't think yours is.' As he spoke he zipped up his jacket and turned up the collar. He was already wearing his gloves and had tucked a dark-blue beanie in his pocket—evidently he didn't seem to think it was cold enough to put it on yet.

Skye slipped her arms into the yellow coat. It was far too big but, under his watchful eye, she rolled up the cuffs to a manageable level and then fastened up the snaps at the front. When she was done he reached around to help her free the hood, and she eased it over her blue hat. Then there were strings to tighten and hold it in place, and he watched her tie them as if she was participating in some sort of test.

This close to him Skye could smell the fresh scent of his aftershave. To distract herself from the odd sensation in the pit of her stomach, she took

note of the stubborn shape of his chin, and the
determined set of his mouth. No, she thought,
Finn could never have stayed in a place where
people were doing the wrong thing, and nor
could he have turned a blind eye. Did Laurie
really imagine he would?

Finished, she tucked a strand of auburn hair out
of the way, and he nodded as if she'd passed mus-
ter. 'Ready?'

Skye took a breath. 'Ready.'

They both opened their doors. Lightning made
a dash for freedom but Finn ordered her back.
'Not you,' he said, with a pat on her head, 'you
stay here and wait. Your paws will freeze and I
haven't got any boots that fit you.'

Reluctantly the greyhound returned to her
blanket, mournful doggy eyes watching them
through the window.

Out here in the sharp, damp air, Skye was better
able to see their surroundings. Finn had parked
the four-wheel drive at the top of a slippery, steep
track that led down into a valley. There were
holes and fallen branches, and it looked as if there
hadn't been any maintenance work on it for a
while. In the summer it might just be negotiable
by an intrepid four-wheel drive, but not today.

The hills glowered all around them, making the
valley seem very secluded and secret. Almost as if
it had been purposely hidden from the outside
world. Mackenzie Crossing was a long way off
the popular tourist trail and even hikers might
think twice about paying a visit. Skye guessed it
was more likely to be somewhere you stumbled

across by accident rather than design.

Either side of the track, saplings and more mature trees stood tall, the understorey a combination of rough-leafed ferns and low scrub. Everything was dripping water, including her. Skye squinted doubtfully at the way down. It looked like a daunting prospect to a girl more used to pounding the footpaths of the Big Smoke. Her boots were going to be ruined, but Skye decided that didn't matter, not when she may never get this opportunity again. She wasn't about to let a pair of suede boots stop her, even if she had bought them on sale at one of the high-end shops.

Reaching back into the cabin, she grabbed her camera case and slung it around her neck. The Pentax was safe inside, although now a trickle of cold, wet water had found its way up her sleeve. She shook her arm with a grimace.

'All right?' Finn looked amused. He was standing waiting, gloved hands jammed in his jacket pockets, his hair already damp and curling slightly. He looked completely comfortable and at ease with the weather and the landscape. Skye didn't know if she envied him or not.

'Lead on,' she said in a Girl Guide sort of voice.

He was smiling as he turned away, and she thought that he was enjoying himself. Or was he just enjoying seeing her so completely out of her comfort zone?

The track was as mucky and slippery as she'd feared. Finn found them a couple of stout sticks, and using his to brace himself, set off, calling to her to put her feet where he did. But after only a few steps, Skye was clinging to a nearest branch, the stout stick more a hindrance than a help. She found it easier to stagger from tree to tree, leaning against the trunks, or grabbing onto the undergrowth—some of which turned out to be prickly—while she caught her breath, before lurching forward again. When she slipped and nearly lost her footing completely, only just saving herself by hugging a sapling, Finn came back for her.

His breath was white in the cold, damp air. He examined her from head to toe with a frown. 'I think it'll be easier if you hang on to me, all right?'

It *was* easier. Any desire she might have felt to assert her independence had already died, and she was grateful for his strength and experience. Trying not to catapult into him, or to grip his arm too fiercely, Skye thought she just might reach Mackenzie Crossing safely. Without sliding into the place on her back, like some bizarre contestant in a luge competition.

That wouldn't be great for her self-esteem, let alone impressing Finn with her mountaineering skills. Not that she was trying to impress him, and anyway, who knew what impressed Finn these days. She suspected it was probably someone tough and hardy and beautiful, like the woman in Neville's photo.

Skye was just getting the hang of it, stopping, balancing and moving forward in a smooth rhythm, using the strength of her legs to keep herself from falling, when they reached the bottom.

A jungle of vegetation blocked their way, and as Finn began to push through it, she could hear the rush of water. A shallow, rocky creek ran the length of the valley, and although at the moment it was only knee-high, Skye was sure it could get deeper and more ferocious at certain times of the year.

'Silverfish Creek,' Finn told her. 'This is what brought in the miners, and then the town. First they were looking for alluvial gold, panning the creek, and later they went underground. You need to be careful, by the way, there are still plenty of mine shafts. They covered them up with saplings and then the shrub grew over, and now they're not immediately obvious. Perfect traps for the unwary. You wouldn't know they were there until you fell in, and some of them go pretty deep.'

Skye tried to watch where she was putting her feet, but she kept getting distracted by the scenery. As far as she could tell this valley was too narrow for a town, unless it was built halfway up the hillsides, though Finn explained that further ahead it widened out into more of a U-shape, and that was where Mackenzie Crossing had been situated.

'It was named for the crossing over the creek,' he said. 'The early track traversed Silverfish Creek at Mackenzie Crossing, and then meandered back up into the hills on the other side. You can walk to Marysville and sometimes hikers go that way, although I doubt many of them even know there used to be a town here.'

It was certainly wild country. They followed the creek, fighting their way through tree ferns and the tangled undergrowth beneath tall, straight trees; Finn pointed out a few of the old mine shafts and the footings of what had once been a battery.

'If you look at some of the old photos the hills are bare. That's because all of the trees were cut down to fire up the battery, as well as prop up the mines. Not much further,' he added, giving her an assessing glance as she stumbled over an obstacle hidden beneath some bracken.

Skye gave him a brave smile, hoping that wasn't doubt she saw in his eyes. She could be tough, she told herself. It was just a shame that after all this effort there wasn't much to see. Skye searched for signs of the town, trying not to feel disappointed. There were areas where the bush seemed to have been slashed back at some stage, and a patch of ground that was uneven and scattered with stone, perhaps remnants of habitation. Skye stepped up onto a fallen log to get a better view, but there was nothing to see.

Mackenzie Crossing was gone.

An old gum tree stood tall and alone, rising above the smaller saplings, and there was something that might have been a water trough, rusted out and returning to the earth. A sodden-looking bird flapped up into the leaden sky.

Skye reached for her camera.

'Archie Manning used to come up here,' Finn was saying, his hands back in his pockets, his face flushed from the cold and the exercise. 'He'd keep this small area clear of scrub. You can see it, here, although it's growing back now. People used to laugh and ask him why he bothered. He said it was respect.'

'Respect?' Skye looked where he pointed, seeing the scattered stones she'd noticed a moment ago.

'That's what he said. Respect for what had once been and for the people who had once lived here. He used to visit quite a few of the old ghost towns, just checking on things, reporting any vandalism. He's not well enough to come up here now, and after he goes no one will. It'll all return to nature.'

'What about his daughter?'

'Nancy? She's not the sort to live in the past.'

'I need to speak to him.' It was a reminder to herself rather than a comment to Finn, so he didn't reply.

Skye walked along the fallen log and stopped to look through the viewfinder at the big old gum tree. Set in the centre of the frame it made a good composition, but off to the side with the hills behind was even better. She took a couple of photos before turning to face the other way, the soles of her boots sliding precariously on the wet surface.

The area Finn had pointed out intrigued her, and she jumped down to inspect it more closely. It was raised above the height of its surroundings, and now she could see that the earth had been piled up and flattened down, as if to create a platform. If she wasn't mistaken, it was about the right size for a house. She began to step it out, just to see, but when she reached the far side, there among the clinging undergrowth, she came upon a heap of tumbled, blackened bricks.

'Are they from a chimney?' she asked, hearing the excitement in her voice. She couldn't help remembering the substantial building in Neville's photograph.

Finn had followed her, and now he looked about, as if getting his bearings. 'I think this was where the old pub was,' he said. 'The creek can rise quickly in the spring, when the snow's melting, so they had raised it up a bit.'

Skye bent to pick up one of the bricks, examining the charring. 'Is this normal, or could it be from the Black Friday fire?'

'The Black Friday fire, I'd think. There weren't many buildings left by then, and all of them were destroyed that day.'

Skye turned the crumbling brick over in her hand. It was a poignant reminder of what had happened here nearly sixty years ago. But more than that, Neville had been here. He'd known this place. Here he'd stood and looked through his lens at a woman with dark hair, and made her live forever.

'Who owned the pub? Do you know?'

'The Mackenzies owned it. They called it a hostelry, but it was a posh name for a pub. It's quite a story, if you want to hear it?'

She gave him a distracted smile. 'Please.'

'After gold mining started to decline in the

early nineteen hundreds, things went downhill. I know it's difficult to believe now, and the Crossing was always an isolated spot even in the good times, but once there was a thriving community here. Hotels, a church, a school, a general store, probably a doctor and a dentist. Anything you could want or need was brought in by packhorse.'

He waited as Skye turned slowly in a circle, struggling to imagine the town in its heyday.

'After the miners left the town slowly began to die. But Big Jim Mackenzie was a determined character, and he fought to keep it alive. He persuaded some of his friends to help finance a couple of sawmills, and that brought timber-getters into the area. He tried to restart the main mine, the Union Jack, but he failed there. He couldn't find anyone willing to invest and he needed money to bring in modern machinery. You can see what a job it would've been for the packhorses. After that the town limped on with just a few of the locals left, as well as a few newcomers who enjoyed the isolation. Big Jim used to entertain locals and travellers in his house, which he'd turned into what he called "The Hostelry", with drinks and food, and a bed for the night. And then Jim died.'

His voice was spinning a spell around her. Skye lifted her camera every now and again, taking memories of the place, while she listened to Finn.

'In the years after Big Jim died, there was only one sawmill still working, but it kept the Crossing alive. Up until nineteen thirty-nine. If the fire hadn't come through then it would've vanished anyway. There are a lot of places like the Crossing, nothing more than ghost towns now. Places for hikers and four-wheel-drive clubs to camp for the night, or for people who are running away from something to hide out in.'

Like Dylan, Skye thought, but she didn't say it aloud. And then she added, *and Neville*. Because hadn't he been running and hiding, too?

'So the, uh, hostelry was still operating in January nineteen thirty-nine?'

He nodded. 'The fire razed the place to the ground. Archie has a photograph in that museum of his. Some reporter took it in the aftermath. There's one of Elysian, as well.'

'Oh.' She started to ask about that and then changed her mind. Best not to get distracted. Archie would be her next project and somehow she would have to persuade his family to let her talk to him.

'What about the inhabitants?' Skye asked. 'I know some of them died—Archie has a list—but there must've been some who survived?'

'There were. A few had the good sense to evacuate to Elysian a couple of days beforehand, but by the time the others knew the fire was going to impact them it was already too late. The wind had picked up and several small fires had joined together to form one massive firestorm. It happened so fast. And in a situation like that, if you run you can get caught in its path, so it's best to try to take shelter. They had no option but to stay.'

'And hope for the best,' Skye murmured. 'God, what a choice to have to make.'

'Have you ever been in a bushfire?'

She shook her head.

'It's a pretty frightening thing. People panic. Run the wrong way, do stupid things.'

As always, Skye tried to imagine how Neville had felt. Traumatised by his experiences in the First World War, and then to face the fury of Black Friday. She couldn't begin to imagine it— she wasn't sure she wanted to.

Better to remain practical.

'So,' Skye said, more of a statement than a question, 'nobody knows whether or not Neville was here on that day. Except I think Archie must know something, although then again it might turn out to be nothing. Is there anyone else I should talk to?'

'There's Mrs Appleby.'

'Who's Mrs Appleby?'

'She's Alison's mother. Alison recently moved her into nursing home in Westcott, closer to her. I'd forgotten she was originally from the Crossing, although it was a long time ago. She's lived in Marysville for years. Her family were one of those already evacuated, so she wasn't here on that day, but she would've heard about it later on. Might be worth a try.'

Skye found herself looking through her viewfinder at Finn as he spoke. He stood where the hostelry had once been situated, the bush rearing up behind him, reminding her it was only a matter of time before all of this area returned to nature. Mackenzie Crossing was wild and lonely, not at all what she'd been expecting, but there was also a beauty about it. A desolate beauty that was beginning to creep into her heart despite herself.

The need for solitude was already a part of her character, so perhaps it wasn't a big stretch to imagine herself in Neville's shoes, when he came here in 1939.

'I hope I can talk to Mrs Appleby before I go home,' she said, stepping back so that she could get the old gum tree into the frame as well. 'Perhaps she'll even let me take a photo of her.'

Perfect. She pressed the shutter.

'That would be something at least,' he said quietly. 'I mean you haven't had much luck so far, have you?'

'No, I suppose not, but I live in hope.' She lowered the Pentax and looked at him properly. 'You've mentioned Archie and Nancy, and I've met Saskia, but what about her father? And her grandmother, if it comes to that. Archie's wife.'

Her fingers felt numb as she fumbled with the camera case hanging around her neck, taking out a soft cloth and using it to dry the camera lens. Now that they'd stopped moving, the chill was creeping into her bones. She had an urge to chatter her teeth. At least the waterproof jacket kept out some of the wind and the rain was reduced to a sprinkle.

It was far from ideal, but then again some of her best photographs had been taken in weather that was not 'ideal'. That was what made hers different—a cut above the common herd—and she was only just beginning to understand it. Like her grandfather she had a signature and one day, if she managed to get her act together, people might point to one of them and say, 'Oh, that's a Skye Stewart!'

Finn finally reached into his pocket and took out the beanie, pulling it over his hair as he answered her questions.

'I think I heard Archie's wife died when their daughter was fairly young. Someone must've told me that, probably Taylor, he knows the family well. Archie brought Nancy up on his own. They're very close, him and his daughter, and she's very protective. I think that's rubbed off on Saskia. As for Saskia's father …' He stopped. 'Do you have to do that, Skye? It's … disconcerting.'

She realised she had crouched down, looking up at him through the viewfinder, aiming for a head shot against the treetops and the clouds.

'Oh. Sorry.' She clicked the shutter and lowered the Pentax. 'It was a good one. I couldn't resist. I suppose it's a bit of a compulsion, to take it now in case I miss out on what could be the perfect photo.'

'I doubt I'm the perfect photo,' he said, although there was a glimmer in his eyes, as if he was amused. 'But thanks anyway.'

She smiled and then remembering herself turned away, lifting the camera again. 'You were talking about Saskia's father.'

'Yes, well, I think he's still around. Lives interstate. Nancy met him while she was working in Sydney and next thing she's home and it's all happy days, but shortly after Saskia was born he was sent on his way.'

'Okay.'

'What I think happened … well, I think Nancy gave him an ultimatum. Fit in with Archie and our lifestyle or …'

'Or on your bike.'

He nodded and looked away, back in the direction of the track. A gust of sleety rain came over them, and he narrowed his eyes and she knew he was checking out the approaching storm and calculating how long they had before he'd have to tell her it was time to go.

Man against the elements, she thought, pressing the shutter. Or man as part of the elements?

'So the Mackenzies owned this place,' she said, thinking aloud.

'Big Jim cast a long shadow. They say he's buried up in the cemetery on the hill. Most of the old Crossing people are buried there. It was closed in the nineteen seventies I think, though it was abandoned long before that. The place is overgrown, barely a headstone that isn't broken or crumbled away. Some of the heritage people came a few years ago and tried to make a list, but I think they only found about three legible names.'

'Was Big Jim one of them?'

'I don't think so.'

'Can we take a look?'

He was looking straight at her now and when he moved forward she stumbled back, almost falling, coming up short against the fallen log.

'You're doing it again,' he said.

'God, am I? Sorry, Finn. It's just habit. A camera

in my hand and I just … it's what I do.'

Remembering something, she reached under her plastic coat for her pocket, and the photocopy she'd pushed in there earlier. She'd taken some other copies of it, so the spots of rain weren't going to be disastrous, but she still sheltered it protectively, her back against the weather, as she came closer to Finn.

'I should've shown you this before,' she said, as she handed it to him.

He bent his head, gaze concentrated on the grainy image. 'Amazing,' he said softly. 'So this is the Mackenzie house? The hostelry. Pretty impressive, isn't it? And this is …?'

'That's the million-dollar question. Well, not really. The million-dollar question is what happened to Neville and was this really the very last photograph he ever took, and if it was, then how did it get developed and then sent in to the missing-persons division in Melbourne in nineteen fifty-seven.'

But he was only half listening. 'She's very compelling, don't you think? You have the sense that you want to know her better.'

'I feel that, too, and Neville obviously did. I think Russell had a bit of a crush on her.'

He chuckled and then looked up, eyes curious. 'Maybe Neville had a crush on her as well.'

Skye stared back at him. She wasn't sure how she felt about that. Neville had left a wife and daughter in his wake, and it didn't exactly fill her with joy to think he might have gone off happily ever after into the sunset. But, she reminded herself, Mary had found a wonderful husband in Louis, and Neville had suffered in the war—she had the hospital records to prove it—so perhaps he had deserved some happiness, before the end.

'I think Big Jim had a daughter,' Finn was saying. 'Or was she a niece? I haven't heard all that much about her. Big Jim was such a larger-than-life character that the stories about him seem to monopolise most of the conversations I've been privy to.' His smile was apologetic. 'It's not that I'm not interested, I just don't have a lot of time for the past.'

'Fair enough,' Skye said. 'And I'm grateful for your help, it means a lot.'

'My pleasure,' he replied, and blew warm air into his gloved hands.

He was being polite, Skye told herself, as she stamped her feet. The chill seemed to be working its way up from the soles of her soggy boots, try as she might to ignore it. But she wasn't going to leave until she'd documented every inch of what remained of Mackenzie Crossing. Determined to finish the job, she turned towards the bricks, taking photos from different angles, concentrating on getting it right. There would be plenty of shots that weren't good enough, there always were, but she hoped the good ones would be really good. She hoped they'd tell the story she wanted them to convey.

Finn was silent now, watching her.

'Would you mind?' she asked, nodding towards the spot where she was guessing the woman had been standing. 'I want to get one of you in the same position.'

He shrugged and went to stand where she wanted him, a bare hint of a smile. She took the photo, and then another one. And then she walked around to the side and snapped one there, with his face in profile against the sky and the encroaching bush.

'How about you?' he suggested. 'I'll take one of you. Do you trust me not to drop the camera?'

Skye hesitated. It wasn't so much that she was afraid he'd drop it, but rather that having him look at her through the lens was going to be a more intimate experience than she'd expected.

Only he'd taken her agreement for granted, and reached for the camera. Skye slipped it from around her neck and he leaned in close.

'So … this isn't your normal camera, is it?'

'No. It's digital, 4 megapixel. A Pentax K1000. I don't need a film and I don't need a dark room to process the negatives. There's a memory card inside that remembers what I've taken, and I can get that processed in a digital–processing machine. And look,' she turned it around so that he could see the screen and brought up the image of him she'd just taken.

'In the old days you had to snap away and hope one of your shots was good, but with digital I can look at them straightaway, and, if I don't like what I see, I can delete and try again.'

He frowned down at his image. 'That's … well, I don't know much about it. I use the old 35mm when I have to take crime-scene photos, which isn't often, usually the Melbourne boys come up for anything major. But, that's pretty good, isn't it? Against the weather like that. I look like I'm about to take flight.'

Skye laughed. 'That was the look I was aiming for.'

He nodded, and listened as she told him what to look through and what to press. It wasn't difficult and he seemed to have a handle on it, so she went back to the same spot and stood waiting.

'Take off your hood,' Finn said, frowning through the viewfinder. She reached up and untied the strings, and slid the hood back onto her shoulders. 'Ah, maybe your hat, too,' he suggested. 'Your red hair against all this would look pretty cool, I'm thinking.'

He had a point. And it would be a very different look from the woman in Neville's photo. She reached up and took off the hat, shaking her hair loose around her shoulders. The wind lifted it and she shivered as the breeze strengthened about her.

'God, it's freezing, Finn.'

'Nah, just another day in paradise,' he said.

She laughed, and he clicked. 'You did that on purpose,' she accused him, putting her hands on her hips.

'Yep,' he said, and took another. 'Good,' he declared, and brought the camera over to her. 'What do you think?'

Skye looked down and he was right, they were good. Somehow she'd relaxed enough with him for them to look natural and interesting. Even more interesting if she placed them beside Neville's photo of the woman, which she was beginning to think might be a good idea.

'Your hair looks great,' he said, his face bent close to hers as they examined the image.

'Yes. I could even heighten the colour a bit, make it redder than it is, and the background greyer. It would really stand out then.'

She was leaning against him, she realised. Resting her body along his as if it was the most natural thing in the world. The realisation was disturbing and she stepped away, pretending to take another photo of the place where the pub used to be. He said nothing, watching her, but she noticed he'd jammed his hands back in his pockets again.

She'd exhausted the cleared area and had begun pushing her way through the bracken, trying to find any hidden debris, when he finally said, 'We'd better go now. Weather's getting worse.'

As soon as he said it she realised how cold she was, and how the gusts of rain had turned into white flakes that could only be snow. Skye held out her hand in astonishment, forgetting herself in a childlike fascination. The snowflakes melted as soon as they touched her glove, but more were falling and soon Mackenzie Crossing would be covered in white.

What a fabulous thought. If she could stay a little longer then …

'Skye,' he was right behind her, and he took her arm firmly in his and turned her around and started walking.

'What, am I under arrest?' she said, trying to make a joke of it.

'Nope, but I can always oblige if that's what it

takes.'

'Ah come on, Finn, just a couple more.'

He looked down at her and shook his head, and he kept walking. 'You know this is what I was telling you yesterday. People that underestimate the weather, or over-estimate their own abilities. You'd be a perfect candidate for a missing person. I'd have to call out half the state to find you, and then more than likely you'd have hypothermia and frost bite, and I'd need a chopper to take you to hospital. Then there'd be reports to write and reporters to avoid, and you'd thank everyone and then turn around and say it was our fault you got lost in the first place.'

She was laughing by now, breathlessly because of the cold, but she couldn't help it. 'Is that what they do when you find them? How ungrateful. No, I wouldn't do that. I just wanted to wait a bit and capture the effect of the snow.'

'Then you'll have to come back another time, when we're more prepared. I might even have to get the skiddoo out of mothballs. I'm not set up for a blizzard today.'

'Tempting,' she said, smiling up at him. She was hanging on to him now, which was surprising because she didn't remember doing that.

'Look, I get how important this is to you,' he said, and suddenly he was serious, that frown drawing down his brows. 'I can tell you love what you're doing. You're really into it and that's a wonderful thing. Good to find a job you love.'

'But ...?' she added after a moment, matching his steps, although she was already out of breath.

The snow was falling thicker now, and she looked longingly behind her. 'What about the cemetery?' she asked, just then remembering what he had said about Big Jim being buried on the hill above the Crossing.

'No way we can do that now.'

'Oh.' She tried not to pout.

Finn heaved a sigh and looked back, too. And then he stopped. 'Go on, then,' he said. 'Take one more. But I mean it about the cemetery, it isn't doable right now.'

She held up the camera. 'Two,' she retorted, and heard him chuckle.

When they started off again, he returned to their previous unfinished conversation. 'There wasn't any "but",' he said. 'You're doing something that makes you feel good, and I think that's important. I wondered … well, I used to wonder what you were up to. I was thinking of you as a teacher with a room full of feral kids. Like we used to be. I never thought of you doing this, but now I've seen you with a camera I can't imagine you doing anything else.'

That was nice, somehow. Skye started to answer and then gave a violent shiver. He put his arm around her and dragged her in close.

'How come you're so warm,' she grumbled, pressing closer.

'I'm used to it,' he said gruffly.

'My toes are numb. And my nose.'

He gave her nose a sharp look and then smiled. 'Looks all right to me. I'll crank up the heating when we get in the car.'

'Photography doesn't pay much,' she said earnestly, after a moment. 'There are a few highfliers who travel all over the world, but most of us just plod along and try to make enough to pay the bills. Working for Fraser is okay, and I *do* like it. There's something about the drama of a wedding that becomes addictive. If I went out on my own, well I doubt I'd make much money. I'm sure there would be days when that would matter a lot, but I don't know, if you're happy in your job, as you say, then you can get around the rest.'

They'd reached the track and Skye looked up with a groan.

He grabbed her hand and held on. 'One, two, three!' he shouted, and took off, dragging her after him. She moaned, but with his momentum she found herself making good progress. For a while, at least, and then the gradient increased and her legs started to ache, and she slowed right down.

By the time they'd reached the top she was gasping for air and her heart was pounding, and although Finn wasn't nearly as done in as her he still looked like he was glad it was over.

He waited patiently while she took some more shots looking down the track and the view of the valley through the trees, and then they climbed inside the car with a relieved Lightning. Finn started the engine, turning up the heating.

'Take off your boots,' he said, when they'd stripped out of their jackets and gloves, and Skye had taken off her hat—the wool was very wet. The windscreen and windows were fogging up and she could no longer see a thing, but the warmth was very welcome.

Skye reached down but her fingers were still numb, as well as the laces being wet and difficult to unknot. Exasperated with her, Finn lifted her feet up onto his lap, one at a time, and divested her of the ruined footwear.

'Cost me a fortune, they did,' she grumbled.

'So it's my fault, is it?' he retorted. 'I thought you weren't going to blame me?'

Skye stretched out her hands to the warm air and sighed. 'It's not. I'm not. Finn, I wish …'

He'd put on the demister and was rubbing a hand over the inside of the glass, but he stopped to look at her. 'What do you wish?' he asked quietly.

'That I could find out what really happened to Neville that day. Do you know what Mum said, one of the last things she ever said? "I wish I knew what happened to him." Well, so do I.'

CHAPTER 17

NEVILLE

Early Thursday 12 January 1939,
Mackenzie Crossing

AT FIRST NEVILLE didn't know what it was that woke him. It was still dark but he sensed it was early morning, a few hours before dawn, and he was usually right. Something stirred in the paddock and he thought that perhaps Aesop had come to his water to drink, or else nudged him through the fence.

'Neville?'

There was no mistaking that voice and he sat up in surprise. 'Georgie?' He'd stripped off his shirt to sleep and now he fumbled to find it, dragging it hastily back on over his naked chest.

She didn't seem to notice. As she stepped closer he saw that she was fully dressed, even wearing her hat. 'I need your help,' she said, the words a little stiff, as if she was worried he might say no. 'I'm getting the Union Jack mine ready, just in case we have to take shelter, and I need your help.'

'My help?' He was on his feet. 'My dear girl, of course I'll help.'

Her shoulders sagged a little with relief, and it occurred to him that she'd thought he may refuse because of the scene earlier. The words spilled out of him before he had time to consider them.

'I sleep out here because I have nightmares, Georgie. Like Tiddler. Bad ones. I'm better off on my own, you see.'

'Oh,' she said.

As the silence stretched out he felt a chill despite the warm night. Words trembled on his tongue but he held them back, aware of all the reasons not to speak. And then she stepped closer and he felt her hand on his arm. It was like last night. The moment she touched him, he had to gather her against him.

'You're wet!' he declared. 'Good God, Georgie, what have you been doing?'

She giggled like a girl. 'What do you think? I've been carrying water up to the Union Jack in kerosene tins.'

'In kerosene tins …?' He knew about the love affair Australians had with the square metal tins that their kerosene was delivered in, how they used them for everything from carrying stock feed and salting meat, to flattening them out for building projects.

'Yes. And that's why I need your help. I have two forty-four-gallon drums I want to take up to the mine and fill with the water.'

Then she told him, keeping her voice low as they passed the cottages where the others were sleeping, that the drums had been appropriated by Big Jim from the truck that had once come calling. In these isolated areas, vehicles carried their own supply of petrol; however, the occupants of the truck had found they needed to lighten their load if they were going to get up the hill beyond the Crossing. Big Jim had kept the drums because he'd thought that one day they might come in handy.

'As they did,' Neville said with amusement.

By this time they were on their way through the smoky darkness to the Union Jack mine, which had been tunnelled into the hillside behind the town. The drums, with their distinctive scallop-shell logo, were awkward and heavy, and the ground was too rough and stony to allow them to be rolled very far. By the time they reached the mine they were both out of breath and dripping with sweat.

'How long have you been at this?' Neville asked her curiously, when he could speak again. 'I mean, preparing for the possibility that you might need to take shelter in the mine?'

She wouldn't meet his eyes. 'A while.'

'Georgie, why didn't you get the others to help?'

She put her hands on her hips. 'And who would help? Hector with his bad leg? Marie, who can barely walk a yard in this heat without collapsing? Peggy and poor Arnold? Or Tiddler, who's already having bad dreams? The able-bodied folk were the first to leave Mackenzie Crossing. There *is* no one to help.'

So she'd taken the burden upon her own shoulders. What a woman she was, he thought. He had the urge to draw her into his arms again, and he might well have done so, if she hadn't spoken.

'Let's finish this before it gets light. I want to be back when Tiddler wakes up.'

There were old timber beams propping up either side of the mine entrance, and although it looked narrow, once inside the tunnel widened out into an area large enough to accommodate the folk of Mackenzie Crossing, even if it would be a bit cramped. The roof was shored up with more timber, but high enough that Neville could stand upright. They manoeuvred the drums into the mine, and Georgie lit a lantern she'd left there, turning it up so that the light sent the shadows fleeing.

Curiously Neville looked around him. 'How far back into the hill does the mine go?' he asked.

Georgie was busy moving a pile of blankets to one side. 'You can't go much further than this. It's quite secure,' she added, seeing his look of consternation. 'They closed up the tunnel as a safety precaution, when the mine was no longer in use.'

Now Neville had noticed the pile of broken palings and stakes propped against the wall, and she explained they were to construct makeshift pens for the animals. 'We can't abandon them,' she said. 'Anyway, Tiddler would never leave Her Majesty.'

'Her Majesty?'

But Georgie simply smiled.

'You've thought of everything.' Despite his

doubts about the wisdom of them staying, he couldn't help but admire her courage and determination.

'I hope so. I told you how the fire went past us in nineteen twenty-six? I remember thinking that nothing bad could happen, not when my father was there to stop it. Now there's only me.'

She looked away but not before he had seen the worry dulling her eyes and the shadows underneath them. Night after night she'd been doing this, all alone.

When they headed back to the hostelry, the sun was rising in a muddy, smoke-streaked sky. Tiddler was already up and came running from the hen house.

'Mr Darling, Her Majesty has laid an egg!' So Her Majesty was a hen, Neville thought with amusement. The boy had an old Arnott's biscuit tin in his hands. 'Georgie! Where *were* you?'

'You'll break it,' Georgie scolded, instead of answering. 'One egg. We are privileged.' And she took the tin from Tiddler, laughter dancing in her eyes.

'Can we have it for breakfast?' the boy asked.

'What, all of us?' Georgie laughed, glancing at Neville to share her pleasure in the moment. He felt slightly dizzy with happiness. Or was it the heat and the hard work?

'Is Mr Darling going to stay?' Tiddler was watching him through his lashes, shy and hopeful at the same time. It was incredible how much he looked like Georgie just then.

Georgie gave Neville a quizzical look. 'You'd

better ask Mr Darling.'

Tiddler repeated his question.

Neville felt as if he was on that cliff edge again, about to test his ability to fly. 'I'm staying, yes. For now at least,' he said. 'Until … well, I'm staying.'

Georgie ruffled the boy's hair. 'There, he's staying.'

They were both beaming at him as if he'd done exactly the right thing, so Neville took the opportunity to make the request he'd been hoping to make ever since he first saw her. 'I'd very much like to take your photograph. Would you mind?'

'Both of us?' Georgie gave the boy a wink. 'Do you want to be famous, Tiddler?'

'Yes, both of you. That was what I meant.' Although he was ashamed to admit it had been Georgie he'd been thinking of.

'Me first!' Tiddler was jumping up and down.

'You'll have to keep still,' Neville warned him. 'Otherwise you'll be nothing but a blur.'

Tiddler dealt with his egg in no time, impatient for this new and exciting experience. Neville found him relatively easy to photograph. Once he was persuaded to stand still, he was a natural. He wanted one of himself and his hen, who turned out to be a brown-and-white creature with an unruffled and regal manner. Neville promised him a copy when it was developed.

Photographing Georgie was more difficult.

Every time he got her nicely framed, she'd tense up and her mouth would tighten and her eyes narrow. This would require patience and sensitivity and Neville had both. He asked her what it was like growing up here. He could tell she was aware of what he was doing, but she answered him anyway, and gradually she began to relax.

'The school at the Crossing was a good one. Mr Wright, the headmaster, had a wife called Elsie, and she helped out in the class. She was a far better teacher than he was. If I have achieved anything in my life, then it's down to her. And my father.'

'You were fortunate.'

'I was.' She took a deep breath. 'Big Jim wouldn't let me stay here once I turned seventeen. I think Elsie might have had a hand in that, too. They thought I'd end up married to some no-hoper with a dozen children hanging off my skirt. Elsie said I was too clever for that and my father used to tell me, "You deserve to make your mark in the world, as I did." I wanted to stay and teach in the school here, but Elsie wouldn't let me, and Big Jim said I was going to Melbourne to a private school there, and that was the end of the argument. Big Jim had friends in high places, you see.'

'A private school in Melbourne?'

'Miss Agostino's School for Young Ladies.' Georgie chuckled at the expression on his face and he wished he'd had the presence of mind to take a photograph right then. 'Not that I saw many young ladies when I was there, but it was obvious they were hoping to be, one day. The good families of Melbourne sent their daughters to Miss Agostino's School and they expected to get their money's worth.'

'And you taught there?'

'I did. For four years. Conversation and English Expression and Spelling, they were my three main accomplishments. It is entirely due to me that the ladies of Melbourne can write out a creditable menu or letter of invitation, and chat with ease at cocktail parties.'

She was enjoying herself, making fun of it all, but Neville wondered if she had been so light-hearted at the time.

'How did you manage in the city after living all your life here at the Crossing? That must have been quite a shock to the system.'

She glanced down with a smile, and this time he did get a photograph.

'It was a dreadful shock at first. I was dazed. Remember, I was only seventeen. Miss Agostino kept an eye on me. My father had known her father when he first came to Australia, and she felt an obligation to him. I don't know the details, but I wouldn't be surprised if there had been something unpleasant happening to Mr Agostino, and it was my father who sorted it out for him. She owed him a debt and she wanted to repay it.'

Neville had noticed that her voice had changed now that she was recalling her days at the posh school. She'd slipped out of her 'Georgie Mackenzie of Mackenzie Crossing' role. She really was a fascinating creature.

'Miss Agostino was very proud of her school's reputation. I didn't realise at the time just how much it meant to her.' She was silent and he wondered what thoughts she was lost in.

'But then you came home again.'

Her eyes were sad and he clicked the shutter, even knowing in his heart it wasn't the perfect photograph. Not yet.

'I came home. I had to. Big Jim was disappointed. I knew that. He didn't have to say it, I could see it in his eyes. He'd wanted me to make my life away from here, but at the same time he was getting old and he needed my help. He could no longer run the town on his own. And this place was his legacy. I knew that, too, and he could never leave it. Why did he expect me to?'

'Because it's a hard and lonely life for a woman?' Neville suggested.

'No more than it is for a man,' she retorted.

'What about your mother? Did she enjoy life here?'

Again that look, and although his fingers itched to take another photograph, this time he restrained himself and awaited her answer.

'I never knew her. She came to the Crossing one day like a stray cat in a thunderstorm, or that was how Big Jim used to put it when he was reminiscing. She was the child of an itinerant Chinese prospector and an Irishwoman, but life hadn't been kind to her. I think my father loved her because she was so different from everyone else, and he could show her off. Did I say she was beautiful? And she loved him because he had sheltered her when she most needed it. But I don't know, really, I'm just guessing. She died when I was born, and Big Jim buried her in the cemetery on the hill. That's where he is buried, too.'

'My condolences.'

She glanced at him curiously. 'It isn't your fault. Things happen. We mightn't ask for them, but when they do we have to get through them as best we can. Such as this fire.'

Georgie looked towards the hills, shading her eyes, and he saw a droplet of sweat run down the side of her neck and underneath the collar where the scar—the scar he didn't want to think about—was hidden. The temperature must be close to a hundred.

If the fire came through here then there would be nothing left. In such circumstances no one could save Big Jim's house, or his town. Surely Georgie knew that? A mortar shell would do less damage and Neville had seen the destruction wrought by them on the French countryside.

Aesop gave a whinny and tossed his big head as Tiddler led him over so that he could be photographed as well. Neville wondered what on earth she was planning to do. Take him into the mine with her and the others?

Madness, he thought, as he took a photograph, and the horse stared back at him like a true professional.

Georgie was watching him. 'I know what you're thinking,' she said, and there was no warmth in her voice now. 'You think I should pack up and run away. Well I won't. I'm going to stay and save the Crossing and its people, you'll see.'

'Georgie—'

She pushed past him. 'Go and take your photos, Pom. That's what you're here for, isn't it? To chronicle the colonials?' And she slammed the door to the house forcibly behind her.

CHAPTER 18

SKYE

Monday 9 June 1997

BY THE TIME they got back to Elysian, the snow was falling thick and fast. Wild winds had given way to a peaceful stillness, and there was already a thick layer of white on the ground. Lightning, finally released from the car, went a little crazy and ran round and round their legs.

Finn was heating up some soup for a late lunch, but Skye was keen to take a look at her photographs, so she left him and the greyhound in the kitchen.

Bringing each shot up onto the monitor and examining it was something she always found absorbing. And there were quite a few of her efforts she already knew would make amazing prints. The weather, rather than being a disaster, had made her visit to Mackenzie Crossing something very special. The monochrome colours were most interesting, and Finn had been right about the startling effect of her auburn hair. A shame she hadn't got more snowy scenes, but reluctant as she'd been to admit it at the time, she knew Finn was right. And it had taken her a long time under the shower to thaw out.

The exhibition, which was now a certainty for her, was constantly in the back of her mind. She thought of it as she flicked through the images, trying to figure out what would work and what wouldn't. It all depended, too, on the theme she decided on, but it needed to be something that would tie the whole event together. Her search for Neville perhaps, or her efforts to follow in his footsteps, from Adelaide all the way to Mackenzie Crossing.

The photo of Finn, with his profile against the wild grey sky, was particularly good. That's why she spent such a long time examining it, or at least that was her excuse. The manner in which he held himself in the landscape made her feel that he was very much alone, and at the same time didn't mind in the least. A maverick, king of his kingdom. Maybe. But she also knew Finn was part of a team.

Skye wondered if he'd like a copy. An enlarged framed copy? And should she ask him, or just do it anyway?

She was still considering the matter when he called out from the kitchen.

'Food's ready!'

Immediately, as if a switch had been flicked, Skye became aware of the appetising smell of buttered toast and hot tomato soup. Her stomach rumbled.

'Some of the photos are really great,' was the first thing she said, walking over to the fire box and holding out her hands. Something about actually seeing the burning log through the smoky glass door was very comforting. She wasn't sure she'd feel the same about ducted heating ever again.

'So you'll use them for your exhibition?'

'I think so. I hope so.' She pulled a face. 'If I can get it all together. I'm still trying to nut out the details.'

'You mean financially or time-wise?' He came and stood beside her. He'd changed out of his wet clothing into a fresh pair of jeans and his faded checked shirt, this time over a black tee. When Skye glanced down she saw he was wearing his favourite Explorer socks.

'Um, both, I suppose. If I could get one of the galleries interested they might be willing to shoulder the cost, but it all depends on whether they think the photos will have enough appeal. They won't do it if no one comes. I mean, who's heard of Neville Darling anyway. Or me!'

'Maybe Melbourne's the wrong place to start. Maybe you should begin small and move up.'

'What do you mean?'

'Well,' he said, 'Neville came here, so why not have the exhibition here? Make it a trial run and then see what happens. You could tweak it if necessary before you take it to the Big Smoke.'

'Here?' She felt herself tense.

His voice went on, even and unhurried, as if what he was suggesting wasn't turning her stomach in somersaults.

'We get plenty of tourists, especially in the summer, and they're always looking for something to do. I'm sure you'd break even, maybe even make some money.'

She didn't know what to say. Was he being helpful or was there some other agenda, or was she losing her mind even thinking such a thing? Their time at Mackenzie Crossing had broken through some of the restraints she'd initially felt about being in Finn's company, but there were still a lot of hurdles to get over before she could feel completely comfortable with him.

If ever.

Face it, she told herself, the past was always going to be there. *Dylan* was always going to be there.

Luckily she didn't have to answer him or make excuses, because Lightning began to bark, and then someone knocked impatiently on the floor-to-ceiling glass door behind them.

They both turned.

'Finn!' came a woman's muffled voice, and there was a face there, looking in, brightly gloved hands cupped on either side.

'Alison.' Finn gave Skye a look that was struggling not to be long-suffering. 'I think a lot of my team, but sometimes …'

Skye couldn't help laughing at his expression. 'Hey, they love you, Finn. Go with it.'

He looked startled, as if these days he didn't come in for much teasing—perhaps no one dared—but then his expression cleared and he gave her a wry smile as he went to open the door.

Lightning followed and stood behind him, wagging her tail in anticipation of more pats.

Alison, a small, wiry woman in her forties, was already removing her padded jacket as she stepped into the kitchen. Her brown hair was topped by a brightly knitted hat, a match for her gloves. Skye recognised the pattern from the shop where she'd bought her own knitted gear.

'What's this about? Who are these detectives from Melbourne?' Alison had launched into a tirade before she realised Finn wasn't alone. Her brows came down, and she gave Skye the sort of stare a mother bird might give an intruder in the nest. But of course Skye had already suspected that was Alison's role at the station, as well as being the keeper of the coffee cups, of course.

Finn introduced them and Skye stretched out a hand. 'Are you feeling better?' she asked with a friendly smile. 'Finn said you've had the flu.'

Alison took her hand briefly, but some of the suspicion left her face. 'Yeah, I'm through the worst of it,' she drawled in a flat, nasal accent. 'I came over to see if you wanted to come home with me and give Finn his house back.'

Well, that was blunt.

'Alison,' Finn interrupted, his voice holding a warning.

'What? You were complaining loud enough before she arrived. Have you changed your mind?' Obviously Alison wasn't afraid to air her views, despite Finn being her boss.

'You were complaining?' Skye looked at Finn, and it was her turn to raise her eyebrows.

'I wasn't complaining,' Finn said, lowering his voice, which only caused Alison to move closer so that she could hear him. 'Or … I mean that was before I …' He heaved a sigh, but Skye refused to help him out. Anyway she was enjoying his discomfort. It probably didn't happen all that often.

'Before what, Sarge?' Alison asked. 'Before you saw her?'

'Alison,' he warned again, although the other woman didn't seem the slightest bit afraid of him. 'No, it was before I realised she was Skye Stewart. We knew each other. A long time ago.'

'Oh.' Alison digested this.

Skye was expecting her to demand the whole story and was grateful when she didn't.

Finn must have been wondering, too, because he jumped in quickly, before she could draw breath. 'Anyway, the point is, now I've been suspended Skye is helping me fill in my time.'

'Is she now?' Alison was one of those people who had the ability to make the most innocent of comments sound faintly sleazy. Although she did grin, to show it was a joke, or at least Skye hoped it was a joke. With her brown eyes sparkling in her freckled face she said, 'Sorry, Skye. I'm used to being the bouncer at the door, guarding my boys' privacy. You wouldn't believe how many single ladies come into town and think they only have to flutter their eyelashes and they'll land themselves a husband with a steady income.'

'You didn't do such a good job with Doug,' Finn spoke in a dry voice. Then, to Skye, 'He fell for a girl in the pub one Saturday night. Alison tried to get him to think twice, but it was too late. They were married last month.'

Alison protested. 'I didn't try to get him to think twice! I just wanted him to be sure. It was very quick.'

'True love can be quick,' Skye put in, and earned herself a curious look from two pairs of eyes. 'Um, well, maybe it was lust.'

Alison gave a snort and whatever she was going to say next was foiled by Finn. 'Would you like some lunch?' He gestured at the pot. 'Tomato soup. It's tinned.'

'Well is there any other sort?' Alison retorted, and dropped herself down into a chair, tugging off her hat and gloves.

Finn gave Skye a wink, which was slightly disconcerting with his black eye, and set about serving up another bowl.

'I heard you were here to find a missing grand-father?' Alison said, resting an elbow on the table and turning to face Skye.

Close up the other woman looked weary. There were smudges under her eyes, her skin was pale, and Skye noticed that her hair hadn't been washed for a while. The flu possibly, working hard probably. Did all of Finn's staff put in hours as long as his?

'Yes, that's right. I'm not sure if I'll find him but I'm trying.'

'Have you got a photo?'

'No. I didn't even know he existed until my mother passed away and … Well, to cut a long story short, my grandmother married again and no one told me her husband was my step-grand-father. My real grandfather was a photographer, like me. Maybe that's why I feel so close to him without having ever known him.' She shrugged awkwardly. 'I do have a photo he took when he was in this area.'

Alison was eager to see it, so Skye went down to her bedroom to get the photocopy. She was on her way back when she heard the two of them talking in low voices. It was impossible to make out the words, until Alison's, '*That's* her!'

Skye hesitated, feeling disorientated. What did that mean? Had Finn been telling everyone about that summer when they were teenagers? It seemed unlikely, but even if he was, there wasn't much she could do about it. It seemed wiser to pretend she hadn't heard, so she picked up her pace and strode into the room as if nothing had happened.

Finn was standing with his back to her, stirring the soup, and Alison was giving a slice of toast her full attention.

'Here it is,' Skye said brightly. 'Taken at Mackenzie Crossing on the day of the Black Friday fire.'

Alison reached for the page. 'My mother came from the Crossing and ... Wow!' She looked up, her gaze going from Finn to Skye. 'You'd think someone would know her,' she said. 'I mean, she's pretty memorable.'

'I thought Archie might know,' Finn said, bringing over Alison's bowl of soup, 'but Skye didn't get a chance to ask him.'

'Couldn't get past the dragon?' Alison asked, and then shook her head. 'I shouldn't say that. Nancy means well. They've always been close.'

Finn glanced at Skye. 'What about your mother, Alison? Is it worth talking to her?'

'Of course it is. Mum would love a chat. I'm not sure she'd know much about your grandfather, but she'd probably know who *that* is.' She tapped her finger on the woman with the dark hair. 'I've just settled Mum into the nursing home in Westcott. Her house was in Marysville and she couldn't cope on her own anymore, and because I'm working here I can't care for her, not properly. I didn't want to move her, but she seems happy. Plenty to do, she tells me, and lots of gossip, so what's not to like?'

'We can drive down there tomorrow. If you want to?' Finn added, giving Skye a questioning look.

'Definitely. Thank you.' She smiled.

Alison was watching them avidly. It made Skye self-conscious, as if she'd done something wrong.

'I don't know how they expect us to carry on without you at the helm.' Alison bit into her toast, chewed and swallowed. 'They have no idea what it's like living and policing beyond the suburbs. Desk jockeys, the lot of them.' She gave Finn a penetrating look. 'I suppose you'll be wanting to go back to Melbourne and find a desk of your own. I wouldn't blame you if you did. None of us get much thanks for the time and sweat we put in.'

Finn ran a hand through his hair. It was still

very dark, but Skye thought she could pick out some silver strands, just a few, caught in the fluorescent overhead light.

'Do we want thanks?' he murmured.

Alison seemed to realise she was heading into an area Finn wasn't keen to explore, because abruptly she changed the subject.

'Taylor's reliable. You know when he says he'll be at work at a certain time then he will. And he's willing to shoulder extra if he's needed.'

'He seems like a nice boy,' Skye offered.

'He wants to buy Mr Rutherford's old place,' Alison said with a laugh. 'Do it up. Maybe live there.'

'Are he and Saskia …?' Skye began, and then wondered if she was speaking out of turn.

Alison nodded. 'Fell in love with her in primary school, I reckon. Never looked at another girl before or since. When she went off to do her nursing degree it broke his heart. I notice she's back again now though.'

'Is there a hospital nearby where she can get work?' Skye asked curiously.

Alison shrugged. 'We have a community health centre and a nurse who visits two days a week. The actual hospital is in Westcott, but most of the staff have been working there forever. So there's nothing nearby, not the way you mean. Jobs are hard to come by around here. Sometimes the only way to get one is to wait until someone retires. Or dies. I don't know what will happen once they've finished training in the Big Smoke. One or both of them might have to commute if they want to base themselves here. Saskia could manage, but I'm not so sure Taylor would, to be honest. What do you think, Sarge?'

Finn shrugged, and Skye thought he probably disapproved of gossiping about one of his team. She decided it was her turn to change the subject, and began to ask Alison about the weather. That led to stories concerning stranded motorists, and she listened in wide-eyed disbelief to some of the hair-raising yarns.

The other woman didn't stay long after she'd finished her soup. 'Better get back and see how Taylor's doing,' she explained, shrugging into her jacket. Finn pulled on his boots and went out with her, and shortly afterwards Skye heard Alison's car drive off.

When Finn returned to the kitchen he began stacking the dishes on the sink, ready to wash.

'Let me do that,' Skye insisted, stepping in. 'You did the cooking. I do the washing up. Isn't that how it works?'

He let her take over but stayed put, leaning back against the bench beside her. 'Alison is a straight talker,' he offered, with an amused glance. 'She takes a bit of getting used to, but her heart's in the right place.'

'That's fine. I like straight talk. It's underrated.'

He glanced at her again, without saying anything, and it occurred to her that he was remembering her refusal to discuss Dylan. To talk *to* Dylan.

But that's different! she wanted to shout.

Couldn't he see that it was different? Being

around Dylan, apart from it being awkward, would bring back the memories she'd pushed away for so long. Did she want to deal with all of that right now? It had taken her a long time to move on from that night and she wasn't at all keen to revisit it. Afterwards she'd been a mess, and worst of all, she'd missed Finn with an ache that had refused to go away.

Her parents hadn't understood that—and they'd been glad to put as much distance as possible between Skye and the Faradays—so how could she have told them?

Taking up photography had given her thoughts a new direction, and Russell had been a good mate to her. She hadn't had another proper boyfriend after Finn, not for years, not until she'd met Fraser. He was funny and easy to be with, and she'd discovered how refreshing it could be to have a relationship that skimmed the surface rather than delving into those angsty, agonising depths.

Love was extremely overrated in her opinion.

Now, seeing Finn again, being with him … Skye didn't know what was happening between them. Perhaps nothing. Perhaps it was all in her mind, some sort of echo of the past. And what did Finn think? Would she ever ask him? Or just wave goodbye at the end of the week and go back to her safe little world.

And now he'd suggested she have her exhibition right here in his town and she didn't know what to say to him.

Skye plunged her hands into the soapy water

and set about washing the cutlery. 'You know,' she began tentatively, 'with you being suspended, you could use your time to go over to Perth and see your daughter. It'd be the ideal opportunity. Why don't you?'

Finn looked down. His arms were folded and his ankles were crossed. The classic defensive pose. 'There are things going on here. I need to keep an eye on them.'

Skye's heart sank. *Dylan*. Why was it always Dylan? But she shook her head at him, trying to make a joke of it. 'Do you really think that everything will fall apart if you're not here?'

But when he looked up at her there was no humour in his face. None whatsoever.

'I know it will.'

CHAPTER 19

DYLAN, FINN AND SKYE

December 1978,
the Bay, Melbourne

AS SOON AS they'd reached the bay, Dylan went whooping down the beach and into the water. It was flat and calm, not a ripple in sight, and the sky was blazing with stars. There were other people here tonight trying to escape the heat, but they were further up the sand, near the jetty, where a bonfire was giving out light and an excuse to party.

'Come on!'

Dylan was shouting at them and waving his arms, but then he lost his balance and toppled backwards with a huge splash. When he came up, gasping and coughing, Finn was doubled over with laughter.

'Help!' Dylan wailed, but it wasn't a real cry for help. He was already laughing again. Or was he spluttering?

'Shh!' Skye looked up the beach at the campfire.

She was worried someone would come running and then see the state of Dylan, but to her relief no one seemed to have heard.

Dylan had driven them here from the park, taking the back streets, and at every corner they'd expected to see a cop car waiting to pull them over.

Because Finn had backed down, given in, just as he always did.

'You owe me, brother,' Dylan had whispered, although Skye knew she was meant to hear.

And after a moment, during which Skye had held her breath, Finn had thrown him the keys he'd only just snatched off him. Not meeting her eyes. Not wanting to tell her why.

'It'll be all right,' he'd said, slinging an arm around her shoulders. 'He's not as bad as he's pretending.'

She knew she could have refused to go with them, but the truth was she didn't want to say no. She wanted to stay here, with Finn, who had his arm around her shoulders and a pleading look in his eyes. Whatever the confusing undercurrents between the twins, she naively thought everything would be all right.

Dylan was still splashing and shouting.

'Here.' She kicked off her sandals and waded into the water in her cut-offs. 'Get up, Dylan. Everyone will hear.'

'Thanks, Skye, thanks for saving me.'

He reached up for her hand but, as soon as his fingers closed over hers, he gave a tug. She fell against him, and then they were both in the water.

She went under, and her shriek was cut short before it had barely begun. For a moment all she thought about was the shark in *Jaws 2*. She began to thrash around, struggling to get back on her feet, but Dylan was cackling like a lunatic and holding her down.

'Let her go, man!' Finn's voice sounded above her.

She felt him pulling at her, trying to lift her, but Dylan wouldn't let go. She took a deep breath that sent her into a coughing fit.

At least the water was shallow. Dylan was hardly covered by it, and Skye was lying on top of him, her clothes wet and clinging. She took another breath and hit out at him.

'You nearly drowned me!'

She was looking straight into his eyes, her own blazing, and then something in his expression stopped her dead. His gaze dipped down to her tee-shirt, which she only realised at that moment was so wet it had become see-through. And just like that she was afraid of him.

He let her go. So suddenly that Finn, who was still trying to free her, went tumbling back into the water, taking her with him.

Now there was sand in her mouth and her hair was all over her face and she was floundering, splashing her hands as if she was going to drown. Because that was how she felt just then. Frightened and out of her depth.

'Hey.' Finn had wrapped her in his arms. He was sitting up so that she was cradled against his chest. 'Hey, Skye, it's all right. You're all right.'

She dragged her hair out of her eyes, scratching herself in the process. Her heart was still pounding and she wasn't exactly sure why, just that Dylan had frightened her. But it was all right now. Finn was here and the water was shallow and quite warm. There was no danger and she even began to think she'd imagined there ever was.

He squeezed her tight for a moment and then he let her go. They could hear Dylan splashing and kicking a few yards away, and then he was singing, 'You're the One that I Want' from *Grease*, hamming it up.

Finn rolled his eyes, the whites showing in the starlight. It made Skye giggle. She was feeling better now. Finn was here, she reminded herself, and it seemed silly to be afraid. Yes, Dylan had been strange. That raw look in his eyes, as if everything in him had been stripped back to just one basic emotion. All the good leached out. But why should Dylan hurt her? He was her friend, wasn't he?

A big cheer went up from the campfire and then a couple of people went running into the smooth, glassy waters of the bay. Skye watched them splashing each other, shouting and laughing. She felt safe here in the darkness with Finn, watching them when they couldn't see her.

Out to sea there was a ship, the navigation lights showing its slow and steady movement towards the heads and the open sea. She watched it, sometimes lifting her fingers to make a frame. She had been doing that a bit lately and she considered whether she might be an artist.

You'd never know the sea was out there, really, the waters of the bay were so calm tonight, just a gentle wash against her legs. She leaned her head sleepily against Finn's shoulder and looked up at the stars. There were so many of them. She did the frame thing again, to see which section of the sky looked the most spectacular, but it was difficult to decide.

'Where's the booze?'

Dylan was standing over them, dripping, his hair a sleek cap on his head.

'In the car, where do you think?' Finn said, and Skye could tell he was fed up with his brother.

Dylan heaved a mega sigh. He splashed past them towards the sand, making sure to turn and heave a great armful of water in their direction.

Finn swore, wrapping Skye up in his arms, but it was too late, and now they were both drenched again. Dylan gave a satisfied chuckle, and headed up the beach towards the car park.

Skye wondered if they should follow him. Couldn't they all be friends again? Why did the brothers have to make everything into such a tug of war? She'd never really understood this thing between them, this mixture of love and hate. The way Dylan always wanted Finn to give in to him, and the way Finn inevitably did.

'Finn …?'

Finn was running his hand over her arm and then he reached up and touched her face, turning her slightly. His lips were warm on her cheek, then the corner of her mouth. She felt a quiver low in her belly, like when she was hungry, only different.

His mouth was on hers now and it was nice. He wasn't doing the sorts of things she'd seen on *Number 96* at Susanne's place—her parents wouldn't let her watch it at home. He didn't stick his tongue in her mouth or mash himself against her. He was gentle, careful, and she began to kiss him back.

They'd kissed earlier, in the park, and yesterday, during *Jaws 2*, before the shark had taken another victim and she'd screamed. But they'd been testing each other then, a little clumsy, bumping their noses together. This time was different, more intense.

The water moved gently around her and the voices from further up the beach faded, and Finn's mouth continued to press softly on hers. When he brushed his fingers across her stomach, above her shorts, she didn't push him away. And when he reached under her tee-shirt and traced the line of her bra, she didn't stop him either.

Maybe it was the alcohol, despite her not having drunk very much, or maybe it was because Dylan had scared her and Finn didn't. Or maybe she just wanted to.

'I love you, Skye,' he said against her neck, his skin warm and salty from the water. They were the words she'd wanted to hear, and they gave her the freedom to share her own secret.

'I love you, too, Finn,' she whispered. 'I do. I really do.'

He drew back and looked into her eyes. His were deeply set, so dark, and his wet hair was slicked back, showing the stark lines of his face, the shape of his nose and chin. The soft curve of his mouth. It was a moment she'd never forget. A perfect moment.

'Ooh!' Dylan was back. '"You're the One that I Want",' he crooned, wriggling his hips around in a parody of Olivia.

'Piss off.' Finn shot his brother a look like a knife.

'Did I spoil it for you?' Dylan asked, but there was something beyond the joking in his voice.

The two boys stared at each other and Skye felt that awful tension growing in the air.

She stood up, crossing her arms over her breasts, feeling the grit of sand against her skin.

'I want to go home,' she said.

Finn also stood up, she could feel him at her back, but Dylan didn't move. He was still glaring over her head at his brother, and his crazy manic mood had given way to something else.

'You owe me,' he repeated.

Finn said nothing, and Skye turned to look at him. The expression on his face frightened her even more than Dylan's strange mood. The warm feeling in her stomach dropped away until there was nothing there but hollowness.

'Finn?' she whispered, and suddenly she was cold. 'What does he mean? What do you owe him?'

'Anything,' Dylan said, and now his gaze was fixed on Skye and the raw look was back. 'And everything.'

CHAPTER 20

SKYE

Late Monday 9 June 1997

THE TELEPHONE IN the kitchen was ringing.

Skye had been looking again at her digital pictures on the camera monitor and had lost track of time. It was late. She glanced at her watch—eleven forty-nine. As far as she was aware Finn had gone to bed hours ago, and she'd only stayed up because she knew she wouldn't be able to sleep. There was too much going on in her head. Too many questions she couldn't seem to answer.

She'd been thinking of making a phone call herself. To Fraser. Why did she want to ring her ex-husband? Well, she wasn't sure, but it just seemed important to touch base. Fraser was good at grounding her, and reminding her who and what she was—as if she'd forgotten after a few days away, which was ridiculous, and yet … The earth beneath her feet was definitely getting shaky, and the past seemed to be rising up around her, assuming an importance it had no right to, not after all these years.

Fraser had a saying: Don't die wondering.

Maybe that was what she really wanted to hear. Then she could give herself permission to behave in a way that was both reckless and reprehensible.

She heard Finn get up and the ringing stopped. She found herself listening, trying to make out the words or his tone of voice. Police business, probably, she told herself. Even suspended Finn would be the go-to man for people in the area.

She'd just returned to the monitor when there was a tap on her bedroom door.

When she got up to open it, Finn was standing outside, wearing the same jeans and shirt as earlier, and looking like a man who'd just been woken from deep sleep and heard bad news. She stepped back, and he followed her into the bedroom.

'That was Taylor,' he said quietly. 'Something's happened.'

She stared up at him, trying to judge how serious it was. Not a hint of a smile in his eyes. Pretty serious, then.

'What? What's happened?'

He was standing very close and she could feel the warmth of his body, but she didn't consider for a moment moving away, although she would have as recently as yesterday.

'You remember Detectives Lois Petersen and Gary Grey? They've been at the station giving Taylor a rough time and now they're on their way here. He rang to warn me, against orders I might add, but I'm glad he did. At least it gives me a chance to talk to you before they get here.'

'Warn you?' Skye repeated. 'About what, Finn?'

'Warn me that they're coming to take me in for questioning on a charge of perverting the course of justice. No arrest yet, but I'm being taken into custody.'

Skye tried to process this information. She felt shocked and disbelieving. This stuff only happened in the movies, surely? 'You mean, for this thing that happened five years ago?'

'They reckon I was crooked five years ago when I was with the Drug Squad.'

'I don't believe it! You wouldn't!'

Her voice had risen and Finn took her arm and led her over to the bed and sat her down, and then he sat down beside her. The bed creaked under their combined weight, and she slid into him so that they were pressed together from thigh to shoulder.

For a moment the past and the present collided. She was back on the beach, in the water, and he was about to kiss her. The sky was a mass of stars and the air was warm against her skin.

And then he said, 'This is about Dylan,' and shattered the illusion.

'Why am I not surprised?' she managed, her throat tight.

He gave her a considering look, as if he had more to say and didn't know if he should say it. Or maybe it was more a case of whether she would listen.

'Skye, Dylan isn't the bad guy in this. He's

come up here to break away from the bad guys, and I've been helping him do that. Because it's my fault he's in this mess in the first place. When I was with the Drug Squad I … Well, it's complicated, but he helped me out, gave information. I told myself I was helping him, as well, but I can't deny it was good for my career. After I moved on, Dylan stayed on as an informant.'

'For the detectives who are coming to question you?'

'Them, and others,' he said. Then, after a hesitation, 'Mainly them. The thing you need to understand is that Dylan's sorting himself out, he wants to step away, but they won't let him. They say he's too valuable to them, but the fact is he knows a lot about what's going on. They'll never let him go willingly. That's why he's come up here, that's why I've got him hidden. He thought he could do some sort of deal, but guys like Gary Grey aren't pushovers.'

'How do they know he's here?'

'How do they know anything? Money changes hands, favours are done, people talk.' He sounded exasperated, though she didn't think it was with her.

'And they want you to hand him back?'

'Yes. That's what my suspension is really about. They're trying to scare me into cooperating, but now that that doesn't seem to be working they've upped the stakes.'

She tried to take in what he was saying. It still sounded like a plot from a movie, but she didn't doubt Finn was telling her the truth, or at least as much of it as he wanted her to hear. Beneath all the talk, the basics were the same. Dylan was in trouble, Dylan needed help, and good old Finn was right there to provide it. Skye felt a flash of anger, burning deep inside her. Didn't it matter to him how his brother's situation affected him? Damaged him? Couldn't he see the harm he was doing himself? But then he never had.

Finn was still talking in that earnest, sincere voice, and she didn't doubt he cared deeply. A pity she couldn't feel the same.

'He isn't dangerous. He isn't wanted for anything illegal. If that was the case then I couldn't have helped him—not without bringing down a consorting charge on my head.'

'I don't trust him,' she interrupted, her voice stony.

'I know you don't,' he said quietly.

She couldn't look away.

'I can't tell them where he is,' Finn went on, and she thought there was a plea somewhere beneath the steely note in his voice. 'I can't risk it.'

'God, you don't mean ... Would they hurt him?' For a moment she forgot her anger at Dylan, horrified by this possibility. 'Do people really do things like that, Finn?'

'Maybe. I don't know. I can't risk it, Skye.'

Skye shook her head in bewilderment. 'Finn, can't you see? Do you really have to be reminded? You need to walk away from him right now.'

Wearily Finn shook his own head. 'I can't do that.'

No, she thought, *you never could.*

'Taylor and Alison don't know Dylan is my brother, they're not involved in this and that's how I want it to stay. And I don't think anyone will question you, Skye, but if they do …'

This was madness. 'Why shouldn't I tell them? If it will help you out of this mess you're in, then why shouldn't I?'

'Because it's complicated,' he said, leaning closer. 'More complicated than you know.' His dark eyes were serious and despite her own feelings, she was compelled to hear him out. 'I've never asked you for anything, have I, Skye? I'm asking you now. I want you to go to him, tell him what's happened. It's important. He'll know what to do.'

'You want me to tell Dylan you're being questioned because of him?' she said in amazement. 'You have no right to ask!'

'No, I haven't. You don't owe me anything.' He was so close she could see his every eyelash. 'But I'd hoped … I thought, you might help me, just this once. Please help me, Skye.'

She rubbed her fingers against her forehead, feeling the beginnings of a headache. The memories of that long-ago night were now crystal clear. He'd said she didn't owe him anything, but that wasn't entirely true. Suddenly, she clearly remembered standing on the road and looking down and seeing his feet, torn and bloody. The image made her feel sick, but it was a reminder that yes, maybe she did owe him. And if she agreed to help him, would it mean the slate would be clean? So that they could walk away from each other and finally forget.

'I must be mad,' she said dully. 'Insane.'

He recognised the signs of her defeat and took a breath, and she could see the vastness of his relief. But it was only a moment and that intense gaze was focused on her again. 'Do you remember how we got there? To Dylan's place?'

She tried to visualise it. She was usually pretty good with directions, but right now she was out of her comfort zone, and in the dark everything would look different. 'I'm not sure.'

'Okay.' He looked around, saw her notebook on the bed and picked it up, and grabbed the pen. He drew the map quickly, adding a few directions, and then he tore off the page and handed it to her, pressing it into her palm. 'Do you understand this?'

Skye looked down, trying to concentrate. 'Desperation Track … Yes, yes, I think so.'

'Good. Here are the keys to the Toyota. Can you drive it?' he asked, frowning.

'Fraser has something similar, so yes, I can drive it.'

'Thank you. It means a lot to me and Dylan.'

'I'm not doing it for Dylan,' she told him, folding the map and placing it in her back pocket.

He wasn't listening. 'Believe me, this wasn't supposed to happen. Not now. I thought I could keep you and him separate, and maybe we …' He gave a harsh laugh. 'I've really cocked it up, haven't I?'

He was talking in riddles and she was too tired to untangle them. As if aware of it, he stopped and tried again.

'Sorry I won't be able to take you to see Mrs Appleby.'

'The least of your problems, I would've thought.'

'Yeah.'

His gaze on her face was making her even more apprehensive and once again she became aware of the warmth of his body at her side. 'Where will they take you?'

'I don't know. The nearest lockup is Westcott, or there's Cumberland. Maybe headquarters for the full treatment.'

'God, Finn, don't get another black eye.' She touched his face, a mere brush of her fingertips.

'Skye …'

He didn't finish whatever he was going to say. He was looking into her eyes, and she wasn't sure what he saw in them, just that she felt as if everything was suddenly laid bare.

Finn leaned in and his mouth brushed hers. Tentatively. She could feel him holding back. Was he worried she might push him away? That this wasn't what she wanted, too?

She slid an arm around his neck, pressing in to kiss him properly, and heard him groan. Their lips clung and opened and the kiss grew more passionate. She felt the heat of it right down to her toes. His arms were around her, her breasts hard against his chest, and in a moment they'd have fallen back on the bed and she was pretty sure about what would have happened next.

The knock on the front door was sharp and peremptory.

His mouth slid reluctantly away from hers.

'They're here.'

'Yes.'

Briefly he cupped her face, his hands gentle and warm. And his mouth was gentle, as he brushed a last kiss on hers. A promise.

'Hold that thought,' he said, and then he was on his feet and walking out of her room.

Skye jumped up, following him. As soon as he opened the front door Gary Grey pushed in, crowding him in a way Skye was pretty sure wasn't legal. 'You're coming with us, Finny-boy,' Gary growled into his face. 'Maybe you'll be more cooperative if we lock you up for a bit, eh? Or maybe I could just throw away the key?'

Lois Petersen had followed her partner inside and noticed Skye watching. She gave him a nudge. Gary looked back down the hall to where she was standing and with a snort of disgusted laughter stepped away. Finn glanced back, as well, but she couldn't read his expression.

'It's all right,' he said, but if he was wanting to reassure her she didn't feel very reassured.

'We're taking your boyfriend in for question-ing,' Lois said, as Finn reached for his jacket. 'Don't expect to see him again anytime soon.'

'What about bail?' Skye demanded. 'Shouldn't I be arranging that? Finn?'

Lois gave a laugh and walked ahead, out to the car. It was Gary who answered her, aggression in every line of his body. 'Perverting the course of justice is a serious charge. If we do charge him, sweetheart, he's not likely to get bail.'

'Where are you taking him?' Not Melbourne,

she thought. His answer was a relief.

'Westcott, for now. Why, are you planning on visiting?' His expression changed, and his gaze slid over her body-hugging shirt and jeans. 'Can I watch?'

For a moment Skye felt dizzy and frightened. And then she felt angry. But before she could answer Finn spoke up. 'Ring Alison and she'll help you get home. Sorry we've had to cut your visit short.'

Home? So he was telling her to go home? Or was that for Gary's benefit?

Skye looked him in the eye. 'Sooner I'm out of here the better.'

He looked a bit shocked, although her answer seemed to amuse Gary. 'Fair enough, Red,' Finn said, and now she knew he was acting. He never called her 'Red'.

'She doesn't like you anymore, Finny,' she heard Gary say as he took hold of his arm and marched him outside to the car. 'You'd better get your act together, mate. You already lost your wife. Tell me what I want to know and I might give you some pointers, yeah?' His voice faded as the engine fired up.

Skye stood there long after the vehicle had disappeared into the distance, until she eventually became aware of Lightning whining and barking from the sitting room. The door was shut—Finn must have locked her in—and when Skye went to let her out the greyhound ran to the front door, claws scrabbling on the polished wood.

Skye began to soothe her, but her thoughts were

already running ahead. Normally she thought of herself as a calm, controlled sort of person, someone who could handle difficult situations. You had to be like that when you photographed big events like weddings, because there was always a certain amount of tension. Sometimes things could go very, very wrong, and while those all around you went into meltdown, you needed to be a sea of tranquillity.

Her sea at the moment was anything but tranquil.

She was angry and upset, so much so that she was trembling with it. Her heart was breaking with it. Because a moment ago Finn had been kissing her and she had been kissing him, and now he was being taken away to jail, possibly arrested, and he would more than likely lose his job and his home and everything he loved. Once again Dylan was going to ruin everything for him, and Finn was going to let him.

Well maybe Finn was, but that didn't mean she had to.

Dylan, she told herself with grim determination, didn't get away with stuffing up Finn's life again.

Skye looked down at the dog. 'Tell me I'm doing the right thing, Lightning.'

Lightning gave an anxious thump of her tail.

Finn's weatherproof coat was hanging on the back of the chair and she put it on, folding up the sleeves just as she'd done earlier today, when they set out down the track for Mackenzie Crossing.

She found she was scolding herself. Berating

herself for her own stupidity. Because she should have known she was in trouble. Even before he kissed her, she should have realised she was sliding deeper and deeper into a situation there was no getting out of. But Skye had underestimated her feelings for him. She'd thought what she was experiencing was just an echo of the past.

The truth was far more dangerous, she admitted, as she picked up the keys to his Toyota from the kitchen bench.

She was in love with him.

CHAPTER 21

NEVILLE

Late Thursday 12 January 1939,
Mackenzie Crossing

NEVILLE HAD SPENT the day doing just what Georgie had told him to do—photographing the Crossing and its surroundings. Documenting a town that might soon be gone in a puff of smoke seemed to him an honourable undertaking, despite her scathing comment. He was aware of a burning desire to show the rest of the world these people as they were right now, because everything was changing so quickly. Even somewhere as remote as Mackenzie Crossing would soon be overtaken by the juggernaut of progress. People like this—and Georgie—would be only a faded memory.

One day this place, and others like it, might be on display in his exhibition. He found himself, rather childishly, imagining Georgie being impressed by that.

The exhibition had become a means of keeping his memories at bay during the dark hours. Visualising his photographs hanging on the walls of the State Library of Victoria, or in some swanky private gallery, and trying to decide which ones deserved to be placed more prominently. Although he always came back to his favourites, he knew he still hadn't captured that perfect image.

Hector and Marie hadn't been averse to being immortalised, and posed on their verandah, with their goat tied up to its usual post. Peggy was flattered to be asked, and hurried to change into her best frock, a cream concoction with orange flowers, and flounces around her ample hips and bosom. Her son, the amiable Arnold, held his two mongrel dogs and grinned so hard his cheeks looked fit to burst. Arnold was a grown man and not a lad, at least not physically, but according to Tiddler he had never spoken a word.

Tiddler himself would have joined them but, as he informed Neville in a despondent voice, he wasn't allowed to take time off his lessons.

'Lessons are important,' Neville assured him. 'When you grow up you'll need a job. Do you know what you want to be?'

The boy looked thoughtful. 'Maybe fly an airplane like Kingsford Smith, or play cricket like Don Bradman.'

Neville didn't let himself smile. That was one of the joys of children, he'd found, their utter confidence in how they would shape their future. Memories of Gertie brought an ache to his heart, and he wished he could see her again, even just for a moment. She'd forget him in time, he knew it, and in a way that was a blessing. Inexorably they were moving away from each other, the gap widening, and soon it would be too wide ever to breach.

He was tempted to climb up the surrounding hills and find the cemetery where Georgie had told him Big Jim was buried. It seemed important to document all the folk of the Crossing, alive and dead. However, the heat was too intense and the considerable effort involved decided him against it. Instead, he walked down to Silverfish Creek with one of Arnold's dogs, and waded in the thin trickle of water that remained, photographing the tall trees against the sullen sky.

When evening came, Hector invited him over for a bite to eat, and later they sat smoking when Marie went to bed and tried to sleep. Neville could taste ash on his tongue, and the Crossing was so still, not a sound to be heard, as if it was holding its breath. The air was stiflingly hot, and the smoke coming from the fires was much thicker, with no wind to blow it away.

It was eerie, and by the time he found his bed, very late.

He hadn't seen Georgie for hours, except from a distance, and he half expected her to come and set him to work at the mine again. Was she still angry with him? When she didn't seek him out, he lay awake and pondered the enigma that was Georgina Mackenzie. There were questions to be asked and he wished he was the sort of man who could simply knock on her door and demand entry. He wasn't a coward, he knew that, not physically anyway, but he understood his limitations. He'd looked for happiness once and failed, and he wasn't at all sure he was capable of doing so again.

Neville must have slept, because when he opened his eyes a few hours later she was there, lying beside him on his blanket. He sat up, aware of an overwhelming sense of relief.

'I hope you don't mind. It's too hot to sleep.' She spoke rather hesitantly, turning to meet his eyes.

'Georgie …'

'You never finished telling me about your nightmares,' she went on quickly, before he could remind her of all the reasons she shouldn't be here.

His nightmares were the last thing he wanted to talk about. Well, no, that wasn't quite true. The last thing he wanted to talk about was the photograph he had taken from Miller Brown, and which was still burning a hole in his pocket. The smiling woman who had captivated him from the first and who he believed was Georgie Mackenzie during her years as a teacher at Miss Agostino's School.

'You don't have to tell me,' she said, and only then did he realise how long the silence must have stretched out. 'I understand, Neville, truly I do. The war left scars on you.'

He lay back down and folded his arms under his head. The words came before he had a chance to stop them, and in fact he didn't want to stop them. Georgie made him feel safe, as if he could say anything to her, and that was surely a dangerous state of affairs. Although right now it felt very liberating.

'Sometimes I wonder how different my life might have been without the war. Would I have done the things that were expected of me? Would I have been happy because I was genuinely happy, or because I didn't know any different?'

'So you don't think things happen for a reason?' she murmured, and again he could feel her gaze on his face.

'What reason could there have been for the destruction of a generation of men? I think we do the best we can in the circumstances. We make our choices and then we have to abide by them. There's no going back.'

'No, there's no going back.'

'Georgie …'

'I didn't plan to come here tonight,' she said quickly, her husky voice breathless. 'I just … couldn't stay away. Do you want me to go?'

Neville turned his head and saw that she was very close. 'I don't want you to go,' he admitted. 'Of course I don't. I think you are the most wonderful girl I've ever met, Georgina.'

She laughed quietly. 'But?' she finished for him.

'I have a wife and child in Adelaide,' he explained a little stiffly. 'I left because I wasn't what she, what Mary, wanted. I tried, but I knew I could never be that man. I disappointed her. I'm better off on my own—I understand that now. It's not that I don't want you … admire you …'

'So you're telling me that you're rejecting me for my own good?' Georgie asked with a touch of humour, which in the circumstances made him admire her even more. 'I don't know whether to be flattered or insulted.' She sat up and he noticed then that her hair was loose about her shoulders. 'Tell me you didn't leave Mary penniless and friendless.'

'No, of course not,' he said, his voice louder than he'd meant it to be. 'She has the house and the business, and her family and many friends.'

'I'm glad to hear it. I knew you wouldn't do that, Neville. You're not the sort. I've seen a lot of men come through the Crossing and so many of them are poor specimens. I know a few have wives they've left somewhere else, but I'm quite sure that their reasons aren't as noble as yours.'

'Noble?' he repeated, sitting up, too, so that they were face to face. He didn't know whether to laugh at her or shake her. 'I assure you there's nothing noble about me.'

She kissed him, a soft pressure of her lips to his. 'Prove it, then,' she whispered. 'Take advantage of me. Please.'

Neville hovered on the brink. Her kisses were like butterfly wings across his cheek and his jawline, and then back to his mouth. He heard himself groan, drowning in the sweet taste of her. Her hair made a cave when she pushed him back onto the blanket and then leaned over him, and he found himself reaching up to hold her, to pull her closer.

He knew now he was very far from noble,

because he couldn't stop. He didn't want to. And if he'd ever thought to turn Georgie into some sort of wronged Madonna, then her earthy laugh and murmurs of unreserved pleasure put paid to that. She was a flesh-and-blood woman, and for this one night she was his.

CHAPTER 22

SKYE

Early morning, Tuesday 10 June 1997

SKYE PAUSED AT the entrance to Desperation Track and let the motor idle. The snow was falling steadily, but so far the wipers were managing to keep it at bay. Luckily she hadn't had to fit the chains. Finn had put them on yesterday. Sometimes when the weather turned bad, the roads were so rough and dangerous that chains were a necessity.

She drove slowly at first, getting used to handling the Toyota, and by the time she'd left Elysian behind she felt she was in control.

Lightning had to stay at home. Skye would have loved the company, but remembering the savage dog at Dylan's gate she thought it was probably safer for them both.

How was she going to get past that brute?

One step at a time, she told herself. First she had to find her way to Dylan's hideout without getting lost or driving off the side of the mountain.

Skye squinted down at Finn's map on the seat beside her. It had seemed reasonably clear when he drew it, and she'd thought she'd remember some of their journey from yesterday morning, but now, everything looked different at night in the snow. To her dismay, she couldn't recognise any landmarks, and in some parts the acacia trees were so dense they gave her the uncomfortable sensation of being in a tunnel.

She slowed down to a crawl, looking for a turn Finn had marked. No need to worry about other traffic—there was none. Empty darkness greeted her every way she looked. Without street lights, and the stars obscured by cloud, she could have been anywhere. The headlights showed her what lay ahead, but even so she found herself leaning forward, staring unblinking.

There it was.

Cautiously she began to turn, but she'd miscalculated and had to reverse to try again. For a moment the wheels seemed to stick and she felt a jolt of panic, but then they freed themselves and she was around.

A deer ran across in front of her and she braked. Hands clenched on the wheel, heart pounding, she reminded herself she couldn't have hit the animal if she'd tried, but it didn't help. Slowly she started off again. According to the map there should be another turn up here. She distinctly remembered Finn having to twist the wheel hard, to avoid a branch that had fallen and been partially dragged off the track to the side.

She checked Finn's directions again. Had she missed it because of her fright with the deer? Maybe she should go back? Skye contemplated the situation, telling herself not to panic. Going forward seemed the more sensible course of action, and then if she didn't find the turn after five, ten minutes, well then she'd go back.

It was a plan. Skye set off again, and was relieved when almost immediately she came upon the turn she remembered. Again it did require some effort to get around, but she made it this time without reversing, and without a scratch on Finn's Toyota. The ground wasn't as firm here, and a couple of times the car dipped, but she kept going, worried that if she stopped she might be here until morning.

Best not to think of that.

The four-wheel drive bumped and edged sideways, but she caught it, steering it carefully back into the middle of the trail. A flicker of light drew her attention and she realised the cottage must be in there, shielded by the bush. By that time she was already past it.

'Crap.' She stopped too suddenly, and the right-side wheels slid into a culvert. Once more her heart began to pound. 'Come on, come on,' she told herself, 'get a grip.' On the second attempt she was able to extract herself, and slowly back up.

This section was even tighter and more churned up than she remembered—how on earth did Dylan get his motorbike in here? A few metres more, creeping along at a snail's pace, and she'd reached her destination.

Skye turned off the engine.

The light from the building was still faint. Was the dog out? Surely Dylan would have it inside where it was warm? Then again what did she know? He might care less about its comfort than the need to be warned if anyone approached.

Skye felt a hard lump of resentment in the pit of her stomach. She didn't want to be here. She didn't want to talk to Dylan as if nothing had happened all those years ago, and he wasn't causing trouble for his brother. Again. If Finn thought she was going to smile pleasantly and pretend it was all rosy ...

She took a deep breath.

Finn had asked her to come. It was as simple, and as complicated, as that. When he'd kissed her she could no longer pretend that nothing was happening between them. The past played a part, of course it did, but what she was feeling now was new and raw and urgent. It left her breathless, and she was still trying to work out whether this was love, real true love, or make-believe.

Even so, running through the tangled skein of her emotions, like a dark thread, was a slow-burning anger, the long-buried need to tell Dylan exactly what she thought of him for what he had done to them that night in the summer of 1978.

It was time.

Skye straightened her jacket, pulled down her knitted hat and opened the door.

The cold hit her like a slap. And it was so still. Not a sound to be heard. The snow was wet and mushy underfoot as she made her way to the gate.

Now she was closer to the cottage, Skye could see that the light came from a small window at the side of the dwelling, but the rest of the place was in darkness. The gate was closed and there was no sign of the dog. She was tempted to stand and shout until he came out, but if there was anyone about and they came to investigate … She told herself that, as little as she cared for Dylan's wellbeing, having him discovered might rebound on Finn. Best not to risk it.

Skye took another gasp of air, feeling the cold seep deep into her lungs, and pushed open the gate. It squeaked and she paused, listening, but there was nothing. She may as well have been entirely alone in the world.

Her feet crunched on the way up the cleared gravel path. Almost at once the dog began to bark from inside, which at least answered one of her questions. It occurred to her that the gravel was a warning, so that Dylan and his dog knew there were visitors.

Too late to change her mind now, Skye thought, as she climbed the step up onto the rickety wooden verandah. Just as the door opened and the dog shot out, barrelling towards her, all teeth and bad breath.

'Dylan!' It was a scream. She fled, throwing herself against the gate and trying to fumble it open. Her fingers wouldn't work, and she turned, thinking she'd rather face the animal than have it jump on her unseen.

'Mojo! Down! Down, boy!'

It seemed to take forever, but at last the dog stopped and dropped down. Those small black eyes were still fixed on her, just waiting for the word. She didn't move. She couldn't with the gate at her back, and now her legs were trembling and her heart was threatening to jump out of her chest. The dog's breath was a white cloud, and so was hers.

'Here, boy. Come.'

Reluctant to give up its prey, or so it seemed to Skye, the dog got up and slunk back to his master. Dylan put a hand on its head. In the darkness it was impossible for her to read his expression.

'Where's Finn?'

He sounded tense and worried. So he should be, Skye thought, fear giving way to anger. *So he bloody should be* …

She moved away from the gate, wondering if it would be imprinted on the back of her thighs forever more. The dog watched her but remained where it was, presumably under control.

'He asked me to come.'

'He—'

'I'm doing him a favour. All right? I'm here for his sake, not yours.'

Dylan seemed to be considering this as Skye shivered, wrapping her arms around herself. His stance relaxed slightly, but he was still just a shadow against the faint light from the doorway.

'Do you really want to have this conversation out here?' he said. 'Come in and we can talk.'

Skye hesitated. Despite the cold she didn't want to go in there with Dylan. Still, she'd set herself this task, and all the way here she'd fed her anger with memories until she felt reckless and bullet-proof. The dog had shaken her a bit, but she was still determined to carry this through.

He'd waited a beat and turned away, vanishing inside. The dog went with him.

Skye followed.

She could see the light was coming from under a door to her left, but the rest of the place was in shadows cast by a glowing fire. Although she couldn't see details, it felt like there was a lot of clutter—boxes piled high. A couple of armchairs were pulled up before the fireplace, and the smell of a meal lingered—maybe some sort of stir-fry with ginger and garlic.

'Come in,' Dylan said. 'You're letting all the heat out.'

That was when Skye realised that she was still hovering on the threshold. She took that final step inside, and he closed the door and threw an impressive-looking bolt across to secure it.

He was standing close to her, so close that she suspected he was trying to intimidate her. Dylan wasn't as tall as Finn, but he was bulkier. He was wearing jeans and a sweater with a reindeer on it, which seemed incongruous for some reason. Then he shuffled past her and over to the chairs, nodding at one of them.

'Sit down.'

Skye had thought to deliver her message, say her piece and go, but Dylan didn't seem to be in any hurry. Besides, she *was* cold—her hands were icy inside her gloves. Reluctantly, she crossed the small space and sat down on the edge of the chair, feeling the old springs sag beneath her. She held out her fingers to the fire, and Dylan knelt to put on another log, stirring up the coals.

Flames flared and she could see him properly at last.

He looked younger than he had in the harsh light of the station, his face less weathered, perhaps less brutal, despite the scars. As if aware of her perusal, he didn't sit down beside her but straightened up, and leaned against the bricked surface of the fireplace. His stare unnerved her, and she assumed he was ticking off the changes in her, too.

'Never thought I'd see you again.' He spoke at last.

'Ditto.'

He gave a snort of laughter. 'So what's this about Finn sending you?' His voice was deeper, with a rasp that made her think he'd smoked a hell of a lot of cigarettes.

'Two detectives from Melbourne have taken him in for questioning.' She watched for his surprise and saw consternation as well. *Good*, she thought. 'If he'd refused to go with them they would've arrested him. They said it was something to do with his time in the Drug Squad five years ago, but Finn told me it was really about you.'

Dylan was silent for so long she had to break the stillness.

'Nothing to say?'

'We both know he won't give me up, Skye.'

And he sat down heavily on the seat beside her, staring into the flames.

'He doesn't deserve this.'

Dylan laughed without humour. ''Course he doesn't. But I don't deserve to risk my life either. I've given them what they wanted over and over again, but they're never satisfied. How do you think it feels to be caught in the middle like that? Looking over your shoulder and wondering who will get to you first? Not a comfortable place to be in, Skye.'

She didn't feel sorry for him. Whatever the situation with Dylan was now, she was pretty sure he'd brought it on himself.

'This is your fault,' she said, and heard the accusation in her voice. 'You sort it out. Finn—'

'He's my brother,' he cut her short, and his glance was full of dislike. 'You don't understand. We always looked out for each other. That's just the way it was in our house. Mum was out of it most of the time and Dad was away driving trucks. Then she brought us down to the Big Smoke and it just got worse. We only had each other.'

'You're right,' she said, 'I don't understand. But right now Finn could lose everything because of you. Isn't it time to repay him for all the help he's given you in the past?'

'Finn owes me more than you'll ever know!' Dylan's raised voice brought the dog from its place near the door. It crept forward, growling softly. Dylan took a breath. 'Sit,' he ordered. 'Sit, boy,' and slowly it retreated again.

Skye, who had felt every muscle in her body tense, tried to relax when all she wanted to do was jump up and run. He frightened her, she admitted it. His unpredictability and sudden rages had always been a problem, a disaster waiting to happen.

Dylan unclenched his hands. She watched him uneasily as he appeared to be silently talking himself down. Maybe, she thought, he'd been on an anger-management course. And maybe he'd read her mind, going by the quirk of a rueful smile on his lips.

'I haven't had a meltdown for a while, Skye, if that's what you're thinking. These days I walk away from trouble.'

Did he want her to congratulate him?

'Like a normal person, you mean?' she said, and watched his smile disappear.

Dylan let his gaze travel over her face, taking his time. He leaned back in his chair, seemingly over his anger. 'What is it to you anyway? What do you care what happens to Finn? You turn up after all these years and suddenly you're the avenging angel?'

'I'm tired of you using him, that's—'

'Finn was crazy about you.'

She felt the jolt, somewhere deep inside, and hoped he hadn't seen how his words affected her. Then she saw that he was smiling again, so yes, he had.

'That was all a long time ago,' she reminded him, trying to be matter-of-fact. 'We were very young.'

'Yeah, it was, and yeah, you were, but that doesn't change the way he felt. It wasn't like a teenage thing. I used to think it was weird, the way you were around each other.' He gave a soft laugh. 'I'd tease him, say I could take you off him if I wanted to. Stir him up about it. I reckon I was jealous. There'd only been us until then, and then there you were. I thought I could show him that you were nothing special.'

'I didn't come here to talk about the past. I came because Finn asked me and—'

'Oh I know why you're here, Skye. Finn is just an excuse. You've been bottling this up for years and now you want to spew it out all over me. Go ahead. Whatever you have to say can't be worse than the things the family of that woman said, when they came to see me in the youth-training centre. I can take it, and if it makes you feel better, then please!'

He opened his arms wide, as if inviting Skye to take a shot at him.

And she realised how much she wanted to do just that. Hit him with her fists until he bled, pummel him until he curled up into a ball and begged her to stop. That night had been like an aching tooth ever since it happened, and although most of the time she could ignore it, pretend it didn't exist, the pain never really went away.

'The doctors I've spoken to suggest I say sorry. That's the big number one. Say sorry and mean it. So let me say it now, Skye. I'm sorry for being the jerk I was to you.'

She stared at him in disbelief. She didn't accept

for a moment that he was sincere. Back then there'd been no counselling for her, no 'get it off your chest'. After a couple of weeks, her parents had stopped talking about it and started acting as if it had never happened. She'd gone along with that, she'd been glad to, but maybe that hadn't helped in the long run. If she'd gone to jail like Dylan she would have received the help of specialist doctors. Wasn't that ironic?

'Your sorry is meaningless,' she said flatly. 'I can't accept it.'

'All right. How about this, then,' he paused a moment, as if he was gathering his thoughts. 'I'm not perfect but neither are you. You shouldn't have walked away from Finn.'

'What? Walked away? Are you kidding? My parents were beside themselves when I came home that night. A few weeks later we moved house. I didn't even know what had happened to you both until I read about it in the newspaper. I wasn't allowed out of the house without Mum or Dad, and even then … My life changed, too, Dylan.'

'Well, poor you.' His expression was steely. 'I've accepted what I did. I'll never forget, but I try. As for Finn … All I'm saying, Skye, is that you could've got in touch if you'd really wanted to.'

This time she shook her head, refusing to answer.

'When I recognised you at the cop shop I couldn't believe my eyes.' Dylan was still talking. 'Never expected to see you again. Finn told me you came to find out what happened to your grandfather. A coincidence.' He laughed, and this time it was more like a real laugh. 'Strange old world, hey?'

Skye sighed, rubbing her hands together. They'd thawed out at last. 'Dylan, what are you going to do about Finn?'

His gaze met hers briefly and then dropped away. 'There's someone I have to call.'

'Someone you have to call? Who?' She stared hard at him, frustration and anger mounting. 'Is that *it*?'

'Back off, Skye. Leave this to the grown-ups.'

'He could go to jail for perverting the course of justice. Lose his job. What would that do to him?' She'd seen how much Finn loved his job, and surely Dylan must also know that.

'There are other jobs,' he said in a dead voice.

Now the anger was bubbling through her every pore. 'You were always selfish,' she began in disgust. 'That night, when you—'

'You don't understand.' He leaned forward, as if he was about to share some important insight with her, but they were interrupted.

'Babe?'

A soft voice came from behind them. Skye hadn't realised that the door—the one with the light shining under it—had opened. A figure stood silhouetted there, a blonde-haired woman, and she was obviously heavily pregnant.

As soon as she spoke Dylan jumped up. 'Sorry, honey,' he said, his voice softening. He went to her, rubbing her back, and there was something very protective in the way he was acting. Skye tried not to stare. 'Did we disturb you?'

'I can't sleep for long, you know that. Too uncomfortable.' Curiously she looked from Skye to Dylan. 'Where's Finn?' she asked.

Dylan gave Skye a look she recognised as a warning, or maybe even a plea. 'He's busy,' he said, silently daring her to contradict him.

'Who's this?' the woman asked. She wasn't all that old, probably in her early to mid-twenties, and there was a gentle reserve in her manner that made her seem younger still.

'This is Skye. She's staying with Finn.'

'Oh.' She gave Skye a tentative smile. 'I'm Ebony,' she explained. 'Dylan's wife.'

Dylan's *wife*? A wife had been mentioned at the station, but she'd thought it was a mistake or maybe some old girlfriend Dylan had staying with him. This girl wasn't at all what she'd imagined. Did she know about his past? But of course she must, if she was hiding out here with him. Skye felt as if her image of Dylan, the Dylan she had known, had shifted out of focus.

Somehow she managed to hold on to her own smile. 'When are you due? Can't be long?'

Ebony grimaced, putting her hand to her belly. 'Two weeks, but I think it's sooner. We had the hospital all booked and everything, and then …' Her gaze went to Dylan. 'Never mind. We'll manage.'

Skye wondered how, and what might happen if something went wrong, but she didn't say it aloud. She was sure both Ebony and Dylan had already gone there.

'Try to get some sleep, babe,' Dylan said gently. 'Skye is going now anyway. She just brought me a message from Finn.'

Ebony nodded. 'Nice to meet you,' she said.

The door closed with a soft click and Dylan took a moment to turn. His face was a study in vulnerability. He looked utterly defenceless.

'Now do you see?' he whispered, coming towards her. 'I want to see my kid grow up. I want to be a good father and husband. That bastard Grey will get me killed, or do the job himself. I just can't go through it. Not anymore.'

And she thought she did understand, she really did, but it still wasn't fair that Finn should be the one to suffer in Dylan's quest for redemption.

'So this call you're going to make. That will sort it out?' she said as quietly as him, but the steel was back in her voice.

'Consider it sorted.'

It was late, and she still had to find her way back to Lightning and her warm bed.

Skye went towards the door, cautiously skirting the dog lying outside Ebony's room.

Dylan unbolted the door but didn't follow her. When she opened the gate she saw his darker shadow standing there, watching her. She should have known he'd have to have the last word. Maybe it made him feel better.

'You staying in Elysian, Skye?' he called out to her. 'Or you running away again?'

CHAPTER 23

DYLAN, FINN AND SKYE

December 1978,
the Bay, Melbourne

DYLAN AND FINN were fighting.

They were rolling over and over, fists swinging, grunting and gasping, more like animals than the boys she thought she knew. She didn't know how to stop them. The violence and rage seemed to have blown up out of nowhere.

She turned, frantic, looking down the beach at the noisy party around the campfire. Why didn't they see something was wrong? Why didn't they come and help?

Dylan rolled over and sat astride his brother and started hitting him again.

'Stop it!' Skye screamed. 'Stop it!'

His fist struck Finn with a slapping noise that sounded sickening. Skye was crying, tears wet on her cheeks. She launched herself at him, pulling at his clothes, his shoulders, struggling to tug him off.

'Go play with your dolls, little girl,' he panted, giving her a push that nearly sent her sprawling.

She came back at him, wrapping her arms around his head, blinding him, dragging him backwards. His arms were flailing, and then his hand caught in her hair. She felt the burning pain as he wrenched, taking some of it out by the roots. She screamed again but she didn't let him go.

'Get off him!' Her throat was raw.

Finn seemed to regain his senses and began to heave around underneath his brother, finally dislodging him. Dylan swore and tumbled backwards onto the ground. His chest and shoulders started to shake and Skye thought he was crying. Stupidly she even thought he was going to say he was sorry, but the next moment she realised he was laughing. He lifted his head and looked up at her, and began howling like a dog.

Finn had rolled over and crawled a few feet away, stopping to cough and spit out blood. Skye followed, kneeling down beside him. She was touching his shoulder, his back, his hair, as if in that way she could heal him. Her hands were shaking, her heart thumping, and she felt completely out of her depth. Violence was not something she had ever seen firsthand before, and certainly not between people who were her friends.

'I'm all right,' Finn was mumbling. 'I'm not hurt.'

'Not hurt?' Skye stared in disbelief at the gush of blood from his nose and the ooze from his mouth. 'How can you say that? You need to go to hospital.'

'Aw, it was just playing.' Dylan was back on his feet, standing opposite her and Finn. He was swaying slightly, his eyes wild with excitement. As if he was enjoying himself. As if a spark had been lit inside him and was burning bright.

'Finn?' Skye held his arm as he struggled to his feet. He didn't seem very steady, so she put an arm around his waist and helped him make his way back to the water, while Dylan trailed behind. Finn dropped heavily to his knees in the shallows and began to splash water onto his face, spitting out blood at the same time.

'What is wrong with you?' Skye asked in a shaky voice, glaring at Dylan. 'He's hurt.' Her head was throbbing, and when she reached up she felt a sticky patch on her scalp. 'So am I.'

Dylan gave an exaggerated sigh. 'Let me see,' he said, but when he took a step towards her she quickly backed away, stumbling into Finn and nearly falling over him.

'Hey,' he grumbled, wiping his hands over his face and squinting up at his brother. His dark hair was sticking up and his shirt was plastered against his skin with a combination of salt water and blood.

Dylan frowned at them as if they were being unreasonable. 'I only want to look,' he told Skye, again reaching out towards her. 'Kiss it better, maybe?'

'You've done enough,' she said and slapped his hand away.

The sound of the contact was suddenly very

loud. Finn struggled back onto his feet. 'Come on,' he mumbled, as if his mouth was hurting, 'let's go and get some fish and chips.'

It was a bizarre thing to say, especially when Skye knew that eating must be the last thing he felt like doing, but then she realised that this was for Dylan's benefit. Finn wanted to give his brother's thoughts another direction, calm him down. Why was he always doing that? It made no sense, not after what had just happened.

She'd had enough.

'I want to go home,' she said, and there was a whine in her voice she didn't like but she couldn't help. She was tired and frightened and any desire to spend time on the beach with Finn had long since passed.

Dylan gave another one of his dramatic sighs. 'Okay,' he said, and slung an arm around her shoulders. Skye stiffened. Finn moved closer to her side. She knew he was watching her, silently pleading with her to pretend everything was all right, to join him in his efforts to placate Dylan. But she wasn't having it.

'Leave me alone!'

She was panting, staring at him, hating him. Instead of yelling back at her or trying to grab her again, Dylan just gave a nasty laugh.

'I get it,' he mocked. He pointed at Finn and then at her, and began to sing the song from Grease. 'You're the one that I want …'

'Shut up,' Finn muttered. 'Do you want fish and chips or not?'

Dylan shrugged, dancing around them as if

he hadn't just been in a fight and was probably hurting—although evidently not as much as Finn was, Skye thought, eyeing him uneasily. If this was a normal situation she'd take Finn home and ring the hospital, but the Faradays were as far from normal as you could get. If she'd suspected it before, she knew it now for certain.

Slowly they walked up from the water and along the beach. Finn refused her help—'I'm all right, Skye, just leave it'—but she stuck close to his side, worried he was going to fall over. The air was so warm she felt her hair drying already, curling around her shoulders, although it still hurt where Dylan had yanked some out.

As they reached the car park and the security lights, she managed to get a good look at Finn; apart from a swollen look to his mouth and nose she couldn't judge how much damage his brother had done. Tomorrow might be a different story, when the bruises would be there for all the world to see.

The car was where they'd left it, skewed across three of the painted lines. She didn't remember Dylan doing that. Maybe she hadn't been very sober after all, because their journey here was a bit hazy, but she'd certainly sobered up now. Everything had a horrifying clarity to it.

Dylan opened the rear door and held it wide. Finn went to get in but Dylan lifted a hand to stop him, shaking his head. 'Uh-uh, ladies first,' he said with a stupid smile. 'In you get, Skye.'

She thought about saying no. She should have said no. Except she was tired and she wanted to go home, and she told herself it was all right. She told herself Dylan was back to normal again, or as normal as he ever was, and soon she'd be able to close her bedroom door and put this night behind her.

So she slid in, expecting Finn to follow her, but Dylan had slammed the door. The next moment Finn was on the ground and Dylan was in the driver's seat, and they were moving.

Skye tried to open the door, and she could hear herself yelling and screaming, but Dylan had locked it somehow and she couldn't get out. She pressed her face to the glass and saw Finn getting to his feet. He was staring at her and there was a look on his face, a mixture of horror and fear, that told her this predicament really was as desperate as she thought. Finn had started to run towards her, but it was too late. She knew he'd never get to the car in time, because Dylan was already accelerating.

A moment later they turned out of the car park, tyres squealing, and headed down the street.

CHAPTER 24

SKYE

Tuesday 10 June 1997

THOUGH IT WAS only eight am, Skye was already up and dressed. There were so many things to think about and she hadn't slept well. As she'd tossed and turned, she'd kept reliving her journey through the dark night, with all of those emotions she'd dragged up from the past churning inside her. Dylan's apology and pop psychology hadn't impressed her, and she'd wanted to hurt him as he'd hurt her. It had been the unexpectedness of meeting Ebony, and seeing him so gentle with her, which had thrown her off kilter. He'd said he wanted to be a good father and husband and, despite her wanting, with every fibre of her being, to call him a liar, Skye had believed him.

And then he'd had to spoil it all as she was leaving.

You staying in Elysian or are you running away again?

She didn't think she'd run away last time. But

maybe Finn didn't see it like that. It seemed ironic that Dylan was giving her a hard time over leaving Finn, considering all the damage he had done to his brother. Who, she asked herself sarcastically, had suddenly made him her conscience?

But the fact was it was a question she needed to seriously consider: whether to go or whether to stay.

For a long time Skye had stared up at the bedroom ceiling as the shadows receded, only there had been no answers there. She tried to tell herself this thing between Finn and Dylan was none of her business. She wasn't here for that, she was here to find her grandfather. And whatever feelings she had for Finn were still in the balance—it was all so new she was afraid to poke at it in case it fell apart.

Her first instinct *was* to run—yes, she admitted that in saying what he did Dylan was right. Because, she had to ask herself, did she really need this sort of complication? Finn and Dylan came as a package after all. And anyway, maybe she'd misread the signals from his side. *Hold that thought* could mean anything, although after the way he'd kissed her, she was pretty sure it meant what she thought it did.

Frustratingly, her thoughts wouldn't stop going around and around in her head, with the consequence that this morning she was tired, worried and stressed.

She'd just made herself a coffee and was about to take a sip, when there was a sharp knock on the window. Startled, she looked up, thinking, just for a moment, it might be Finn.

The depth of her disappointment at the sight of Alison's face, neatly framed by her brightly knitted gloves, shocked her.

It was a moment before Skye got up for her visitor.

'Bloody cold out there. I wondered if you were ever going to let me in.' Alison seemed to take in Skye's sleepless night at a glance, as she reached down to pat Lightning. 'I know about Finn,' she said bluntly.

'Oh,' seemed the safest response.

The woman was wearing the same patterned hat and gloves as yesterday in a different-coloured wool. Maybe she had a set for every day of the week.

Skye slid the glass door closed against the frozen air. She'd already been out with Lightning and, although the greyhound had enjoyed her run over the snow-covered grass to the creek, they'd both been glad to return to the warm house.

Alison was frowning like a thundercloud. 'They're idiots. As if Finn could do anything wrong! He was cleared last time and he'll be cleared this time. I reckon someone's got it in for him. I know he's stepped on a few toes over the years—he doesn't tolerate fools.'

Skye considered her reply. Obviously Finn had been true to his word and hadn't told Alison what was going on, just as he hadn't told Taylor. It wasn't up to her to enlighten them and she certainly wasn't going to breach Finn's confidence.

'It was a bit of a shock,' she admitted. 'Do you

know when they're going to let him go?'

'No,' Alison answered with a frown. 'Our friendly detectives aren't sharing anything.'

Alison sat herself down as Skye found another coffee mug. 'When he rang me this morning, I told him he needed a legal representative or at least someone from the union, but he said he was okay for now.'

'He rang you?'

Skye tried not to make it sound like an accusation.

Alison grinned. 'He wanted to know how we were managing without him.'

'And how are you managing?'

'Doug's okay, but I think his mind is elsewhere.' She rolled her eyes. 'He's still on his honeymoon … well, they never had one, so I suppose that's it.'

Skye smiled despite herself. 'And Taylor?'

'That boy's pure gold.'

Alison watched as Skye spooned in the instant granules and then poured in the hot water. Skye brought the cups over and Alison added her own milk and sugar. Finn had stocked up the fridge and cupboards for her stay, but she needed to replenish some of the foodstuffs. She couldn't swan off home to Carlton and leave him with nothing in the house.

If she did go home, that was.

Wearily, she ran a hand through her curls, pulling them to her nape. And what about Lightning? Who would look after the greyhound if she left?

No, it was pretty obvious she wasn't going anywhere, at least not until Finn was out of jail.

Slowly Alison stirred her coffee. 'Finn said he was planning to take you to Westcott today to see Mum, that right?'

'That's right. I wanted to show her the photograph, the woman, remember? And I was going to ask her if she knew anything about my grandfather.'

Alison took a sip. 'Good brew,' she said appreciatively. Then, 'I'll take you. Taylor can hold the fort and Doug is more than capable when his brain's not below his belt.'

Skye considered whether she should refuse—maybe Alison was needed at the station—but in truth she didn't want to. Finding Neville was important to her—he was the reason she'd come here in the first place and he deserved her full attention. Besides, she hoped that concentrating on him might help her to forget her other worries, for a while at least.

'Are you sure?'

'Yep. Get your stuff. We'll drink this down and then hit the road. I rang yesterday and told Mum you were coming,' she added with a grin, 'and she'll be disappointed if you don't show up.'

Lightning followed them to the door with such a hopeful expression that neither of them could say no. The greyhound was missing her master and had been sticking close to Skye, refusing to let her out of her sight. An awkward situation when she was trying to take a shower, with the dog outside the door whining and scrabbling at the door with her claws.

Alison arranged Lightning's blanket on the

back seat of her station wagon while Skye collected her camera, and soon they were on their way.

Once they'd left Elysian behind, the sun came out. The snow had stopped falling sometime early this morning, and although it was very cold, the brilliance of the day seemed to make up for it.

Amazing, Skye thought, how sunshine cheered one up.

Westcott was north of Elysian, and the road seemed to alternate between stretches of bitumen and areas of unsealed gravel. Despite that, Alison said it was well maintained and should be okay, but it was a different matter in the dead of winter, when the snow was heavy. If the snow plough couldn't get out to clear it, then sometimes the road had to be closed.

'You've got no idea how people take risks up here. Not the locals, usually they know better. The number of times Finn's had to go out on a night you wouldn't send a dog into, just to find someone who's got themselves lost or hurt. And usually it's because they've thought they didn't need to pay attention to the weather warnings. Some people just think they're invincible.'

Skye was secretly glad the other woman didn't know about her adventure last night, although surely if Finn had thought she was incapable of making the trip he wouldn't have asked. He had confidence in her, he trusted her, and actually now she thought about it, that was a nice feeling.

She listened with half an ear as Alison told her a couple of terrifying stories, but she was more interested in the scenery. The mountains looked pristine in this light, their peaks etched against the blue sky, rolling away endlessly into the distance. The snow was already beginning to melt closer to the road, where views of rugged hilltops and bush-covered slopes and valleys were constantly catching her eye. Black cockatoos flew up in a cloud and Skye reached for her camera.

But a sideways glance at Alison gave her second thoughts. Alison wasn't really the sort of person you could ask to stop the car so that you could snap away. Finn she might have been able to persuade, Alison on the other hand, was focused on the task ahead—and she took the corners even faster than Finn.

'Have you always lived here?' she asked, to break the silence.

'Not here but in the mountains, yeah, although I spent some time away when I was younger,' Alison answered easily. 'It can be a bit like living in a fish bowl. Same faces, some conversations. After a while you long for a change.'

Skye could just imagine how in a place like Elysian everybody would know everybody else's business. 'And yet you came back?'

'I missed it.' Alison shook her head in disgust at herself. 'I had a good job, too! But, I don't know, I just felt so … anonymous. One day I got up and I just knew I couldn't stay away any longer. Homesick like you wouldn't believe. A friend of a friend said there was a job at the Elysian pub, so I ended up making beds and cooking breakfast for the tourists. Then the police station had its big refurbishment, and they were looking for someone to answer phones and wash dishes. I applied. I figured I had experience in the latter, anyway. And surprise, surprise, I got the job! I've been there ever since.'

'So that was before Finn arrived?'

'Yeah, I've seen off two of his predecessors, and good riddance. Finn's the best of them by far.'

'You're not biased, are you?'

Alison gave her a little smile. 'A bit, maybe. But seriously, this place doesn't know how lucky it is to have him, and when he goes … And it might be sooner than we think, if those two fools from Melbourne mess up his career for him.'

They wound down into a valley and through another small settlement, this time only a couple of houses, and a parking area with a toilet and a picnic bench, before climbing again.

Skye turned to stare at the buildings, barely clinging to the hillside, and hoped she'd be able to get Alison to stop on the way back. It seemed a shame to miss out on some great shots for her exhibition.

Surprised, she realised she was beginning to think about her dream as if it was a reality. Instead of a tribute to her grandfather, it was now *her* exhibition, and it was no longer *if* but *when*.

'You all right?' Alison had noticed her restlessness. 'These roads can make some people motion sick.'

Skye smiled. 'No, I'm fine. I never get motion sick—land, air or sea. I have a cast-iron stomach. I should've been an astronaut.'

'Is it too late?' Alison asked with a laugh.

'I think it might be.'

'Pity,' Alison said dryly. 'Finn never gets sick either. Maybe you and he could orbit the moon together.'

Skye wasn't sure how to answer that, so it was just as well that they'd reached the outskirts of Westcott.

Westcott, according to Alison, was the administration town for the area that encompassed Elysian. Set in the foothills, it consisted of a number of substantial, Victorian-era buildings and busy shops, as well as a couple of beautiful old pubs and modern cafes. Alison gave her a quick guided tour from the car.

Skye half expected her to point out the jail. The thought that Finn was close and yet unreachable was unexpectedly painful. But she reminded herself that there was nothing more she could do for him. Whatever was happening between him and Dylan would have to play itself out in its own time.

The nursing home was on the far side of the town. Over this way everything looked very new, including the home, and there were no views of the mountains. Skye wondered if Mrs Appleby, like her daughter, grew homesick.

Once inside, they made their way to a large common room, where a cluster of grey heads sat around a table, taking part in a craft session. A chirpy woman held up the object they were supposed to be copying—brightly coloured buttons had been glued onto a picture of a green shrub, giving the impression of flowers.

'Mum?' Alison mouthed, and was pointed through a doorway. She gave a wave of thanks as she led Skye into a sunroom. Visible through the glass door was a brick patio, where a few vegetables and flowers were being grown in tubs and wooden planters. Everything looked a bit cold today, but Skye imagined that in the spring it would be a pretty sight.

There was only one occupant in the room, a small, fragile woman rugged up in a woollen skirt, thick stockings and fur-lined slippers, with a multicoloured cardigan completing her ensemble. She was seated in a wheelchair, and staring out at the view with a forlorn expression.

'They won't let me out,' she complained, as Alison bent over to kiss her cheek. 'They're in there making those silly cards, and I want to plant some winter lettuce, but they won't let me out.'

'Mum it's too cold! There'll be better days for planting lettuce.'

Mrs Appleby didn't seem to find any comfort in this observation.

'Anyway, you haven't got time for gardening now,' Alison added brightly. 'I've brought your visitor.'

'Visitor?' Mrs Appleby had blue eyes, unlike her daughter's brown, but they were full of the same bright curiosity.

'Remember? I told you about it on the phone? This is Skye Stewart. She's looking for her grandfather. He was at the Crossing and took a photo.'

'Why would anyone want to take a photo of

the Crossing?' Mrs Appleby muttered, gaze still firmly fixed on the patio.

Alison gave Skye a frustrated grimace. 'When she gets something into her head it's hard to shift,' she murmured. 'Perhaps if you showed her …?'

Skye removed the folded photocopy from her bag. It was starting to look a bit tatty and she smoothed it out, wishing again that she had the original.

'Mrs Appleby?' Drawing up a chair beside the older woman, she sat down and placed the page on the tray attached to her wheelchair. 'This is a photograph my grandfather took. His name was Neville Darling. He was at Mackenzie, uh, at the Crossing, in January nineteen thirty-nine.'

Mrs Appleby needed a moment to adjust her thinking, and shift her gaze from the longed-for garden and down to the image before her.

Frowning, she slipped on the glasses hanging from a chain around her neck, and reached out shaky hands to lift the paper nearer to her eyes. Skye waited, hoping, while simultaneously not allowing herself to expect too much. Better that way, she thought, then she wouldn't be disappointed.

'Oh!' The woman's exclamation made them both jump.

'Mum?' Alison put a hand on her mother's shoulder. 'Are you all right? What is it? Do you know who this is?'

'Yes, I do. That's Georgie!' her mother declared, beaming at them. 'Georgie Mackenzie!'

'Nowhere like the Crossing,' Mrs Appleby was saying, and nodded her head so vigorously her glasses jumped up and down.

'Oh, it's the Seventh Wonder of the World *now*, is it?' Alison drawled, but she was smiling.

'We went over there yesterday,' Skye said. 'Or at least where it used to be. I found some bricks that came from the chimney of the hostelry, before it was ...' Her words drifted off when it occurred to her she might upset the old woman.

Mrs Appleby had no such qualms.

'Before it was burned to a crisp on Black Friday,' she said matter-of-factly, her pale eyes a little more watery than they had been. 'I wasn't there when the fire came through. My parents had already taken us to Elysian. My mother was always very nervous about bushfires. She'd be out, sniffing the air, and at the first hint of smoke she'd want to go. A week before it happened she told my father we were leaving, and she always wore the pants.'

'Strong women in our family,' Alison supplied with a grin.

'But you *do* know a bit about that day, don't you, Mrs Appleby?' asked Skye, trying not to sound as desperate as she felt.

'I do, dear. There was a water tunnel in Elysian and we sheltered inside it with people from all over the place—some who'd been evacuated and others who'd just come because they didn't feel safe where they were. More chance of surviving in a place like Elysian than the Crossing. Everyone was frightened. I was a child, but I remember it very well. The smoke got into my lungs and I had a cough for months afterwards.'

Skye found it difficult to imagine such an event in a young girl's life. Trauma like that could cause all sorts of mental and physical problems, and yet Mrs Appleby didn't seem to bear any scars. She seemed bright and vivacious, and was certainly having no trouble speaking about her experiences on that day.

'What about Georgie?' Skye tapped her fingertip on Georgie Mackenzie's enigmatic face. 'Was she in Elysian with you? I know this photo was taken at the Crossing, but that doesn't mean she didn't leave shortly afterwards. If your mother knew the fire was coming then surely so did Georgie?'

Mrs Appleby thought about it for a moment. 'No, I don't think she was in Elysian. You see, dear, some of them waited too long and then they couldn't get out. The fire was very fast, very fierce. People just had to take shelter wherever they could and hope that somehow they'd survive.'

'*I* don't remember her,' Alison said, frowning at the image.

'My family shifted away from the mountains after Black Friday.' Mrs Appleby smiled at her daughter. 'My mother wouldn't stay a moment longer than we had to, so we moved in with relatives. I didn't think I'd come back here, ever, but then I met your father. He was a mountain boy and he wanted to come home, so we did. He had a job as a timber-mill foreman near Marysville. His father, Phillip, had been one before him, and …' For a moment she looked sad, and then she shook her head. 'Well, you don't want to hear about that. We felt at home so we decided to stay.'

'And you don't remember seeing Georgie Mackenzie anywhere later on?' Skye asked again, knowing she was clutching at straws.

'No. And it wouldn't have occurred to me to ask about her. You just didn't. Things were different then. I knew people had died, but my parents never mentioned it. Some things weren't talked about in front of the children. Not like they are today, dear.'

'So you have no idea what happened at the Crossing on Black Friday?'

'Poor souls. That's what my mother used to say whenever the subject of Black Friday came up. "Poor souls, best not to dwell," and then she'd close her mouth like a trap and refuse to say another word.'

Skye allowed the silence to lengthen. Another disappointment, although she tried not to see it that way. Every little piece of information helped to fill out the picture, she told herself. And at least now she had a name, that was a big step forward.

'I haven't been much help, have I?' Mrs Appleby said at last.

Embarrassed she was so easily read, Skye began to protest. 'Of course you have. Thank you so much.'

'Yes, you have,' Alison added her voice. 'Skye can put a name to the face now. Georgie Mackenzie. Did she always dress like that?' she added, with an expressive sideways look at Skye.

Her mother chuckled. 'Oh yes. She was a character, was Georgie. You've made me wish I knew now what happened to her. Although I suppose I had my own family to think of then. I took my mother's advice and didn't dwell on it.'

'I can understand that,' Skye assured her, but she couldn't help wishing she had.

'And there have been other bushfires since then. We've had some bad ones. You worry, of course you do, but,' she shrugged her shoulders, 'you get on with it.'

They stayed for morning refreshments. The tea was strong and hot, and the muffins, according to Alison's mother, were homemade. The conversation turned to lighter matters. As they left Mrs Appleby was once more looking anxiously through the window at the patio and its collection of tubs and planters.

When they got back to the car, they found Lightning patiently waiting on the back seat. Skye let her out for a quick rest stop.

'Rightio,' Alison said.

Skye looked up, surprised by the note of determination in the other woman's voice, and was disconcerted by her direct stare. 'Rightio what?'

'Now we're going to see the Sarge.'

Skye felt her heart begin that strange push and pull that had been happening ever since she had stepped out into the emptiness of Lockington and come face to face with Finn. She knew she was staring back at Alison like a fool but she couldn't seem to help it. 'How? I mean, will they let us in?'

''Course they will.'

Skye didn't know what to say. Did she want to see Finn in those circumstances? The whole thing would feel very uncomfortable.

Alison was watching her curiously. 'Don't you want to see him?'

'Yes. I … It's just … I'm not sure he'll want to see me. It must be awful for him.'

She knew she sounded lame, but she wasn't going to explain her private thoughts and doubts to someone who would be sure to take Finn's side.

'He's tough,' Alison said bracingly. 'Come on, hop in.'

It was clear she would brook no arguments, so Skye did as she was told. On the drive back into the town she saw mature trees lining the green strip in the middle of the main street, and there was a rotunda in a small park that only needed a brass band and an audience in long skirts and top hats to take her back to the last century.

Alison began to give her a history lesson, and she tried to pay attention, grateful for the distraction.

'During the gold rush there was a military gold escort from Elysian to Westcott. Once the gold arrived safely, they'd lock it up in the bank vault until they could get the Cobb and Co coach to transport it to Melbourne. There were plenty of opportunities for bushrangers to hold up the escort and steal some gold for themselves. Dangerous times. Later on, when the gold started to peter out, the military escort was dropped and it was just the lowly Elysian policeman who had to make the trek over the mountains. Him and his packhorses. He needed to keep his wits about him, that's for sure. I think he did get knocked on the head once or twice, but he put up a fight, and not one ounce of gold was ever stolen.'

'You make it sound like the Wild West.'

'Oh, it was. Still is, in a lot of ways. People come up here to hide out, or go a little crazy, and we have to keep them from breaking the law. You need to be a strong person to do that. When the Sarge first arrived he wasn't as sure of himself as he is now, but he's grown into the job. With some help from me, of course.'

Skye smiled, knowing that despite the jokes, Alison clearly thought the world of her boss. And why not! He was a good person—Skye knew he was a good person—it was just that there were an awful lot of questions still to be answered. And baggage. God, there was a lot of that as well. Not to mention their wildly differing lifestyles. So many ifs.

And the biggest 'if' of all was definitely Dylan and the fact that he was still getting Finn to bail him out of trouble after all these years. It made her anxious whenever she thought about it, and it made her back away from any commitment to a workable future.

Westcott police station was an antique. Unlike the modern building in Elysian, this one obviously hadn't undergone refurbishment since the nineteenth century. Built of red brick with an arched doorway and slate roof, it stood solid against changing times.

Inside the air smelled stale, and there were the usual notices pinned up on the wall. A pair of rusty handcuffs was displayed in a glass case, along with a weapon that Skye decided was definitely a relic from a bygone age.

The middle-aged, balding constable on the desk recognised Alison and gave her a look that seemed to suggest he knew exactly why she was here.

'I told you I wasn't sure you could see him,' he said. 'We have our orders, Alison.'

'You know those orders are rubbish. Come on, Leonard, just let me have a word with him,' she reasoned. 'Something's come up and everyone else is clueless. You know what a control freak the Sarge is. We'll all get it if this isn't handled just right.'

Leonard hesitated, almost convinced, and then his eyes flicked to Skye. 'What about her?' he said.

'This is his cousin,' Alison lied with breathtaking ease. 'Mother's side.'

Leonard didn't believe it, but evidently he didn't require proof, just a credible answer. He took a bunch of keys that looked as old as the building from a drawer under the desk, and led the way through a door and down some worn stone stairs.

'Ned Kelly spent some time in here in eighteen seventy for horse stealing,' he said, giving Skye another glance. 'In the very same cell as your cousin, so he's in good company.'

Alison snorted a derisive laugh. 'I'm not sure that's very comforting, Leonard.'

'Well at least we don't hang our prisoners these days, Alison,' was the laconic reply.

Down below was an open area with a table and chair, and three metal doors leading into cells. It did indeed look like something Ned Kelly might have spent some time in. Through the open grille in the first door, they could see Finn, sitting on his mattress, head in his hands as if he was in deep thought. Or perhaps despair.

'I thought he was here voluntarily,' Skye said and heard the anger in her voice. She couldn't seem to help it.

Finn looked up.

Skye's stomach went hollow. She could tell he hadn't slept much by the shadows under his eyes and the line etched deep between his brows. She was having a hard time reading the expression on his face and deciding whether or not he was glad to see her.

By now Finn had risen to his feet and approached the door. 'Alison? Is anything wrong?' he asked. 'Doug?'

Alison snorted. 'He's fine. Lording it over us. But,' and she glanced at Leonard, 'there *is* something we need to ask you. In private. Can you open the door, Constable?'

'I'm not supposed to—'

'He's here voluntarily, isn't he?' Alison repeated Skye's words. 'And he outranks you. Open the door, Leonard. Nothing is going to happen.'

Leonard rolled his eyes, before he unlocked the door and opened it. The cell looked even less inviting up close—it might be historic but that wasn't a recommendation in her opinion. 'You have five minutes so hurry it up. I'm not losing my job over this, Alison Appleby.' And he turned and climbed back up the stairs, his back very straight.

Finn stepped out.

Alison moved closer. 'Do you know when they're going to let you go?' she demanded. 'I mean there are still no charges, are there? They can't hold you, Sarge. This is a complete stuff-up and they must know it. Let me ring the union and—'

'No.' He cut her short.

Alison shook her head. 'I don't understand, Finn. *What* is going on?'

'Look,' he softened his voice, 'trust me, Alison, I know what I'm doing. Everything will be all right.'

'Will it?' she snapped, and looked worried.

Finn's gaze went to Skye, who was standing back, awkwardly waiting. 'Can I have a moment alone?' he said quietly.

Alison looked from one to the other of them and then gave a loud sigh. 'All right. I'll be over there, *trying* not to listen.' She went to the stairs and stood with her back turned ostentatiously to them.

Skye moved in closer. Her legs felt shaky, but she told herself that was because she'd never been in jail before.

'Did you see him?' Finn dropped his voice as low as he could, glancing towards Alison.

'Yes. He knows what's happening. He said he was going to call someone.' An angry note of scepticism had leaked into her voice. 'I don't even know if that's true or if it was just something he said to get me off his back. Finn, give him up, he's not worth it.'

Finn looked down at his boots. He was wearing the same clothes he'd been wearing last night, and he needed a shave. But despite all of that it was as if he was giving off some invisible magnetic force because she was finding it a struggle not to reach out and wrap her arms around him.

'He has Ebony to think about now,' he said, as if that was an explanation. 'She's good for him. Did you meet Ebony?'

'Yes, I met her.' Skye shifted her feet. 'Why is it always about him?'

'Skye—'

'No, Finn, I won't buy into it. You shouldn't have to spend your life protecting your brother. Whatever happened to him, he brought it on himself.'

Maybe she was being one-eyed, but she couldn't seem to help it. Seeing Finn locked up in this antiquated cell was … upsetting.

He shifted his stance, sliding his hands into his pockets. 'Skye, that isn't true. You can't say—'

'I can say it. I am saying it. You can't be his keeper all his life.'

Amusement warmed his eyes.

'You know what I mean,' she retorted. 'He told me he wants to be a good father and a good hus-band, but what about a good brother? He's letting you down. If he doesn't want to help the cops anymore then he has to tell them to their faces.'

'And what do you think will happen to him then?' he asked with a heavy hint of irony. 'You're being naive.'

'I don't know what will happen to him,' she said stubbornly, 'and I don't care. That's for him to sort out.'

'Skye—'

'Would you really lose your job and go to jail for him?' she asked, and heard the ache in her voice. Because if he did this then how could there be anything between them, no matter how much she might want it? She couldn't be with a man who thought his own life was so worthless. And yet she wanted to. She hadn't realised just how much she wanted to until this very moment.

The silence went on for so long Skye thought it might be time for her to go, but then he spoke again and he sounded surprised.

'You're angry,' he said, as if he'd just realised the truth of it.

Exasperated, Skye whispered, 'Yes, I'm angry. Of course I'm angry. I thought … I hoped …' She took a deep breath. 'Look, I know it's your decision, he's your brother, but I can't pretend I'm going to sit back and smile while you ruin your life. If you do get charged and go to prison then …'

'Then?' He was so close now their faces were

nearly touching.

'Then I'll never see you again.'

He searched her eyes. 'Are you giving me an ultimatum, Skye? This is too complex for a single yes or no answer.'

'It always is!'

'Do you think you could trust me?' That intent look, as if he could win her over by the sheer force of his will. 'I'd like to take you into my confidence but it isn't safe. Besides,' and remarkably, in the circumstances, he managed a smile, 'I'm not very good with ultimatums.'

'Finn—'

'Right, time's up!' Leonard shouted from the top of the stairs and they heard him start making his way down.

Skye took a step away, and then another, and, frowning, Finn watched her go.

Alison was back, and gave Finn's arm a pat. 'See you soon, Sarge,' she said, injecting a hefty dose of confidence into her voice.

Then Leonard arrived and ushered them back up the stairs, while behind them they heard the cell door close with a reverberating clang.

Skye felt hollow. *I'm not very good with ultimatums.* What did that mean? But she was pretty sure it meant no. And as for *Do you think you could trust me?* That would require her to put aside all of her prejudices where Dylan was concerned, all of her memories of the past, all of … Well it was an awful lot to ask.

Instead, Skye's inner voice began to inform her that she should have known as soon as she set eyes on Dylan that this was never going to work. Her and Finn. It hadn't worked last time and it wouldn't work this time. Whatever it was the two brothers shared it was exclusive and she wasn't a part of it. So what was the point in wishing for something she was never going to have?

Naturally she was hurt and upset. Good sense had gone out the window, and she'd indulged herself by believing in a future for them. She'd opened up her heart to Finn in a way she hadn't done since, well the last time, and if she was feeling miserable then it was her own dumb fault.

'Stupid, stupid, stupid …'

'Did you say something?' Alison was eyeing her curiously.

'Merely offering myself some advice.'

'Ah-ha.'

Back at the car, Lightning needed another toilet break, and Alison tipped some water into a plastic carton for the dog to drink. The sun wasn't as warm as it looked, but Skye lifted her face and closed her eyes.

'The Sarge has mentioned you,' Alison's voice interrupted her effort to clear her mind of all things Finn.

'I don't want to hear it.' She kept her eyes firmly shut.

'One night we were celebrating an arrest,' Alison began, ignoring her. 'Some loser growing weed in one of the old mining culverts. We'd all had a few too many and the Sarge started telling me about a girl called Skye. That *is* you, isn't it? The redhead who burned herself into his heart.'

Skye's eyes snapped open. 'He didn't say that!'

'Maybe not those exact words, but near enough.'

'It wasn't …' She bit her lip and started again. She was using her haughty voice, as Fraser called it, reserved for clients who were asking her for more than the moon she usually provided. 'You don't know what you're talking about, Alison.'

'Don't I? You need to work out where your loyalties lie, Skye, and if they aren't with Finn then you should go back to wherever it was you came from.'

The advice was blunt and shocking. It rocked Skye, pushing her beyond familiar territory and into somewhere totally foreign and unsafe. Things were no longer neat and tidy, as she liked them. She had a feeling they were about to get very, very *un*tidy.

'I'm not going anywhere,' she heard herself say.

Her inner voice, however, wasn't having it. *Unless Finn gets arrested and you never see him again. Have you forgotten that?*

Alison wasn't privy to her inner voice, and this was obviously the answer she wanted to hear. Her lips had curled into a satisfied smile. 'That's more like it! Now we're clear on that, we just have to work out how to get the Sarge out of that cell before he grows a beard and begins to *look* like Ned Kelly. What do you say, Skye, got any ideas?'

She was fishing and Skye knew it. She used Lightning as a distraction, reaching down to pat the dog, while her fingers received a thorough licking.

It was a temptation to blurt out the truth. She

could lay it all on Alison's shoulders and walk away. That was the sensible thing to do. And yet, Skye found she couldn't break Finn's confidence.

Trust me. It wasn't an easy decision to make, it was complex and testing, and she had to drag herself kicking and screaming all the way to the line, but it looked like she was going to do just that.

'No,' she said to Alison, 'I haven't.'

Alison tipped her head to one side and sighed. 'I don't believe you. You're as bad as him.'

'Believe me, Alison, if I could tell you I would,' and the words were heartfelt.

'Hmm. All right. I'll leave off pestering you for now. Let's go and have some lunch.'

CHAPTER 25

NEVILLE

Eight am, Friday 13 January 1939,
Mackenzie Crossing

HE'D OPENED HIS eyes to the glare of sunlight through a hazy dawn. For a time he lay on his back, smoking, thinking of Georgie, and watching the world wake up to another breathless day. Aesop came to look at him over the fence and then wandered off again to his tree.

After she'd left him he hadn't slept well, drifting in and out of dreams. Most of them seemed to be about Georgie, and that was a big improvement on reliving the horrors of the trenches. All the same he didn't quite trust himself to sleep with her and not wake up screaming. Maybe it showed an inordinate amount of pride, but no matter what she said, Neville didn't want Georgie to think badly of him, he didn't want to see in her eyes the same expression he'd seen in Mary's.

Eventually Tiddler appeared, scampering over to him and flopping down on the ground. 'Georgie says to come in for breakfast,' he said with a glance from under his fringe. 'There's another egg. Her Majesty must like you.'

Suddenly, Neville could smell the food, as if the words had unlocked his olfactory senses.

'Rightio. Come on, then. Ready, set, go!'

The boy giggled as they set off in a race to the pub, but he soon sprinted ahead. 'I win, I win!' he shouted, dancing on the spot, while Neville leaned against the wall, groaning.

'You must both be mad,' Georgie declared, standing with her hands on her hips. She was in her trousers, held up by the tooled leather belt, and button-up shirt, her hair once again in its long plait. He wondered how he could ever have mistaken her for a boy. As he now knew, there were too many curves beneath that loose clothing to make her anything other than a woman, and a beautiful one at that.

'Good morning,' he said politely, while their eyes spoke a more intimate language.

'Good morning,' she murmured in return, a smile playing about her mouth. Had they been alone he might have kissed her.

'It feels hotter than ever,' Neville continued the conversation as he followed her inside.

'As long as the wind doesn't strengthen.' She glanced at Tiddler, worried he might have overheard, but he was engrossed in some game or other with his marbles.

'I thought I might go up to the timber camp today. Phil Appleby invited me to take photographs of the men.'

'I'm sure they'll be happy to pose for you.' She reached for the pan and slid the contents—fried bread and some of Hector's tomatoes—onto their plates. 'Will you make them famous, Pom?' she teased.

'Perhaps not as famous as Phar Lap, but you never know.'

'Ah, so you like a flutter?' Her exotic eyes fixed on him with interest.

'I used to, when I had the money to flutter with.'

'There is that, I suppose.' She lifted the neck of her shirt up and down, trying to create a breeze. 'There's more smoke this morning. I think I might tether Aesop closer.'

After breakfast, he watched her bring the horse from his paddock. When he took out his camera she sighed but graciously consented to him taking some more photographs. He didn't think he'd ever have enough of her.

'Me now, me now!' Tiddler said, jumping up and down.

Georgie laughed, and then her face grew serious. That expression—melancholy and yet passionate—made it clear to him that here was a complex woman to be reckoned with. And in contrast to her obvious strength of character, there was a vulnerability in the curve of her cheek and the way her long dark plait lay across her shoulder.

He remembered last night, with her in his arms, her hair loose around them.

She was looking directly at him and he thought

she was remembering it, too. He knew when he pressed the shutter that this would be the perfect photograph he'd been dreaming of. And it was. The best he'd ever taken.

Afterwards, Neville collected his camera bag, securing the strap over his shoulder, and set off. Georgie was already busy with the day's tasks, as if she'd put what happened between them away for later. Folded it neatly and practically into a chest of drawers. The image made him smile. Tiddler followed him for a few yards, plainly wishing he could come, too, but Georgie called him back and told him he had school work to do.

The school that used to be here at Mackenzie Crossing was long gone now. Neville supposed the nearest was probably in Elysian. Tiddler could have ridden Aesop there, but it seemed Georgie was prepared to teach him herself, and from what he had seen of the boy's mathematical skills she was doing an excellent job.

The bush was still, breathless, and there was little sound apart from the crackle of dried leaves and twigs under his feet. Phil and his men had trodden a path over the hills, from their camp to the hostelry, so there was no chance of getting lost. He could also hear the sound of an axe ringing through the trees above. Neville knew something about the industry, mainly gleaned from conversations during his travels.

By the late 1920s the more accessible timber, those coupes closer to the larger towns and settlements, had been cleared. So the sawmilling businessmen had expanded out into the inaccessible regions, and that had brought with it the problem of how to transport the logs back to civilisation.

He'd seen the rough wooden tramlines running along the tracks and on rickety bridges over creeks and gullies. These were what was used to haul the timber back to the mills. Roads were too expensive to build in such rugged terrain, and the timber-getters had become adept at making do. Up here, above the Crossing, horses were used to drag the sawn logs on trolleys to the tramline junction along the Elysian road, which eventually connected with a tramline to Warburton.

Phil had told him the other night that his mill was a small, portable one, and most of the work on the timber was done firstly by hand. The life these men lived was lonely and hard in the extreme, and he didn't wonder they looked forward to Georgie's smile.

He paused a moment, resting his hand on the straight, smooth trunk of a sapling, new growth where the timber had been harvested before. Looking up into the canopy, he saw that the leaves hung down, trying to conserve moisture in these stifling temperatures. There were no birds, or if there were any, then they were keeping their own counsel.

Over time he'd grown used to the noisy Australian birds. The shrieks and squawks and screams. Even the laughing kookaburra no longer shocked him. Nor the shy and amazing lyrebird, which he'd known to imitate the sound of the very same axe he could hear now.

Neville became aware of the men at the camp before he saw them. Their voices were loud and carefree, apart from the foreman's occasional growl at them to get moving. When Neville appeared along the path, they all looked up, their heat-flushed faces filled with pleasure. Any diversion was a good one on a day like this, he imagined.

'Pom!' Phil came to shake his hand, his own hot and damp. 'You've brought your camera? We're all wearing our finest, as you can see.'

There was general laughter at that. They looked a rough-and-ready lot, but then that was what he wanted. Reality, not the poised pretence of his studio back in Adelaide. 'Want some of our brew, Pom?'

Neville accepted the offer of some strong black tea, and the banter of the men—referring to the liking of Englishmen for their tea—with good grace.

In the end it turned into a quick session. The men stood in a ragged group, the younger ones with new beards, some of the older men with faces so weathered and lined, they might have been composed from the earth itself. One of them, old Patrick, informed Neville proudly that he had been born in the bush and, when the others quizzed him as to whether that had been in a wombat burrow, muttered that they were all silly young buggers. Then they went off to their allotted tasks, and only Phil lingered behind with his cuppa.

'The boss has asked us to stay and finish,' he

explained. 'Then we can load up the logs and run them down to the junction on the Elysian road. They'll be as safe there as anywhere, and we can head into the town. We'll be the last lot to go.' He seemed proud of the fact.

'So the fire is coming?' Neville asked anxiously.

'Probably not. No need to fret, Pom. Just a precaution.'

Neville looked at his tea. 'I wasn't fretting for myself,' he said with quiet dignity. 'I was thinking of Georgie and Tiddler.'

'That Georgie, she's a dark horse,' Phil said, giving Neville a sideways glance. 'What do you make of her, Pom?'

Neville wasn't going to tell Phil what he thought of Georgie Mackenzie. Even if last night hadn't happened, he was the sort of man who respected another's privacy, and it felt wrong to gossip.

However, the need to be polite—the curse of the English—was also part of his nature.

'Is it true her father founded Mackenzie Crossing?' he asked, as a sort of compromise.

'Sure did.' Phil grinned. 'Not that there's much to be proud of in that! Although I believe in the old days, when gold was first discovered around here, it was much bigger than it is today. Hundreds set up camp. Thousands. Big Jim thought he'd hit the bonanza.'

Neville nodded and sipped his tea despite it being too hot for this weather. At least it was wet.

'You know Tiddler's her son, don't you? Even though she pretends he's a cousin, everyone knows.'

Neville said nothing. He'd already worked that out himself, and was about to change the subject when Phil went on.

'Funny thing is, a lad from one of the other coupes dropped in yesterday. He was in Elysian last week and he said there was a chap asking about her.' He looked up, his expression more puzzled than worried. 'A policeman, or so he claimed. He wanted to know where she was living. 'Course no one who knew Georgie would tell him. Even if we didn't all think the world of her, it's none of his business, is it?'

'A policeman?' Neville frowned. It was Miller Brown, it must be.

'So he said. Then on Monday he popped up at another coupe, strolling through the bush as if he was on a picnic, asking questions, nosing around.'

Neville had never imagined Miller Brown might still be looking for Georgie, not in the circumstances, not with the fire so dangerously close. Now he realised he should have. He should have been more alert. 'Did this man give his name?'

'If he did the lad didn't remember it. Thin bloke, face like a fox, he said.'

Retired Detective Inspector Miller Brown, it had to be. Neville felt every muscle in his body tense. It might mean nothing, Brown might finally have left the area by now, but he was fearing the worst.

'Why would a policeman want to find Georgie?' he asked casually, his heart banging as hard as it used to just before a sortie through no-man's-land.

Phil shrugged, scratching his chin. 'Well, Pom, I assume it was Georgie he was looking for. Half-Chinese woman living in the mountains, that was what he said, and Georgie is the only one I can think of who more or less fits the bill. Said he was from Melbourne, so maybe it was to do with her time there. You know she was a teacher in a posh school? Big Jim wanted her to get away from the Crossing, he said she deserved better. She was bright, too. I heard she was gone for a few years, and then one day she turned up with the boy. He was little more than a baby, but she said he was a foundling. The cousin story came later.'

'Her father …?' he began tentatively, ashamed he was indulging in this vice he loathed, but suddenly it seemed more important than upholding his own ethical boundaries. 'He let her stay?'

'Didn't throw her out, do you mean?' Phil chuckled. 'Nah. Took her back with open arms. A year later he was dead from lockjaw. Cut his foot in the stable. Georgie assumed responsibility in his place. There was talk of the Crossing emptying out, as if Big Jim was all that was keeping it together. Georgie started wearing his clothes, ordering people about, as if she was trying to be him. I'm used to it now, but it was bloody strange at the time, so they say. Now there's talk of our sawmills closing—the money's not there anymore—but I know she'll fight that tooth and nail. With the Union Jack mine gone, we're the only thing keeping the Crossing alive.'

Neville thought about that. It made sense. Georgie taking on her beloved father's persona and her ownership of the Crossing. He'd been telling himself that she wasn't the type of woman who would commit a murder, but he knew now that he was wrong. Because this was exactly the type of woman who would do anything—even murder—to protect her own.

'She didn't want to go back to teaching?' he asked at last, forcing some more tea down through his constricted throat.

'Couldn't, not with Tiddler.'

'She could've given him away, handed him off to someone else. There are plenty who do,' Neville said.

Phil shook his head. 'I don't think she'd do that, not Georgie. She loves that boy fiercely. And she thinks that if she goes then the Crossing will disappear, and she's probably right. She's the last of them. If you don't count her boy.'

'Aesop … the horse?' Neville asked randomly, scrambling to make sense of it all.

'Big Jim named the poor bugger.' Phil laughed. 'Used to be Socks, I recall, when we had him. She bought him back, but he just stands in that paddock and eats his head off. Still, she won't part with him.'

'Why do you think that is?'

Phil gave him a look. 'He was her father's horse. Sold off after he died. Georgie wanted him back again, I reckon. He was part of her family, and she's ferociously protective of her family.'

It *was* Georgie the ex-inspector was hunting.

Neville refused to believe that it was as cut and dried as the man had tried to make out during their chat at the Elysian Hotel, but he had an awful sense of time running out for the woman who had held him spellbound from the moment he'd laid eyes on her.

'The scar on her throat.' Phil casually tossed the dregs from his mug into the fire. 'You've seen it, right?'

Of course he had. Last night he had kissed her there more than once, but he hadn't asked her about it. Not then. He hadn't wanted to spoil the moment and he'd told himself she would tell him herself when she was ready.

'That happened in Melbourne,' Phil continued. 'She never talks about it. I've tried to draw her out—just being kind, you know—but nah, noth–ing.'

'I expect she feels ashamed,' Neville replied quietly, musing aloud. 'Women sometimes do if a man has hurt them. They believe it's their fault.'

Phil looked surprised. 'I hadn't thought of it like that. Thanks, Pom.' He clapped him on the back. 'I'll have a bit of a word to her next time I'm down there. She's all right, is Georgie. I'm a widower and I wouldn't mind, well …'

Neville choked and Phil clapped him again, nearly breaking his ribs, and then stood up.

'Better get on with things if we're to finish today,' he said. 'Those buggers will be waiting for me to tell them what to do.' He hesitated a moment. 'Tell Georgie that bloke is asking after her, will you? Just in case she needs to lay low for a bit.'

Neville realised then that even if Phil didn't know the whole story, and perhaps didn't want to, he knew enough. He and his 'lads' were protecting Georgie with their silence, but they could only do so much.

'I will.'

Phil nodded and kicked out the fire, covering it with earth, and stamped on the coals to make sure they were out properly. 'Bye, Pom,' he called out, as he walked away. 'Don't forget to send me a copy of that photo.'

Neville remained there after he'd gone, finishing his tea and thinking. He was trying to clear his head, decide what to do. The first thing he must do was tell Georgie about Brown. He wasn't going to stand by and let her be arrested.

The strange thing was, even accepting Georgie had killed someone made no difference to how he felt about her. Whatever she'd done he believed there was a good reason for it, and yes, even murder could be a choice forced upon someone. He needed to hear her side of the story, but he doubted it would alter his conviction.

Eventually, he tossed the dregs from his tin mug onto the ground and stood up. He heard a soft rustling and noticed the leaves stirring above him. The wind was picking up, and it was a northerly, hot as hades. He thought that probably wasn't a good thing. The fire had been marking time and now this wind was going to blow it somewhere.

Time was running out in more ways than one.

Neville quickened his pace as he started down

the path through the bush, back towards Mackenzie Crossing.

CHAPTER 26

SKYE

Tuesday 10 June 1997

B Y THE TIME they got back to Finn's house
the light was already fading. After lunch,
there had been time to stop off at the supermar-
ket. Skye wanted to stock up on groceries—she
would need to, she thought, now that she wouldn't
be leaving for a while.

And what was Fraser going to say about that?

Of course, he wasn't expecting her to return
to work until next week, and perhaps she would
have thought of a good excuse by then. Or perhaps she wouldn't need to. Finn might have
been released from jail, and ten minutes later
they might have decided that the whole thing
was completely unworkable and impractical, and
what the hell had they been thinking.

A moment of madness, because of their memories of the past, which was over before it had
really begun.

And why did those rational thoughts leave her

feeling so flat? It wasn't as if she had come up here with the hope of romance, and she certainly hadn't imagined she'd see Finn again. It was just a momentary glitch, she told herself, and normal service would be resumed as soon as possible. But in her heart she knew that what was happening between them wasn't so easily explained away.

Her decision to trust him had flung her into unfamiliar territory. No wonder she was floundering around like someone in a strange land with the lights off.

After Alison had dropped her and Lightning home, Skye was too restless to stay inside, and besides, she thought the greyhound deserved some free time after being cooped up in the car all day long.

Finn had explained to her that contrary to common belief, greyhounds didn't need a great deal of exercise. They were sprinters not marathon runners. All the same, Lightning clearly enjoyed her freedom, circling Skye a few times and then bounding off towards the line of trees at the bottom of the yard.

Skye followed her down, and found herself on the bank of a shadowy creek. It was shallow and fast, skipping over pebbles and cascading through larger stones. She supposed it was fed by the melting snow in the spring and that it could turn into a raging torrent in some weathers.

Not today though. Today the sounds it was making were soothing, and she took some photographs, and several of Lightning as well.

Earlier, over lunch, as Alison had tucked into

her bruschetta, she'd spoken about Finn and his career, and the police force in general.

'There've been rumours,' she'd said. 'About the Drug Squad, I mean. Some of them think they're outside the law. Hard to tell which side they're on.'

'Not Finn though.'

'God, no. The Sarge is as straight as they come.'

Except when it comes to Dylan, Skye thought now, watching the rippling water. Although Finn hadn't actually broken the law for his brother, it was a fine line. And yet here she was falling in behind him.

By the time she'd wandered back from the creek it was nearly dark, but she paused to admire the house. The interior lights shone gently through the big kitchen windows, making rectangles on the mown grass where only a dusting of snow remained. A fire break, Finn had told her, when she'd commented on his lawn.

Fire was an ever-present and constant danger during the hotter months, and she had never really understood that before. Neville had witnessed the horror of it firsthand. Georgie Mackenzie, too—the fact that neither of them had made it out seemed to be gathering momentum. Had they run at the end, desperately trying to survive, or had they stood and allowed themselves to be consumed?

Skye shivered at the images her thoughts had evoked.

She wasn't particularly hungry, but she supposed she should cook something. And she'd bought some of her favourite ingredients, so it would be no hardship to make up a vegetable stir-fry and jasmine rice. She'd never been a neat cook, and afterwards there were pots and plates everywhere.

Skye had just finished eating and was thinking about washing up—what would Finn think if he could see his neat kitchen now?—when a knock on the front door heralded unexpected visitors.

Definitely not Finn, he wouldn't need to knock. Maybe Alison had come back, although the kitchen window was her usual entry point. It was only as she reached the door that she remembered Dylan. Would he dare come calling on her? Her hand hesitated over the deadlock.

'Are you going to let us in?'

It was Taylor! She couldn't hold back a smile of relief as she opened the door.

'Brrr,' Taylor greeted her. 'Cold enough to snow again. What do you think of life in Elysian?'

'Surprising,' she said wryly. 'Yes, surprising about covers it.'

'Why surprising?'

Skye was just thinking up an answer when Saskia stepped out from behind him. The girl appeared nervous, her gaze meeting Skye's and then darting away, and she tucked her hand tightly in the crook of Taylor's elbow as if for courage. But Skye was so glad to see Archie's granddaughter, it must have been obvious to them both how welcome they were as she invited them in.

'You know Finn still isn't home?' she said, as they took off their outside gear. Taylor was in jeans and a sweater, while Saskia had on her short skirt, teamed with her sapphire sweater, black tights and Doc Martens.

Taylor gave a frown reminiscent of his boss as they made their way towards the kitchen. 'Idiots,' he declared. 'What are they thinking? He's the best cop we've had here since ... well he's the best cop.' Saskia squeezed his arm and he reigned in his rampant partiality with an apologetic smile. 'But that isn't the reason we're here. Saskia has something to show you.'

'Yeah. In a little while though, Taylor. Give me a minute.'

Skye was tempted to demand to know what it was, but once again Saskia avoided her eyes, and she decided she'd be better off waiting. She didn't want to blow what may be her last chance to interrogate the natives about Neville.

'Well, come in. I've eaten or I'd offer you dinner. I do have coffee and cake?' She looked from one to the other, and decided she'd hooked Taylor.

'Coffee and cake would be good,' he said. 'Tea for Saskia. Herbal if you've got it.' And he gave the girl a fond look of exasperation, as if he considered her refusal to drink caffeine a sweet quirkiness of character.

Skye searched the cupboards, finally finding some chamomile tea that wasn't past its use-by date. Maybe Laurie had been a herbal-tea drinker, or perhaps Finn had a need for its calming qualities. Taylor and Saskia were having a quiet conversation but stopped as soon as she brought their mugs over. The cake was rainbow with sticky pink icing, and she cut some slices and handed them around.

'What are the two of you doing out tonight?' she asked with a smile. *See how harmless and friendly I am?*

'We were at a footy meeting,' Taylor explained. 'The local team are hoping to do better than bottom this year so they're trying to rally up some support. There're a lot of players who'd like to play, but they work outside the area and have to commute. Anyone really good gets poached away to the bigger towns.'

After a moment the conversation came around to which team Skye followed.

'I'm not much of an AFL fan,' she admitted. 'When I first came over to live in Victoria—I was from Adelaide—I tried to fit in by choosing the same team as my friends.'

'What team was that?'

'Collingwood.'

Their howl of disgust had Skye laughing and covering her ears. She'd discovered a long time ago that if you were a Collingwood Magpies supporter then it was always an us-and-them situation.

'That's Sergeant Galloway's team,' Saskia commented, when the racket had died down.

'Yes, he was one of the friends,' Skye admitted wryly.

The other two exchanged a glance that Skye pretended not to notice. Was gossip rife in the town? Was everyone speculating on how good a friend she was with Finn and whether they'd jumped into bed together yet? But then she supposed she was new meat for them.

'You don't mind being on your own?' Taylor queried her, reaching down to pat Lightning, who had taken up position beside his chair, eyes on the last piece of cake. 'You could always stay with Alison, you know. She wouldn't mind. She says the house is too big for her.'

'She should move to a smaller place,' Saskia put in. 'Somewhere newer. Not so many cobwebs and spiders.'

'Old houses are good to live in,' Taylor interrupted, not quite meeting her eyes, and Skye remembered his plans to buy Mr Rutherford's house. Evidently he hadn't shared them with Saskia quite yet.

Taylor held out a bite-sized piece of cake to Lightning on the palm of his hand, which she took neatly with her tongue. She was a very well-mannered dog, Skye thought fondly, even her wake-up kisses weren't overly slobbery. And her company had certainly helped during the time she'd spent here alone.

The silence lengthened and Skye tried to hide her impatience. Why didn't they tell her the real reason for their visit? She cleared her throat. 'How is your granddad?' she asked with studied casualness.

Saskia wasn't fooled. Carefully she set down her tea. 'Ah … he's okay. You remember he was going through Mr Rutherford's junk? Well he's also been cataloguing some of the stuff in the museum and that keeps him busy.'

Skye smiled again, but she could see that Taylor was looking edgy and Saskia was staring down at her hands. The girl spoke up first.

'I'm sorry about Sunday. I know you were upset and it must've seemed strange. I just … I couldn't risk Granddad getting agitated. Mum would kill me.'

Skye knew she was only telling the truth as she saw it. 'All right.'

'Actually,' Taylor said, with a nudge against Saskia's arm. 'We've brought something to show you.'

The girl gave him an uncertain look, eyes pleading. 'I don't know, Taylor. Mum won't be happy with me. And what if Granddad finds out and gets upset? You know how she is. Maybe I shouldn't do this.'

Taylor didn't back down. 'You thought it was a good idea before we got here, Sask. You agreed with what I said.' He looked at Skye. 'I reminded her that she has Archie, but you're still looking for your grandfather.'

Saskia appeared torn. She put her fingers to her mouth as if she was about to chew on her fingernails, and then stopped and quickly returned them to her lap. Maybe that was something else her mother would kill her for, Skye thought.

'Saskia, come on,' Taylor said, exasperation creeping into his voice. 'We'll have to go soon. You said you couldn't be away from Archie for too long. It's now or never.'

Saskia lifted her shoulders and then let them

drop. 'All right,' she said.

'All right what?'

'Let's show Skye what we brought.'

He smiled, giving her a one-armed hug. 'Come on, then. Let's go and get it.'

She smiled back but Skye decided the girl was definitely out of her comfort zone. Nancy Manning must be a fierce woman to inspire such trepidation in her daughter.

Taylor and Saskia were only outside for a short while, and when they returned, they were carrying something large and flat in a taped-up plastic bag. It was the size of a painting, Skye thought, sitting up straighter.

Saskia caught Skye's glance, and her own skittered away. 'Taylor …'

'It'll be fine,' Taylor assured her. 'Anyway, your mum'll kill me first, so you'll be able to run away.'

Saskia bit her lip. 'Not funny,' she muttered.

They laid the object on the table. 'It used to hang above the counter in the museum,' Saskia explained a little breathlessly, 'but one day someone was asking questions about it and … well Granddad took it down. The one that's up there now is of Elysian after the Black Friday fire. You saw it, didn't you?'

Skye was waiting impatiently for the girl to finish unwrapping whatever it was they'd brought. 'Hmm, not really. The light was shining on the glass and I couldn't see it properly.'

'Oh.' Saskia pulled off the last bit of covering. 'It' was also a photograph, framed, with glass over the top that looked smeary. Taylor gave it a bit of a wipe with his sleeve, but Skye had already forgotten them. Because what she was looking at took her complete attention.

It was a scene of utter chaos.

She stood up. There was just something about it that seemed to demand she rise to her feet.

'I found it the other day when I was helping Granddad sort out Mr Rutherford's collection,' Saskia's voice came from a long way away. 'He had to go into the other room and I was alone in the storage area, and it was leaning against a pile of books. When I turned it around, well, there it was. I didn't mention it to him. I remembered what Mum had said about him getting upset when it used to hang above the counter in the museum.'

'And then I arrived and started telling you about my grandfather being a photographer who hadn't been seen since Black Friday in Mackenzie Crossing,' Skye finished the story for her.

'Yes,' Saskia agreed.

Skye couldn't take her eyes off what was in front of her. She didn't recognise this scene from her visit to the Crossing with Finn, not with the swirls of smoke making everything ghostly. In the background there were some straight lines—cottages, and the two-storey building she now knew was the hostelry—and blurred movement that could have been people running. But her attention wasn't on them. Her gaze was focused on the figure of the woman in the foreground, standing and staring into the camera lens. Almost as if she was looking right through it, and into Skye's eyes.

It was the same woman. This was Georgie Mackenzie, she was certain of it.

A blanket was wrapped around her shoulders and over her head, leaving only her face visible. Her skin appeared oddly colourless and her eyes were dark hollows, and Skye was reminded of the old masters and their paintings of the Madonna.

It was powerful. The impact was undeniable. Breathtaking and heartbreaking.

And she knew who had taken it. There was only one person in the world capable of such heartfelt sincerity and eloquence.

'Where did Archie get this?' she managed, her throat raw with emotion.

'Granddad's had it ever since I can remember,' Saskia said, and she was on her feet, too, standing beside Skye. 'It was hanging in the museum for ... well, forever. Until he took it down and put it out the back in the storage room.'

'This is a Neville Darling.'

'But ...' Saskia looked worried. 'Are you sure? Granddad always said it was taken by a journalist who was covering the nineteen thirty-nine fires. He discovered it in an auction room in Melbourne. According to him he also found a whole lot of other photos by the same journalist and bought them for a song.'

Skye felt her eyes widen in shock. If that was true ... Did that mean there were more of Neville's photos? She searched for words, fighting through the jumble of questions that required answers.

'What else does Archie know about the journalist?' she managed at last. 'His name or …?'

Saskia bit her lip, giving Taylor a look that seemed to be asking for his help and which he ignored, pretending sudden interest in cake crumbs. Tough love? Skye wondered.

'I-I don't know anything more. Really, I don't. When you started to tell me about your grandfather and that he was a photographer, I remembered this, but … I couldn't tell you about it then. I didn't want you to talk to Granddad and upset him.'

Skye's shock was fading and excitement had taken its place. She'd found Neville's footprints, she was sure of it, and all she had to do was follow them. Obviously this photo had been taken during the first impact of the fire on Mackenzie Crossing, and although it didn't prove he'd survived, it told her that someone had. His camera must have been okay and the photographs in it had been developed, and surely whoever did that must have known him or what had happened to him?

Perhaps there would be clues in the other photos. She needed to see them.

'That's a woman, isn't it?' Taylor was frowning down at the image in the foreground. 'Do you recognise her? It's not old Mrs Appleby's mother, is it?'

'When Alison drove me to Westcott to see her mother today, Mrs Appleby said her family had evacuated to Elysian well before the fire reached the Crossing,' Skye explained. 'But I think I know who it is.' She took another look at the shape of the eyes, and those gorgeous high cheekbones. Yes, she was sure she was right.

'Wait here!' she said, and, startling them, hurried off down the corridor to her bedroom.

When she returned with her crumpled likeness of Georgie Mackenzie, she placed it on the table next to the framed photo.

Obediently, Saskia and Taylor shuffled closer to stare down at it. The girl made a sound of surprise.

'I know her!' she said.

'Do you?' Skye asked carefully, trying to remember to breathe.

Saskia's brow furrowed. 'Well, when I say ... I don't really *know* her.'

The anti-climax was acute, but before she could ask what she meant, Saskia went on.

'I've seen this photo before though, or one like it. It was with the others I was telling you about, in the box that Granddad brought home from the Melbourne auction.'

'Are you sure?' Taylor murmured.

'Yes, yes, I'm sure!' she said with an impatient glance. 'I remember her because I thought it was so weird, her being dressed like that. And they're old photos and—'

'So you've actually looked through them?' Skye interrupted. 'You know where they are?'

'Well,' she tucked a strand of hair behind her ear. 'I noticed them in his room a few years ago, when I was searching for his good suit. There was a funeral and ...' She waved a dismissive hand. 'Anyway, I opened the box—it's about this big,' and she made a shape about a metre by two-thirds of a metre. 'I didn't think it was private or anything, it was shoved under his dressing table. As I said, I was looking for his suit. Anyway, I opened the box and saw the photos and had a look through them. I remember I was surprised by how good they were. How interesting. So I told Granddad what I'd seen and he went a bit odd, as if he didn't want me to see them. No, that's not right,' she said with a frown. 'As if he didn't want me to ask *questions* about them. He changed the subject and when I brought it up again, later on, he pretended he'd forgotten. But I could tell he hadn't. He never forgets anything.'

Bewildered, she looked from Skye to Taylor. 'I don't understand,' and she pointed at the photocopy of Georgie. 'Where did *you* get this?'

So then it was Skye's turn to explain. 'The letter with it was sent from Elysian in nineteen fifty-seven,' she finished, 'but no one ever followed it up.'

'Nineteen fifty-seven,' Saskia repeated thoughtfully. 'I'm not sure exactly when Granddad came to live here. But anyway, why would he write a letter to the police about a man he'd never met? A man he'd never heard of! No, it can't have been him.'

This was turning into a multi-layered mystery, Skye decided.

'And you're sure you've never heard of Neville Darling?' she asked. 'Sorry, but I just want to be sure I've covered all bases.'

Saskia shook her head emphatically. 'No, I've

never heard the name.'

Skye looked again at the two images, side by side, knowing in her heart and soul that Neville had taken them both. The question was, who had developed his film, and who had sold his photographs at auction in Melbourne? Was it possible that a journalist had found them sometime after the fire and passed them off as his own? But if that was so then why hadn't they become more well known? In her opinion these were the sort of iconic images that should be familiar to all Australians.

'*If* I showed this to Grandad,' Saskia said, smoothing her finger over Georgie's face, 'he might tell me who it is. If he knows. But I can't promise anything.'

'I know who it is,' Skye replied. 'It's Georgie Mackenzie of Mackenzie Crossing. Mrs Appleby recognised her this morning.'

'Oh.' Saskia shared a glance with Taylor, and they both shook their heads.

'Do you think I could come and talk to your grandfather? Or your mother? When will she be home? I wouldn't do anything to upset them, at least I'd try not to, but I do need some answers.'

Saskia looked dubious.

'I promise to be very gentle with them.'

'I'll ask. That's all I can do. Okay?' She'd started chewing her fingernails and this time she didn't take her hand away. 'She's formidable, my mum,' Saskia added.

Taylor nodded without arguing.

Skye knew she should be grateful for this

information, and the possibility of more, but the answer to what happened to Neville seemed so tantalisingly close. It wasn't enough, and she knew it wouldn't ever be enough until the whole truth was spread out before her. And as for more of Neville's photographs for her exhibition … If they were as good as these two she knew it would be a roaring success. Her dream of bringing Neville Darling to the world was starting to look like it might actually become a reality.

Saskia took the framed photograph with her, saying she dared not leave it in case someone noticed and her mother found out what she'd done. 'She's a great mother,' the girl insisted, when Skye looked doubtful, 'really. Just … strict, you know?'

'Saskia's family have always liked to keep things confidential,' Taylor added. Reading between the lines Skye thought that might mean they were particularly sensitive about their privacy, and there could be all sorts of reasons for that.

When Skye closed the door on them, Lightning came to lean against her leg. She reached down to stroke the dog's smooth head.

'I know,' she said aloud. 'Frustrating doesn't cover it, does it? But we're making progress, girl. Bit by bit.'

Lightning didn't have much to say to that, but Skye thought she could see the wisdom in the dog's eyes.

CHAPTER 27

NEVILLE

Eleven am, Friday 13 January 1939,
Mackenzie Crossing

THE HEAT FELT even more oppressive as Neville made his way back down the track to the Crossing. And the sky had turned a strange colour, as if the smoke was getting too thick now for the light to filter through as it should. The wind was one of those hot northerlies that the state of Victoria dreaded, blowing down from the inland deserts.

He imagined he could taste the grit on his tongue.

For a moment he hesitated, wondering if he should go back to warn Phil and his crew, but he decided against it. They'd lived here longer than him, and they'd surely know when it was time to take shelter. He'd rather get down to Mackenzie Crossing, to Georgie and Tiddler, and see them right.

The thought gave him pause. In truth he hardly

knew Georgie and Tiddler. A few days ago he hadn't heard of them, and even now a sensible man would think of preserving his own life first and fleeing the mountains. Besides which, he could no longer ignore the fact that Miller Brown was looking for Georgie to ask her about a murder.

Well, perhaps he wasn't a sensible man, he told himself, because even knowing what he did made no difference to the way he felt.

Down in the valley, the wind wasn't as strong, but the air was smokier, certainly worse than it had been when he left to go up to the timber camp. He found Georgie busy inside the hostelry, and she glanced up with a fraught expression as he came through the door. For a moment he thought she looked relieved to see him, but almost at once she turned away again.

'I thought Phil might have put you to work cutting down trees,' she said with dry humour.

He saw she was packing a rather weather-beaten suitcase with what looked like clothing and personal items. An old teddy bear went in on top, so worn it must have belonged to Georgie herself before it was passed down to her son. 'I don't want Tiddler to see this,' she murmured, 'but there mightn't be time later on.'

'I think the wind is strengthening. Perhaps we should go now.'

She looked at him as if she thought he might know something she didn't, and then shook her head. 'No. Fire might not get here, or the wind might go around. Better to stay in case we need to put out spot fires. If we can save the buildings then we should.'

'You've done this before, then?'

'Not like this. I've seen fires and I know what can happen. But no, Neville, not like this.' She closed the suitcase and tucked it away in the corner.

He tried to tell himself that maybe Georgie was right and the fire would turn. Was it selfish of him to wish terror and havoc on some other place, if it would keep Mackenzie Crossing safe?

Behind them the window rattled as a blast of air came in, sending the curtains spinning. Georgie hurried to close it while Neville carried his camera outside. Even in the short time they'd been speaking the atmosphere had changed for the worse. Wind gusted and he saw the treetops higher up the slopes moan and bend. The smell of smoke and ash in the air was suddenly stronger, stinging the inside of his nose, and there was a sensation as if the skin on his face had begun to dry out and shrivel.

Neville didn't consider himself a fanciful chap, but he had an ominous feeling, like the end of the world was coming. Shocked, he looked through the camera lens at the darkening sky. 'Is it too late for me to get them all to Elysian?' he asked himself aloud.

'I'm not leaving.' Georgie had come up behind him without him hearing and now she was staring at him as if he was the enemy. 'I won't go. I won't leave the Crossing. This is my home and it's all I have.'

Neville's heart ached for her, but he still had the presence of mind to take a photograph. 'What about Tiddler?' he said. 'Shouldn't you be thinking of your son?'

Georgie's eyes flared and she took a step closer. 'Who told you that? Phil Appleby, I suppose!'

'I knew already. He's very like you.'

She looked torn in two. He expected her to argue some more. Instead, she said in a firm, no-nonsense voice, 'He'll be safe in the mine. We'll all be safe.'

He realised then that, like the troops on the Western Front, she'd dug in and was about to make her stand.

Another blast of air and she half closed her eyes against the heat of it, tendrils of hair dancing about her face. The way the wind tugged at her clothing, outlining her figure, reminded him of the photograph of the woman on the pier. It had been in his pocket all this time, and Neville knew that he couldn't wait any longer. He had to speak.

'Phil Appleby told me something else, Georgie. There's a policeman from Melbourne asking after you.'

Her eyes fixed on his and he had never seen such a whirlwind of emotions in one woman's face. 'Policeman?' she repeated, her voice a croak in the dry heat.

'Don't worry. Phil said they haven't told him where you are. They're your friends; they're protecting you.'

'Bloody fools.' She looked around as if she expected to see the representative of the law bearing down on her.

For a moment Neville was confused. Could he have been mistaken? Had she really nothing to hide? Was she innocent after all? He tried to believe it and found he couldn't.

'Actually I met him myself when I was in Elysian. At least I think it was the same man. His name is Miller Brown.'

She was staring at him and he could see she was wondering why he had said nothing to her. Why he had kept the secret to himself.

'He showed me this.' He reached into his pocket for the photograph and held it out to her. 'He thought I might recognise the woman in it, but of course I didn't. How could I?'

For a long time she gazed at the grainy image as he tried to read her face, and when she looked up again there were tears in her eyes. 'You know, don't you? Oh, God, you know.'

'Georgie …'

'I was such a fool, Neville. Such an innocent.' She laughed a little wildly. 'I wish I could make you understand why I—'

Whatever she was going to say was never finished. Something fluttered past her face and fell to the ground.

Burning leaves from a tree, flung far ahead of the fire front now bearing down upon them. Georgie gasped and hurriedly stamped them out, looking about her anxiously for more. The smell of fire and ash was more intense, and the sky was black beyond the hilltops that before now had seemed to protect the town.

She blotted the sweat from her face with her sleeve and handed him back the photograph. She seemed to have regained her equilibrium, or perhaps fear of the fire had negated all others. 'Why did this policeman let you keep it?' she asked him curiously.

'He didn't,' Neville admitted. 'I stole it.'

She started to laugh and then changed her mind. 'Do you pray, Neville?' she asked him breathlessly.

'Not for a long time. Not since before the war.'

'Big Jim was religious. Prayers every Sunday, and then the congregation would sojourn to the hostelry for the drink of their choice. He figured the former cancelled out the sin in the latter.'

'It sounds like he gave it some thought,' he said, watching her.

Georgie smiled. 'Big Jim believed in salvation,' she said, and he could see that she did, too.

He opened his mouth to ask her to explain about the policeman and the sin she had committed and needed to absolve.

Just as someone began to ring the fire-warning bell, the sound echoing starkly over Mackenzie Crossing.

CHAPTER 28

SKYE

Two am, Wednesday 11 June 1997

SKYE HAD TAKEN a long time to get to sleep after the visit by Taylor and Saskia. The possibility of more Neville Darling photographs had fully occupied her thoughts, which was a good thing, because it had stopped her thinking about Finn. But eventually she had drifted off, and then she was dreaming.

In the dream she tilted her head back and looked up, and the black cavernous sky was awash with stars. At the same time she felt the warm water against her ankles, and when she looked down she could see the smooth waters of the bay. Only they were reflecting the stars, too, so it felt as if she was adrift among them.

Floating in space.

Was it the night Dylan and Finn had fought, the night it all went so wrong? She'd always felt some guilt about that, as if it was her fault that it had happened. Perhaps some of it was. She'd caused a chasm to form between the brothers, although she wasn't sure they wouldn't have fought it out anyway, eventually. Sometimes the tension around them was palpable. There was always the chance it would erupt into violence.

'Skye …?'

Finn was there after all. She remembered his arms around her, and the touch of his lips against hers. And as if thought could become reality, he was kissing her, his lips soft and gentle, the rasp of his unshaven cheek against her skin …

Huh?

Skye's eyes flew open.

'Finn?'

He was sitting on the edge of her bed, his broad shoulders and the tilt of his head silhouetted against the light from the hallway outside her door. 'Hey,' he whispered. 'Sorry to wake you.'

She pushed herself up until she was half sitting, propped back against her pillows. 'Finn! How did you … I mean, they let you go?'

He nodded, turning his head slightly, so that now half of his face was lit while the rest was all hollows and shadows. She could see the gleam of his eye and the line of his mouth. He wasn't smiling, but he wasn't far off.

'Did Dylan …?'

'Yes. He called up a friend of mine. The traffic cop I told you about, who put me on the right road when I was heading for trouble. He's quite high up in the police force these days. After Dylan contacted him he had a word.'

He made it sound easy, but she had her doubts

about that.

Skye narrowed her eyes at him. 'You knew this would happen all along, didn't you?' she said, remembering with embarrassment how she had carried on in the jail in Westcott, issuing ultimatums. He must have been laughing at her.

His answer was decisive enough to convince her. 'I didn't, I promise you. I hoped so, but I didn't know how it was going to end up.'

'But Dylan knew,' she said accusingly.

'He knows what's going on, yes, but I couldn't reach him to let him know I was being taken into custody. That's why I asked you to visit him. I wanted him to be ready in case I had to tell Gary and Lois where he was. I didn't intend to, I thought I wouldn't have to, but you never know. You've met Gary,' and he gave her a serious look, 'he's pretty much capable of anything.'

She had met Gary, and she hadn't liked what she saw. She shivered. 'You asked me to trust you,' she reminded him, 'and I do. Why can't you tell me what's happening?'

He sighed. 'It's an ongoing operation. It's probably safer if you don't know. Safer for you.'

'I trust you, Finn. I want you to trust me, whether it's safer or not.'

He didn't answer immediately, but she waited, knowing he was thinking things over, choosing his words. She wriggled back against her pillows to get comfortable.

'Okay,' he said at last, 'I'm going to tell you what I can. But you need to be careful, Skye. Seriously, you need to be very careful.'

'I'm a careful person,' she assured him. 'Law abiding, too.'

The look he gave her said he did not appreciate her levity.

'Sorry, I'm listening.'

'Okay, here's the thing. Gary and Lois have been skimming drugs from the busts they've been making. They've been doing it for years. Dylan knows the details. He can give evidence against them if it ever got to court, which they would do almost anything to stop happening. They're not alone in this, there are others involved, and they're protected by others even higher up. They all get their cut and none of them want it to come to an end.'

'It sounds serious.'

'Yes, it is.'

'So when you said they wanted to find Dylan, you meant they might want to …'

'Get rid of him? Make him vanish? Yes, that's what I meant.'

'God, Finn …' She thought for a moment, watching his face. 'Can't you just …?'

He must be able to read her more easily than she could him. 'Get all the good guys together and fight it out? Let justice and truth win the day? Me and my friend are going for something slightly less ambitious, but we're hoping it might kickstart some sort of inquiry. This corruption is entrenched and longstanding, and it won't be cleaned up in a day or even a year. Our idea is for Dylan and Ebony to go into protective custody, but if that doesn't appear to be a possibility, or it's taking overly long, then I'll get them a change of identity.'

He sounded as if he meant business.

'Thank you for telling me,' she said, 'but can I say something you're not going to like?'

He sighed. 'Why change an old habit?'

'Exactly.' She waited a moment, watching him, but he was waiting too. 'You're willing to risk your job, even your life, for Dylan. To get him out of the trouble he got himself into. How do you know he's not going to do it all over again? He's like an addiction, Finn, that you can't let go of.'

'I suppose it looks like that.' He met her eyes and seemed to be considering her words. She thought for a moment he might tell her whatever it was that held him and his brother together like glue, but as the silence went on it became clear that he'd changed his mind. And maybe it was nothing more than the usual bonds between twins, she told herself, trying not to feel disappointed. Or maybe he wasn't ready to tell her, and she shouldn't push him.

'So,' she said softly, trying for a smile, 'why don't you like ultimatums?'

It was only when she saw his shoulders relax that she realised how tense he'd been. 'Well, I've had a few in my time. Yours was mild, believe me.'

He meant Laurie, she suspected. An imploding marriage could be a messy business, as Skye was well aware, and blame games were all part of its rich tapestry.

'I just …'

'Just what?'

She shook her head. She didn't want to talk

about Dylan and the past, not now. Finn was here with her, and considering all that was going on, he could be arrested at any time. She should be making the most of him.

'What about tomorrow? Is it work as usual?'

'I reckon Doug can handle things for another day.'

He didn't quite say he wanted to spend the day with her, but he may as well have. Nerves made her wriggle around a bit more, and she began to tell him all about Taylor and Saskia's visit, and the photo they'd brought of Mackenzie Crossing.

'So I still don't know whether Neville survived or not,' she added in a rush. 'I need to talk to Archie, but I'm not sure I'll be able to. I'm hoping. Maybe if you were there, they might be more forthcoming.'

'If I put on my serious cop face, you mean?'

She giggled and then bit her lip. God, it must be the nerves, she wasn't normally the giggling kind.

'It'd be a marvellous addition for the exhibition,' she told him, regaining her maturity. 'And the others. I haven't seen them yet, but if Neville took them they have to be good.'

'Your eyes shine when you talk about the exhibition,' he said, and she could see he was smiling again. 'So you are going ahead with it?'

In the kitchen the phone began ringing.

Finn groaned and pushed himself to his feet. After a moment Skye heard him answer it and then the murmur of his voice as he responded to whoever was on the other end. She waited, wondering if he was going to head out again to save the world. Or Dylan. When silence returned and he didn't come back, she got up, pulled on her sweater over her pyjama top, and went to find him.

He was in the kitchen, standing with his back to her, staring out at the darkness beyond the windows. Skye saw her own reflection hovering behind him but wasn't even sure he knew she was there until he spoke.

'Skye.'

'What is it?' He sounded so strange she was worried. She came up behind him, almost touching him but not quite. 'Who was it?'

'It was Laurie.' He turned then, and Skye read the pain in his expression, but also the relief.

'What's happened?' She glanced at the clock and saw that it was nearly two am.

'It's about midnight in Perth,' he said, seeing her glance. 'Laurie was always a night owl. When I spoke to her the other day I asked her to make a decision she's been thinking about for quite a while now. Nearly two years. She's made it, so she thought she'd give me a ring with her answer. We're getting a divorce.'

'Oh.' She decided it was better to be cautious with her response. 'I'm sorry.'

'Don't be. I'll make sure I get access to my daughter, even if it means conceding everything else. I know Laurie will drive a hard bargain,' he added with a bleak smile.

'But coming now, on top of everything else …'

He laughed. He actually laughed while she

stared at him in confusion. 'Nah, it's the least of my worries, Skye.'

Skye was struggling to keep up, but there was something in his smile as he moved closer and rested his hands lightly on her shoulders. He smelled of coffee and soap, and she felt a longing that threatened to catapult her into his arms.

'Laurie and me got married because it seemed like the thing to do, but I knew it was a mistake as soon as I started making excuses to stay at work. She wasn't who I was looking for.'

'Finn …'

'When you moved in next door, there was something about you. At the risk of sounding like a dangerous lunatic, you were in my head day and night, Skye. Life for me at that time wasn't the greatest, but you were by far the best thing in it. Seeing you again, that sense of you, me, us, that we're special together, hasn't changed. Now you're going to ask me to drive you to Alison's, aren't you?'

His dark eyes were intense and she couldn't look away. Didn't want to. 'I don't want to go to Alison's,' she retorted softly, and reaching up, slid her arms around his neck and drew his mouth down to hers.

She'd been telling herself his kisses from the other night couldn't be as good as she'd remembered, but as soon as his lips touched hers she knew they were that good. Better. It was as if a flame ignited and suddenly it was raging.

His hands slid over the curve of her back, down to her waist and her hips, smoothing the warm, bare skin where her pyjama bottoms had slipped down. When she leaned in closer against his body, she could feel him harden. Her heartbeat ratcheted up a notch. It had been a while, but she thought she remembered the basics.

Unexpectedly, Finn broke the contact, just far enough so that he could rest his forehead against hers, yet still close enough for her to be aware of his heart hammering wildly.

'I need a shower,' he said. 'The cell in Westcott isn't as clean as mine.'

Skye laughed and heard the tension in her voice. 'So not everyone is as scrupulous about their cells as you, Finn?'

'You bet.'

He hesitated again, and then said aloud what she already knew. 'I want you, Skye. Will you come and scrub my back?'

Skye bit her lip. Her mouth was warm and tingly from his kiss and she was already feeling her body heating up in all sorts of places. He was right, there was something going on here, but they were older and as a grown-up she knew that giving in to passion had consequences.

He ran his fingertip down the side of her face, as if reacquainting himself with its shape. 'I know we have a few things to sort out.'

'A few,' she said, and her voice cracked on the laugh.

'Well, more than a few. But I'm pretty sure I'm not going to wake up tomorrow and leave town. What about you?'

Definitely not, Skye thought. God, she really

wanted him. She must be just as crazy. Still, with her practical genes reasserting themselves, Skye opened her mouth to begin listing the issues that they would need to address—she always liked a good list—until he stopped her by kissing her again.

And after that there wasn't really anything left to say.

The air was frigid. The fire box in the kitchen must be out. Skye shivered and turned over, ready to cuddle up to Finn, but the space beside her was empty. He was gone and she was alone in a cold bed.

It felt like a metaphor.

See! You can't go back, that practical voice in her head informed her. *You can never go back.*

'Oh, God.'

'You all right?' And there he was, climbing beneath the quilt and in beside her, his body chilled as he slid his arms around her and drew her against all that naked skin and lean muscle. 'I had to get the fire going,' he explained. 'I forgot about it last night.'

Somewhere in the background her practical voice was still warning her about all the things that might go wrong, but she was no longer listening.

'I didn't know where you were,' she said, her cheek against his chest. Fraser waxed his, but Skye liked the feel of those rough hairs against her skin, tickling her nose. She sneezed.

'Bless you,' he rumbled. 'Lightning wanted to go out for a moment. Looks like we're going to get some more snow. The house should warm up soon. It's only six am. Plenty of time before we have to get up properly.'

Skye wondered if he planned to stay in bed all day. Not that she was complaining.

'Skye?' Finn stroked her hair, indicating he wanted to see her face, but she smiled and burrowed deeper into his chest. 'Am I talking too much? Mum always said I talked too much when I was happy.'

She thought about ignoring the opening, but the question would have to be addressed at some point. 'What happened to Melissa?' she asked carefully.

He stared up at the ceiling. 'She died of an overdose.'

'Oh, Finn—'

He spoke over her, as if he didn't want to hear her sympathy. 'After Darryl went back to jail, and Dylan and I ... well, she took up with another loser. She'd been clean for a while, but he got her back onto the smack.'

'I'm sorry.'

'It was a wasted life. She had her chances, but she wasn't strong enough to break free, or maybe she just didn't want to.'

Skye opened her mouth to say something, and then kissed his shoulder instead. And then it felt so nice she kissed him again, nuzzling against his neck.

He made a noise in his throat that sounded like a big cat purring.

'I've never felt the urge to take drugs,' he said. 'Well, I had a bit of a fling with alcohol for a while, and I've learned to respect it. Dylan was in a bad way for a few years, but he's clean now. Ebony wouldn't put up with any of that crap, though to be fair, he'd stopped before he met her.'

To Skye it felt like he was discussing another world. Her parents had been ultra-conservative and she'd never thought of rebelling, not in that way. The Faraday brothers had been her one and only rebellion, and the consequences of that had dissuaded her from ever wanting to do it again.

He shifted his head and searched her eyes. 'Are you thinking this was a mistake?' he asked her. That was the thing about Finn, he'd always liked a straight answer to a straight question. Well almost always. When it came to Dylan the answers weren't quite as forthcoming.

'A mistake?' Skye wriggled further up beside him, resting her head on her elbow so that she could look down into his face. 'Are *you*?'

'No,' he said firmly. 'I've been wanting to do this ever since I saw you standing on the road in Lockington in those amazing skin-tight red jeans. And then when you got into my car and I smelled your perfume,' and he made a sound suspiciously like a growl.

Skye didn't think she'd been wearing perfume; it sounded so sexy though, she didn't want to quibble.

He reached up to draw her head down for more

kisses, but she resisted. She felt as if she should put up at least a token protest, before they were in this too deep.

'Do you really think this is a good idea? I mean, stepping back into the past like this?'

'I don't think of it like that,' he said in surprise. 'Well, maybe a bit, but this isn't then, this is now. We're making something new together.'

'You know I'll have to go back to Melbourne. I have a life there. And yours is here.'

'Cars are wonderful things, Skye. They can take us from one place to another remarkably quickly. There's no hurry to make up our minds about the details. And I promise we'll take it nice and slow.'

So was this taking it slow? she wondered, as he kissed the swell of her breast. Her breath quickened, and when he ran his tongue around her nipple and drew it into his mouth she tried not to pant.

She was leaning over him and now he reached up to draw her body to completely cover his. At first it was an ungainly sprawl, but they soon wriggled into position. So he liked her on top, did he? Skye thought, both bemused and amused.

'Skye,' he groaned.

She looked down at him, enjoying the view. And then he was moving and so was she, and that quickly the passion overcame them again. Which made her think that this thing between them, old or new or a bit of both, wouldn't burn itself out for a good while yet.

She had time. To get used to him, to get her

head in the right place, to make concessions. To make the decisions that needed to be made.

And yet, like a worm wriggling at the back of her mind, never quite going away, was still the thought of Dylan. And what damage he could inflict this time.

CHAPTER 29

DYLAN, FINN AND SKYE

December 1978,
the accident, Melbourne

A S THEY ROUNDED the corner, the car tipped so far over that Skye thought they were going to roll. She screamed, clinging to the seat while Darryl's handyman box opened and the contents scattered all around her.

Dylan laughed.

She'd been about to grab him around the neck from behind, but he must have seen her in the mirror because he spun the wheel to throw her off balance. The car only just righted itself, speeding along the increasingly busy road, heading in the direction of the city.

Her heart seemed to have lodged in her throat. She twisted around so she could kneel on the seat and see through the dust and grime on the rear window. The road behind them stretched out, and any occupants of the houses on either side were hidden behind drawn curtains.

Dylan took another corner too fast, but this time Skye held on with gritted teeth. Because she'd seen him. Finn. Just before a milk bar on the corner had obscured her view, he'd appeared in the middle of the road. Running.

'*Wheee!*' Dylan avoided a couple of oncoming cars and mounted the kerb, all to the chorus of horns blaring. The car came down again with a thud. Skye heard something underneath the chassis go *clunk*. She held her breath, fingers digging into the cracked vinyl, hoping it would all stop. *Please let it stop.* But the vehicle kept going, except now there was a metallic clanging and bumping sound, as if some part of the engine was hitting the asphalt.

'Dylan!' she shrieked.

He seemed to be enjoying her terror. His face was a grinning mask. 'Skye!' he roared, and spun the wheel again, making the car pirouette several times while she screamed at the top of her voice.

When he gunned the engine this time, she was huddled in a ball with her eyes closed. The noise from under the car was deafening and she could smell smoke. Maybe they'd blow up. She felt sure she was going to die.

And then Dylan yelled, 'Stupid bastard!'

Skye sat up and opened her eyes. And that was when she realised that after Dylan had spun the car, he'd set off back in the direction they'd just come. Because there, right in front of them, was Finn. He was standing on the white line, and they were heading right for him.

She didn't even scream this time, just launched

herself over the front seat, scrabbling for the wheel, fighting Dylan for control. But he knocked her backwards with his elbow, striking her cheekbone, and she felt something crack as she fell once again into the back seat.

The pain filled her head and then seemed to recede into cold horror. They were going to hit Finn. Dylan was going to kill him. She couldn't let that happen.

In desperation she scrabbled around on the floor for something to use, and her hand closed on what she thought was a hammer. Only it was just the handle of one, broken, like everything Darryl owned.

Even as she thought about finding something else, she looked up and realised it was too late. Finn was right there. 'Stop!' she screamed in fury and despair.

Dylan jammed on the brakes, sending her crashing forward against the back of his seat. The tyres screeched and smoked, and the car rocked to a stop.

At first she didn't move. Her body seemed locked into paralysis. The knowledge that Finn must be dead had taken away her will to save herself. As if from a distance, she heard Dylan fumbling with the gears, swearing, and hitting the shift with his fist, and realised something must have stuck.

Someone pounded on the window beside her.

Her head jerked up and for a moment she couldn't believe her eyes. Finn was standing there. His face was a bloody mask, but he was alive.

'Skye, Skye, get out!' he was shouting. At the same time he was wrenching at the handle and Skye, hands clumsy with fear, began to push hard from her side.

The door flew open.

Just as Dylan managed to put the car into gear and jammed his foot back on the accelerator. She felt the vehicle move and knew she'd be carried along with it, and in desperation leaped out. She felt Finn's hands reaching for her, but she was moving too fast, propelled by the car's momentum, and he couldn't hold on. He did slow her down a bit, so that when she hit the road she only skinned her elbows and knees, instead of breaking bones.

For what seemed a long time she stayed put, feeling dizzy and sick. However, the revving motor wasn't far away and with it came the nightmare vision of Dylan turning around and heading straight for them as they lay here, helpless. Skye struggled up, looking around for Finn.

He was lying on his back on the road a few yards from her. Someone in a passing car slowed down as if they were thinking of helping, only to change their mind and speed up again.

'Finn, get up!'

When he lifted his head, she saw his swollen eyes and bloody mouth. There was a thin trickle of watery stuff from his nose, and he wiped it on his sleeve with a groan. 'You all right?' he tried to say, his words muffled by his injuries.

She crouched over him, saying urgently, 'Finn, please, please, get up. He's coming back.'

At first he didn't seem to want to move, but she wasn't about to leave him. Slowly, and with her help, he managed to get to his feet. He'd been running after the car without his shoes, and his feet were cut, one toe with a mangled nail. When she saw that her heart ached, and it hurt more than her cheek and the other bits of her that had been bruised or scraped or torn.

Clinging to each other, they staggered over the kerb and then across the dried strip of grass to where someone's low-brick fence offered them a place to lean against when they sat down.

Somewhere in the distance a siren sounded; neither of them moved.

'I thought you were dead,' she sobbed. 'I thought the car hit you and you were dead.'

'I jumped to the side,' he said. And then, his bloody face filling with rage, 'When he drove away with you I wanted to kill him. I will kill him. When I find him, Skye, I will.'

'He's crazy.' Her throat was starting to hurt from screaming, as if it was raw. 'Why would he do that, Finn? Why?'

Finn looked at her as if he was going to answer, and then shook his head. Even though they were sitting down he seemed to lose his balance, nearly toppling over, and she slid an arm around his waist. He gave a shudder and let his head fall back against the bricks, still warm from the sun. His eyes were closed and he was breathing through his mouth.

'Can we just go home?' she whispered. And then, remembering, 'What about the car? What will Darryl say?'

'We can say it was stolen,' Finn mumbled, as if it was something that happened to him every day.

'Tell him Dylan took it.'

Finn tried to meet her gaze, but one of his eyes was almost closed up and the other one not far from it. 'Skye—'

'He nearly killed us, Finn. You know he did. He should be arrested.'

He looked torn, powerless, as if he wanted to do what she said only something was stopping him. Still, she thought she might have won him around, if they hadn't been interrupted.

Behind them a porch light had come on. 'What do you think you're doing?'

They hadn't heard the man walking across the yard behind them, but now he was there. Elderly, wearing a white singlet over his bulging stomach, and grey shorts at half-mast.

His eyes widened in alarm at the sight of her face, and then fairly bulged when he saw Finn's.

'You're hurt!' Instead of reaching out to help he backed away. 'Stay here,' he said. 'I'll call for an ambulance.' And then he was shuffling towards the open door of his house as fast as his thongs would allow him.

'Come on,' Finn said, as soon as he'd gone.

Was he serious? Skye shook her head. 'He's right, you need to go to hospital.'

'No,' he said, steely determination in his voice. 'I need to find Dylan.'

'Find Dylan?' she squeaked in horrified amazement. 'I never want to see Dylan again!'

Skye wondered what her parents were going to say. It wasn't as if she could hide the truth, not this time. Maybe she could play it down, for Finn's sake, but she knew whatever happened she'd never forgive Dylan.

Another siren sounded, shrill and urgent, and it occurred to Skye that there'd been an accident. As they crested a hill they could see down to the intersection at the bottom. There *had* been an accident. Several cars were scattered across the road at odd angles, and the flashing lights of the ambulance and a police car were illuminating the scene.

Finn's body tensed.

'You don't know he's there,' Skye whispered.

Finn didn't answer, just started to speed up, lurching to one side and only just stopping himself from over-balancing.

'Finn!' She got to him, again using her arm around his waist to keep him steady. 'Finn, don't,' she begged, but he wouldn't turn around.

They stumbled down the hill, closer and closer to the action. Skye felt herself shaking, and Finn was gasping for air.

'That's Darryl's car,' he croaked, pointing.

She didn't know how he could tell. The two vehicles were crumpled against the metal pole which held the traffic lights, and it looked as if they'd collided and then slid across the road before coming to an abrupt stop. Jagged metal hung off the side of Darryl's car, and the window of the other, newer model was smashed out, with ominous dark stains on the bonnet. Several metres away, on the median strip, was a shape covered in what looked like a picnic blanket.

Skye was sure it was Dylan and he must be dead. And she didn't know if it was anguish she was feeling or relief. Finn was holding her hand so hard it felt crushed. And then he made a sound and she looked up, following his gaze. Dylan was sitting at the back of the ambulance, his shoulders hunched and his head bowed. He looked diminished and his arm was in a sling, but it was him.

'Hey, mate, you can't come in here.' A harassed-looking cop in uniform stepped in front of them.

'He's my brother,' Finn mumbled.

The policeman took in the state of him. 'Were you in the car as well?' His eyes narrowed suspiciously.

'No.' Skye found her voice. 'He wasn't. Just Dylan.'

'I'll need a statement,' he began. 'We've got more officers on their way and—' Someone behind him called his name and he turned. The distraction was enough for Finn to push past, only to come to an unsteady halt in front of his brother.

'Dylan?'

There were several shell-shocked-looking witnesses milling around, and only two policemen. Skye heard a woman with a Farrah Fawcett hairstyle say with incredulity, 'He tried to do a U-turn in the middle of the intersection. In front of the oncoming traffic.'

Skye followed Finn to the ambulance but

stopped at a distance. Not wanting to get too close to Dylan, not trusting him. Hating him. He'd lifted his head now and she could see how white his face was, and the deep cut through his eyebrow, just missing his eye.

Seeing them at last he said, 'Hey,' his voice barely more than a whisper. There was a look in his eyes—bewildered, confused. As if he was the innocent party in all of this. But it didn't fool Skye.

'Are you okay?' Finn was eying his brother warily. His hands were clenching and unclenching at his sides, and, worried, Skye edged closer.

Dylan's gaze had wandered over to the body under the blanket. Tears began to leak out of his eyes and down his cheeks. He wiped his face on his sleeve, and spoke in a shaky voice. 'They said she's dead.'

'Who's dead?' Finn spoke as if he couldn't take it in. 'Who?'

'I don't know her name. She's dead, Finn.' Dylan sounded so young, and he was looking at his brother as if expecting him to make everything right.

Finn stared at him, clearly lost for words. After a moment he went over and sat down beside him. Dylan dropped his head to his chest and began to cry, and as Finn put an arm around him, he looked up and saw Skye standing there.

She could see he was torn apart, shattered, and she wanted to go to him. But she didn't. He'd chosen Dylan, she thought to herself. He'd made his choice.

When she turned away the policeman asked her if she was all right and what had happened, and would she like to sit down and tell him.

Soon afterwards she was taken home, and when she got out of the car and saw her parents' faces she was pretty sure she would never see Finn or Dylan again. And right then she was relieved.

CHAPTER 30

SKYE

Wednesday 11 June 1997

FINN PAUSED AT the entrance to Desperation Track, engine idling. The light had gone and the weather had closed in, but it wasn't that causing the chill inside the Toyota. Finn glanced sideways at her, and Skye wondered whether he was going to tell her once more that she wasn't coming with him. He could try, she thought obstinately, but short of throwing her out of the vehicle, she wasn't moving.

Things had been very different earlier in the day.

They'd stayed in bed until lunchtime, and then they'd held hands while they ate. It was silly, really, but it hadn't felt silly. And he'd kept touching her, as if he couldn't help it, and it was the same for her. She remembered sitting on his knee and smoothing a finger along his freshly shaven jaw, and then leaning in to kiss him, feeling high just from the scent of his aftershave.

They were crazy, she'd decided at the time, but by then it had been too late for second thoughts. If there had been a moment when she could have taken a step back from him and caught her breath, then it had long gone. She'd told herself she was in love, wildly and madly in love. Pelting along at top speed like a child on a roller coaster. If she came off the rails then she was insane enough to think it might even have been worth it.

Then, like some sort of omen, it had begun to snow again.

Lightning had been sleeping by the fire, but every now and then she'd opened one eye to look at the window, as if she knew all of this couldn't last.

Taylor had already rung to say that Doug had been called out to an accident about thirty kilometres away—a motorcyclist who'd come off his bike and broken his leg.

Finn had reassured her with the comment, 'I've told them that it'd have to be something pretty serious to call me in.'

She'd tried to look fierce when she said, 'Good.' But it only made him laugh.

So when the phone sounded again, Skye had known it must be important, and there was no way he wasn't going to answer. She'd watched his face as he'd listened, and his gaze had gone to hers and held it, just for a moment, before he'd turned his back.

Was that because she was a distraction, or was it because he hadn't wanted her to see what he was thinking? Her doubts hadn't boded well for a quiet night in, and she hadn't been at all surprised when, after he'd hung up, he was frowning.

'Another accident?' she asked.

'No. It was Taylor. He wanted to let me know that Lois Petersen came into the station. She's worried. Her partner Gary Grey went out hours ago and hasn't returned. She wanted to know if we'd heard from him, or if ...' He shook his head. 'If we thought he had met with Dylan. Of course Taylor didn't know who she was talking about, but he told her he'd talk to me.'

'But ... do they know where Dylan is? Lois and Gary, I mean,' Skye said, and jumped up to follow him as he strode from the room. 'I thought his whereabouts were all hush-hush?'

'That was the idea.' He went into his bedroom and peered around, opened the wardrobe door and closed it again.

'So how could Gary have called in to see him?' An exasperated note was creeping into her voice, mostly because Finn wouldn't stay still. Now he was in her bedroom, and after a cursory look around, he bent and peered under the bed.

'Here they are,' he muttered, and pulled out his boots. He sat down on the bed they'd only recently vacated and paused to look up at her. 'Skye, as far as I know Dylan is safe. I was the only one who knew where he was and *who* he was. I've been careful.'

'You don't think they followed me when I went to deliver your message?' she asked anxiously.

'No, I don't think that,' he reassured her. 'Gary and Lois were with me, heading to Westcott, and

I know they didn't double back. Gary was too busy telling me what he'd do to me if I didn't cooperate. Maybe one of the locals has let something slip that made Gary think "Mr Tennyson" was actually Dylan.'

'So what are you going to do?' she asked, standing in front of him while he finished tugging on his footwear.

Finn stood up. 'I'm going to drive out to Dylan's and check on him and Ebony.'

'Okay.' Skye nodded her head slowly. 'I'm coming, too.'

And that was when the argument started.

'I can't risk it,' he said.

'Well I'm not risking you going alone,' she retorted. 'And what if you need help with Ebony? What if she goes into labour from the shock of you arriving and telling Dylan that Gary is out there, looking for him? Women are better at these things.'

His look told her what he thought of that pathetic effort at psychology. 'Gary Grey is a dangerous man. Capable of anything,' he said, and the quietness of his voice conveyed that point better than any raised tones and arm waving might have done.

'I'm going with you, Finn. I promise not to get in your way, but I want to be with you.'

He stared at her as if he was considering various ways of stopping her, and she stared back. For once Skye out-stared him. 'I'm not happy,' he told her. 'Dylan—'

'It's exactly because this is about Dylan that I'm

staying with you,' she retorted.

That silenced him, but he still didn't look happy, and she wasn't sure he'd given up.

She could have backed down, Skye supposed, but she didn't want to. She felt as if she'd been here before, and last time she'd walked away. Well she didn't want to do that again. Finn was worried about his brother and she was worried about Finn, and she had an inkling that if she let him put her aside now then he'd keep doing it. And if they were to have any chance of being together then she needed to assert herself where he was concerned.

Finn was just too good at compartmentalising his life, and Skye knew she wanted it all. All or nothing—however much nothing would hurt. She wasn't going to make do with only the bits he was willing to share.

As for Dylan, well he would always be there, always, and one way or another she would have to learn to live with him. But she wasn't going to let his presence in Finn's life push her out.

After what seemed a long time sitting and saying nothing, Finn turned the vehicle into Desperation Track and Skye felt her shoulders relax a little.

The stuff hitting their windscreen was a combination of rain and sleet and snow, and the four-wheel drive ploughed through the slush on the track, heading deeper into the wilderness.

'Do you think we should bring Ebony back into town with us?' Skye broke through the silence. 'I mean, she shouldn't be stuck out here.

What if something goes wrong?'

'They were only supposed to be there for a few days, until we sorted something out. It's taking a lot longer than I thought.' He didn't sound angry, but then she remembered he rarely did. He withdrew, that was Finn's defence. He pulled up the drawbridge and locked the gate.

'They were going into protective custody?'

'Yes. That was the idea. My friend who's high up in the force wants to move on the corrupt element. He has to keep it quiet for obvious reasons. Dylan was going to give him information and in return he was going to be looked after. Only he started to get nervous. He didn't trust the men who'd been chosen to look after him. He didn't feel safe, he said. So I said I'd take care of him until all of the arrangements were in place.'

'But somehow Gary and Lois found out and came up here after him?'

'Which just goes to prove that Dylan was spot on when he said he didn't feel safe.'

She thought it through. It made sense, and she wished Finn had shared some of this with her in the beginning, but she also understood why he hadn't felt able to—he was well aware she wasn't Dylan's best friend.

Just for a moment Skye let herself imagine Gary Grey holding Ebony hostage, and Finn storming into the room to find Dylan lying dead on the floor. But she pushed that awful real-life movie out of her head and told herself not to be melodramatic. Surely things like that didn't actually happen? And yet she was beginning to think that maybe she'd bitten off more than she could chew by tagging along with Finn.

'Too late now.'

'Huh?' He turned to look at her, his face all shadows in the greenish glow from the dash-board. 'Having second thoughts, Skye?'

'Of course not,' she said firmly.

She thought he smiled, but she might have been mistaken.

The next moment the lights from Dylan's dilapidated hideaway shone dully through the trees and Finn pulled up out the front and turned off the engine. They'd climbed out of the Land-Cruiser and were making their way towards the gate, when the door opened and Dylan himself, rugged up in a jacket, appeared on the verandah.

'You couldn't have come at a better time, bro!' he called out, and there was a mixture of excitement and anticipation in his voice that didn't seem to suggest he was in imminent danger.

'What's going on?' Finn's tone was sharp as he met him halfway down the path. Inside the building they heard the dog give a gruff bark and fall silent.

'Ebony's having contractions,' he said, and his grin was almost wide enough to split his face in two. Then, with a puzzled glance from Finn to Skye, 'Why are you here anyway? I don't remember asking you both to the party.'

'We might have a problem,' Finn spoke quietly, as they began to walk back to the cottage.

By the time Skye followed them inside, the two men were standing together by the fire, heads close. There was something of deja vu in the moment, something that twisted in her stomach, and rather than joining them, she went in search of Ebony.

She'd expected to find the other woman lying down but instead she was in the kitchen, fussing around a large pan with a roast chicken surrounded by a variety of vegetables. Although small and cramped, the room was freshly painted and surprisingly well stocked.

'Shouldn't you be resting?' Skye asked.

Ebony gave a start and turned around. 'Oh, Skye! Great. You can help us eat some of this food. I seem to have cooked an awful lot,' she added with a puzzled glance.

'Dylan said you were in labour,' Skye ventured.

'I think I am.' She smiled. 'Early stages though. Time to do a few things before baby arrives.'

She seemed so calm and together that Skye was impressed. She couldn't imagine herself being so relaxed in the same circumstances. 'Perhaps you should sit down and I'll finish making the meal for you,' she offered, stepping forward and trying to look competent.

Ebony shook her head. 'I've been sleeping most of the day,' she said. 'I don't need to sit down. Really. But thank you for the offer.'

'Ebs, Skye is right, you really should be resting.' Dylan had come up behind them, unheard. His gaze lingered on Skye's face for a moment, before he slid his arm around his wife.

Ebony sighed and rolled her eyes. 'I want to get this done, then at least you'll have something to eat later on. The baby might take a long time to come, and you'll need to keep your strength up.'

Finn had followed his brother and was standing in the doorway. When Skye caught his eye she could tell that this time they were both on the same page. 'Ah, so what were you planning to do?' he asked. 'Ride into town on the back of Dylan's bike?'

Ebony laughed. 'No, I was going to have the baby here. I know what to do. My sister had a couple of home births, so it's not new to me.'

'But, what if something ...' Skye stopped herself, not sure whether she wanted to be the voice of reason here.

It was clear Dylan wasn't as comfortable with the decision as his wife. He tucked a strand of her fair hair behind her ear and bent down to look into her face, his voice gentle. 'You know, babe, I think it might be better if we go to Westcott. My baby-delivering skills need a bit of work.'

'That's all right,' she said, 'I can do it on my own.'

He shook his head at her in wonder, and once more it was obvious to Skye how much he loved her. 'I bet you can, but I need you to trust me on this. There's been a ... a bit of trouble and Finn thinks we'd be safer away from the cottage for a little while. Nowhere safer than a hospital, is there?'

Her mouth turned mulish, as if she was preparing for a fight. 'Dylan, this wasn't part of the plan.'

'I know it wasn't. I'm sorry. We need to leave.'

Ebony looked as if she had more to say about

that, but whatever she saw in his face changed her mind. 'What about all this food?' she protested.

'It'll keep,' he said confidently. 'Come on, Ebs, get your suitcase. We need to go.'

This time the words he had spoken earlier seemed to sink in. 'What is it?' she asked him, her gaze searching his. 'You said "a bit of trouble". What does that mean?'

'A possibility, that's all. This is just a precaution. You know what Finn's like, scared of his own shadow. We can talk about it later. Come on, Ebony, let's go!'

Ebony looked at Finn, but he smiled and nodded, and she groaned in frustration. 'I'm pregnant not an imbecile,' she muttered, as she pushed past and went towards the bedroom.

There was an uncomfortable silence.

'So, has Gary been here?' Skye asked.

'No,' Finn answered her.

Dylan gave her a cool look. 'No secrets between you two, then? Cosy.'

'Dylan,' his brother warned. 'Skye came in case Ebony needed her.'

'Ebony doesn't need anyone except me,' Dylan retorted. 'I've been taking care of her up until now. We should be somewhere in the sun, Finn, that's what I was promised when I agreed to give evidence to your important friend. Instead here we are in the middle of Alaska.'

'You asked for my help,' Finn reminded him mildly.

'I didn't think it was going to take a lifetime.' Dylan sounded frustrated and disgruntled. 'That's what happens when you put your life into other people's hands, Finn. It's a risk. Sometimes it's better just to deal with it yourself.'

'Now's not the time to do this.' Finn glared, clearly just as frustrated. 'If you're not happy then I'll make sure the people who need to know are told. But right now we have to get to Westcott so that I can keep you both safe.'

Dylan pointed a finger at him. 'You don't need to keep us safe, I can do that. What I need from you is a deal and that you have so far failed to deliver.'

'It takes time,' Finn said, the strain evident in his voice. 'You know it takes time. I'm doing what I can.'

Dylan's gaze rested on Finn's face. 'You owe me,' he said quietly. 'Remember?'

Finn seemed taken by surprise. His body tensed and his head came up, but to Skye it looked as if he'd been punched. 'I'm aware of that,' he spoke at last, as if it was an effort. 'You don't have to remind me.'

'Don't I?' Dylan shook his head in disgust. 'I'll go and see what Ebony's doing. Probably baking a cake,' and he shot a smile at Skye, as if the argument had never happened.

Finn hadn't moved. Skye put a hand on his arm and felt his muscles bunched up. 'What did he mean? Finn?'

He shrugged awkwardly, pretending it was nothing. 'You know Dylan. The king of riddles.'

She might have pressed him for more, but Dylan and Ebony were back. Ebony looked a little pale and was chewing her bottom lip. 'The contractions are getting stronger,' she explained. 'I'm glad you two turned up, maybe I'm not so keen to do this on my own after all.'

'We'd better get going,' Dylan put in, a pleading look in his eyes. 'You ready, Finn?'

He was scared. Skye realised that's what the arguing and aggression was all about. Dylan was frightened and it was his way of bolstering himself up, and Finn just happened to be there.

Finn didn't answer him, reaching out instead to rest a gentle hand on Ebony's belly. 'Hold on a bit longer, nephew,' he said. 'Just till we get to Westcott.'

Ebony giggled. 'I've told you, it's a girl!'

Finn shook his head. 'Nope. Dylan's getting a boy. An exact replica of himself. Only fair.'

Briefly he rested his gaze on Dylan, who was the first to look away. And then they were moving towards the door. Dylan paused to check that the fire in the hearth was safe, and put out extra food for his dog, before they went outside to the Toyota.

'I wish we could've had a proper visit,' Ebony said, with a shy glance at Skye. 'It's nice, sometimes, to chill out with girl stuff. You know? I miss my friends.'

Skye did know, but she asked herself how much worse it must be for Ebony, hiding out here with Dylan. And what about the future, that must be an added stress, when they didn't even know what it was going to entail. A new name, a new town, and always looking over her shoulder.

No wonder Dylan was a mess, but Skye didn't like him taking it out on his brother. Finn didn't deserve that. And that crack about him owing him? Wasn't that something Skye had heard before? Had it always upset Finn? She couldn't remember the details, but she was sure of one thing. This time she wasn't going to ignore it. This time she was going to find out the truth.

After they'd all made themselves comfortable in the cabin, Ebony in the rear with Dylan, Finn turned them around and headed back. If anything the weather was worse, the wipers going at full tilt, and still failing to clear the windscreen.

Finn was concentrating on his driving, and silence had fallen in the back. Skye cleared her throat. 'So where did you two meet?' she asked curiously, hoping the answer wasn't going to be 'in prison'.

'He ordered a coffee in the place I was working at, and we got talking,' Ebony said with a laugh. 'Corny, I know, but we've been together ever since.'

'Best coffee I'd ever drunk,' Dylan added. 'How could I let her go?'

Ebony gave him a smile and for a moment they seemed lost in each other's eyes. Skye looked away, pondering if it had really been that cut and dried. Love at first sight? Perhaps for Dylan, but Ebony seemed like the sort of girl who could be choosy when it came to men. Although Skye could remember him being good company, some of the time, and a lot of the girls at school had fancied him. He'd been funny, too, when he wasn't being crazy.

'I'm lucky I came along at the right time,' Ebony added from the back seat, sounding utterly serious.

'Lucky?' Skye repeated.

'Yeah. That he hadn't been taken.'

Evidently Dylan knew what Skye was thinking, because he spoke up unexpectedly, his tone dry. 'Skye is having trouble with that one, babe. She only remembers me from my dickhead days. It took me a bit longer than Finn to grow up. But when you came along, Ebs, I was in a good place, and now I'm in a better one.'

Skye felt her face heat up. 'I'm sure Ebony is right,' she said stiffly.

Dylan gave a soft laugh and silence fell once again, and this time Skye left it alone.

Once they got onto the Westcott road things went smoother, and Finn made good time. There wasn't any traffic, and those few vehicles they did meet were being cautious. A couple of times Ebony murmured to Dylan and shifted about, trying to get comfortable, but she didn't seem to be overly stressed.

However, the hospital staff didn't take matters so lightly, and Ebony was swiftly booked in. By then Finn had arranged for a constable from Westcott to provide security, promising that Doug would take over when he got back from the accident. Dylan was caught up with Ebony, helping her settle in, but he said he'd be out to talk to Finn in a moment.

Finn and Skye waited in the lobby. The snow

had stopped and it was very cold outside. Just looking at it had Skye huddling into her woollen coat and blowing warm air into her gloved hands.

'I should get myself some proper winter clothing,' she said aloud, and gave Finn a sideways glance.

He was standing with his hands in his pockets, staring out at the car park. 'Does that mean you'll only be visiting me in cold weather?' he asked. Although he was smiling, she thought it was a struggle. Something was wrong. Was it just that he was worried about Dylan and the whereabouts of Gary Grey, or was it more than that?

She moved closer, resting her body against his, and murmured into his shoulder, 'Why is everything so complicated?'

He bent and kissed the top of her head. 'Tell me about it.'

'Do you think if we'd just met, and there wasn't all that stuff from years ago, that we'd feel the same?' she wondered aloud. 'I mean, if we were strangers.'

She lifted her face and searched his eyes for the same doubts she was feeling, but all she could see was calm certainty. 'Yep,' he said. 'We're destined to be together, Skye, the stars are aligned.'

'You think it's fate then? I wish I'd known that when I'd arrived, I wouldn't have tried so hard to be aloof.'

He laughed properly this time, and put his arm around her to give her a squeeze, and it was a moment before they realised Dylan had come up beside them. He shot them a tentative smile.

'Happy days, eh?' he said, with a glance at Finn, and Skye realised he was probably trying to make amends for his earlier behaviour. 'Glad to see you guys back together.'

Finn nodded without responding. Skye looked from one to the other, not understanding any more than she had all those years ago.

'How's Ebony settling in?' she asked instead.

'She'll be fine. She's strong.' He turned to his brother. 'You staying?'

'I thought I should, just in case,' Finn spoke at last. 'A constable from the local station will be here soon.'

'I appreciate it,' Dylan said, and it was obvious he did. 'Look, Finn, you know how I get. I didn't mean—'

'Sergeant Galloway? Alison in Elysian wants to speak to you urgently.'

They all turned at the sound of the voice. It was the woman on reception, her eyebrows raised, holding up the telephone receiver.

'Now what?' Skye murmured, as Finn went over to take the call. He spoke with his back to them, and it was impossible to tell what was being said.

'Finn's good in a crisis. Better than me,' Dylan said, rubbing his hands together to warm them. The hospital heating seemed to be lacking down here.

'I suppose it's his job,' she replied evenly, treading carefully.

'I tend to react. Now that I have Ebony, I worry more than I used to. I couldn't bear it if anything happened to her.'

'That's understandable,' Skye began, but stopped when she saw Finn was coming back to join them.

'There's a situation.'

'What sort of "situation"?' Dylan demanded impatiently—evidently his good intentions had already gone out the window.

'A car has gone off the road and down the side of a mountain. It's jammed against a tree, next stop Silverfish Creek. The guy who saw it and called it in didn't notice any movement, but he thinks there's someone still in the car. Could be serious injuries.'

'What are you going to do?' Skye whispered.

Finn was watching his brother, but now he turned to her. 'I'll call out the tow truck, though it might take them a while to get there, and the helicopter pilot who's dealing with Doug's motorcyclist is going to make his way over as soon as he's done. A couple of hours probably.' He shook his head wearily. 'But for now I'm it. The best I can do.'

'Where *is* the car?'

'Off the road to Mackenzie Crossing.'

'Mackenzie Crossing, eh? That's your place, isn't it, Skye?' Dylan said, and there was a light in his eyes Skye didn't like, as if he was enjoying this.

Finn ignored him, concentrating on Skye. 'I'll drop you off at home when the constable arrives,' he told her. 'Sorry about this, Dylan, but there's not much I can do. I'll make sure he knows about Gary Grey, and I'll be back as soon as I can.'

Dylan snorted. 'You can't go out there to rescue the guy on your own, bro. I'll come with you.'

There was speculation and doubt in Finn's expression, but also something that suggested to Skye he was tempted to say yes. 'You're a police witness about to go into protective custody. If we're going strictly by the book—'

'You need my help. Who cares about the book?'

Another pause and then at last Finn nodded in agreement, but Skye could see the tension was back in his shoulders.

'Then I'll come, too,' she announced, as if it was all arranged. 'Maybe I can man the radio or something.'

If she had been expecting Finn to try to dissuade her this time she was surprised. 'Are you sure?' he asked, unable to hide his relief. He wanted her there. Or maybe he just didn't want to be alone with his brother.

And why on earth was she thinking that?

'Sure I'm sure,' she said.

'If our resources weren't so stretched …' he began, and then shrugged irritably. 'Can't be helped.'

'I brought my camera,' she remembered. 'I thought I might get some photos of Dylan and Ebony. Anyway, I can take some of the scene. Isn't that what you usually do?'

Just then a police car pulled into the car park outside, and Finn moved towards the door to meet the constable, saying, 'Back in a minute.'

Skye watched the two men talking outside. She couldn't hear what they were saying, but their serious faces seemed to suggest Finn was making certain his fellow officer understood the situation.

'What about Ebony?' she turned to Dylan. 'Shouldn't you let her know what's going on?'

'Just about to,' Dylan responded. He hesitated, and then added, 'Come and say hi.'

'Okay,' she said. As she walked beside him she found herself speculating if there was a reason he wanted her with him, or was she just being unnecessarily suspicious? Surely not everything Dylan did or said had an ulterior motive.

'So you decided to stick around, did you, Skye?' Dylan turned his head to look at her as they climbed the stairs. 'I'm glad. I want Finn to be happy.'

'Do you?' She couldn't read his face, although she thought he was sincere. 'I hope that's true.'

'Why wouldn't it be?' he asked with a smile that didn't reach his eyes.

She looked at him curiously. 'You seem very relaxed suddenly. I thought you were worried about Gary Grey? Shouldn't you stay here with Ebony? You could ask Finn to take the constable with him instead of you.'

'Nah. I trust him. And if I can help then I should. A few gold stars against my name won't go astray.'

Again Skye felt puzzled. There was something not right about him and what he was saying, but she couldn't work out what it was.

They'd reached Ebony's room and found her sitting on the edge of the bed. She looked up with relief as Dylan entered. 'There you are!'

Dylan sat down beside her. 'Ebs, there's something I have to do.'

Ebony glanced from him to Skye and back again, her eyes narrowing. 'What could be more important than your baby being born?' she said, and Skye knew then that Dylan had brought her along to try to prevent a scene. He was looking over at her now, wanting her to jump in on his side, but she folded her arms and remained silent. With a sigh he turned back to his wife.

'Babe, it's Finn. I have to go with him.'

'Dylan, this isn't the way it was supposed to be,' Ebony said, her voice rising. 'First you drag me out into the back of beyond, and now you're not even going to be here when your baby is born.'

Dylan looked at Skye again. 'Give us some space, would you?'

She was tempted to say no, and to ask him why, if he had something to say, he couldn't do so in front of her, but Finn would be waiting. 'Bye, Ebony,' she said with a smile. 'Take care.'

'Yeah, thanks.' Ebony drew a deep breath to calm herself.

Skye closed the door. Almost immediately their voices started up, Dylan's low and persuasive, and Ebony's louder complaints, so that she quickened her pace down the corridor, until they faded into the usual hospital sounds.

At the top of the stairs she paused. Finn was in the lobby with the constable, no doubt giving him some last-minute instructions. By the time she reached reception the man was on his way up to guard Ebony's room.

'Where's Dylan?' Finn asked.

'Just saying goodbye to Ebony. She wasn't very happy with him.'

'He knows he can stay,' Finn said with a frown.

'And yet he seems keen to come,' she replied, meeting his eyes. She knew then that there *was* something else he wasn't telling her, and if she'd insisted he might have done so, but just then Dylan arrived.

'Stay if you want,' Finn told him. 'The guy in the car might be dead for all we know, which would mean there's nothing urgent about the call-out. But just in case he's hurt and needs help, I need to go.'

Dylan looked down at his boots and then shook his head. 'Ebs is okay—she says we have a few hours before anything really starts happening. I want to come with you and make myself useful.'

It sounded plausible, but Skye thought Dylan wasn't telling the whole truth. Neither of them was. Perhaps she should stay behind, stay out of it? But they were heading towards the door now, and Finn turned around to see where she was.

'Coming?' he asked. He wanted her there with him, she could tell, and she wasn't going to let him down.

CHAPTER 31

NEVILLE

One pm, Friday 13 January 1939,
Mackenzie Crossing

THE WIND HAD lifted the temperature beyond unbearable. At one point Neville searched out his camera and, in between his efforts to help, began to take photographs. It seemed important to him to record what was happening.

Georgie was busy wetting sacks and blankets for protection if the fire came through. She'd even started a bucket brigade from the creek, tossing pails of muddy water onto the walls of the hostelry, in the hope it would keep them safe if the time came to shelter within. She was still hoping the fire would pass over them. Neville wasn't so sure anything would save them from the conflagration if it decided to descend upon them, but at least it gave them something to do.

Hector limped past, and Neville saw that his face was as red as one of the tomatoes he grew in his garden. Georgie's clothing was damp with sweat and water from the creek, and her hair was a tangle beneath her drooping hat. She looked up, towards the hill behind the town, and Neville automatically followed her gaze.

The sky was dark with a red glow, as if all the world beyond was ablaze. It was one of the most frightening things he'd ever seen and his heart sank.

'Where's Tiddler?'

Georgie's voice was a shout, because the noise of the wind was increasing. Neville looked about him, turning a full circle, but the boy was nowhere to be seen.

Peggy had arrived with another bucket and she pointed past the hostelry, up the track Neville had travelled this morning. He only caught bits and pieces of what she was saying; however, he was able to put it together. Tiddler and Arnold had gone to fetch Her Majesty, so they could keep her safe, but she'd taken fright and run off. Arnold stayed but Tiddler went after her. 'I told him not to go far, Georgie,' Peggy wailed, 'and he promised.'

Georgie went still. Neville could see her thoughts flitting across her face, all of them bad. He reached out to grasp her arm and when she looked at him her eyes were full of doubt. And he realised once again how much effort it was taking her to keep up her appearance of ironclad courage. She might be fooling the others, yet Neville could see she was very frightened indeed.

'You won't leave me, will you?' she said.

For a second he didn't know what she meant. Leave her to deal with this situation on her own or leave her afterwards when it was over and whatever was about to happen had happened? And then he realised that the answer to both questions was the same. Somewhere in the past few hours his decision had been made and there was no going back. 'No,' he spoke with absolute certainty. 'No, I won't leave you.'

'Tiddler …'

'I'll find him and bring him back,' Neville said, his voice full of the sort of confidence he'd once displayed in the army, and set off at a run before she could say another word. There was no time to waste.

As he climbed up from the Crossing towards the timber camp, he tried to tell himself there was still a chance everything would be all right. Even if they ended up in the Union Jack mine, this place had escaped disaster before and he wouldn't be at all surprised if Georgie could perform miracles. If anyone could do it then it was she. His job was simpler. He just had to find Tiddler and bring him home.

The track appeared different from this morning, when he'd set out to photograph Phil and the others. All around him, the smoke was getting steadily thicker, and when he called out for the boy his voice sounded like a husk in his raw throat.

When it failed altogether, he swallowed and tried again.

How far should he go? The boy could be anywhere, he thought in sudden panic. What if he couldn't find him? What if he had to go back without him? It didn't bear thinking of. For a moment the past washed over him, the sound of the guns in the trenches, their pounding making the ground beneath his feet shudder, while his men followed trustingly behind him. All the way across no-man's-land.

And suddenly he knew this was just another mission. Instead of overcoming enemy trenches, he had to find Georgie's son, and he couldn't go back without him. It was as simple as that.

'Tiddler!'

This time he thought he heard a response from further up the slope. He must be almost at the campfire site now. His leg muscles burning and his eyes stinging, Neville pushed on, pausing only occasionally to cling to the rough bark of a sapling and catch his breath, coughing from the smoke. A wallaby bounced past him, blind with panic.

'Mr Darling!'

Thank God, thank God, it was Tiddler.

From somewhere, he found the extra energy to break into a run, and quickly reached a dip in the track before it rose upwards again. A shape was approaching him through the murk. Confused, he knew it was too tall to be Tiddler, but a moment later he understood there were two of them, and Tiddler wasn't alone.

'Mr Darling!' Tiddler shouted, and ran against him. The boy was holding Her Majesty is his arms, the hen looking worse for wear, but then none of them were particularly spick and span right now. 'She ran away,' he said, sounding achingly young and scared, although being Georgie's child he was trying his best to hide it.

'But we found her, didn't we, son?'

The voice was familiar. Slowly Neville looked up, his mind coming to grips with this new problem, wishing he was mistaken even as he knew he wasn't.

'We meet again,' said former Detective Inspector Miller Brown. His thin face was dripping sweat and smeared where bits of ash had dropped onto him from the wind, and yet he stood ramrod straight, like a soldier on parade. And something about that straight back convinced Neville that here was a man who was willing to do anything, even risk his own life, in order to bring Georgie to justice.

'We need to get back, Tiddler,' he said quietly. 'Thank you for looking after him, Mr Brown.'

But when he turned, half hoping the man would go back the way he'd come, Brown followed after them down the track. 'Is this your son, then, Mr Darling?'

'No, he's not my son.'

A gust of wind blew from behind them, so hot Neville felt as if the skin was peeling from his body. He noticed Her Majesty's beak was open and she was sagging in Tiddler's arms.

'He says he comes from Mackenzie Crossing. Is that right? That's my destination.' He sounded pleased with himself. 'It seems as if I've been going around in circles for days and then finally

I had a spot of luck. Someone pointed me in the right direction. I was told it was too dangerous to get there today and to go back to Elysian, but I refuse to allow some bad weather to prevent me from doing my duty.'

Neville's cheek was stinging and he put a hand to it, realising a falling ember had produced a blister. Tiddler tripped and nearly fell, his hands full with the hen, so he put an arm around the boy's thin shoulders to steady him.

'Nearly there,' he murmured, bending closer. 'Georgie has some water in buckets she got from the creek. You need to wet down Her Majesty.'

Tiddler gave him an anxious smile. 'Should I go ahead?'

'Perhaps you should. But be careful!' he called out, as the boy started to run down the slope as if he wanted to get back to the Crossing as soon as possible.

The smoke lay over them like a fog, and Neville could imagine what that meant. Somewhere beyond the hills behind them a fire was moving swiftly in their direction. Driven on by the wind, it was eating up the tinder-dry bushland with insatiable appetite.

A knot formed in his throat and he swallowed it down. He needed time.

Brown was keeping pace behind him. 'The spot of luck I mentioned,' he said, seeming satisfied. 'Remember the story I told you that day at the Elysian Hotel? I showed you the photograph that was found among the murdered man's belongings and ...' He gave Neville a curious glance.

'Why did you keep it?' Then, before Neville could think of an answer, he waved a dismissive hand, eager to complete his story. 'Never mind that now. What matters is I've found the woman I was seeking.'

Neville moved ahead, hoping to outpace him, but then the track widened and he came abreast of Neville again, and his curiosity had turned to suspicion. 'But you must know her, if you're staying there.'

Neville shook his head. 'I've only just arrived. I've been taking photographs. I don't know much about the place, and the boy—someone sent me up to find him.'

'Ah,' Brown said, apparently swallowing the lie easily enough. Or perhaps he was just impatient to continue with his story.

Neville barely had to ask, and then a word here and there was enough to keep Brown's voice flowing.

'For almost nine years this case has haunted me,' Brown went on. 'It happens sometimes, and it's rare there's a resolution, but this time an informant has come forward. The landlord of the rooms in Fitzroy in which the body was found, the rooms in which the woman and the murdered man were meeting, has always claimed to know nothing about the matter. When I visited him several weeks ago, he finally admitted he remembered the woman, and his description of her matched that of the photograph. And he mentioned something more, that she had spoken to him one day and told him her home was in the mountains, near Elysian. That was what brought me here, Darling.'

'It seems little enough. How many women could fit such a description? I don't—'

'Let me finish,' and he held up his hand as if Neville was an impertinent underling. 'When I saw this gentleman he told me he was not long for this world, and I suggested he clear his conscience before it was too late. I left him the name of a colleague. Two days ago he visited that colleague and made a formal statement. I received a telegram at the Elysian Hotel.' He tapped his pocket. 'It's all here. The woman's name is Mackenzie, Miss Georgina Mackenzie, and she was a teacher in a girl's school. Turns out the murdered man was involved in the running of the school. He was also a bit of a Lothario—he'd used those rooms before for the same purpose. The landlord has admitted he was privy to this, but the man paid well, so he was prepared to turn a blind eye. Except that this time the girl was different. She was young and naive, and the situation made him feel uncomfortable. Still, he continued to take the money, even when he discovered she was having a child.'

'A son.'

'Yes, a son.' Brown didn't seem to notice the slip. 'Our chatty friend believes that on the day the man was murdered, it had been arranged for him to take the boy away. See to his adoption. It was impossible for a single woman like Miss Mackenzie, a teacher, to keep him. I can only guess what happened next, but my belief is that when the father came to take him away, Miss Mackenzie wouldn't allow it. They fought. She produced a knife. In the ensuing struggle he was killed.'

'A mother's love for her child can make her a fierce opponent, Brown.'

The other man nodded, but his voice was brisk and emotionless when he went on. 'Murder is an evil business, Darling. I can't condone it. The father may have been wrong to seduce her, but they had an agreement. Whatever he may have done, he didn't deserve to be slaughtered like a sheep.'

Neville slowed his steps. The air was full of the smell of burning and he knew he didn't have long. 'Why wasn't she arrested at the time?'

'Because she fled the scene with the child. We didn't know who she was until now. I did what I could to find her, but it was as if she'd vanished into thin air. Of course she must have had help, possibly this Miss Agostino, who owned the school, although she's dead now so we won't be able to charge her.'

'Indeed.'

'I'm on my way to make an arrest that's been nearly nine years coming, Darling, and let me tell you it gives me a good deal of satisfaction.'

The truth was worse than Neville had imagined, but he couldn't believe it was as simple as Brown had said. He couldn't. Georgie would not have agreed to give up her son willingly, and even if she had, when Tiddler was being taken, she must have felt so desperate. She had saved herself and the boy the only way she could. Perhaps he was smitten or a fool, but he could not imagine it any other way.

'You didn't consider just letting this go?' he asked quietly.

'Did we give up on the Somme?' Brown said proudly, with that straight back. 'No, we fought to the last man, and I'd be happy to do so again.'

Neville knew then that it would be pointless reasoning with him. Anyone who spoke of that war with pride instead of the horror it deserved was not a reasonable person. The choice before him was stark.

He could let Brown have his way and, assuming the fire missed the Crossing, Georgie would be arrested and perhaps hanged, and Tiddler's future would be thrown into chaos. In the short time he had known them he had grown to love and admire them, to see in them something that was lacking in his own life. He'd felt a connection and a glimmer of hope for a future that until now had seemed a bleak and lonely prospect, and to have it taken away from him in such cruel circumstances was not to be borne.

Or he could stop Brown now.

And that was when Neville realised he'd already made up his mind.

He turned and looked at Miller Brown. The man's eyes changed, grew wary. 'The law is the law,' he said firmly.

'But is it justice?' Neville replied.

Once you'd killed a man, he told himself, what difference did another make? And he had killed many. But it wasn't easy, it was never easy.

It was just something that had to be done.

CHAPTER 32

SKYE

Wednesday 11 June 1997

THE AIR WAS frigid, and Skye's breath came in puffs of white, and even with the gloves on, her hands ached with the cold. She stamped her feet, trying to prevent her toes from going slowly numb. Behind her, the Toyota was parked so that its headlights gave some illumination to the crash site.

Finn was edging his way towards it, slow and easy, testing each step on the snow-covered ground beneath his feet. Every now and then he'd stop and look behind him, catch his breath.

Skye had already shot some photos with her Pentax—just general views of the car and the area it had come to rest in. The vehicle was halfway down the steep slope, and only the trunk of a battered-looking tree and a clump of scrub had stopped it from going all the way over the edge and into Silver Fish Creek. Just beyond the bonnet and front wheels was the lip of the ravine and clear air.

How was Finn going to get a badly injured passenger out of there? He'd explained to them that he normally had a safety harness he used in situations like this but it was currently in the police vehicle with Doug.

When they'd arrived he'd wanted her to stay in the car. She'd refused. Partially because she'd thought that was what Laurie would have done, stay put and keep warm. Although then again Laurie wouldn't have been here in the first place. But the point was Skye wanted to know exactly what it was Finn did in these situations. She wanted to understand the good and bad of being Sergeant Galloway, top cop in Elysian.

Knowledge was power, wasn't it?

Skye stamped her feet again, trying to put aside her doubts, telling herself that Finn had probably done this a hundred times before. Ignoring her stomach, queasy with nerves.

Dylan was standing beside her, his shoulders hunched in his thermal jacket, his red beanie pulled down to his eyebrows. Like Skye, his attention was focused on the man moving closer to the wreck.

Finn was keeping close to the ground, crouched low to stop from slipping. A few more scrambling steps and he was opposite the passenger-side window. He lifted his flashlight and shone it inside. They could see the beam moving about and then it stilled. He seemed to keep it there for a long time.

'What's he doing?' Dylan muttered. Then, 'Can

you see anything?' he called out impatiently.

Finn looked up, his face a pale oval beneath his blue beanie. 'A man,' he shouted back. 'Not moving.'

'Not moving,' Dylan murmured.

'Dead, then?' Skye glanced sideways at him, but he was so engrossed with what lay below he didn't seem to hear her.

'Should you wait for the tow truck?' Skye called out in her turn, feeling the cold biting into the skin of her face where it was exposed.

Finn didn't respond, but a moment later he began to climb back up the slope towards them. Skye watched him get closer and closer, each step increasing her feelings of relief. Dylan reached out at the last and hauled him the final few metres, and then he was standing beside her, his face flushed and his chest heaving with effort.

'Okay?' she asked, touching his gloved hand.

He nodded and caught his breath. 'It's steep but there's plenty of grip. The car's caught against the tree but not by much. Could go at any minute.'

'He's dead, then,' Dylan spoke up, 'the guy in the car?'

'Looks that way to me.'

'Are you sure?' Dylan asked.

'I'm sure,' he said, and didn't elaborate.

'So, is it an accident?' Dylan again, suddenly interested. 'I mean, the guy went off the road by accident?'

It seemed a strange question.

'Looks that way,' Finn replied, met his eyes briefly and then looked away.

Dylan nodded. 'Any idea who it might be?' he asked.

Finn shook his head. 'No. I couldn't …' a glance at Skye, 'didn't recognise him.'

'Stranger, huh?'

'Tourist, maybe. Joy rider, although it's not the sort of vehicle I'd expect for someone looking for thrills. Someone lost?' He shrugged.

'Wrong place at the wrong time?' Dylan was pushing the point.

There didn't seem to be an answer for that.

Dylan groaned in frustration. 'Come on, Finn, that's bullshit! It's Gary Grey, isn't it?'

'Gary Grey?' Skye looked from one to the other in shocked amazement. 'What do you mean?'

Finn said nothing, but he didn't dispute Dylan's accusation.

Dylan shook his head. He looked like he wanted to hit someone. 'He thinks I did it,' he said, pointing a finger at his brother, and Skye noticed it was far from steady. 'Come on, Finn, admit it. You looked through that window and saw Grey and you thought I did it.'

'It crossed my mind,' Finn said quietly. 'I won't apologise for that, Dylan. You knew he was in the car long before I did. As soon as you heard about the accident your concern for Ebony went way down the scale. You didn't want to stay with her, you wanted to come out here with me, and don't tell me it was because you wanted to help.'

'I thought it might be him,' he admitted. His eyes were sore looking, his face tired. He seemed to have aged years. 'Whatever I say you won't believe me,' he muttered. 'Why should you?'

'Did you do it?' Skye burst out.

He looked at her and seemed to be considering his words, but in the end he just shook his head and said a simple, 'No.'

'Dylan,' Finn reclaimed his attention, dark eyes intense. 'Try me. What is the truth here, because I have a dead cop in a car and I'm going to have to tell someone pretty soon. After that it's out of my hands.'

'Okay, okay.' He pinched the bridge of his nose and squeezed his eyes shut, as if he had a headache. He gave a shaky laugh. 'What a mess. Right, here's the thing, Lois Petersen came to me a couple of months ago. She said she was worried about Gary and she needed help with him. He was unstable, taking too much from each drug bust, wanting more money. Erratic. So she wanted to get rid of him, and she wanted me to arrange it—well, she probably thought I'd do it myself, but that wasn't going to happen.'

He gave them both a hard look, as if daring them to dispute it. When neither said anything he shook his head again and went on.

'I said no. She said if I did it then I wouldn't have to help her anymore, she would leave me alone. I didn't believe her, and anyway I didn't want her help. I said, "No thanks" and then I contacted Finn.'

'But you didn't tell me this particular part of the story,' Finn reminded him.

'I was saving it up for a rainy day,' he retorted. 'Well that's not true, I suppose, I was saving it up to use as leverage, in case Lois came looking for me. And then she did, and now Gary's dead and it looks like I did it. Thanks, Lois.'

'Where were you earlier today? I'd say he's been dead a few hours.'

'I was at home with Ebs.'

'She said she slept most of the day,' Skye murmured, and earned herself an angry stare. She shrugged, not intimidated. 'I'm just telling you what she told me.'

'I was with my wife,' he repeated, but there was a note of desperation in his voice now. As if he knew he was losing the battle. In an instant the hostility seemed to drain out of him. 'Help me, Finn. Save me one last time and I promise never to ask for anything ever again.'

Skye was waiting for him to say 'You owe me'. Strangely he didn't. Finn must have been waiting for it, too, because she felt the tension in the arm pressed to hers.

'Gary looks like he's been shot,' he said at last. 'Do you own a gun?'

Dylan snorted. 'Not the one that shot him.'

'Then we need to document the scene. We have to do everything by the book from now on. Skye,' he said, turning to her, 'I'm going to need to borrow your camera.' When she didn't answer him, he said, 'I'll be careful.'

'God, Finn, it's not the camera I'm worried about,' she blurted out.

She lifted the camera from around her neck and handed it to him, and he slipped the strap over his head. 'Thanks,' he said softly, and kissed her cold cheek. 'Stay here. Truck should arrive soon.'

'What about me?' Dylan asked.

'I'm still working on that,' Finn said, frowning. 'You shouldn't be here. You must have known how that would look?'

'I was worried she'd leave something in the car that pointed to me. She probably has.'

Unless he'd left it himself and that's how he knew, Skye thought, but she bit back the words.

'I'm coming with you,' Dylan said. 'This is down to me and you're not going on your own, Finn.'

'No.' Finn gave him a look, and then without another word he began to descend, backwards, once again testing each step, pausing every now and then to look over his shoulder and get his bearings. He was moving incredibly fast really, covering a lot of ground, and he *was* careful.

'Always the hero,' Dylan muttered, and launched himself forward and down the slope, so quickly she had no chance of stopping him.

'No, no …' she whispered, frantically taking a few steps along the verge and then turning back again. But there was nothing for it, she had to follow, although what she could do if there was a fight she didn't know.

She only just kept her balance. It was very steep, and her boots were wrong, they had no tread. Dylan was already far ahead, keeping low on his haunches, finding foot and handholds in the churned-up snow Finn had already travelled.

Finn had reached the car and was getting the camera ready, using his flashlight to check the mechanism. He must have heard the noise of Dylan's approach, because he looked back. Skye couldn't read his expression, but there was something in his stillness that warned her of trouble ahead.

Suddenly, she became aware of a distant rumble away to her left. The approaching tow truck. The ground seemed to shake. Relieved, she turned to look, hoping to see the headlights streaming through the trees. It would be all right now, wouldn't it? More people meant Dylan would have to behave himself.

Then a shout came from below. Skye turned back and the first thing she saw was the flashlight spiralling along the ground, the light sending out crazy glimpses of tree and snow, and Finn pressed against the side of the car and Dylan holding onto him.

'Finn!' she screamed.

There was a grinding sound and the wrecked car was moving, twisting. As if in slow motion it began to slide, picking up speed as it freed itself from the safe embrace of the tree trunk. It began to tip over the ravine, and then seemed to pause, like a high-board diver going for the ten-point dive.

Dylan let out a shout, and she saw he had Finn by the arm, and then they both fell forward.

The next moment it was gone, metal grinding and screeching, all the way down to Silverfish Creek. In the Toyota headlights, she could see the bare sweep of snow, and someone crouched near to where the car had lingered before it fell.

Jacket and jeans, a beanie over dark hair ... It could have been either brother, and it was only when he turned and lifted his face that she realised who it was.

Dylan.

She couldn't do anything. Shock held her completely still.

Finn was gone. She'd only just found him again and now she'd lost him.

And then she was on the ground, sliding, tumbling, moving down the slope. It was stupid and dangerous, but she couldn't help it. The thought of Finn falling, injured, *dead* ...

'Skye! Skye, stop!'

Dylan was standing up, waving his arms at her. It took her a moment to understand what he was saying.

'The truck. They'll have a winch. Finn's okay, he's on a ledge, but we have to haul him back up.'

She'd managed to slow her momentum. Panting, she lay a moment, torn between believing him or not. Maybe he knew it, because he knelt down again, leaning over the lip of the ravine, and when he turned back he called out, 'He says your camera is fine and the exhibition can go ahead.'

A laugh came out of her that sounded more like a sob. He *was* alive. Only Finn would say something like that.

'It doesn't look all that secure,' Dylan shouted again. 'Maybe we should hurry.'

There was a strained note in his voice.

That did it. Skye turned and started back up

the slope she'd just descended. It was quite a hike, but by the time she reached the top, the truck was in sight. It pulled in beside the LandCruiser and two men jumped out to meet her.

Moments later, with her heart in her throat, she watched as Finn was hauled up over the lip of the ravine. Dylan had hold of his brother's arm, and despite the guys with the truck telling him they had it and he could let Finn go, he wouldn't.

'Hey, this is my twin brother!' he shouted back. 'I'm the eldest by five minutes and I'm not letting him go.'

Finn was laughing, which made her doubt if either of them was quite sane.

As they got closer she could see that Finn had a scrape on his cheek and there was a tear in his jacket, but otherwise he didn't look any the worse for wear. All the same she put her arms around him and held him tight.

'What happened?' she whispered.

'We were looking through the window and then the truck came. I think the vibration was enough to send the car off. Dylan jumped out of the way but my jacket caught and I … It tore free as I went over.'

Skye clung tighter.

'What was the silly bugger doing out here in this weather?' One of the guys from the truck spoke up behind them. He pointed towards where the car had gone over. Heads were shaken at the stupidity of tourists and city folk.

Finn went to call Taylor on the CB radio and he was gone a long time. Dylan was standing beside Skye as they waited, and this time when she shivered he put a tentative arm around her. Earlier she might have shaken him off, in fact she was certain of it. Now, although she didn't exactly return his hug, neither did she pull away. She was remembering the sound of his voice and the look on his face as he had helped Finn back to solid ground.

No matter what had happened in the past and would happen in the future, she could no longer doubt Dylan's love for his younger brother, and it seemed to have tipped the balance where Skye was concerned.

Soon the helicopter arrived, spotlight leeching the colour out of the landscape as it rested above them.

'Hang on,' she told Dylan, and went to fetch her camera.

The helicopter was still circling, and the juxtaposition of light and dark was striking. She took several photos of Finn, too, covert shots, unposed. And one of Dylan standing watching his brother.

Taking photographs always calmed her. Whether she'd ever use these she didn't know—perhaps legally she wouldn't be allowed to. The helicopter had taken a look over in the ravine and the pilot had reported that the car was down there, and recovery would have to wait until morning.

'You need to go home.' Finn found her at last, seated in the vehicle now, trying to get warm. He crouched down on the ground looking in the open door, eyes taking in her weary smile.

'Home?' she whispered, thinking he meant Melbourne.

'Dylan needs to get back to Ebony, so maybe you can take him there first. I don't know when I'll be home, Skye. My friend at head office has got in touch, but there're going to be lots of hoops to jump through. I have to wait until the team arrives from Melbourne.'

'I can also wait,' she said quickly, relieved he didn't want her to set off for the city after all.

He shook his head. 'Better if you don't. Lightning needs you.'

She managed a chuckle.

Dylan had come up behind his brother. 'We ready, Skye?' he asked, and she thought that of course he would be concerned about his wife and the baby.

'Name him after me,' Finn said, as he straightened.

Dylan looked puzzled for a moment and then his face cleared and he gave a genuine laugh. 'I won't be naming *her* after anybody. She'll be her own person to make her own mistakes, but hopefully not too many.'

'Hopefully,' Finn murmured.

CHAPTER 33

NEVILLE

Two pm, Friday 13 January 1939,
Mackenzie Crossing

TIDDLER HAD A wet blanket wrapped around his head and shoulders, and another strip around a disgruntled Her Majesty, who was tucked up safely in a small basket. The suitcase Georgie had packed earlier was on the ground at his feet and beside it, the brass lamp with the yellow glass shade. By the time Neville got back he was gasping, beginning to think oxygen was in short supply, and he could tell the others were having similar problems.

'Where's Mr Brown?' the boy asked in a croaky voice.

'Mr Brown?' Distracted, Georgie turned to look at him. She had a blanket as well, and now she handed one to Neville, and he could feel it was heavy with water. 'Put that on. We're going up to shelter in the old Union Jack mine. Just until the fire makes up its mind,' she told Neville, for Tiddler's sake. Her gaze slid to her son's worried face. 'It's a precaution, that's all. Everything will be all right. Isn't that so, Pom?'

'Tickety Boo,' Neville said, wrapping himself up in his own blanket. Tiddler began to tell him about the lamp and how Big Jim Mackenzie had brought it with him from Scotland, and that it had been lit every evening as long as anyone could remember. Neville pretended not to know, asking lots of questions to distract the boy.

He'd noticed his camera case and his swag, set beside the suitcase, and now he picked them both up. He couldn't resist getting out the Leica and taking some photographs—the concentration needed to frame the shots allowed him to conquer his panic. His nerves were jumping, and looking through the viewfinder and making images seemed to steady them.

Tiddler, however, had other ideas.

'Mr Brown said he was a policeman,' the boy was explaining to his mother, between coughs. His usually bright eyes were bloodshot. 'He helped me catch Her Majesty.'

Georgie's panicked gaze went to Neville's and he could see her quick wits had already jumped ahead.

'He decided to head back to the timber camp,' Neville casually answered the question he'd hoped to avoid, and took another photo so he didn't have to continue to meet her eyes. 'He said he didn't like the odds down here.'

Georgie nodded slowly, still watching him. 'Then he's a fool,' she said quietly, sounding as if she genuinely meant it. 'We're safer here than up at the camp.'

The wind was gusting around them, giving the impression it had come straight out of an oven.

'Come on!' Suddenly Georgie made the decision and reached down for the lamp, before pushing Tiddler firmly in front of her. 'Don't forget Aesop,' she called, turning to look at Neville, but he already had the horse's tether. All around them the last remaining inhabitants of Mackenzie Crossing were bringing whatever was most precious to them as they stumbled forward through the smoke. Neville noticed that as well as Aesop, there was the goat and Arnold's two dogs, and a parrot in a cage.

It felt a bit like a colonial version of Noah's Ark.

Hector had hung back, his wife, Marie, hovering behind him. He obviously wanted to have a word with Georgie on her own. 'Why not shelter in the creek?' he said. 'With the mine, well, the roof might have fallen in. And what about all the timber in there? Timber burns. I don't care how well prepared you think you are, it's a death trap.'

His hostility was due to fear, Neville knew that. He'd heard it before, and now he stepped closer in case he had to intervene. But Georgie didn't need his help. She answered with quiet authority. 'The mine is perfectly safe. I've been in there to set things up for us.'

Marie nodded. 'That's good enough for me,' she said, and hurried off after the others.

Hector wasn't convinced. 'You've been in there already? I thought you said no fire would ever put an end to the Crossing,' he said belligerently. 'Have you changed your mind now, Georgie?'

She looked him in the eye. 'I haven't changed my mind. It's what Big Jim would've wanted me to do. He always said the Union Jack was the safest place to go if there was a fire in the mountains.'

He stood a moment, looking as if he didn't know whether to rant or weep. His gaze strayed towards his house, and his expression became bleak, and then he nodded and disappeared into the smoke after Marie. Georgie gave a relieved sigh, turning to Neville as if she thought she might have to persuade him as well.

'You'll get no argument from me,' he reassured her. 'I'm coming with you.'

At least he'd made her smile, he thought, as they followed after the others, and it was amazing, in the circumstances, how much pleasure that gave him.

Night seemed to have fallen in the middle of the afternoon. Neville's eyes stung and he wiped a hand over them, and then paused to check that the wet cloth tied around Aesop's eyes was still secure. The old horse whinnied in fear and pulled against Neville's restraining hand, but seemed to respond to his soothing words.

He tried to keep an eye on Georgie's slender back in front of him, knowing how easily one could get disorientated. And getting lost would probably end in death. Although he doubted she'd let him go astray. He was aware of her constantly turning and checking on her little flock, making sure everyone was all right and following orders. She'd have made a good commander, he reflected, and couldn't help giving a chuckle. He thought with surprise that he might be somewhat lightheaded.

The Union Jack mine's narrow entrance was a welcome sight and everyone was eager to get inside.

The problem was Aesop.

The old horse wasn't too keen on being forced into a dark, smoky mine tunnel, and although the blindfold meant he couldn't see what was before him, he seemed to sense the unfamiliar surroundings. Georgie, on the other hand, was determined to make up his mind for him, and after much pushing and exhorting from behind, and tugging from the front, eventually they got him in.

They led him to where the roof had caved in to form the back wall. The palings and stakes that had been brought up earlier by Georgie were now used to make a makeshift pen for the animals. Tiddler found a wetted sack to put over Aesop's head and neck, which the horse immediately objected to, trying to remove it with a violent toss of his head.

'No, Aesop,' the boy scolded him. 'It's to keep you cool and help you breathe.'

But the tunnel was already full of smoke, and once the fire came over them—and despite Georgie's optimism Neville was sure it would— things would only get worse.

The others were busy settling themselves, and Georgie made her way among them, stepping around bodies and bundles, stopping to give someone a needed word of reassurance. Neville watched her. He'd had a murmured conversation with Hector, and they'd inspected the timber roof. Neville let him have his say about how they should wet down the wood, and listened to his fears about fire catching and taking hold.

'We'd need to get it out as soon as possible. You're the man in charge of that,' Neville informed him, with just the right note of confidence.

Now Georgie had a couple of wet sheets, and she was making her way to the tunnel entrance. She was obviously planning to hang them up as a makeshift curtain, in an effort to stop any more smoke from entering, and hopefully the fire as well.

Neville followed her, and stood peering out into the darkness. For a moment the smoke shifted and he thought he saw the Crossing spread out on the valley floor in front of him. Or perhaps it was just an illusion—a mirage created by a brain affected by the heat and the lack of clean air. Or maybe everything was a dream, and he was still at home in Adelaide, waking up in his bed to Mary's nervous glances, and hoping he hadn't screamed too loudly in the night and frightened Gertie.

'Here, let me,' he said, taking the sheet from Georgie and holding it up so that she could hammer the nails across the top. The old timber was as hard as iron and she swore as the nail bent.

'Do you think we've forgotten anything?' he said.

'No,' she answered him, trying for another nail.

'We can only wait now, and hope. Not that I'll tell them that,' she added, with a glance over her shoulder. '*I* told them they should stay here, that *I* would keep them safe. I can't very well let them down now, can I?'

'No, you can't let them down.'

'My whole life is in that house,' she murmured, finally getting the nail into the wood, and starting on the next one. 'Big Jim's, too, and my mother's wedding dress is in a box under the bed. I thought of bringing it, but it seemed ridiculous, and … and although I know you don't believe me, I still think the Crossing will be saved.'

'Georgie …'

She caught his look and stopped, eyes searching his face. He wondered what she was looking for, though he was fairly certain he knew. Georgie was too clever by half.

'What did the policeman say, Neville?'

'Not much. He just wanted to talk to you.'

'You're lying,' she chastised him softly, and there was a note in her voice that warned him she wasn't to be denied. 'Tell me the truth. Quickly. Before Tiddler comes.'

He took the hammer from her and finished putting in the last nail, and then he stood back to survey their handiwork as best he could. One sheet done and one to go. It occurred to him that if the fire didn't get them then the smoke would suffocate them, so what did it matter if he told her some of it now?

'He said you had murdered a man in Melbourne and then run away. The rooms you used … the landlord has made a statement. I don't know how true it is, but it was enough to send Brown out hunting for you. He wanted to see you hanged. He's a great believer in the rule of law.'

Georgie was staring at him, and he conjectured whether, despite everything, she was going to deny it, pretend he'd made a mistake or he was a lunatic. But Georgie Mackenzie was no coward.

'He wanted Tiddler,' she said, and although her voice was steady she turned her eyes away, as if she couldn't bear to see what he was thinking. 'I didn't know that was why he was there. Miss Agostino had arranged it. Between them they'd decided. It didn't seem to matter that I was the child's mother. *She* had her school's reputation to consider and *he* had money and a position, and he couldn't risk it all for a bastard got on a half-caste Chinee. Those were his words, Neville. So after I said no, and he laughed at me as if I was insane, I knew the only way I could keep my baby was by force. I had a knife, I forget why, I think it was a bread knife. He got it off me and cut me. He was so angry … There was so much blood and I thought I was going to die, but I kept fighting and then, well, he was dead. I was in a terrible state. I had nowhere to go, so I went to Miss Agostino and told her what I'd done. She bandaged me up and said she'd help me. She said she was sorry, that she'd meant it for the best. But now she remembered the promise she'd made to my father to keep me safe.'

'Did you tell Big Jim what had happened?'

'Oh yes.' She managed a smile, despite how very

pale she looked in the shadowy light. It occurred to him that she probably hadn't spoken of this since she'd told her father, that he was the first, and there was an odd sort of pleasure in that.

'When I came home to the Crossing I told him everything. I said I would go to the police if he asked me to. I literally put my life into his hands.'

Neville knew he should start on the next sheet, hammer in another nail, and then he changed his mind. This felt more important. 'He took you and Tiddler in.'

'Yes, he did. He said he would keep me safe and make certain my son was never taken away from me. But we had to be careful, pretend Tiddler was a foundling. As he grew older, though, everyone could see the resemblance, so I said he was a cousin.' She gave a mocking laugh. 'Silly, I know, but if it meant fewer questions being asked, then where was the harm?'

He brushed her cheek with his fingertip. She'd taken off her hat and her hair was grimy and tangled, her skin streaked with sweat and ash, but he thought she was the most beautiful woman he had ever known.

'I've seen things … done things,' he paused, searching for the right words, so that she would know he understood. He thought of the fighting in France, the horror, and yet he'd known at the time there was no other way.

'Sometimes to save that which is most precious to us, we must fight and fight hard. It might be difficult, horrible, and we might question the morality of what we are doing, but the alternative is so much worse that we do it anyway.'

A tear ran down her cheek. 'Yes,' she said. 'That's it exactly. We do it anyway.' She gave a rough laugh. 'I never thought I would be the sort of person who could kill a man, but I did. In that moment the choice was simple.'

Then she looked up at him, and he could see the question she wanted to ask and he'd hoped she wouldn't. And at the same time he hoped she would, because he knew once it was spoken of between them then they would be bound together irrevocably.

'Neville,' she began softly. 'What did—'

And then he heard it. The roar of the fire, like a hundred freight trains all at once, and the heat of it, and then a great gob of flame sprang from the hilltop above and down into the Crossing. The hostelry was ablaze in an instant.

He caught hold of Georgie's arm to stop her from running out. She struggled with him for a moment, but she must have known how impossible it was to save her home. There was a whoosh as the rest of the fire came roaring down the hill, so intense they could no longer stand there. Georgie stumbled back, sobbing. Behind him in the tunnel, above the incredible noise, he could hear Aesop screaming and Tiddler's shouts. Neville gritted his teeth and held up the sheet in what he now knew to be a futile effort to save them, and began to hammer it in place.

CHAPTER 34

SKYE

Thursday 12 June 1997

FINN HADN'T WOKEN her when he came in and she didn't even know if he was at home, but when Skye peeked around his bedroom door she saw he was flat out on his stomach on the bed, dead to the world. She had taken Dylan to the Westcott Hospital and stayed briefly, but Ebony was sleepy and thought she wasn't in labour after all, and so she had headed home.

That had been well after midnight, so God knew when Finn had got in.

Skye let Lightning out for a bit of a frolic, fed her, and then made coffee. When she returned Finn was still asleep.

'Finn?'

Nothing.

She put the mug on the bedside table and sat down on the mattress beside him. His head was turned towards her, comfortable in his folded arms, with his face buried in the pillow. The room was shadowy, with drawn curtains, but it looked bare, just like the rest of the house. Maybe Finn liked it that way, paring his life down to the absolute minimum, but she thought Laurie's leaving might have had something to do with it. Even though she'd been gone a while, he hadn't had the time or cared enough to fill his home with all that was missing.

What was it about the nape of his neck? Skye asked herself. So vulnerable and so tempting. She gently brushed aside some strands of dark hair and bent down to press her lips to his warm skin. He made a noise. So she did it again. This time he turned his face and she could see he was smiling, although his eyes still weren't open.

For an awful moment it occurred to her that he might think she was someone else, that he might call her by another name. Fraser had done that once and the ache in her stomach had stayed there for days.

'Nice,' he mumbled. 'Do I smell coffee?'

'Yep. What time did you get to bed?'

'Late, very late. I didn't want to disturb you.'

So, she thought, he probably knew who she was. But just in case … She ran the tip of her tongue along the corner of his mouth and this time he turned over properly and pulled her down into his arms.

'Hey, beautiful,' he murmured, after a long, satisfying moment.

His eyes opened and, no, he didn't display any surprise at seeing her. All good, then, Skye told herself, and leaned back as he pushed himself up and reached for the coffee.

He watched her over the lip of the cup as he sipped, his dark eyes sleepy, the bruise a rather attractive pale mauve mixed with lemon over-tones.

She reached out to touch it with her fingertips. 'Still sore?'

'Hardly notice it.' His smile was back. 'There are other places that need your attention though. If you're feeling in a charitable mood.'

'I'll bet. I hate to spoil the ambiance, but how did it go last night?'

He pulled a face. 'The team from Melbourne turned up eventually, and then Doug arrived, so I left him to it. Dylan and Ebony have gone into protective custody and Lois Petersen is under arrest.'

'They're gone?' Skye picked out the one thing that seemed the most important. 'Already? Did you get to say goodbye, Finn?'

'I did. I went to tell them the news.'

'Oh.'

'Looks like I'll have to wait a bit to see my nephew, but at least they're safe.'

He seemed calm about it, and Skye questioned what she felt. Was she sorry not to have spent more time with Dylan and his wife? She was only just beginning to heal some of the old wounds and now …

And then there was the thing that Dylan had said to her, when he had walked her out to the hospital car park, just before she'd left.

Ask Finn about the laundry, Skye. It's time he told

you. And don't let him put you off, it's important. And when you ask him, tell him he doesn't owe me anything. Not anymore.

She watched Finn as he took another swallow of coffee and set the mug down. Was this the moment? And yet the words seemed stuck in her throat, probably because she knew that once she asked the question, she could never go back. This was a secret that, like a tidal surge, was going to have after-effects.

Lightning whining outside the door was an excuse not to take the plunge, and Skye got up to let her in. The greyhound gave Finn several wet kisses that, he said, were almost as good as Skye's.

He swung his legs out of the bed and onto the floor. He was wearing a pair of pyjama bottoms and nothing else. They hung low on his hips, and she liked the way the line of dark hair ran down his flat belly and under the waistband.

'What happens now? To you, I mean.'

'There'll be an investigation. Gary and Lois and their murky secrets should come to the surface, and maybe a lot of smaller fish will get caught in the net. I'm not sure about the bigger ones, they have a habit of slipping away.'

'Oh.'

'Don't worry,' he said, watching her face.

'I'm not. Well I am, but …'

He held out his hand and Skye slotted her fingers into his. 'I've told them I'm having the day off,' he explained.

'Oh?' She pretended to be shocked. 'What did they say?'

'Alison said she was pleased to hear it.'

He tugged her down onto his lap and she made herself comfortable in the circle of his arms, while her head rested on his shoulder. She thought about telling him how frightened she'd been when he'd vanished over the edge of the ravine last night, and how relieved when he was safe, but she didn't want him to think she'd be that sort of woman. Always worrying about what might or might not happen to him during the course of his job.

So she took a breath, thinking it was time to ask about Dylan's cryptic words. The puzzle she wanted to finally put to rest. 'Finn, Dylan said something to me last night. Something about …'

He frowned. 'Dylan says lots of things, Skye.'

'Well he does, but I just thought …' She looked at him again and decided that after all now was not the time. 'Never mind,' she whispered, and kissed him instead.

'I was worried you might have decided you'd had enough and headed back to the Big Smoke,' he told her, when they came up for air.

'Were you?' She felt surprise and a guilty twinge of pleasure. 'Why?'

He shrugged a shoulder. 'I suppose I was having a bit of a bleak moment.' He shifted restlessly, trying to explain. 'Dylan and Gary and the car going over the side. My job. Nothing in particular.'

'Well I'm still here, so next time you have a bleak moment, remember this,' she said, and nuzzled into his neck, and then kissed him along the line of his jaw, until he made that purry sound again.

'Don't you get lonely?' she asked, pausing. She gently twisted a strand of his hair around her finger and tucked it behind his ear. 'You're a long way from civilisation.'

'Beyond the black stump.'

'And after five years, maybe it's too late for you to assimilate back into society?'

He shook his head and laughed, then flicked a glance at the digital clock. 'We don't need to get up yet, do we?' he asked her innocently.

'Well, no. I've fed the dog and put some more wood in the fire box. Unless you have something important you need to be doing on a mountainside somewhere?'

From the urgency with which he took her in his arms, it seemed that he didn't.

After they'd dressed and showered, they set out for a walk down to the creek. By then Skye told herself she had forgotten Dylan's words and her abortive effort to ask Finn about them, but she hadn't, not really. Rather, she'd pushed them aside until a better moment presented itself.

The weather had improved. It was one of those clear days with a blue sky, although the air was still frigid and she was glad of her woollen gloves.

To her surprise it was Finn who brought up the subject she was avoiding.

'What did he say last night?' he asked her, slowing his stride to match hers. 'Dylan, I mean.

You were going to ask me something and then I diverted you.' He shot her a sideways look.

'Was I?' Skye let her gaze slide over his profile, his straight nose and strong chin. The wear and tear of the years. She was almost tempted to say it didn't matter and let's not allow the past to interfere with the present anymore, and yet …

'You said Dylan wanted you to ask me something.' He spoke patiently.

She turned to look at him properly and this time she thought she understood. He *wanted* her to ask him. He *wanted* to tell her.

'Okay,' she said, and took a breath. 'Dylan wanted me to ask you about the laundry. He said it was time you told me. And he said you didn't owe him anything, not anymore.'

She noticed his hands were clenched. That wasn't a good sign. Once again she was having doubts.

'Look, Finn, you don't have to talk about it,' she went on quickly.

He nodded his head to show he'd heard her. They'd reached the creek and he stood staring into the water while she waited. And waited. She was ready to suggest they go back to the house, and even Lightning was giving him odd looks, when he finally heaved a sigh and began to speak.

'I've never told anyone this,' he admitted, and there was something stirring in his dark eyes that made her panicky. 'I've never wanted to. Especially you. I couldn't tell you back then. It would've been impossible. I knew you thought it was weird, the way me and Dylan were together, and how I was always making excuses for him, but I couldn't explain. And I was worried, too, that if I did somehow find the courage to tell you that you'd walk away from me. You were the only thing I really cared about, the only good thing in my life, and I couldn't risk it.'

'Oh, Finn. Whatever it is—'

'It was unfair on you, I know that now. Putting that pressure on you. All my focus. Like sunlight through a magnifying glass on a poor bloody butterfly.'

'Come on,' she reached out her hand and squeezed his fingers when he responded. 'Just tell me, okay? I promise I won't run screaming back to the city.'

Her heart was beating faster, and there was that squirmy feeling in her stomach, as there used to be all those years ago when Dylan did something that seemed likely to blow up into one of their dangerous arguments. She knew that whatever Finn was about to reveal was going to be big. For both of them.

And then he just launched into it.

'Mum and Dad split up when Dylan and me were little. When we met you it was the second time we'd gone to live with her. We used to bounce around between the two of them a fair bit. The first time …' He cleared his throat and she knew this was hard for him.

'You were how old?' she asked, thinking questions might help.

'Six. We were six. Dad was always away working and he decided we'd be better off with her.

He didn't know what was going on in her life, or maybe he didn't want to look very hard because then he'd have to have us back, and give up work and … Well, anyway.'

He looked at her then and something in his eyes warned her that at some point along this journey she might want to ask him to stop.

'Finn, what happened?'

'Mum had a guy hanging around the year we went to live with her. That first time. When we were six. A real bastard.' His mouth had turned grim and the frown was pretty serious. 'He was a kiddie fiddler.' And he waited, as if asking her again whether he should go on.

Oh, God. Skye wondered if her face had drained of colour. It certainly felt like it. 'Didn't she … didn't she know?' she managed, her voice sounding rough.

'I don't think so.' He paused and gave it some thought, and she realised he hadn't before. 'She wouldn't have put us in harm's way intentionally, no. Well, not that sort of harm. But she was drinking heavily and so out of it most of the time she didn't even notice what was going on. He was another Darryl, well, kind of. They'd get drunk most nights and the weekends were a write-off. Because of that he was more important to her than we were.'

'God, Finn, that's … this is.' She swallowed, knowing she wasn't helping.

'You still want to hear this?' His expression was bleak.

Skye almost said no, but she knew she couldn't

do that. He had brought himself to the point of telling her something from his past he would probably rather forget, and she must be brave and do him the courtesy of hearing him out.

'Yes,' she said with sincerity, 'I do. Really.'

He nodded again, and she saw his throat move as he swallowed.

'I haven't thought about it for a long time, you know. But being with Dylan again, and then him saying I owed him. It all flooded back. Suddenly, it was as if I was looking through a tunnel into the past, seeing myself as a kid, and it was so *fresh*. Maybe because you were there, when he said it. The three of us together. And I remembered how it used to be between us. There's been a lot of damage done, Skye, and I want to start mending it. If I can. If you'll let me.'

'You were always making excuses for Dylan,' she replied quietly. 'I could never understand it. And then, on that night we went down to the bay, when he was behaving like a complete nut-case. You were both so *angry*. I used to think you hated each other, but I also knew that whatever Dylan did you were always going to forgive him.'

'Yeah. I thought—I hoped you might visit me, afterwards, but I understood why you didn't want to.'

'Finn …'

'No, it's all right. Probably better you didn't. Skye, let me finish this now or I mightn't be able to.'

His eyes were pleading and all she could do was nod.

'Right, so, this … guy had tried it on with me a few times, but I always got away. Jinx, that was what he called himself. I don't think that was his real name. I looked him up on the police database once—broke all the rules to do it—and I couldn't find him. I sort of hoped he was dead.'

'Shark attack,' Skye murmured, and drew a brief smile from him.

But there was no stopping him now.

'I don't know why he liked me best,' he went on. 'It made Dylan and me laugh. Like it was funny. I suppose we had to find a laugh from somewhere. It didn't seem real.'

'Couldn't you tell Melissa?'

He gave her a look that made her heart ache for him.

'I get the feeling this story doesn't end well, Finn,' she said, in a voice that strove to stay unwavering. She thought she might start to cry, but she was determined not to. This was his story, and love him though she did, she didn't have the right to swamp him with her pity. He wanted her to listen and that was what she was going to do.

'The laundry was a little room at the back, a bit of an addition to the place, with a door into the kitchen and another one to the backyard. One night he got me trapped in there, both doors were shut, and Mum was wiped out in the bedroom and couldn't hear a thing.'

She wanted to close her eyes but she didn't think that was fair, so she kept them open, her gaze on his face. Perhaps her imagination was just too good because she could visualise the scene despite his sparse description of it, and it was all the more horrific.

'Dylan was banging on the kitchen door, I could hear him, but I was so bloody scared I couldn't move. He had my shorts down … and then the door flew open. Maybe Jinx didn't close it properly or the lock was faulty, but the next moment Dylan was in there and he was climbing on the guy's back and punching him in the head, and it was bloody chaos.'

'Dylan came to your rescue,' Skye murmured, understanding at last.

Finn nodded. 'There's more,' he said. 'Jinx went berserk and grabbed hold of Dylan and threw him against the wall. He hit the washing machine with his head and just … I thought he was dead. So did Jinx, because he took off out of there and we never saw him again.'

'But he was all right? Dylan, I mean?'

He ignored her question, keeping on with his story. Perhaps he had to tell it like this, perhaps it was just too awful to stop now that he'd started and he wanted to get it out there between them at last.

'I woke Mum up, it took a while, and then I got on the phone and rang for the ambulance. They didn't know what to make of me at first, howling into the mouthpiece. But they came and rushed Dylan to the hospital. He was unconscious for a long time, and then they were worried about a brain injury. Later on they said he was okay, but I don't think he was ever the kid he was before that. He took more risks, you know? And he got angrier than he used to. So whatever happened when he hit his head, it changed him, and I always knew it was because he'd put himself on the line for me. So do you understand now why I have to do the same, Skye?'

She looked into his eyes. 'Yes,' she said. 'I do understand.' She reached out to touch his arm, rubbing the thick jacket he was wearing as if it was alive. He looked shattered. This big, tough man was completely wrung out.

He reached up to cover her hand with his and it was shaking. 'I could never tell you before. How could I tell the girl I loved that a thing like that had happened to me? When you're young you're so uncertain, so vulnerable.'

'I don't think it's only when you're young,' she said wryly.

'Maybe.' He took a deep breath and sighed it out. 'I'm glad it's been said.' He looked at her, and this time there was a hint of a proper smile. 'I told you you were a bit of a witch.'

Skye stretched her arms around his chest to give him a hug, cuddling into him.

And for a time they said nothing, just content to hold each other.

'She never told Dad,' he said, when finally they began the slow walk back to the house. 'Mum, I mean. I think she was ashamed. She said she was sorry so many times it became a sort of a joke, and maybe she thought because I was laughing I was over it, or I'd forgotten. I wanted to forget, and I think eventually I did. For the past fifteen years I've hardly thought of it at all. Until last night, when Dylan said I owed him, when it all came roaring back into my head.'

Skye shivered. She hadn't noticed the cold during the telling of his story, but now she leaned into him, enjoying his warmth. 'What happened afterwards? I mean with your mum?'

'She sent us back to Dad. She said Dylan was too much for her, which by then he was. By the time we came back down to live with her the second time we were older, and you were there.'

They reached the door into the kitchen and when Finn opened it, Lightning pushed through first.

'It all makes sense now.' She sighed. 'Everything. Thank you for trusting me, Finn.'

He nodded, but she could tell he wanted to put it aside now, let it go, and that was fine with her.

'I wondered if you wanted to go and see Archie and Nancy Manning,' Finn said, as they stepped into the warm house. 'She's home and she's willing to meet you, according to Taylor.'

'Really?'

'I don't know how helpful it'll be but it's worth a try. You still want to find Neville, don't you?'

Neville had taken a back seat recently, but he had brought her here to Elysian, and because of him she had found Finn.

She nodded. 'I'd like to know what happened to him. Draw a line under the story.'

'And there's your exhibition.'

There was a question in his face and she no longer had any doubts about giving him the answer he wanted. 'You'll have to give me some ideas for a suitable venue.'

'Here?'

'Yes. You were right, there's nowhere else I'd rather it be. Well maybe Mackenzie Crossing, but Elysian will do.'

And it would do very well.

CHAPTER 35

NEVILLE

Four pm, Friday 13 January 1939,
Mackenzie Crossing

'WHAT DID YOU do to Mr Brown, Neville?'

She was watching him, but he didn't meet her eyes. The heat in the mine was now so oppressive every breath was a chore. There was more oxygen closer to the ground, and so they lay down. Kept low. Tiddler had smoothed mud over Aesop's sides, and now the old horse stood with its head hanging between its forelegs. The other animals had fallen silent.

Marie had been singing a hymn, but her voice had also drifted into silence. They couldn't do anything but stay put and try to survive. Outside the fire was raging, and a couple of times Neville managed to get to the entrance and throw water over the sheets. Hector helped, and they both put out a fire when the ceiling caught, but he wasn't sure they could do it again. Staying alive had become a struggle, and none of them could hold out much longer.

'I wish I'd known you before,' Georgie went on. 'I wish we could've met years ago, Neville.' Her voice was rambling, and he wondered if she was delirious. She hadn't been drinking enough water, worrying about everyone else. He looked around for the billy can and dipped the metal cup into it.

'Here, drink,' he croaked. 'Drink it, Georgie.'

She took the cup and tipped it up.

'Rest,' he told her, watching as her head sank down, as if she no longer had the strength to hold it up, and her cheek pressed to the ground.

'What did you do to him?' she muttered. 'Mr Brown, what did you—'

'Hush,' he said quickly, worried someone would hear her. He put his hand over her mouth, and almost immediately regretted it and began to take it away. But she clung to him, pressing her lips into the hollow of his palm.

'Thank you,' she breathed. 'Thank you, Neville.'

His heart ached at the sight of this proud, strong woman so humbled.

'Tell me why you're here with your camera? Are you running away, too?'

So he told her. How he'd set off for war as one man and come home as another. How he'd run away to Adelaide, and then run away again when he discovered he wasn't suited for marriage or fatherhood. And how gradually the journey had turned into something more, and he'd begun to heal.

'Will you go back to your family one day?' she asked him, and then spent some time coughing.

'I think about it, of course I think about it.' Or he had before he'd met Georgie and Tiddler. Before he'd met Miller Brown.

'And what have you decided?' she asked, and then in the same breath she said, 'Mary might have someone else now. People move on.'

Neville met her eyes. 'Yes, they do.'

Suddenly, there was a scuffling at the entrance to the tunnel, and when he pushed himself upright he saw someone trying to fight their way through the sheets. Above the roar of the flames they could hear shouting, and then sobbing.

Neville helped the man inside and, when he fell to the ground, turned him over. For some reason he thought that it was Brown. That he was alive and had come looking for them. In that moment his heart was in his throat.

But of course it wasn't Brown, it couldn't be. This man had grey hair singed into tufts and his clothing was burned in places and torn in others by his fight to survive. Through the blistered skin and grimy sweat on his face, Neville thought he recognised one of the older timber-getters from the camp this morning.

'Thank God,' the fellow muttered through raw lips. 'Thought I was a goner for sure, until I remembered Big Jim's mine.'

'Patrick?' Georgie was bending over him. She scooped up some water from the billy can and trickled it into his mouth. He drank thirstily, and then lay back as if the thought of moving again was beyond him.

Neville and Georgie helped to drag him further into the tunnel. They thought he was unconscious, but when he heard Aesop and the goat his eyes widened, the whites all inflamed.

'Jesus,' he whispered, crossing himself with a shaking hand. 'Is this the Ark, Georgie? Have I died and ended up in heaven somewhere?'

'No, Patrick, you're not dead. It's just the people from the Crossing. And I couldn't leave Aesop out there now, could I? Tiddler has his hen and Marie her goat, and there are dogs and a parrot. For a while we had a wallaby with us, but I think he decided to leave.'

'Jesus,' Patrick said again in astonishment. When they had him comfortable, he said, dropping his voice, 'It's bad out there. Phil and the rest of us tried to make it to Elysian, but it was too late, so then we set out for the millpond. We were halfway there when I got lost, and then the fire came through and cut me off. God help 'em, Georgie.'

One of the dogs started to bark while the other one panted. The air had been getting steadily hotter and Neville was beginning to wonder if instead of saving them, the mine might cook them all slowly until they were done.

Georgie wet another blanket from their dwindling supply of water, and lay it over Patrick's prone form. He'd closed his eyes, his lips moving in silent prayer, or maybe he was remembering the names of those poor souls from the timber camp.

Neville thought of Phil Appleby and the others,

the young men with their shy smiles for Georgie, and the older, harder men who had sought the solitude of the bush for their own reasons. Were they all dead now?

But a lesson he'd learned in the trenches was that it was useless worrying about the dead. Not when he had his hands full with the living.

'There's more breathable air near the ground,' he said, loud enough for everyone to hear. 'Lie down if you can. Put a wet blanket over your head.'

'Once the fire is gone we'll be able to go out-side,' Georgie added.

'There'll be nothing left,' Patrick muttered. 'That fire is like something unleashed by the devil.'

In the end it was the heat and smoke that drove them out. Tiddler was worried Aesop would fall down and die, and it was a job to get him through the entrance again. By the time he was on the other side he had blood running down his flank, but Georgie said that was the least of their worries and they could patch him up later.

Tiddler was hollow-eyed and clinging to his mother, but he still had Her Majesty, even if she did look as if her feathers were singed beyond repair.

The wallaby Georgie had mentioned to Patrick hadn't gone back out after all. He was still in the tunnel, and sat watching them, exhausted, as they headed down to the Crossing.

Neville didn't think words could describe what was before him. Everything charred and smouldering, the hostelry unrecognisable, apart from the chimney. The whole valley had been devastated—it was as if a giant hand had swept across it and left nothing but blackened stumps and air putrid with burning. Mackenzie Crossing was gone.

He knew he must look as strange as his companions, his face white with ash, and the blanket still clasped about him like a shroud. The ground felt hot through the soles of his shoes and he knew the animals' unprotected feet would soon be blistered.

Georgie stumbled and he caught her, sliding his arm around her. She leaned into him, silent, grieving. She'd done all in her power to keep Big Jim's legacy alive, no one could have done more, but in the end even she had recognised the hopelessness of trying to save the town. And people, after all, were more important.

The others were moving towards what had been their homes, as if they hoped by some miracle that something had survived the inferno. Patrick couldn't walk far and Neville doubted he'd survive the experience. He was blinded and needed to be guided.

'We have to get to Elysian,' Neville said. 'We'll get help there.' And, although he didn't say it aloud, there was nothing left for them here at the Crossing.

Georgie was despairing, her eyes empty. Now the hostelry was gone, and all of Big Jim's legacy with it, she was adrift in an unfamiliar world. She stepped away from him as if she had somewhere to be and then realising there was nowhere, stopped again.

'Come on, Georgina,' he said, holding out his hand. 'We need to go.'

'We?' But she said it with a lilt of hope, and that gave him the courage to speak aloud the thoughts that had been running through his head while they were in the mine.

'There are other places, Georgina. I know they won't be the same, they won't be Mackenzie Crossing.'

She looked back at what had been her home, but he couldn't see her face and he wasn't sure he wanted to. 'I don't know what to do, Neville. All I am is here. I think if I went away then I would lose myself. I'd be a stranger.'

'No, you wouldn't.' He stepped closer. 'I know who you are. I know better than anyone, Georgina Mackenzie. And I think you know me. We've found each other, and I have no intention of losing you again. Or Tiddler,' he added, looking over at the boy, who was stroking Aesop's singed nose and looking disconsolate.

Georgie bowed her head, but he waited and at last she nodded. 'Do you think it's possible to be happy?' she asked him, as they led the raggle-taggle bunch down the blackened valley. 'Do we deserve happiness?' she added on a whisper.

'I don't know,' he said, and put his arm around her. 'Let's just take one day at a time.'

She was holding the lamp with the yellow glass shade in her blistered hands, and it was so absurd for a moment that he stared at it. He tried to assemble his thoughts. He'd been through war and now this, and he was still alive. It seemed like a miracle, and if he was a religious man like Big Jim then he'd think there was a reason for it. That it was meant to be.

Perhaps he was alive, not for his own sake, but for Georgie and Tiddler? He allowed that idea to sink into his heart and mind. Turning it over and over, examining it from all sides. And it looked solid and indisputable; it looked like pure gold.

'I want more than a day.' Her voice was weary and painful and barely recognisable, and yet the determination was all Georgie.

Neville's blistered face hurt when he smiled and yet he did it anyway. 'So do I,' he told her. 'My dear girl, so do I.'

CHAPTER 36

SKYE

Thursday 12 June 1997

BY THE TIME they set out for the museum, the blue sky had clouded over and it was snowing again. Flakes drifted silently upon the surrounding landscape, and the ground was soon coated in a fresh layer of white.

'Now that is beautiful,' Skye said, smiling.

'Do you want to take some photographs? I can stop.'

Her smile broadened. 'Maybe afterwards. I want to talk to Archie first.'

The lights in the museum were on.

Finn drew up and sat a moment, hands on the wheel, looking at Skye. 'You ready for this?'

'As I'll ever be.' Truthfully, though, she didn't know if she *was* ready. What if Archie didn't know anything or wouldn't talk? Could she let it go or would it always be there, like an unhealed sore, reminding her that one day her grandfather had walked out on his family and had never come back?

Lightning had come with them, although Finn had warned her she may not be welcome. 'This is not a dog-friendly place,' he'd advised her sternly, to which she'd responded by wagging her tail.

As they walked up the path to the front door, Skye stopped herself from looking through the large bay windows, in case Archie was peering back at her. She didn't want to frighten him.

But it was Nancy Manning who opened the door.

For a brief, strange moment Skye thought she recognised her, although the resemblance was too fleeting to pin down. Something about the strong chin and high cheekbones. Nancy was of a similar height to her daughter, her dark hair smoothed back into a chignon, but whereas Saskia seemed to favour short skirts and Doc Martens, Nancy wore dark slacks and a matching jacket over a cream sweater. She may have been born and bred in Elysian, but she wouldn't have looked out of place in the Paris end of Collins Street.

Her stare was rather unnerving, and her arms were folded in the classic defensive position.

'Saskia told me what you want,' she said in a polite, firm voice. 'I'm sorry, I don't think we can help you.'

It wasn't a hopeful start.

Skye glanced at Finn. He shrugged. This was her show, he seemed to be saying, and it was up to her how she handled it.

'Did Saskia explain that the photo you have of Mackenzie Crossing was taken by my grandfather? Well, of course she did,' she said quickly, before Nancy could open her mouth and give voice to the irritation in her hazel eyes. 'She explained that your father found them at an auction in Melbourne, but I was hoping you knew the name of the auction house, or the journalist who owned them. And I hoped, I know it is a lot to ask, but could I see the other photographs?'

Crap, she was going to say no. Skye could tell. And then she was going to have to beg, or scream, or both.

'Skye is a photographer herself,' Finn said mildly, his voice a welcome interruption. 'She's holding an exhibition up here in Elysian. It would be good for the town, bring in more tourists. Good for Archie's museum, too.'

Nancy looked at him and then back at Skye. 'I thought you were only here for a few days,' she said with a slight frown.

'Well I was, but, uh, my plans have changed.'

Nancy glanced at Finn again and for a moment Skye thought the woman was actually going to smile. 'All right,' she said, though it wasn't a surrender, more like a regrouping of her forces. 'Come through. Dad is resting so I'd be grateful if you'd keep your voices down. He doesn't know you're here and I don't want him disturbed.'

Skye tried not to take offence, and tried not to get her hopes up. If the best she could do was take a look at the box of photos then she decided she could be happy with that. It was more than she had ever expected when she had made her pilgrimage up here into the mountains, following in Neville's footsteps.

And if Nancy agreed to her using the amazingly atmospheric photo of Mackenzie Crossing in her exhibition, well, she'd be ecstatic.

They followed the woman down the narrow path between the clutter of artefacts. 'This is completely over the top,' Finn murmured. 'A bit of a fire hazard, I would've thought.'

'Hmm,' Skye said. 'Maybe you can threaten them with closure if they don't give me what I want?'

Nancy turned before he could answer. They'd reached the door that Skye remembered from her last visit, and Nancy put a finger to her lips, before opening it and taking them through.

The building was much larger than Skye had thought. Archie had had an extension built onto the back, and the room Nancy took them into now was very modern looking compared to the museum. There was a sitting area, with a sofa and chairs, and a large flat screen television. A fire bank on one wall was sending out much-needed warmth, and on the other were floor-to-ceiling windows giving a view of a steep backyard, rising up to one of the timbered hills enfolding Elysian.

The only thing that might be classed an antique was a lamp with a yellow glass shade, sitting on a table against the wall.

Nancy closed the door. 'Sit down,' she said briskly.

Finn had told her that Nancy was a solicitor, and Skye didn't know why she found this surprising. Perhaps because she imagined there wasn't much chance of her practising law in a place like Elysian. She was biased and if she was going to make a life here then she would have to work on that.

Nancy had placed herself in a chair with a straight back, so Skye and Finn took the sofa. It was smaller than it looked, and she found herself squashed up against him. Not that she minded. In fact, leaning against Finn's warm, strong body was just what she needed to remind her that whatever happened here, whatever she learned or didn't learn about her grandfather, she'd already achieved an awful lot.

'I have a photograph I want you to see,' she said, fumbling the photocopy out of her bag. She'd even brought her camera, in case, except she had a feeling if she got it out now Nancy would evict them.

Once more she began to explain how the newspapers had run an appeal for information on Neville Darling, and how a letter had arrived in response to that, and how it had been too late for the police to consider looking into it.

'Nineteen fifty-seven,' Nancy repeated, her eyes widening slightly. 'I don't think my father was a resident here then, if that's what you're suggesting?'

'No. No, I'm not suggesting anything. I thought perhaps, with the museum, that he might have heard something?' She shrugged helplessly. 'I'm not expecting a miracle, Ms Manning. My grandmother remarried to a lovely man called Louis, and my mother had a loving father who made up for the years without Neville.' Skye frowned. 'When she was dying my mother spoke about Neville, though. She wanted to know what had happened to him, and I suppose so do I. Apart,' she added, 'from believing his photographs deserve more recognition—and I might be biased, I admit, but I'm a professional photographer myself and I don't think so. As a photographer he's quite remarkable.'

When finally she held out the image of Georgie Mackenzie, Nancy seemed to hesitate before she took it briskly, reaching for a pair of fashionable red-framed glasses that were on the table.

Skye thought her face became still, but it was hard to tell what Nancy was thinking. She seemed to be adept at hiding her feelings, and to be fair that might be because of her profession, although Skye didn't think that was the whole story.

She kept talking, softly, hoping to break through Nancy's rocklike facade. 'I didn't know Louis wasn't my biological grandfather, not until I was clearing out my mother's things and found her birth certificate. It was a bit of a shock, actually.'

'Funny how these things come back to bite you,' Nancy murmured cryptically.

Skye paused briefly, but when Nancy had nothing more to say on the subject, she carried on. 'When I found the photos Mum had kept, I realised where my own passion came from, and it seemed important to try to find out what had happened to Neville.' She leaned forward. 'That's why it'd be wonderful if I could see these other photos Saskia mentioned and—'

Finn squeezed her hand. She broke off, turning to look at him, and he nodded towards Nancy. Skye had been so full of her own need to persuade the woman that she hadn't really noticed how fixated Nancy was by the crumpled image of Georgie.

'Do you have the copy of the letter, too?' Finn suggested. 'Show Nancy. She might recognise the handwriting.'

Skye pulled out the copy of the letter, but Nancy was already shaking her head. She looked pale. 'I don't want to see it,' she said in that voice that brooked no argument.

No wonder her daughter was afraid of upsetting her, Skye thought. With Nancy Manning it would always be her way or the highway. Skye's parents had been strict, but she had the feeling Nancy had taken strictness to a whole new level.

There was another silence. Nancy lay the photograph down on the table carefully, as if she was finished with it, and met Skye's gaze. She was waiting to hear whatever other arguments Skye might have and then she would say no, sorry, and show them the door.

'Do you think I could see the photographs now?' Skye said, trying not to sound desperate. 'I can see you're busy, so if I could just have a look now I'll leave you to get on with it.'

Nancy picked an invisible piece of lint from her sleeve. 'I'm sorry, I should've said before, but I can't find the photographs Saskia told you about. She saw them some time ago and it appears my father put them away somewhere else or got rid of them.' She spread her hands. 'I'm sorry, I can't find them anywhere.'

She was lying. Skye knew it and from the look in his eyes so did Finn, but there was nothing they could do. For some reason Nancy Manning was refusing to allow them to see Neville's photographs, or help them in any way, and it was beyond frustrating.

'Oh, that's a pity,' Skye began, and then, hearing the anguish in her voice and yet unable to stop, 'He—Neville—really did have a remarkable ability to reveal a subject's innermost thoughts. I don't think I'll ever be as good as he was. Not many people are. This one, for instance,' and she gestured to the photocopy on the table. 'She is absolutely fascinating. Not just because of her clothing or her situation, but her expression. Her eyes. So strong, so determined, it's as if she's about to step forward and speak.'

Did Nancy's face soften? Was it possible she was winning her over?

'I agree, it is a remarkable photograph,' the other woman said and cleared her throat. 'I wish I could help you, Ms Stewart, but I can't.'

There was nothing more to be done. Finn stood up and slowly, reluctantly, Skye looked up at him, aware that her heart was in her face. She tried to swallow down her tears, to tell herself not to give Nancy the satisfaction, but it was tough.

'I wish …' she began.

'You may not be able to help her, Nancy, but I can.'

The voice came from the doorway. Archie was

standing there, and behind him, eyes like sau-
cers, was Saskia. No one had heard him come in,
they'd been so enmeshed in their own struggles.

'Dad,' Nancy said, and for the first time she
sounded uncertain. She stood up and moved
towards him, obviously intent on sending him
back to his room.

It was Saskia who came to the rescue. 'He heard
you talking. Mum, he wants to explain to Skye.'
She came out from behind her grandfather, and
although she looked pale and nervous, it was clear
that she was actually standing up to her mother.
Her gaze flickered before Nancy's hard stare like
a faulty lightbulb, but she didn't look away.

'Saskia, you don't understand,' Nancy began,
reaching to take her father's arm—Archie was
wearing the same green cardigan Skye remembered from last time—and ease him back through
the door.

'No.' This time it was Archie who resisted her,
his voice querulous. Skye couldn't help but notice
how drawn and unwell the old man looked, and
she had the sense that she should just say, 'No,
Nancy is right, go back to bed', and walk out. But
even as she considered it, she caught the pleading
look in Saskia's eyes and held her tongue.

'Let him,' the girl said. 'It'll be all right, Mum. I
mean, where's the harm in talking?'

Nancy gave her a disbelieving look. 'Saskia,
you don't understand, now please stay out of this.
Dad, you're not well. You need to—'

'I need to tell this young lady what happened to
her grandfather,' Archie retorted, raising his voice

over hers. 'My mother kept the secret, and then so did I, and now you, Nancy. Enough is enough. What does it matter anyway? It was years ago. We don't need to protect anyone, not anymore. I think it's all become a habit and it's time to stop.'

Archie shuffled further into the room. He was wearing slippers and he looked shrunken even from the last time Skye had seen him. Again she felt remorseful for persisting, but then she noticed the same strong chin on Archie as his daughter, and decided the elderly man was probably tougher than he seemed.

'I always felt guilty,' he said, looking fixedly at Skye. 'I felt as if we took him away from his real family, despite him telling me he was happy to be with us. "Everything is Tickety Boo," that was what he used to say. That's why I wrote that letter to the police, because I was worried Neville's wife was still looking for him. Grieving for him. But no one came to ask questions and so I let it go. I'm sorry.'

'No,' Skye said, 'don't be. I mean, my grandmother remarried and …' She blinked. 'Are you saying that you *knew* Neville?'

Archie chuckled. 'Oh yes. He was my father, or the nearest thing I had to one.'

Nancy made a sound, as if this was the final straw. 'Sit down, Dad, before you fall down.'

He looked at the chair she was pointing to and shook his head. 'I'd rather stand, love.'

'I'll hold your arm if you need me to, Granddad,' Saskia stood close to him, giving her mother a defiant look, while Archie sent a fond smile in her direction.

'The worm has turned,' Finn whispered, and raised his eyebrows at Skye.

Nancy was obviously struggling with her need to take charge, but she must have realised it was too late anyway. Archie had well and truly spilled the beans. 'All right, then,' she said. 'You have the floor, Dad, but remember what your mother always said.'

Archie grinned. 'How could I forget. *Never, never tell anyone!* That was what she used to say. *If you do then we'll all go to prison.* I believed it. I knew it might well be true. But she's dead and so is Neville, so who are they going to send to jail?' He gave Finn a wink. 'And actually,' he rubbed his hands together briskly, 'it's a relief to finally tell someone about it.'

With his eyes shining, sparkling with life, it was easy for Skye to forget how frail and ill he was supposed to be. He nodded at her.

'You look like him, you know. Pom. That was what everyone called him. 'Cause of his accent. Real posh it was, too. Real gent was Neville. And a good man,' he added with quiet reverence.

Surreptitiously, Saskia slipped her arm through his, letting him lean against her as he went on. 'Georgie Mackenzie was my mother. She was a strong woman. Ironclad. But she loved Pom. I mean, really loved him. If he'd left her I think she would've willed herself to death. As it was …' He bit his lip, tears filling his eyes. 'Well, he loved her just as much. They made a promise after Black Friday. We'd gone to Elysian afterwards. We had nothing, just the clothes on our backs and Mum's old lamp, and Aesop and Her Majesty.'

'Granddad,' Saskia was eyeing him with concern.

'No, I haven't lost my marbles,' Archie reassured her. 'Elysian had been hit hard by the fire as well, and people no longer had a home, or anything much, and they were on the move. If you've lost touch with friends and family, well it's simple enough to vanish. So that's what we did. Changed our name to Manning and vanished. Then I got sick with rheumatic fever and they thought I might die. By the time I was well again we'd settled into our new life. But I never forgot the Crossing—Mum wouldn't let me. I was a Mackenzie, and so was she, and it was our birthright. So when she died in nineteen fifty-seven, I came back here to bury her, and then I stayed.'

'Georgie Mackenzie is buried at the Crossing?' Skye said, feeling the tremble of excitement and emotion deep inside her. 'And Neville … Pom?'

'He's there with her. Both of them are near Big Jim. I'll take my place with them soon, I reckon. Tiddler Mackenzie,' he added, and chuckled as if he'd made a joke.

'Oh, Dad,' Nancy murmured, and there was a glimmer of tears in her eyes. 'Not for a long time yet, I hope.'

'Well not until I see this one happy with Taylor, eh, Saskia?' he said, giving his granddaughter's hand a pat.

'I think Saskia graduating is more important than Taylor,' Nancy responded tartly.

Saskia looked from one to the other and rolled her eyes. 'Can't I do both?' she asked.

'Sorry.' Skye waved her hand. 'Sorry to interrupt. But why did Neville and Georgie vanish? I understand Neville was still married and times were different, but surely that could've been overcome? And people pretend to be married every day, why should it have been so difficult for them?'

Archie looked a bit cagey, and seeing it Nancy gave a humourless laugh. 'There now, Dad, how are you going to answer that one?'

Archie straightened his back proudly. 'I'm going to answer it truthfully, Nancy. And, I think,' he moved towards the chair at last, 'I'm going to answer it sitting down.'

When they finally left the museum, Skye felt as if she was in a daze. Clutching a cardboard box full of Neville Darling's photographs, she noticed the list of names on the wall inside the door, the names of those who had died in the Black Friday fires.

Miller Brown was among them.

Finn steered her towards the LandCruiser.

'When did Neville die?' she'd asked Archie, one of her final questions. It was obvious the old man was very tired now and Nancy and Saskia were hovering.

'Nineteen fifty-five. He'd been ill with pneumonia, and he couldn't shake it off. Georgie buried him in the cemetery above the Crossing, and prepared to join him.'

'Is there a stone? A marker? Could I find them if I went there?'

Archie gave her a weary smile. 'Just look for the highest point.'

She wanted to ask him what he meant, but Nancy had sent Saskia to get the photographs and at that moment the girl returned, placing them in her hands.

When she opened the lid the first one she saw was Georgie in front of the hostelry, and the next, Archie as a boy with a hen in his arms.

'Look at them when you're alone,' Nancy said with an anxious glance towards her father. 'And there is a condition attached to them.'

The condition was that she must not use the story she'd been told as part of the exhibition, and if she did then Nancy would sue her for defamation.

Skye wasn't sure how she was going to get around that. And anyway, she wasn't sure she wanted everyone to know what Neville had done for Georgie. That he had killed a man for love she had no doubt, and yet some people would not see it like that. Some people might call him a cold-blooded murderer.

'What about Aesop?' Finn asked, when they finally stood up to leave. By then Nancy was nearly pushing them out of the door.

Archie smiled, his tired face lighting up. 'Aesop was fine. Bit of singed hide here and there, but he was a tough old fella. Her Majesty the chook was good, too, thank you for asking. Probably shortened her life by a bit, but it was an adventure not many hens can live to talk about.'

They laughed. Saskia gave Skye a hug, which was nice, but she didn't expect one from Nancy, and nor did she get one.

Now, driving home, she remembered again the sense that she had seen Nancy before. Of course it was the photograph of Georgie. There was a resemblance between them, and perhaps in character as well as features. Both strong, determined women, both willing to do anything to keep those they loved safe. A very different woman from Mary, her own grandmother. Neville and Georgie, one of the great love stories, and she wasn't sure she could ever tell it. Not all of it, anyway.

Once they arrived home, Lightning was out in a flash, running around to the back and down to the creek, leaving paw prints in the snow.

Inside the heat was waning, so Finn went to stoke up the fire, while Skye sat down and opened the box, shuffling through the photographs.

She stopped at a small image. Not a Neville Darling, and nothing special. Except to her. She slipped it out and into her hand, blinking back sudden tears.

Two people were smiling at the camera, a man with a lined face and a twinkling smile, and a woman with her dark hair in a braid and exotic eyes. They were holding hands. She glanced on the back and read the scrawl: 'Pom and Georgie 1955'.

'It must've been just before he died,' Skye said, her voice wavering with emotion.

Finn watched her for a moment and then went and poured her a drink and brought it back. 'Here,' he said, pressing it into her hand. 'I don't normally advise people to drink alcohol, but you've had a shock. Several.'

Skye laughed, taking a sip of the whisky, and leaned back in the chair, closing her eyes.

Her mind was alive with all the things that had happened. The story of Pom and Georgie seemed to play out before her dazzled, amazed brain. The fire and the journey to Elysian with young Archie, and then their decision to vanish. It was a happy ending, but a unique one, with a dark thread running through it.

And it was very different from anything she could have ever imagined when she had made the journey from Melbourne to Lockington.

It wasn't until Finn sat down beside her that she pulled herself out of her dream and sat up. 'I was thinking,' she assured him. 'I wasn't asleep.'

'Never said you were.'

He was watching her carefully, though whatever he saw must have reassured him that she really was all right.

'I'm going to use the photos for my exhibition,' she told him, 'but I'm not sure how much of the story I should tell.'

Finn took a few seconds to consider the problem. 'Maybe you should do it on your own. Just your photos. Neville is gone and his secrets with him, and I don't think you should dredge them up again. He murdered a man, Skye. Whatever the circumstances. That won't go down well in some parts of the community.'

'You mean my photos alone? But he was brilliant, Finn! I'm just …'

'I think you devalue yourself,' he said. 'You're pretty brilliant, too.'

'But you're biased.'

'Yep.' He examined her expression with a smile. 'Do you want something to eat or do you want to go to bed?'

'Well there's a choice,' she teased. 'Can't I have both?'

'Not sure.' He leaned in and kissed the corner of her mouth and her stomach took a dive. 'Once we're in there I may not come up for air for hours. But if you're hungry …'

'Not for food,' she breathed, and turned her face to kiss his mouth properly.

'I'm taking it slowly,' he said, reaching out a hand for hers.

'This is slowly?' she asked, as he pulled her to her feet. 'Not that I'm complaining, Finn. It's been a while since a man was willing to forgo his dinner for my body.'

'You're kidding?' He gave her a hard stare. 'Skye I'd live on bread and water for a week for you.'

She leaned into him, wrapping her arms around his neck. 'You say the most romantic things,' she whispered, pressing her body to his hard, lean one. 'But then you always did.'

She could see he didn't believe her. At sixteen most boys weren't interested in romance, but

Finn had been different even then, or perhaps it was just that together *they* had been different.

She turned to tell him so over her shoulder as she reached the bedroom, only to find he was already stripping off his sweater and flinging it on the floor behind him.

'What?' he asked innocently. 'Saves time.'

'Well I'm not going to throw off my clothes,' she reproved.

His gaze slid all the way down her body and back up again, and the look in his eyes stopped her heart. 'That's because I'm going to undress you myself, piece by piece.'

Skye wondered if her legs would hold her up as far as the bed. Anyway, she didn't need to find out because Finn lifted her into his arms and carried her.

CHAPTER 37

SKYE

A year later

THE OLD MACKENZIE Crossing cemetery was closed to burials now, the stones worn smooth and illegible in some cases, broken in others, while the bush continued to encroach. Skye hadn't been able to visit here to pay her respects for a while, there'd been too much happening. Setting up the exhibition had taken up most of her time, and then to her surprise it was such a success that a gallery in Melbourne had contacted her, offering to run it for several weeks.

That had meant being away from Finn.

She'd learned then, if she hadn't known it already, how much she loved him and wanted to be with him. He'd driven down to stay with her in Carlton when he could, but it wasn't enough, and anyway she'd begun to grow fond of the mountains of Elysian.

Fraser thought she was crazy wanting to live in the middle of nowhere, although he'd admitted

Finn was a cool guy, and words like that from Fraser were a rare gift. Milly the cat had made her choice and was remaining in Melbourne. And Russell, whose research had sent her to Elysian in the first place, was determined to take the credit for bringing her and Finn together.

Dylan and Ebony had had a daughter. Despite their still being in protective custody, a letter was sent without a return address, and enclosed was a photograph. Dylan's smile had never been bigger. Finn said the court case seemed further away than ever and the investigation was proceeding, and he hoped that eventually the truth would come out. One day.

Lightning was sniffing about the graveyard, investigating the scents and trails of other animals. Behind her was her new friend, Mojo. The big black dog hadn't been able to go with Dylan on such short notice, and when Skye had learned he was being kept in the confines of the cell at the police station in Westcott, until it was decided what to do with him, she had felt so sorry she'd offered to take him. To her relief he wasn't the vicious creature she'd imagined, in fact he was just a big softy, and Lightning was a good influence.

Or so Ashley, Finn's daughter, had said. She'd just left after a two-week holiday in Elysian, the first time since the wedding that the three of them had been together, and Skye found herself missing the girl. She'd promised to send Ashley some photographs, and Ashley—who had shown a real interest in Skye's work—promised to send some in return.

The wind whipped across the high ground, making Skye's eyes water. The clouds had that greenish look that seemed to precede snow, and she had seen Finn looking at them, also.

He caught her glance and smiled. He seemed to smile a lot these days, or so Alison informed her. Taylor and Saskia were living in Melbourne, but they came up when they could. Nancy had sold the museum to an incomer from Cumberland, a former historian who had written several books, and he seemed to have slotted into the community without any trouble. Everyone felt Archie's treasures were in good hands.

The photographs were Skye's now, left to her at Archie's request, and she was still planning an exhibition of Neville's work. She wasn't certain how she would tell his story, but the urge to do so was strong and she knew it would happen. The right time would come.

'This is a beautiful place.' She sighed. If she stood up she could see down into the valley that was Mackenzie Crossing. The settlement was long gone, but the memories remained, and as long as Skye was around she was determined they would not be forgotten.

When they'd first visited the graveyard last year, Skye had found that most of the stones weren't the originals. The place had been burned out by the bushfires that had come after Black Friday, and although some people had replaced them, often they didn't. Time went by and descendants forgot, and so did locals, until no one remembered who was buried here.

But she'd recalled what Archie had said about looking for the highest point, and that was when she'd found the boulder.

It rose up from the surrounding area like a stylised teardrop, the top pointing at the grey sky, and it was only when she'd pushed back the brush that had grown up around it that she'd found the words carved into the stone.

Here Lies Big Jim Mackenzie, founder of Mackenzie Crossing, a man of integrity, much loved and much missed. His wife, Eileen, gone too soon, forever remembered.

Also Neville Manning and Georgie Mackenzie Manning, exiles in life, come home in death.

Now, a year later, another name had been added.

And their beloved son, Archie, safe in their arms.

Skye traced his name with her fingertips and smiled. Archie—Tiddler—the boy who had lived through so much and in the end been strong enough and brave enough to share with her the truth. Saskia and Nancy had asked her to be present at the private burial ceremony up here, and she had felt like part of their family.

She *was* part of their family. She and Pom Darling.

Now she lifted her camera and took a photograph. And then, because she could never take just one, a couple more from different angles. The view looking over the cemetery to the distant mountains was also worthy. Georgie and Pom's resting place was beautiful and isolated, but it was also peaceful, and if they had craved peace, she knew that they had found it now. Pom from his nightmares of the war, and Georgie from her fear of being found out, and her son being taken from her.

It was true, they had come home in death to the place that had brought them together, and she hoped that somewhere, somehow, they knew it.

Lightning came up to her and gave a shiver, while Mojo flung himself down, panting, at her side. 'I know, I know.' Skye sighed. 'Just let me lay the flowers and then we can go home.'

They were wildflowers picked from the surrounding bush, and she set them down beside the stone.

Finn walked over and stood beside her.

'All right?' he asked, wrapping an arm around her, holding her close as he always did. 'Can we go home now?'

'Yes.' Skye nodded. 'Yes, let's go home.'

ACKNOWLEDGEMENTS

MY GRATITUDE GOES once more to Sue Brockhoff and the team at Harlequin Mira Australia, for their continuing support and for making writing such a pleasure. Also to my editor, Alex Nahlous, who has done an amazing job with this book, just as she did with my other two. To my agent, Selwa Anthony, with endless thanks for keeping me on track and for being so understanding when I told her I was writing the wrong book and needed to start again. I think the seed for this story was sown long ago when I was a child, and my grandfather used to speak of Black Friday, and how, when he looked out from his home on that day, the sky to the north was black, as if the whole state was burning. For my research on the bushfires of Black Friday, 1939, I used the excellent ABC website, and also the book written by *Herald* journalist, W.S. Noble, titled *Ordeal by Fire: The Week a State Burned Up*. Many thanks go to the Information Services Team at the State Library of Victoria, who once more provided me with invaluable information on life in the 1930s and the types of cameras in use at the time. Both Mackenzie Crossing and Elysian are fictitious towns, an amalgam of places in the Victorian Alps. They are also the product of a holiday my family took several years ago. Lost in the eerie darkness, driving white-knuckled on unfamiliar roads, it felt as if we were all alone in the world, and then we came upon the small town of Wood's Point, where we were welcomed at the hotel with open arms. I am greatly indebted to Leading Senior Constable Ken Dwight, stationed at Wood's Point, for his help in understanding policing and life in such a remote area, and for sharing his copies of the local newspaper *The Mountaineer*. I have tweaked some things for the sake of the story, and any mistakes are my own. Also gratitude must go to Rick of Rick Bentley Photography, who helped with cameras and weddings, and taking the perfect photograph, and was endlessly patient with my questions. And finally, thanks to Jessie Ngaio, for explaining to me how an exhibition is put together.

AUTHOR BIO

KAYE DOBBIE HAS been writing profession-
ally ever since she won the Big River short
story contest at the age of eighteen. Her career
has undergone many changes, including writing
Australian historical fiction under the name Lilly
Sommers, to romance written as Sara Bennett
and published in the US and Australia. Her books
have been translated into many languages. She is
currently writing under her 'proper' name, Kaye
Dobbie, and is published by Harlequin Mira in
Australia and Weltbild in Germany. Kaye lives on
the central Victorian goldfields, where she creates
her stories and in her spare time researches her
family tree.

www.ingramcontent.com/pod-product-compliance
Lightning Source LLC
Chambersburg PA
CBHW070152120726
47909CB00001B/76